Dead Fish Jumping On The Road

Dead Fish Jumping
On The Road

W.L. Liberman

Chapter One

June 9th, 1966—my very first dead body—as an adult. Norma Jennings drowned off Roach's Point in Rattlesnake Bay. Aged 22, she stood five feet three inches tall, weighed 118 pounds and wore her long blond hair in a ponytail. Norma had fallen out of a speedboat, a Shark 235 with twin Johnson 75's. The boyfriend drove. They'd been fooling around.

Norma rode the bow backward while dangling her feet in the water, letting her heels kick up from the hard surface not suspecting that tragedy would strike. I pictured her smile and the brightness of her eyes, heard her brazen laugh. She wore a white bikini that barely covered her ample figure—a cheerleader's body. The boyfriend, Blake Rothwell, spun the boat's wheel at full speed, pushing it to 22 miles per hour, slewing through the waves at blunt angles. What a blast, he might have thought, high on the motion and velocity and thrill of doing something dangerous, something far out on the edge. Just the look of her made him push it to the limit. He wanted to be bad without knowing or caring or even understanding what bad was. Bad was in that summer.

Norma teetered this way and that, moving with the motion, still laughing, grabbing at the edges and missing, breaking a brilliantly lacquered nail, too drunk to be afraid. She held a Mickey of scotch in her left hand and tilted it to her lips as Blake continued to throw the boat around in its own wake. I could picture the heave of her white bosom, the pout of her full lips and see how she wiped her mouth after each pull on the bottle. I heard her titter as the liquor ran down her chin and dribbled into her cleavage. Her shrieks of laughter brayed out harshly over the wind and currents.

I could imagine Norma on that boat but in my real life I reported the facts. Five foot ten inches. Black hair. Blue eyes. One hundred sixty-pounds soaking wet. Twenty-six years old. Pugnacious attitude. Scarred childhood. That's me, Joe Simpson, reporter. How mundane it sounded. Just the facts, please, just the facts, bud. How many times I'd uttered that dreary phrase and how the facts as I often knew them, bored me to tears. But then, some stories came along and changed all that. I tried to escape from just such a story that had no ending…and then I landed in Applewood. Only partially on my feet.

Boyfriends named Blake always screwed up. The whine of the powerful outboard screamed in his ear. The boat slammed into a massive roller thundering forward like an avalanche. The Shark's hull dipped dangerously to the starboard side, slipping down to the varnished gunwale. Water the colour of slate licked the polished chrome fittings as, suddenly, Blake stared at an escalating mountain of boat over his left shoulder. He fought the rising motion for balance, struggling to keep the boat from flipping over and threw in a prayer for good measure. After a suspended eon, the Shark's hull leveled out with a thump slapping the water like a surfboard riding a high curl and that's when he grabbed the throttle and cut it dead. Blake felt victorious. He'd conquered the Bay and filling his lungs let out a piercing rebel yell. What kicks, he thought. But then Norma had gone. She'd gone for good. He hadn't even heard the splash or seen the upturned kick of her pretty white legs. Afterwards, we found broken shards of the mickey stuck into the surface of the polished hull dripping traces of her blood. AB positive.

The water lay 94 feet deep where Norma disappeared, too deep for the divers to have any chance of finding her but they went out anyway knowing all along it was useless. Roach's Point is a rocky knoll thrusting outward into the Bay. A flat shelf of granite extended out seventeen feet where the water stood waist high but dropped off crazily. Not a few had stepped off it into oblivion, hence its name, Dead Man's Plank. Blake's boat tore up the water no more than 35 yards offshore. But the night had been balmy and rough, the wind at 14 knots with swells of two and a half to three feet rolled in and pounded the beach. The water temperature leveled off at seventy degrees Fahrenheit—skin puckering cold. Currents moved in a vicious counter-clockwise vortex sucking up everything in their path, then spewed their miserable victims on to the pebbled shoal.

And that's what happened to poor Norma. She'd been sucked down to the bottom. Her tangled, semi-nude body rested peacefully at the water's edge as if the Bay had vomited it up whole. The Bay embraced her, swathed as she was in lacy strips of weed and marsh grass. Black clay and snails and leeches filled her cheeks, minnows kissed her eyes and lips and in her tightly-closed fist we found half a translucent clam shell. I still have that shell. I keep it as a sad and angry memento, the single remnant of a lush young woman who died foolishly. It was kicks too, she'd thought. And that seemed to characterize the atmosphere all that summer.

In the bleak dampness of an early June dawn, grey-coated shapes hovered around her, moving and talking mechanically, wishing they were somewhere else. They longed for a joke, a ray of light and for an easing of their burden. I'd gotten a call at 4:32 am. It was Hal Bigelow, one of the local cops.

"Norma's washed up," he said softly, and gave me the location. Then he hung up taking care not to bang the receiver in my ear.

Under threatening skies, the four men seemed anonymous, squinting into the weak light, their hats and faces slick from the moist Bay air. As I approached, Doc Seaton bent low over the body, no mean feat for Doc since describing him as rotund was being generous and he looked to be at least eighty years old. I saw him remove and wipe his gold wire spectacles with a handkerchief he'd managed to tug out of his back pocket. Having finished scrubbing the shiny lenses, he stuffed the soggy rag back into his coat. The others stood stock still hanging their heads, hats in hand, like members of a funeral procession waiting for the corpse to descend into a freshly dug grave.

I picked out Hal Bigelow's enormous bulk right away since he stood six feet eight. Beside Hal, primping like a prissy, pampered mouse, perched Alistair Macafee, the mortician's sleek assistant. Steff Randolph, the mortician, stood looking like an upright cadaver himself. Steff had brought the hearse. He and Alistair waited on Doc Seaton's say-so, then they'd slide a gurney out and artfully arrange Norma's broken body on it. After which, she'd be transported to the Applewood town morgue where Doc would perform his standard autopsy, producing the standard results. Blake Rothwell reported Norma missing six hours after she'd sunk into the still, frigid waters of Rattlesnake Bay.

Standing with the group, we'd become five faceless citizens witnessing a little bit of horror together. I thought I caught Alistair smile ever so slightly as Doc gingerly probed one of Norma's shoal-scraped breasts and I wanted to flatten his smug, oily weasel face. But Doc wasted no time.

"Okay boys," he said. "You can load Norma up now." Doc stood up groaning and stepped back from the body. "Oh, hello Joe. Didn't hear you come up."

"Doc."

Doc puckered his lips, then clasped his hands on his round belly, clucking like a desiccated turkey.

"Such a shame, a pretty young woman like that." He reached into his trench coat and fished out a packet of Sweet Cap's and offered them around. Hal and I each took one. Steff and Alistair busied themselves with the details of collecting their newest client. Steff brought out some threadbare field blankets and neatly covered Norma up, working delicately as if she were merely sleeping and he didn't want to wake her accidentally. Hal extended his lighter and we all drew from it.

"I delivered her, you know. I delivered a lot of them. And sometimes, I get them back. Kicks," Doc snorted, blowing smoke. "Makes me sick."

Doc and I felt the same way about it. But then every town boasted a fast crowd and Applewood crowed as loud if not louder than most.

"Cause of death, Doc?" I asked sheepishly.

"Accidental drowning," he drawled.

"You can get the blood alcohol reading from the police report," Hal said to me from behind a paw as he dragged on his smoke. I nodded, pressing my hand in close so that the stub almost burned my nose. The smoke brought quick tears to my eyes. It was the smell of her, like soft, rotted flesh decayed into a jellied tub of corruption. To my everlasting gratitude, Steff and Alastair lifted the stretcher and picked their way carefully over the wet stones to the hearse. I spotted a flash of muddied, yellow hair, just before the door clamped shut. Steff gave us a flagging wave, showing his exuberant side, then he and Alastair climbed into the impassive black machine. They drove slowly off down the sandy, pitted track toward the main highway back to town. Hal flipped the collar of his coat down onto his shoulders, unbuttoned the front and looked skyward.

"Looks like it's gonna be a decent day, after all," he said.

Chapter Two

"Sassafrass!" spat Theodore Graff, as I bulled my way into the meagre offices of the *Applewood Gazette*, paid circulation 12, 331, balancing a cup of coffee and an apple danish in one hand and a brownie bag containing all my writing stuff—pencils, pads, erasers, and leaky pens in the other. At short arm's length, Teddy, who wasn't tall but almost excessively squat, blew out his apple cheeks, pursed his thick lips and scrutinized the front page of the afternoon edition as he leaned over the composing table in the middle of the room. By the severity of his scowl, I could tell instantly he disliked the results.

The cigar he'd been sucking on for the past week jutted from his rubbery lips as he closed one eye and stared hard at the page, then did the same with the other.

" Crooked," he muttered disgustedly. Then roared at the top of his lungs, "Stumpy!"

"Hi Teddy," I said.

He swiveled his thick head about to unleash a blast in my direction. Just then, however, Stumpy Butler, the ancient, wizened pressman, his Popeye-like forearms hanging helplessly at his sides, black ink smeared up to the elbows, leaned in from the composing room.

"You called, Teddy?" he asked in a querulous, innocent voice, as if he might have heard someone call him from a long distance off but wasn't sure and decided to check, just in case. Stumpy owned about three teeth and appeared frequently bamboozled if not drunk. The typesetter broke down the week before and while repairs were effected, Stumpy knocked in type the old way, by hand. Except. With Stumpy, that word lay there, except.

"Crooked again, Stumpy," Teddy growled at him, doing his best to snarl and curl his lip upward.

"How do you mean?" Stumpy asked in his quavery way.

"The type is crooked, goddammit. It's very simple, Stumpy. It isn't straight. How can I get out an edition when the type is all over the place, man? We'll drive our readers to blindness. We've got standards of excellence to maintain. Get it?"

"Yes sir."

"Do it, again. And I want absolute precision."

While following this riveting exchange, I managed to sling my coat over a chair, dump the bag onto my desk, take a bite out of the Danish and get in two or three slurps of coffee, steeling myself for the wrath of Teddy; whole rage fomented out of him because it could. The image of Norma fractured my mind and I thought simple, mundane tasks might wipe it away. Warily, Stumpy ducked back into the composing room to give the type another go. I could hear him whacking the letters into place.

Teddy leveled his bushy brows at me while I continued to consume breakfast. "Where the hell have you been? We're on a deadline here."

"Asleep," I answered truthfully. "But from 4:15 to 5:30 a.m., I was in the company of Norma Jennings." Teddy's creased his brows more tightly knitting a dense bush across his forehead.

"Description," he commanded.

I wiped the apple glaze off my chin with a paper napkin and swallowed before answering. "Bloated and ugly. A putrified mass of flesh. Brought half the Bay in with her. Steff, Alistair, Hal and Doc Seaton were there too. It was pretty grim. That bastard, Alistair, smiled like a voyeur when Doc touched her," I said. I held my fist up and shook it. I didn't mind a fight. I'd been in plenty as a kid.

Teddy merely grunted. "And the Rothwell kid?"

"Nothing yet. He'll probably be charged with careless and dangerous operation of a motorboat or some damn thing. He waited six hours before reporting Norma missing."

"So soooon?" Teddy remarked sarcastically.

"That means he'll beat the drunk rap for sure. He showed up at the station with Freddy Oliveira in tow. Released on his own cognizance. Told to stick around, the usual crap. She used to be a beautiful girl, Teddy, I mean really beautiful. The whole thing stinks. It just stinks," I said, shaking my head in disgust.

Teddy hooked his thumbs into his suspenders and ran them up and down. For once, his white shirt looked clean. "You remember now—"

"Yeah, yeah, I know. Stick to the facts. Just stick to the facts."

"You got it, Joe. That's what we're here for. You write up what you've got and then we'll see what a mess Tommy can make of it. Then I want you to run out to the Beatty place. His sow dropped 12 piglets last night."

I grimaced. "Now there's a story."

"It is around here," Teddy replied in a threatening tone, daring me not to like it.

I lit a Sweet Cap perching on the corner of my desk. Teddy had turned back to examine the layout on the composing table. He glanced over his shoulder.

"You still here?"

"Yup…I was just thinking—"

"I don't pay you to think, Joe. I pay you to report. Sounds simple enough, doesn't it?"

I shrugged, trying to swallow my anger with the apple Danish that now sat in my gullet like a hard lump. "You're the boss."

"And don't you forget it."

"Wouldn't dream of it," I murmured.

"What was that?"

" I hear you, Teddy."

"Good. Now scram."

Before I could vamoose, I needed to pluck my courage up and ask Teddy for more dough. I owned a black 1960 Chevrolet Biscayne convertible. It had looked sweet and gleaming on the dusty used lot. When I bought it a few months ago, the original whitewalls were still on the car. Within a week, however, two of the tires had blown, the transmission had acted up and the brakes squealed louder than I imagined those baby piglets ever could. Barney Diggle from Diggle's Gas Bar sold it to me. Barney had a reputation as a bit of a crook but I needed a set of wheels cheap to get around, especially when stories popped up in the backwoods. The repairs set me back a few hundred and my rent was due.

"Teddy….I need a raise….badly…"

His back stiffened so tight I though his suspenders would snap. He swiveled back to me. "I told you not to buy that damn car, didn't I? But no, you didn't listen to me, did you? Smartass kid who thinks he knows better, aren't you?"

"Hey, I'm twenty-six." Teddy had a point. I probably bought the car because Teddy harangued me about Barney Diggle. "Besides, I don't know about that...."

"I do..." And he thrust the stub of putrid cigar in my direction. I steeled myself.

"What's your point, Teddy? If I sell my car will you give me a raise?"

Teddy choked on his bile. I could see it in the sudden red flush that repainted his face from its normal pink to a severe purplish hue. "Don't be a damned fool, Joe. Of course I'm not giving you a raise. Do you know how—"

"—Lucky I am to have this job? That there are at least sixty, eager young newshounds waiting in the wings. Waiting for my demise, waiting for me to falter, waiting for my miserable ballpoint to blow up in my face. Isn't that what you were going to say, Teddy?" I asked him.

I had what the others didn't. A mother in prison, serving life for murdering my father. Norma's body was the first I had seen in the flesh. But I couldn't forget seeing the outline of my father's corpse under a sheet hastily thrown over him just after my twelfth birthday. Nice present. I saw the blood dripping into the cracks of the floorboards, the pale, flushed expression as my mother, wild-eyed, frantic, her expression pleading, the cops dragging her out of our apartment, a third floor walk-up on a 19 by 120-foot lot on Borden Street in Toronto. A guy in soiled coveralls wheeled the covered gurney carrying my father's body down the long hall of our building. And like Norma, my father's arm flopped out from under the starched sheet. The fingers splayed, the back of his hand grimy with black hair. I remember one of the detectives in a rumpled suit, fedora crushed on his skull, saying, "Jeezus Harry, get the kid the hell outta here." A large, blue policeman carried me down into the street. I kicked and cried, beat my hands against his massive chest. It felt like striking a stonewall.

Like me, my dad reported the news. He worked the crime desk for the Toronto Mercury and wrote lucid stories that were simple and powerful in their brutality— that is, when he was sober. He blamed it all on the War, of course. Said he came back from Germany damaged. My mother sulked. They only kept each other company when they hit the bottle. Then all of the suppressed rage spilled out of him and she loomed there, right there in front of him. And he had to punish someone.

She used a steak knife from the kitchen drawer. The serrated blade broke off in his chest. In this regard, being 'special' sucked.

Knotting the clump of greying sagebrush that marked the beginning of his forehead, Teddy shook his foul, shredded cigar stub in my face.

"I'd watch it if I were you, Joe. You're getting too damn big for your britches. If you weren't such a good reporter, I'd have kicked your butt out of here a long time ago."

"That and the fact you haven't given me a raise in two years," I said.

"Two years?" he grunted. "What is your salary now, Joe?"

"Eighty-seven fifty; gross," I replied, shoving my hands into the pockets of my scuffed chinos, looking at him in a brash sort of way. As brash as I could muster, blowing smoke to the ceiling.

"Eighty-seven fifty," he repeated. "You know when I started out that would have been a king's ransom. You could have fed a family of ten on that wage and had plenty left over."

"This isn't 1925," I replied.

Teddy smiled dangerously. "No," he said. "No, it isn't..." he said.

"I'm not talking about anything outrageous, Teddy. A hundred a week would do me fine."

"A hundred a week, eh?" he said quietly, prelude to a welling torrent of outrage. "Just a lousy twenty percent increase, that's all you're asking for?"

"Um, fifteen percent actually."

"Sure," Teddy smiled sweetly. "Just fifteen percent. Uh-huh. Sounds reasonable to me. I mean, after all, there are steel plants and coal mines closing all across this country..." Listening to this twaddle, I sighed. "...family farms are packing it in and moving to the cities to go on the breadline, the soup kitchens are working overtime, little kids are begging in the street and you want me to give you a fifteen percent raise while all of this abject poverty, this undiluted misery is swilling its black hopelessness all around us?"

I looked out the picture window into the street. It was deserted, no line-ups, no ragged kids pressing their noses in. "That's right," I replied.

"And where do you think that money's going to come from? You expect a new advertiser just to waltz in here and plunk down a wad of cash for a stack of advertisements? Or maybe we should trim some of the fat around here?"

I shrugged. I really didn't know, or care if the truth be known.

"Perhaps, you'd like me to cut Stumpy's pay? Stumpy," he roared and Stumpy Butler's bewildered visage, pale and dripping with sweat, popped out of the composing room.

"Yes, Teddy?" His jaw went slack dragging his mouth open.

"Stumpy...how would you like to take a cut in pay?"

"Wwwhaaaattt?" Stumpy swallowed. "What for?" I'd seen lame animals look less pathetic.

"Why...to accommodate Joe here, who feels he's the most deserving of a raise."

Stumpy looked even more miserable, if that was possible and scratched his meager scalp. "Well, I, uh..."

Teddy cut him off. "Nadine," he snapped and Nadine Morgan, the chain-smoking office manager who'd heard every word, raised her beehive above eye level to peer over her cubicle.

She breathed smoke. "Yeah?"

"Maybe you'd like to make a fiscal sacrifice for Joe here? What do you say?"

Nadine snorted. "If anybody should make a gesture here, it's you, Teddy."

Teddy raised his finger and pointed it heavenward. "Of course, of course. Take the food out of the mouths of my children."

"Your kids are grown up and left home ages ago," Nadine snorted, shaking her head.

"But still...it's the principal that's at stake here," he insisted.

"Unbelievable," Nadine muttered. "All this over a few measly bucks," she said and shook her lacquered head some more. Not a wisp stirred.

The toes of my shoes had become increasingly more interesting. Just when I thought he would explode, I looked up. "So do I get the raise or not?"

"You think you're pretty smart," he hissed back.

I knew Teddy would try it on. He always did and in the past I'd usually cave but not this time. This time I was determined to see it through.

"No, I just need a raise, Teddy. And it has been over two years."

Teddy suspended his performance on a dime.

"All right, Joe," he said very quietly. "We'll play it your way," he added in a tone that told me this wasn't the end of it.

But I didn't care about the consequences. "That's a hundred a week, effective today," I said happily. "Right?"

Teddy nodded. "Now, I've wasted enough damn time," he said grumpily. "I've got a paper to put together here."

Stumpy stood aghast.

"Well, I'll be," he said scratching his sparse head. And then he had an idea, I could see it growing in his eyes, moving slowly downward from his forehead to his chin, until finally his entire face lit up.

"Say, Teddy..?"

"Not now, Stumpy," Teddy hollered. "I've got work to do." Stumpy swallowed hard, crestfallen, then slunk back into the composing room, muttering to himself at his missed opportunity. With Stumpy it was often difficult to know just what he was thinking. Maybe he'd lay Teddy across the metal type and threaten to whack him on to the front page if he didn't get a raise too?

"Say Joe, didn't I give you an assignment?" Teddy asked.

I nodded, basking in my newfound prosperity. "Yup."

"Well, hop to it." Now that the crisis was over, he'd become reasonable...normal.

"I'm leaving, I'm leaving. Er, I expect Doc's autopsy report on Norma might be ready by now."

"That's pretty quick work," Teddy growled.

"Well you know Doc Seaton. He's a fast worker. Listen can I....?"

Teddy waved his hand in disgust, as if he had a sudden bad taste in his mouth and resumed sucking on the cold stogie to take it away.

"No. Piggies first. Autopsy after. Go on, get going," he said.

"You've made me very happy."

"Sure."

"I'll name my first born after you."

"Yeah. Yeah."

I went to open my mouth again.

"Get outta here," Teddy yelled. I grabbed my jacket, patted Nadine's wrinkled cheek. She raised her head far enough to give me a wan smile, picked up my brownie bag and left slamming the door.

Chapter Three

I drove out of town trying to shake off those childhood memories but that was like saying time stood still and the sun never rose each morning. My old man used to say that he could feel a big story coming on, that he'd get this tingling feeling in the back of his neck. Jack Simpson. Had a nose for the news, his buddies used to boast. The only times I saw him smile, even whistle under his breath sometimes was when he slapped a copy of The Mercury on the kitchen table and pointed to his byline on the front page. "Best feeling in the world," he'd crow and my mother and I would smile shyly with him, wondering how long the euphoria would last. Never long enough. Maybe the only good thing I got from him was the same intuition. My neck had been tingling ever since Norma's body washed up on shore. In truth, it was a curse but like my old man, I couldn't leave go of the big one when it came along. I realized, that in my own way, I was competing with him even though he lay in a box below ground, shamefully dead.

On a busy day it took no more than seven minutes to escape Applewood and the countryside opened up like a spring flower. I followed Highway 26 north for six miles, then turned on to Nottawasaga Road 8, heading west, intending to make my way out to the Beatty place and report on the blessed coming of the divine piglets.

The road opened before me empty and infinite, except for a car coming up quickly in my rear view mirror. I glanced at it, then looked ahead. The sun soared. A mild breeze blew. I had begun to relax, slipping into that state of semi-reverie on a pleasant, summer day. The black car raised dust as it fish-tailed around the curves. Guy's going awfully fast, I thought. I gripped the wheel a little harder as the car loomed larger in my sphere of vision. My Chevy was a big, solid car and could move when I wanted it to but the road narrowed and wound around this far out in the country. A solid line split the pitted tarmac. No passing allowed.

The dark car drew nearer, edging up. I knew by its low-riding chassis that it was a Corvette and heard the throaty growl of its engine. The driver pulled up close, just back of my rear bumper. What the hell was he playing at? Guy should be reported but I couldn't make out any details to report. Couldn't make out the driver as the windshield had been blacked over. In fact, the entire car was black from top to bottom. Some kind of joker, I figured, thinking I drove like a knock-kneed tourist or an old-age pensioner. He inched closer, dropped back, then moved up again, boosting the gas. I began to think the guy was nuts. Some psycho road hog having a thrill.

I eased up on the accelerator hoping the Vette would pass but it dropped back. Then, I pumped the brake lightly to warn him off but he hung back for a second then charged up again playing kissy-kissy with my rear bumper. I squared up behind the wheel then trod on the accelerator watching the guy fade in the rear view... but not for long. He swooped up then pulled out beside and slightly behind me as we accelerated around a hair-pin. I felt the Chevy's tires spin on the gravel shoulder. The foghorn blast from a logging truck made me jump out of my skin. The Corvette dropped back quickly tucking itself neatly behind me. I caught a flash of the flushed face and angry, flexed jaw of the driver. He jabbed a rigid thumb up in the air. His obscene words swallowed by another blast of the air horn. Just as the rig blew by, the dark car moved up again inching its way forward. The harder I pushed, the faster he went, matching me effortlessly. We balanced neck and neck charging down the twisted road at 80, 90, then 100 miles an hour, faster than I'd ever gone before. Faster than I thought possible. I felt like the guy was laughing at me. Playing some stupid but dangerous game. What the hell was I doing? My hands locked on the steering wheel. My arms had gone rigid, fused into iron bars.

I heard it before I felt the impact.

A bang erupted behind my head. The car rumbled and shuddered and rocked on its springs. I wrestled the wheel with all my strength lifting my foot off the accelerator... the rear left had exploded. The back end of the Chevy jerked sluicing on loose gravel and sand rabbiting dangerously. The front end swung left. The scream of rubber filled the air or maybe it was me doing the screaming... I wrenched the wheel to the right and felt the car careen toward the shoulder.

The Chevy left the road shooting up a hill where it jounced and bounced in the ruts and gullies of the boggy grassland.

I gripped the wheel with all the strength I could muster as the car dove to a stop in the gully of a lumpy slope where I cracked my head on the dashboard. A creak, then a groan teased out of the metal carcass as The Chevy began to roll backward toward the road. Dizzily, I stomped on the brake forcing some steel into my leg. The car's jerking progress stopped just short of the gravel shoulder before exposing its rear end to the highway. When I finally managed to look up, the Corvette, pristine in its throaty power, vanished around the next bend. I jammed the transmission into park, kicked in the parking brake and switched off the engine letting my head loll back on the seat. I lay like that for a long time panting and moaning although probably only two minutes had lapsed. In the rear view, I could see a nasty lump forming on my forehead where the skin had broken and was rapidly turning green and blue. The Corvette had no license plates. A cipher.

I examined the damage. The right front fender looked banged up pretty good and a long, sickening scrape scythed across the doors where I'd plowed through a stand of prickly scrub and saplings. Now that my head pounded to beat the band to match the damage, it was all just about perfect.

I kept a spare in the trunk. After much huffing and wheezing, I changed the tire. I looked at it in disgust. The blown whitewall seemed beyond repair, shredded into oblivion. And then I wondered what had happened. I shook my head. I really didn't know. I did know that a nice goose egg formed on my head, my hands were covered in grease, my elbow smarted where I'd skinned it on the tire jack and I'd sweated through my short-sleeve, button-down, cotton shirt. And now, I had to see a man about pigs.

I swung the car onto the road feeling a bit numb. The front right tire clanged against the crumpled wheel well.

Turning up a gravel road, I spotted the dented mailbox marking the Beatty place and bumped along their dirt drive, hearing the squeal of extremely animated pigs and worse, smelling the stench of filthy, mud-slopped bodies. They heard my car. No sooner had I cut the engine than Jan Beatty, blonde and apple-cheeked, wiping her large, reddened hands on a calico apron and Evan, stout as a fireplug in his bleached coveralls and a fierce expression shielded by a ratty-looking straw hat pulled low on his dark bearded face, waddled down the steps of their porch.

"'Bout time you got here," fumed Evan. "We've been waiting on you. Expected you to show up over an hour ago." Then spat a stream of tobacco in a black arc at my feet splattering my socks.

"Now Evan," scolded Jan as I wondered what Ozark nightmare they'd crawled out of, "there was no call to do that. Mr. Simpson'll think we're uncivilized. How about some cold lemonade, Mr. Simpson? I make it myself. It is such a warm day." Her voice resonated with that ever-present nasality that city slickers come to expect in country folk. I wasn't disappointed. You could hitch a hay wagon to it. Jan stood on the porch steps and turned to await my reply before disappearing inside the farmhouse.

"That'd be swell," I said, resisting the urge to wipe my socks in front of Evan. His eyes formed dark orbs rimmed with white. He had the look of a wild stallion about to rear up and stomp something or someone into a pulpy mess. His thick beard had been trimmed into a round bush by a pair of garden shears but his upper lip remained clean. Surprisingly delicate nostrils pulsated like vibrating flanges as he snorted in anger. He spat again and leaned in close. I smelled his acrid, tobacco-filled breath. He gave me a dead-eyed stare. Spooky. I was still trying to shake off the effects of the near-death experience I'd just had in the car. Evan began to murmur in a muttering, accusatorial tone pointing a stubby finger in my direction. He sniffed the air then shrugged violently as if physically assaulted by some odious shape.

"I smell it, boy and I smell it on you," he said.

"Smell what?" Had my deodorant let me down?

"Slime. Evil slime. It burns the air around me. I choke. I gag. I want to clear my throat and spit it up. It's here around you and I say, get it gone from me."

"Well, when you find it, whatever it is, let me know."

He gathered himself up to blather on when the porch door flew open with a frightening bang. Evan nearly left his boots standing in place. So did I. The resounding knock of wood on wood made me realize that for a working farm, the Beatty place had become uncharacteristically quiet suddenly. Eerily quiet. The grunting undercurrents of the piggies surged through the hazy air. Jan marched down the stairs carrying a broad tray…a wooden tablet embroidered around the edges with a cyrillic-like script…laden with a frosted pitcher and tall glasses. I heard the rattling of spoons as she clumped along. She lay the tray across the flat end of an upturned log. In her best hostess manner, she poured out three glasses handing one to Evan and me where we stood virtually toe-to-toe in mute enmity. She looked at us curiously.

Jan asked, "What's the matter with you two?" Hands on ample hips, scolding us as if we were rapscallions up to no good.

"Oh, it's nothin'," Evan muttered darkly and slurped his lemonade in the manner of a horse watering at a trough. I seemed incapable of moving, morbidly fascinated by what was becoming another episodic moment hashed into the day.

"How do you like it? Is it cold enough for you?" It took me a long moment to realize it was me Jan addressed. I took a sip and she watched me raptly, eagerly awaiting my pronouncement. Jeee—zus and the hepcats! Never in my existence had I tasted anything so sour. My palette had gone dry as the arroyo. I couldn't even swallow let alone talk. I would have dearly loved to spit the noxious beverage into Evan's warthog face. I nodded with false enthusiasm stretching shriveled lips as wide as possible. "Mmm…aahhh…eerrggg…"

Evan stared mightily with his accursed eyes. Even Jan felt his intensity.

"Evan. What's got into you? You're acting most peculiar. Don't mind him, Mr. Simpson. He's in one of his moods. They come and go, just like the seasons. And sometimes just as slow too," Jan said, dimpling her plump face with a smile.

Perhaps it was the lemonade, perhaps not but while verbally paralyzed, my mind raced on toward some distant intellectual nebula. Maybe I had simply been concussed. And suddenly, silence blanketed the world. The silence permeated the air, drenched it. I felt my ankles and feet melt into the earth, then slowly take root. My hosts stood, shoulders touching then began to merge, while sheer white light emanated from their direction. But it became a benign hue not dazzling and not stinging to the eye. As seconds ticked off, the Beattys formed the light, that is, it came through from behind them and gradually achieved an elevated state of phosphorescence obliterating all else nearby. The radiance then sprang forward as if seeking a new host and moved behind my eyes, probing my ears, my senses, my mind. I couldn't hear anything but a low crackling, wireless hum. Fragments of the landscape zoomed into my foreground, then out again. Zoom. I strained to hear. Dead leaves crunchless underfoot. Zoom. Calves lowing silently in the meadow. Zoom. A crop duster soaring lazily in the mute distance. Zoom. My voice bellowing a dumb scream to the cotton-wadded atmosphere. But the world had been framed and screened and the big knob controlling the volume had been switched to off. Who was watching? And could they hear my thoughts?

Then, I heard it.

Solid, basso-profundo lines... musical notes. Music the like of which I'd never felt before—shattering and powerful. Chords struck for an eternity touching and surrounding my person like an everlasting truth. It was then, in a single, peerless second that the utterly simple significance of nature came to me as if the notes contained a secret hieroglyph meant only for me. It was a pattern. I was to un-make it. An oratorio of voices descended like a fluttering cloud and mingled freely with the music. Its form so powerful that a massive city could rise up on its own underpinnings without fear or concern for physical danger. Each popping molecule pressed in around me but instinct indicated there was no cause for alarm. Clouds lightened then darkened spasmodically like the clench of a heart, moving quickly across the pulsating sky in staccato fashion. The sun winked at each rapid fire uncovering, flickering with the intense pulse of a disco strobe fuelled by juiced up circuitry. As sound and sight melded with my throbbing blood, my worldview tilted dangerously. Somehow, I'd landed on the ground just as the cosmic pandemonia frothed to their collective apex; the voices withered, the sky dissipated and my senses boomeranged back to normal perspective as I stared uncomprehendingly at Evan's manure-splattered boots.

Jan exclaimed, "Oh my goodness! Evan, help Mr. Simpson up. He's had a fainting spell. Let's get him into the shade. Probably a touch of heat stroke, I'm sure."

Evan glowered some more but complied with his wife's request as I felt myself yanked upright and dragged to a cooler locale under cover of the barn's slanted roof where the world continued to congeal into proper view.

"Wow. Some lemonade," I rasped, feeling my burning face.

"I expect you got too much sun," Jan said reassuringly. "Your face is quite bright, you know. And that lump."

"I'm feeling better, thank you."

"Well, if you're sufficiently recovered, let's go see the piggie-wiggies, shall we?" Jan cried, desperately hoping the sight of them might restore her moment of glory. She beckoned me to follow her broad back and shoulders—shoulders sloped from fetching slop pails, rolling hay bales, mucking out stalls—around the side of the weather-beaten barn. Evan, stolid as an A-bomb, strode darkly after.

The grunting and snorting sounded menacing as we approached the large pen, all bedecked with ribbons of pink and blue.

"There they are," declared Jan proudly. I peered in. An obese sow lay on her side as her offspring recreated a rugby scrum pushing and shoving, digging in their little hooves for better traction to get at her swollen teats. A collection of squeals rose up as the victors fought successfully to their prize.

I asked, "What do you call them?"

"Maisie."

"Maisie? They're all called Maisie?"

"Easier to remember," Evan said with quiet menace. "We've got a lot of animals here. Can't always remember their names, you know."

"No, of course not," I agreed, edging away from Evan and his strangeness. "I guess you're both tinkled pink."

"Actually," Evan interjected, "there were thirteen but I strangled one at birth. Thirteen is bad luck, an evil omen."

"Oh Evan. Don't be so strange. He's so superstitious, Mr. Simpson. There's nothing to it, really. Why, he's always looking out for black cats and ladders and things. Sometimes, he just gets carried away, don't you Evan?" she cried.

"No," he replied dully.

I desperately wanted to get the hell out of there. "Say, why don't I take a picture for the article, then I'll just beat it."

"Don't you even want to know their birth weights or how long poor Maisie mommy was in labour?" Jan asked, disappointment etched keenly on her face.

"Sure, sure, okay," I replied as she promptly began to list each one in turn. "Why don't you just tell me the average birth weight, Mrs. Beatty? I'm not sure how much space we're going to have, you know, including the picture and everything."

I managed to coax a nice smile out of Maisie mommy and her brood, even composed an orderly tableaux with a proud Jan and a glowering Evan and then tore the hell out of the Beatty place as Jan waved enthusiastically and Evan stared out from under the brim of that ratty hat. I could see the rims of his eyes and their wildness chilled me as I rammed the gear lever into reverse, trod the accelerator shooting shards of gravel and stones into the air as I peeled out of there. Once back on the main road, I relaxed my foot and eased off the gas pedal still shivering. Now the sun shone heatless. Checking the rear view mirror, all the colour had drained from my face except for the pulsating lump. If for a scant millisecond, I'd thought I understood nature, it had been a sad mistake. I saw Norma Jennings' rotted face staring back at me as I tore away and nearly lost control. Control of everything.

Chapter Four

On the way back to town, whizzing past rotted fence posts, grazing heifers, sun-dried fields of peaches'n cream corn, waffling oaks and heat dissipating off the tarmac, my brain suffered gridlock. I was entranced without being able to assimilate anything that had happened yet alone wonder about the meaning or possible origins of such ungodly events. Maybe I was just a dupe, a sap and that was it. The Big Guy simply laughed at me.

And what about fate?

You walk down the street and a flowerpot hits the sidewalk in front of you. Or you stroll in the woods and suddenly you hear a tremendous crashing sound, something smacks you in the head, your knees buckle, your vision goes dark. After a moment, your senses return. Instantly you're up to your armpits in the branches of a fallen maple tree. You are standing where the main part of the trunk forks and it is only by some random aura you aren't smashed to kindling. My mother had not committed a random act. I damned my father to hell. I hated him for what he'd done, for the marks he'd left on me but I loved him too. I just didn't want to be him.

Some hundred yards ahead, I spied a wiry figure perched atop a fence post. I slowed the car to get a better look. There came that now familiar feeling. I reached into my jacket pocket and rubbed Norma's clamshell. For good luck. I saw a middle-aged man—gaunt as a scarecrow, ably balanced, hugging his bony knees to his skinny chest, swaying minutely. He looked deeply tanned and wore torn fatigues, an over-sized white T-shirt with a pocket over the left breast and black high tops with no socks. His ankles seemed sharp as chiseled flints.

The strange man appeared to be whispering to himself while staring ahead, his gaze frozen on some fixed point. The surrounding area remained unpeopled, just rumpled fields merging into dense forest. His hair was iron-grey and cut close, shaved around the sides and back like most of the farmers in the area. The typical bowl cut.

I pulled on to the grassy shoulder and stopped. At the squeal of the brakes, the man's head began to swivel like a machine gun turret on a Sherman tank; smoothly checking for signs of the enemy. His eyes reminded me of wet cement, vacant and opaque. For a second, I thought he might flap his arms and try to fly. But he didn't. We both sat there and I watched him continue to swivel his head while wondering what to do.

He frightened me a little and I tried to remember if there were any asylums nearby. I couldn't just sit there forever and I didn't want to leave the poor guy, I mean what was his story? I began to write the copy up in my head. Seemed more newsworthy than a bunch of piglets, that's what instinct signaled to me. I leaned out from behind the wheel and unhitched the door carefully. I left it open in case a quick getaway was required. Steady and slow—I approached. I didn't want to rile him but made sure he saw me too. I was surprised to discover that, the birdman, as tall as he was, kept his perch so easily. He looked healthy enough with that ruddy complexion and although lean didn't seem undernourished in any way. What he was, however, meant being somewhere else in his mind. Part of me wanted to join him.

As I drew near, I heard him talking to himself in a parrot-like manner, to the point of mimicking the scratchy pitch of the bird's voice.

"Did you see him? He was so tall…above the tabernacle. His hands were on fire…Did you see him? He was so tall…above the tabernacle. His hands were on fire…", he said repeatedly in that nasal tone. No squawking or screeching though.

I approached. "Sir?" The head swiveled. The voice nattered. "Sir?" No reaction. Oh well, what the hell. "Polly?" That got his attention. He stopped and then wet his lips. I was stumped. Now what?

"Polly…want a …banana?"

As it happened, I didn't have any crackers but I did have a banana in the glove compartment of my car. Meant to eat it but just forgot it was stuffed in there. If he'd been out here for any length of time, I reasoned astutely, he was bound to be hungry. Something in his face told me he was receptive to the idea, a kind of quizzical look. I reached out my hand.

"Come on, Polly. Come on down now and I'll give you a banana."

The birdman cocked his head to the right, then the left and unfolded one leg like a stork until it touched the ground, whereupon taking his weight fully, released the other and stood in a half-crouch, with his hands cupped forward in front and elbows tight to his sides. His long neck stood outstretched and as I took a step toward him, he pulled it in sharply lifting his thin lips, exposing yellow teeth.

I held up my hands. "Okay. Okay, Polly." I backed away slowly.

"Why don't you come with me and get the banana? Come on. Come on, Polly." I coaxed him bit by bit to the car…he duck-walked along the shoulder of the road. The sharp smell of freshly laid tar wafted up. I opened the passenger door and he stepped in, standing then crouching on the seat where he resumed his perch, head and shoulders above the line of the windshield. Over on the driver's side, I opened the glove compartment, removed the banana, peeled it and held it out to him. He examined it for a few moments and then reassured it was what I said it was, took it in his hands holding them like talons and began to peck at the mushy fruit eagerly, head bobbing rhythmically. I put the car in gear and drove carefully back to Highway 26.

And so we drove into town, this creature on my right pecked at a banana ready to take wing if he were able, as I contemplated how this might look to the so-called sane world. Then I decided, to hell with the sane world. What had it done for me lately?

I skirted the town perimeter and came up through the alleyway behind the police station. Now I had a problem. Should I lead him inside or leave him in the car and bring somebody out? Might he fly the convertible? By now, he'd finished the banana and resumed the swivel routine. Instinct told me he'd stay put for at least a little while.

"Polly. I want you to stay here in your perch until I get back. Do you understand, Polly? Polly, do you understand?" I don't know if he heard me but I stepped over the door of the car praying that Hal Bigelow hadn't finished his shift yet. I was in luck. He sat behind the main counter filling out forms. In his meaty fist, the pencil looked like a toothpick.

"Hal, we've got to parley. Outside."

He barely looked up. "Simpson. Back again. Why don't we give you a desk or maybe you'd like an office?"

"Hal look. I don't have time to explain but you've got to come outside with me right now. I've got something to show you. It's in my car." His eyes narrowed suspiciously showing concentrated mental activity then flitted to the mound of paperwork in front of him. "Hal, when I say now, I mean now."

He sighed, fingered his chin, then slapped the pencil down on the clipboard. "Okay, okay." he groused, rising, taking the elevator to his full height. "What's up? You got some fancy hubcaps or something?"

"Come outside and try not to fall flat on your kisser, wise guy."

I literally pulled him out the door. It was like dragging an elephant stuck in the mud. We went out back. I feared the birdman had taken off or been driven away. To my relief, there he sat, maintaining his perch in the front seat, swiveling his head, scanning the unseen horizon for the figure in his terrifying vision.

"Have a look-see," I said.

Constable Bigelow stopped dead and gaped. "What the hell? What's he doing?"

"You know this guy?" I asked.

"I sure do. It's Ellis Boston."

"The guy who planted a hoe in his wife's back?"

"Yeah. Say. How did you know about that? The public announcement hasn't gone out yet. It's all been on the QT."

"Never mind."

"What the hell is he doing?"

"Being a bird," I replied.

Hal said, "Come again?"

"He thinks he's a bird, Bigelow. A bird. What'd you think I said?"

"Don't ask," he muttered and stepped gingerly toward Ellis Boston who affixed him with a piercing stare. Hal stopped several feet in front of the car. "Ellis? Ellis? What the hell are you doing? Ellis, can you hear me?" The only response he elicited was a muted squawk.

"He won't answer you. But he was mumbling something when I found him. Something like,"Did you see him...above the tabernacle. He was so tall. His hands were on fire." Or words to that effect," I said.

Hal clawed at his scalp. "I don't know who's more nuts here, us or him. Where did you say you found him, Joe?"

"Perched on a fence post up 26 about three miles north of Nottawasaga."

"That'd be about seven miles from his place."

"Wonder if he flew?"

"Funny, Simpson. Very funny. We've had patrol cars combing the county for him." Hal didn't laugh, however. He didn't even look as if he thought about it. "Come on, help me get him inside. We'll have to put him in a lock-up until we can get Doc Seaton to have a look at him."

"Okay," I replied, opening the door. "You know, it occurs to me, that if a guy wanted to beat a murder rap, this might be a pretty neat way of doing it."

"Save the analysis, okay Joe?" Then Hal began to croon as if he'd been talking to human birds all his life. "Come on, Ellis. Come with me now. We'll take care of you. Come on. That's it." And the birdman allowed himself to be helped out of the car and led awkwardly inside.

I said, "He seems to like bananas."

Watching Hal lead Ellis into the stationhouse reminded me of Gulliver and his pet—quite touching in a way. Once inside, the officers and clerks and a lone forgotten prisoner sitting on a bench against the wall sipping coffee, kept about their business. Gradually, however, the standing workaday hum dropped to the level of a whisper as, one by one, a voice, then another, ceased and bodies stilled, scribbles halted in mid-sentence, calls were cut short after three digits, and twenty pairs of eyes turned to stare in astonishment at Constable Bigelow and his quirky charge, who continued to swivel his head spraying the large room with his sightless gaze.

Chief McKie chose that moment to enter. He was a short, bow-legged man with dark wavy hair greased with pomade brushed straight back from a narrow forehead. Hazel eyes squinted suspiciously at the world. Everyone had a flaw, a hole in their character where, Chief McKie surmised, as a result of reading the one criminology text he could understand—*The Criminal Mind; A Lawman's Guide to Deviancy*—offered the potential for each individual in society to do no good. That's why children torched houses, husbands brutalized wives, charities and churches were robbed with abandon, priests committed carnal sin and so on. Apart from that elevated tome, Chief McKie remained fixated on such intellectual reading material as *Police Gazette* and *True Detective* to satisfy his informational urges.

And when the illustrious chief, his wide face festooned with razor nicks, saw Ellis Boston looking to the entire world like an ostrich on a string—his greasy eyebrows nearly disappeared into his gooey hairline.

"Jumpin' Jehosephat," he exclaimed, quoting his favourite cartoon hero, Yosemite Sam. "What the tarnation's going on here?" he twanged.

"It's Ellis Boston, Chief," replied Hal.

"I know damn well who it is, Bigelow. What's the matter with him?" growled the Chief, flicking his plump little hands. His short sleeve, blue shirt had creases sharp enough to sliver cheese.

At that point, I couldn't help but jump in. "He thinks he's a bird, Chief."

The Chief's scrinchy eyes flitted angrily in my direction. "What the hell do you know about it, Simpson?"

"Nothing much. I just found him and drove him in. That's about all, I guess."

"Found him where?" barked the Chief.

"On a fence post not more than 6 miles up Highway 26," I replied.

"And what was he doing at that time?"

I shrugged. "Nothing much. Just sitting there in a perched position talking to himself."

"Well. What'd he say?"

"He said…"Did you see him…above the tabernacle. He's so tall. His hands were on fire." That's all," I replied.

"Tabernacle? He said, tabernacle?" cried the Chief, who was a Baptist. The idea of a bird uttering such a noun was unthinkable and shook his shiny head in utter disbelief. "If that don't beat all. If that don't beat all."

Hal said, "Uh Chief. I think we'd better get Ellis down into a cell where it's a bit more peaceful and people won't stare, don't you think?"

I said, "Maybe you ought to call Dr. Hillside, the Vet."

The Chief blinked twice, started to open his mouth to say something then decided the best course of action was to ignore me. Probably right too. He nodded.

"All right. But you'd better get Doc Seaton here right away. Ellis needs looking over." Then glaring at the stupefaction around him for the first time, hollered, "Go on, you robots, back to work. There's nothing worth staring at."

The hubbub returned albeit reluctantly as people's minds raced around the possibilities.

"This'll be all over town in about two minutes," the Chief muttered miserably. He turned his mealy gaze on me for a moment and started again to say something, then changed his mind, cheeks flinching with nervous irritation. He thought I could badmouth him in the paper, which of course, I'd done previously and enjoyed it. Instead, he spun with military decisiveness on the elevated heels of his tan cowboy boots, and strode down the corridor quickstepping into his office slamming the door. Lord knows how any crime got solved in this abandoned parish, I thought. I watched Hal Bigelow lead Ellis Boston carefully to the basement where the cells were located. On his way, he asked Juanita Barnes, the dispatcher, if she'd be good enough to fetch a sandwich out of Hal's desk, in case Ellis felt peckish. I took this as my cue to skedaddle.

I said, "I'll just be moseying along."

"Coward," Hal replied, concentrating on Ellis. "Oh Joe?"

I stopped. "Yeah?"

"Is there something else, something you're not telling me, maybe?"

"Now, why would you think such a thing, Constable?" I said.

"Well, you look like you've been run over by a herd of sex-crazed cattle, for one thing," Hal said, grinning.

"It's a cultivated look, copper. Something a bumpkin like you wouldn't understand," I replied.

"That goes along with the egg on your forehead, the axle grease on your hands and the bashed in fender I spotted outside?" Bigelow asked.

"Something like that. Now, if you don't mind, I have some pressing commitments."

"Sure. Give Teddy my regards. I'd like to hear him tear a strip off you myself but you look a little beat up. He may go easy."

I sighed. "Yeah. He might." Ellis continued to swivel his head, then ducked his beak under his arm for a second, then popped back up. "Native is getting restless," I said.

Hal led Ellis away…twenty pairs of eyes trailed after them.

Chapter Five

I left my jalopy behind the cop shop thinking it would be as safe there as anywhere then stopped into my apartment to change my shirt and get cleaned up. I had axle grease on my hands and dirt and sweat encrusted in my face. The damn tingling didn't stop so I did what I always do—stuck sheets of paper up on the walls—nothing on them anyway, not a poster or a painting or a photograph—and wrote down Norma's name on one and Blake Rothwell on the other. Listed what I knew about each as well as any questions that popped into my head, such as, why did Blake wait such a long time to report Norma's drowning? How fast was he going? Was he drunk? Fragments of ideas that I hoped would gel into a bigger story. Heck, then I decided to put up another page and wrote Jan and Ned Beatty's names on it just because they were so weird and another page with Ellis Boston and the word, birdman, underneath. What happened to him? How did he get to the fencepost so far away from his farm? I surveyed the messy collage then decided I needed to hoof it back to The Gazette. I was anxious to get hold of Doc's autopsy report on Norma Jennings. I'd pass right by the town morgue on my way. Thinking more about Ellis Boston and what he'd become, left me puzzled and frightened. How did a man transform himself into a parrot? But then I thought about how people loved to gossip and hear it bantered about. It wasn't as if people didn't mind repeating things they'd heard time and again. Not in a small town like Applewood—a community of parrots.

Next to the police station sat the new post office—a chunky concrete structure, then the A&P where I shopped, Charlie's coin laundry where, no surprise, I took my dirty things, then the Moon Glow Restaurant that served Chinese-Canadian cuisine. I wasn't entirely sure what that meant even after eating there once or twice. Further south came Searle's department store where you could buy socks to sequins to seat covers; even live goldfish you could take home in a plastic bag for a quarter apiece. Adjacent to Searle's stood the Country Kitchen donut shop where I stopped for coffee and something to snack on just about every morning. I never made time for breakfast at home anymore.

I paused at the corner of Tecumseh and Geraint streets. After crossing Geraint, a fairly imposing professional building came into view. It housed accountants and lawyers offices and in the basement, a couple of fortune-tellers and masseurs. The Lantern Restaurant stood in as the local greasy spoon and was favoured by the professionals, as well as, the grease monkeys and farm hands in town. After which, came Hillside Veterinary Clinic, Dr. Wayne Hillside presiding, who had a special affinity for birds, warblers, parrots and pintails, in particular. Not that he didn't tend to dogs, cats, chickens, horses and cows but Dr. Hillside had a natural preference for anything with feathers.

On the corner of Brook Street, I passed the oily eyesore called Diggle's Gas Bar staffed by goggle-eyed, droopy-mouthed men who seemed to be the product of inbreeding far back in the hill country somewhere. Charlie Diggle himself looked after my Chevy Biscayne. When the whitewalls began to blow in succession like so many firecrackers on Queen Victoria Day, Charlie gave me a decent discount on new tires out of pure regret and goodwill. At least I liked to think so.

I told myself I was only paying a visit to the dead not joining them but as I trudged along Tecumseh St., I needed to be convinced. Until now, I'd had no occasion to visit Doc Seaton in his frigid lair deep within the morgue. When the opportunity had arisen, Teddy had stepped forward to accept the honours, something he danced into with ghoulish delight. Eyeballing the most shattered remains from a head-on collision or the charred, smoking remnants of a five-alarm house fire never seemed to bother him. He'd stand back with a sanguine and detached eye scribbling notes as Doc worked away like a mechanic, reaching for various drills and saws and pliers. Teddy told me he enjoyed the morgue experience and autopsies in particular. Hmm.

Marching along the rapidly dwindling blocks, my spirits began to lift in the warm, June sunshine. People gave me funny looks. I guess it had something to do with the lump on my forehead. I found it hard to believe, almost unfathomable, that early the very same morning, I'd seen Norma Jennings' broken body washed up out of Rattlesnake Bay.

I came abreast of a new record store that had opened up within the past couple of months called Sky High Records & Tapes. 'For What Its Worth' by Buffalo Springfield blasted out the doorway causing most of the older citizens of Applewood to cross to the other side of the street. The owner went by the name of Wishbone Jones. He had the dubious honour of being the town's very first authenticated hippy. He wore his fair hair long and braided in the back and sported enormous moustaches that seemed to fly up his skinny nostrils. The storefront featured a large peace symbol emblazoned on the plate glass window. Wishbone appeared in Applewood one day and before anyone could blink twice, he'd opened up the store. I'd heard no end of rumours about him—that he'd been an American draft dodger, a Vietnam vet, or in fact, a French Canadian dentist impersonating an American frontier character, and finally, the heir to the J.P. Getty fortune but had rejected his wealthy roots. Who Wishbone really was burned my curiosity.

Acquisitive teenagers constantly jammed Wishbone's store eager to scoop up the latest popular music. Somehow, he managed to get rare imported records that these kids would do anything to get. He featured a decent selection of jazz and classical records but more importantly, an outstanding collection of vintage blues artists like Robert Johnson, Meadowlark Lemon, Muddy Waters, Howling Wolf, Bessie Smith and Big Mama Thornton among many others. Favourites of my old man's. Jack Simpson cursed me with his vocation and his taste in music. Anyway, that's how I met Wishbone, looking for the blues.

I couldn't even begin to guess his age. He could have been thirty-five or forty-five. I couldn't penetrate that persona with all its flamboyant trappings. His brow and cheeks were deeply furrowed indicating he'd spent a good deal of time out in the sun or done a lot of worrying or both. Another puzzling thing about Wishbone— his capacity for attracting gorgeous women. It seemed almost uncanny that this unkempt, skinny, hawk-faced man could draw such winsome beauties like lovesick bees high on the scent of nectar. I'd never seen anything quite like it. They'd just show up from somewhere as if summoned and then some weeks or months later, simply disappear. Not long after, another cool beauty would take her place.

As I was strolling by, Wishbone lounged in the doorway of his shop, one eyebrow cocked as he observed the world with an air of jovial irony. A young woman in her middle 20's named Beverly, worked the cash. Just a few days earlier, she just showed up looking rather prissy, hair in a bun, shapeless skirt, baggy blouse. Now, her glossy dark hair rose like an inferno piled on top of her head. She moved languidly, owning the world around her. She sang softly to herself and her voice made you want to cry. Somehow, Wishbone had done something to her too. I marveled at the change in her. Before, no one would have given her a second look. Today, she'd cause a vicious pile-up on Highway 26 merely by showing up. Wishbone continually yammered on about inner beauty waiting to be released, all it took was the right combination of life forces, he said and I guess he had something there.

The store was jammed with pimply teenagers who simply wanted to speak to Beverly but didn't have the nerve. Naturally, while they were pining over her, each one bought at least two albums each, sometimes more. I concluded from all of this that Wishbone Jones was really a marketing whiz and could teach the button-down set a thing or two about moving product.

Wishbone offered me his palm.

"Joe Blow, gimme five," he drawled and his moustaches fluttered in the soft breeze. I gave him a hand slap and let him do mine. A particularly gruesome scar ran from the heel of his hand in a giddy, jagged line up his forearm to the crook of his elbow. Got his arm caught in some barbed wire was all he'd ever say about it and once again the spectacular scar fuelled talk of his past with three schools of thought prevailing. The first pegged it as a shark attack while surfing off Malibu. The second claimed it was the result of a vicious dog bite during an anti-segregation march in Selma or possibly Birmingham. The third harkened back to the war and some shrapnel he'd taken in Vietnam that earned him an honourable discharge from the USMC, possibly a bronze star too. If anybody looked less like a marine, it was Wishbone, and that's why I tended to believe that theory over the others.

"What's happening, my friend?" he asked, grinning the grin of the enlightened.

"Nothing much. The usual. Reporting, you know," I answered lamely.

Wishbone cocked his head toward the store's interior. "I've got a Dylan you'll be wanting."

"Oh yeah, why's that?" I asked, curious because he knew I didn't really care for Dylan—too nasal, too self-interested.

Wishbone grinned. One of his front teeth had been badly chipped, the result of a bar fight he'd said, someone who'd made fun of his long hair. Somehow, he had the air of a man who could look after himself.

"'Cause Big Mama Thornton's doing the singing, that's why. It'll shake you up, Joe, wait and see. Besides, you oughta give Dylan a chance. He's better than you think," he said.

"Okay," I conceded. "I'll come by later and give it a spin." He had a way of convincing without pushing it, sort of like the Quaker idea of friendly persuasion. But then I remembered that Richard Nixon was a Quaker too.

Wishbone nodded and tapped me seriously on the back. "You won't be sorry, Joe."

"Hi Joe." It was Beverly who'd come up from behind and peaked around one of Wishbone's pointed shoulders, draping a tanned arm around him. "What'd you do to your head?"

"Oh. That. Uh, had a little road accident."

Wish sniggered. "You should be more careful, Joe. A lot of crazy drivers out there on the road. Maybe you need to pay more attention at the wheel."

"Yeah, maybe," I conceded.

"Let me take a look," Beverly said. She came in close and probed the lump on my forehead pressing her strong fingers.

"Yeow."

"Sorry. Didn't mean to push so hard. That's nasty. You should get it seen to."

She had moved in close and her full on womanhood suddenly made me feel foolish and uncomfortable. I felt like one of the pimply kids in the shop.

"That's right. You tell him, Bev," Wish said.

"Actually, I'm on my way to see Doc Seaton now."

Bev said, " Good. Hey. You must be writing about the latest goings on? I don't know what to think about that girl drowning—and the boy driving the boat? He must have been pretty careless, wouldn't you say?" She looked at me expectantly. Suddenly, it felt like an interview question, that I was supposed to make a comment.

I sidestepped. "Well, I don't think we've got the whole story yet."

She cocked her head. "Don't you think you've outgrown this place, Joe? Wouldn't it be better if you headed to Toronto to work for a larger paper?" Bev couldn't have known how I felt about the big city papers. I remembered the screaming headlines and lurid pictures of my mother's bewildered face as the cops arrested her, hustled into a patrol car and the ambulance pulling away from the curb with the old man's corpse. It fueled my desire to escape and when

I thought about it, I gagged, remembering the skinny, twelve year-old kid with no parents anymore.

Bev held me in her gaze. The fact that she oozed some potent kind of sensuality made it difficult to look away. I shivered.

Suddenly, she jammed Wishbone in the ribs with her elbow knocking the wind out of him. "Hey, I've got a great idea. Why don't you invite Joe to one of your parties, Wish? He'd have a great time. Wouldn't you like to come along, Joe?"

"Not sure. I might," I managed.

After Wishbone straightened up, he curled one of his moustaches, nodded sagely, as if listening to a brief during a session of the Supreme Court.

"Bev's right, Joe," he concluded. "My parties are very loose. And you know the music is guaranteed to be out of this world. Listen, I've got one set up for tomorrow night, just a few people, you understand. Why don't you stop by the store about eight? What do you say?"

"I'll see, Wishbone. I'm not sure what's happening yet."

"Oh come on, Joe," Beverly said. "You'll have fun. That's a promise." She gave me a wink.

Ouch. That current was strong. I started to leave. "Well, I'll do my best."

Wishbone just nodded in agreement. "Whatever, Joe. Whatever."

"Look after that lump," called Beverly, as I backed away.

I raised a hand in farewell and then turned my back on them. It seemed pretty clear to me that Wishbone and Beverly had a relationship that went beyond employer and employee. I also wondered how long the more conservative elements in town would turn a blind eye to Wishbone Jones with the rumours flying like a summer tornado around him. Already some understanding and compassionate individual had spray-painted the kind and charitable message—Faggot Queer Go Home—on the store's window. Like mass murder, suicide and even something as common as arson, intolerance can occur anywhere. Applewood seemed like a sleepy community but you never knew what percolated down below.

Chapter Six

Doc Seaton's receptionist abandoned her post for lunch. The desk lay empty.

I plunged into the underworld. A blast of cold air hit me as I descended concrete steps. After the warm sunshine, it gave me the creeps.

I looked right, then left. A doorway glowed with eerie light. I heard some faint murmurings. Ungluing my feet, I tiptoed in that direction. The door stood ajar and with some trepidation I'll admit, nudged it open.

The room surprised me. It looked very much like a modern operating facility with stainless steel counter tops and sinks, immaculate linoleum flooring and white linen covering the nastier bits. Soothing classical music emanated from an elaborate tape machine. The plume of a dying cigarette curled upward from a substantial ashtray carved out of black onyx. I counted only two slabs.

Norma Jennings lay on the slab closest to the door. At least, I assumed it was her by the colour of her hair. Thankfully, a long, white sheet covered her bloated corpse. Except for her delicate, white feet, now badly discoloured and broken. I noticed her toenails were painted pink, reminding me of the clamshell I'd taken after it dropped from her lifeless hand.

Doc Seaton stood with his round back to me, hunched over the second slab engrossed entirely in his work. Above the prone body, hung a microphone on a long, spindly cord. Doc murmured into it as he worked, I could see his elbows jerking and occasionally, he'd reach up and steady the mike with bloodied fingertips.

I found my voice. "Doc?"

What the…?" he gasped, straightening up and clocking himself on the crown with the mike that began to sway menacingly to and fro, swiping at his nose as he tried to duck out of the way. Doc didn't seem to recognize me at first. His pale eyes remained unfocused and he looked supremely annoyed.

"Don't creep up on me like that, Joe. You damn near scared the crap out of me. God knows I don't want to end up like them," he said and gestured broadly to his silenced companions. "That'll happen soon enough."

"Sorry, Doc," I said, humbled by his anger. "I didn't mean to give you a fright."

"Well you can't imagine a lot of people traipsing through this place, do you Joe? We don't get many visitors down here and that's a fact." I could see he was beginning to calm himself now. "Your boss is one of the few who likes to hang around down here. Even the cops can't stand it."

"Yes, I can see that. Sorry," I replied.

"Well," he grumbled and pushed his spectacles up the bridge of his nose with a free elbow. "Now that you're here, what do you want, Joe?"

"I was wondering about the autopsy report on Norma. Hal Bigelow said there'd been a snag of some kind."

Doc nodded, then wiped his hands on a clean towel and having finished, removed his spectacles and rubbed them in an absent-minded way on the smock.

"Not a snag, exactly, Joe. Just something I didn't expect. But there's always something. Now, why don't you wait down the hall in my office while I finish up with Lizzy here." And he indicated the body he'd been working on. "That's Lizzy Boston," he began as if introducing us. I almost said, how do you do. "Her husband, Ellis, claims that Lizzy must have passed out while gardening and fell onto her hoe, which according to Ellis, that is, explains the puncture marks in her back. They look like they were made by a hoe, all right, so I'll give Ellis that much anyway."

"You don't believe him, Doc?"

"Well, I didn't say that exactly, Joe and this is off the record, by the way. I guess it's a matter of what she passed out from, isn't it?" He shook his head. "The whole thing just seems strange. Ellis claims it looked like heat stroke but he couldn't be sure. It's no more than seventy-seven degrees out there today and Lizzy was wearing her hat like she always does. Besides, she's a pretty healthy fifty-two year-old from what I can see. It'll depend on the angle of the wounds, too, you see, Joe. The angle is pretty important."

"You think he did it, Doc? Ellis?"

Doc smiled and replaced his spectacles. " Chief McKie will have to find him first and then ask him. It wouldn't be the first time a husband struck his wife out of anger or the opposite, now, would it?" he asked in a dry voice.

"No, I guess it wouldn't," I conceded. "Speaking of which...."

"Yes?"

"They need you up at the police station."

"Why's that?"

"It's about Ellis..." and I nodded toward Lizzie Boston.

"Ellis? What about him?"

"Something's happened to him...gone a little strange in the head. I guess he went a bit loco after Mrs. Boston had her...well, died." I shrugged. " He's in a holding cell. They need you to take a look...give your opinion...."

Doc sighed and tched under his breath a little, shaking his head and his wattles along with it. "There's lots of news today, isn't there, Joe? Now you go and wait for me in my office and we'll talk about that report, okay Joe?"

"Okay, Doc."

"I'll just be a few more minutes with Lizzy, here."

I found Doc Seaton's office at the far end of the hall. I sat down in a creaky leather chair opposite his desk and lit a Sweet Cap to rid the taste of stainless steel and formaldehyde from my palate. Smells that reminded me of dissecting frogs in science class, after which, I never ate another dill pickle and couldn't look at one without feelings of disgust. I expected to see a skull sitting on top of Doc's desk but instead there were boxes of tapes neatly stacked and labeled. The tapes were cross-referenced to file numbers on a group of folders also piled high. Detailed autopsy reports and tapes of the autopsy results recorded live. Somehow I'd never thought of Doc as being so meticulously organized and it surprised me.

Medical books and journals and reports—all lined up in glass cabinets right way around the room from floor to ceiling. The little remaining wall space, was taken up by large colour charts of the major body organs displayed much like others would hang calendars or maps. To me, the organ charts resembled exotic locales with canals and arteries and chambers brightly coloured—all unexplored by the general populace. It would make for a different kind of trip, all right and suddenly I thanked providence the medical field had never proved a temptation. All I could think was, these hands buried in human goo all day long? No thanks, I'd take paper and ink anytime.

"Sorry, I was so long, Joe," Doc pronounced upon entering, and waddled around his desk sinking that prodigious bulk into his chair with a satisfied smile creasing his round face. "Oh, that feels good. I've been on my feet since early this morning. It feels damn good to take a load off."

I sympathized. "I can well imagine, Doc. Sure makes for a long day."

"As a physician you get used to it, Joe. Your family doesn't but you do, you haven't got any choice. Now then, you wanted to know about Norma, didn't you?"

I nodded. Doc opened the file he'd been carrying under his arm when he came in. "Now let's see here," he muttered to himself, as if he were reading it for the first time. He scanned through for a moment, then abruptly slapped the folder closed. "Before we start, I've got to ask you, Joe, not to draw any conclusions from this. What I mean is, conclusions that haven't been substantiated by fact. That's a matter for Chief McKie and his boys. If any charges are pending against Blake Rothwell, then it's up to him to make that determination. At the least, we could be looking at a coroner's inquest based on what I see here."

I shrugged innocently, thinking that Chief McKie couldn't substantiate his own shoe size.

"Okay Doc. Whatever you say." I was burning with curiosity now. I hadn't expected Doc to be so edgy and that meant he found something pretty important.

"And you have to swear, Joe, not to write any of this up before it goes over to the stationhouse, too," Doc commanded sternly.

"Sure, Doc. I'll hold off until we get the official go-ahead. You know that's how it always works. Teddy prides himself on cooperating with the authorities, you know that," I replied.

"I just want it to be clear," he said sharply and continued, "The first thing I discovered—Norma Jennings was pregnant, about eight or nine weeks along, I figure."

I nodded, not really taking it in fully but the news made me feel worse.

Doc forged on.

"Norma's alcohol level was .15, about double what it'd take to get her really soused. On top of that we found some kind of chemical in her bloodstream."

"Chemical?" I asked.

"Right, Joe. The lab in Hazelton, where I'd sent out for the blood analysis, phoned to let me know. So far, they haven't been able to figure out what it is but it's plenty evident all right. And when they find out, they'll call right away. So you see, all of this might put a different complexion on things than it would if it was just an accidental drowning. I'm not saying it still isn't, you understand. But there are other factors now to consider," Doc said.

"What factors?" I asked.

"I couldn't possibly speculate," Doc replied casually, drumming his fingers on top of the cardboard folder.

"But...."

"And that's it," Doc concluded.

"That's it?" I asked.

Doc grinned. "For now."

He pulled a manila envelope out of his desk drawer, dropped the folder into it, and sealed it with an official looking stamp.

"Maybe you wouldn't mind dropping this off to Chief McKie for me? I was going to do it myself but if you're passing that way...?" He handed it across his desk.

"I'd be happy to, Doc. What about Ellis?"

"Thanks son. Just leave it with the Chief. I've got to get back to Lizzy there and besides, I'm too old to be running all over town at my age. As soon as I finish with Lizzie and a few other things first. I've got my chickens in the run out back to take care of, haven't checked the nests yet and then, I'll be over to take a look at Ellis. Doesn't sound like he's going anywhere."

"No, I guess not." Then held up the report. "Don't worry, Doc. I'll get it there," I promised.

"Thanks, Joe." He smiled beatifically and as he tilted his head upward, the lenses of his spectacles went opaque.

Chapter Seven

No sooner had I stepped inside the office than Teddy jumped me growling like a pint-sized tiger in a feeding frenzy, gnashing the cigar stub, flicking his suspenders in irritation.

"Goddamit, Joe. Where the hell have you been? Do you know what time it is?" Teddy started talking to himself, thinking aloud, I guess. "The kid goes to write a little piece about some goddam pigs and comes back four hours later. What the hell takes four hours when you're writing about pigs?" He turned his attention back to me. "Tell me, I'd sure like to know. What the hell took you so goddam long?"

"Teddy. You've been knotting your undies too tight again. Listen, you're not going to believe the day I had, honest. You're just not going to believe it." I'd run back from the morgue and sweated through my clean shirt.

"Believe? You'd better hope I believe or believe me when I tell you…" He stopped suddenly staring me in the face for the first time. "You're a mess, Joe. Where'd you get that egg on your forehead?"

I touched the swollen spot then winced. "Uh, little accident on the road. Some guy ran me off it doing about 100 miles an hour."

"You don't say?" Teddy exclaimed, although he looked skeptical. Maybe he was thinking that I was capable of self-inflicting said lump to avoid his wrath and ire.

I nodded. "If you don't believe me, take a look at my car. It's banged up pretty good."

At least that was something that Teddy could understand. Getting your car dinged meant serious business. He frowned. "Much damage?"

"Scrape along the driver's side, crumpled up wheel well, blown rear tire and the bumper probably will need replacing."

Teddy let out a long, low whistle. "Mmm... doesn't sound good."

"It isn't. Guess I know what I'll be spending that raise on."

As it happened, our "society" columnist, Paisley O'Toole, sat nearby toiling over her weekly column, not much for the well-heeled to do in Applewood but Paisley remained determined to change that sad state of affairs. A well-groomed woman of 40, Paisley served on every committee Applewood had to offer and was married to one of the town's wealthiest citizens. Seamus was fifteen years her senior and known as a gruff blackguard in business circles. Her smooth face nearly shriveled inside itself when she glanced up at me.

"Why Joe," she cried. "Don't let anybody ever tell you that body odour is sexy," and wrinkled her cosmetically rearranged nose, which, even I admitted, was kind of pert.

I replied, "Don't you know it's the smell of death and destruction? Fire and brimstone, Paisley dear. I reek of it. It's in my pores. I have it on good authority from an expert in the religious field. Don't come too close. It'll ooze out of me and will pollute you," I said. She turned away, repelled by my impudence. I grinned, not kindly.

"You're a nutcase, Joe Simpson," Paisley said.

"Listen Teddy, you wouldn't believe what's been going on around here," I said trying to get things back on track.

"It'd better be pretty damn spectacular, Joe. We're talking fireworks and rockets here. Get me?"

Marching behind Teddy's hunched shoulders to his office, I noted the plume of his shirtsleeves billowing out around the elastic bands he wore up on his biceps. Keeping his cuffs neat and tidy. The surface of his desk looked like rats had been rumbling on it—galleys strewn about, the wreckage of stories he'd been marking up, mine included and remnants of what could have been lunch or even breakfast. He waved me brusquely into a chair and a few of the wayward pages fluttered in the breeze he created. I sat.

"Now give," he demanded, jamming the cold cigar butt into his face and squinted at me through make-believe smoke, vapor trailing the mortar blasts in his eyes.

I feigned innocence. "I almost don't know where to begin."

He said, "Find a spot. How about, what happened when you left here at 12:30?"

I filled him in finishing with a flourish. " Listen to me, Teddy. I know it sounds crazy but something is going on around here. Something peculiar."

"Yeah?" His eyebrows shifted. "Like what?" He was sniffing for a story and he'd look under any rock or in any parched riverbed to find one.

"I don't know, exactly. Not yet."

"So?" He thought I was wasting his time and didn't shrink from letting me know. He began to sift through the crumpled pile on his desk.

"Just look at all the things that have happened in a short space of time" I counted them off on my fingers. "Norma goes in the drink. Doc finds some weird chemical in her blood he can't identify. Someone tries to run me off the road for no reason in some sort of monster car with blacked out windows..."

"Now that could be someone from your deep, dark past, Joe. Or just a kid out joyriding for a cheap laugh."

I shook my head emphatically. "Don't think so. This guy knew exactly what he was doing. He knew how to handle that hot rod, I'm telling you."

Teddy sighed, then said something that sounded like, "Eerphh..."

"Then Lizzie Boston gets a hoe planted in her back...don't you see? All this stuff happening practically at the same time?

"Facts, Joe. I need facts. We can't report any of this cock-and-bull stuff. We'd be laughed out of the whole county."

Like I cared. But I decided to zip in one more fastball. "You're right, Teddy. I mean, when you're right, you're right. Nothing more to say, is there? And in keeping with the peculiar, I guess you know then that Ellis Boston thinks he's a bird." Teddy snapped his head back in surprise.

"What's that?"

I pulled it out slowly like a little kid trailing gum. "When I was driving in from the Beatty place, I swear to all the gods in the universe, I found Ellis Boston perched on top of a fence post posing like a parrot. He was mumbling to himself with his hands tucked to his sides like folded wings. And if you don't believe me, call Hal or Chief McKie and see what they have to say about it. Now when I say something peculiar is going on around here, do you think I'd just make it up and expect you to swallow it whole?"

Without a word, Teddy picked up the phone and dialed. "Chief McKie, please. McKie? Graff here. What's this I hear about Ellis Boston being a bird?" He paused. "Yeah. Uh-huh. Yes. I see. Okay. Sure. Why not? Fine, bye." He hung up the receiver thoughtfully, then cleared his throat. "Doc Seaton is with him now. Running some kind of tests on him. They've called in a shrink from the Montauk Mental Hospital too." He rose slowly from his chair, leaned the heels of his hands on the edge of the desk thinking for a moment, then looked at me somberly.

"Ellis and I used to be good friends once. We were in the same year at school. We used to go fishing together for smallmouth bass up at Forget-me-not Creek. Hell, I even dated Lizzie once or twice. Not my type as it turned out." He sighed, "You might as well write it up, Joe. It'd better be in the paper tomorrow, 'cause half the town's talking about it, already, Chief McKie says."

"But Teddy, don't you think all this is more than just a coincidence? I sure as hell do."

"I don't know. All we've got is a distraught husband, possibly a killer, who's off his nut. But we've got to approach this whole thing in a sober and responsible way. The big city Tabs'll turn it into another"Kidnapped By Aliens" story. You can follow it up but don't let go of the other things. You know, Norma and Lizzie and now, I guess, Ellis too. And the Rothwell kid's going to be called to a coroner's jury, you know. Starts the day after tomorrow. There's a hot shot coming up from Toronto to head the inquest and Doc'll be called to testify. Maybe you will too, if they could get any straight talk out of you. Goddammed if I can. Meanwhile, because the kid's old man is so powerful, some of the Toronto boys are coming up for it, I'm told."

"The competition."

Teddy circled around behind his chair. He broke out into a radiant predatory grin. He snapped his red suspenders. "Competition. Hah! We'll eat'em alive," he said, as if rolling the words on his tongue. "Oh yeah, I can't wait." And he hammered the top of his chair with a meaty fist.

I left him reveling in his self-induced fancy. Sir Teddy and the Dragon—a fairy tale for children of all ages. It was now five o'clock and I had to write up the Beatty story, Norma's autopsy report, do a piece on both Lizzie and Ellis, get home, shower and change in time for my date with Darlene Norris, at 7:30 pm. I sent our photographer, a brash, chain-smoking, hard drinking kid named Dusty Rhodes, over to the police station to get pics of Hal, Ellis, Chief McKie and anybody else he thought interesting. After which, Dusty had to develop the film I brought back of the Beatty's churlish piglets and print up some copies.

Then he'd put on an apron and roll up his sleeves and help Stumpy Butler sling type together in time for tomorrow's edition. Dusty was a whiz with a camera and I knew he wouldn't be hanging around this outcrop long. He put in extra time building up his portfolio.

As I pounded away at the keys of the beat up Smith-Corona that resembled a typewriter, something tickled the back of my neck. I recognized the nails. She was the only woman in the office who had any to speak of.

"What do you want, Paisley?" I said without pausing to break from the story. Teddy said he'd return after dinner to proof them before going to press so I had to work fast and didn't want to be interrupted.

Paisley leaned over and purred in my ear. She was the type who could purr and get away with it. I felt her hair brush my neck and smelled her perfume—a lilac scent. "Don't be so gruff, Joe. I just want to know what's going on, that's all."

"Nothing that society cares about, Paisley."

She was rubbing my neck now. Her fingers felt cool to the touch. "Come on, Joe. You're typing like a speed demon."

"I got a hot date and I don't want to keep the little lady waiting."

"With whom?"

"Darlene Norris."

"The assistant bank manager?" Paisley let loose a small laugh, more like a tinkle. "Oh Joe, you can do better than her."

I paused to give her a dirty look. " I'm not debating my social life with the likes of you, Paisley. You want to know something? Ask me a question. But I've got to finish this stuff as we go." And let my fingers hit the keys hard.

She said, "Tell me all about Norma Jennings."

My fingers froze momentarily while I thought about Paisley's interest in Norma. I turned around and took a long, hard look at her. What was she doing in this rural backwater when she could easily cut it in Toronto, Montreal or further afield, New York and London? An elegant, handsome woman with a slim figure, a small face in the shape of a perfect oval, delicate mouth, sharp cheekbones and captivating green eyes. Her chestnut hair looked hard enough to withstand a good whack from a hockey stick but it was a nice colour. She was wearing a pink ruffled blouse tucked neatly into a tailored white skirt that showed off her figure. The wide black leather belt cinched her narrow waist. She had very pretty ankles. Her make-up was perfect. Just enough to give her face colour, enhance the poutiness of her lips and bring out the green of her eyes. The pearls around her slender neck were large, long and real. I imagined she could have her way with just about anyone and her old man wasn't just anyone.

I replied, "What's to know? She's dead. You read it in the paper."

"What about the autopsy report?"

"Since when do society ladies care about autopsies?"

Her voice hardened. "Joe."

I sighed. "Okay doll. High level of alcohol—the usual kicks. Drinking and boating. Happens all the time."

Her face clouded. "Any talk of charges yet?"

"I don't know. Not my department. Say, you wouldn't be interested because there's talk of your husband doing business with the Rothwell kid's old man, would you? Now that would be big news. Along with the snot-nosed kid, who incidentally, is making an appearance Thursday at the coroner's inquiry? That sort of publicity wouldn't be very good for any business, would it?"

Paisley smiled but there was no humour in her expression. "I'll forget you said that, Joe."

"Hey, I never said a thing." I turned back to my typing.

"What else can you tell me, Joe?"

Without pausing, I said, "Read about it in the paper tomorrow, Paisley. And incidentally, give Seamus my fondest regards." She came around in front of the desk her heels clicking along the floor like a flamenco dancer working a pair of castanets. "You know, Joe. I could be very helpful to you. When you need it." She gave me a steady, unflinching look that was supposed to be full of meaning.

"Help me how?"

"Get out of this town and get a job on a real paper, for one thing, maybe in Toronto or Montreal."

"Toronto's too expensive and I don't speak French. Besides, I like it here in Applewood. It's becoming more and more interesting all the time." I wasn't going to tell her either that I ran away from the big city.

"Don't kid me, Joe. I can see you've got a bit of the crusader in you. I like that. Just remember, though, Joe darling," and she ran her beautifully manicured fingernail down my cheek just hard enough to leave a disappearing mark, "that crusaders often get burned at the stake."

"Oh Paisley. Didn't I tell you? I wear asbestos underwear."

She laughed. "Not funny, Joe. Not even clever." She picked up her alligator skin handbag, then wrinkled her patrician nose at me like a cat smelling a liver dinner. Paisley. Stupid name but a lovely woman.

After Paisley left, I decided to sneak a peek at her desk. Her leather bound diary sat primly in the top right corner. I flipped it open and leafed through a couple of pages. A snooper never has regrets I told myself. Bingo. A dinner party on the books with the Rothwells no less. Hmm. Wonder what they'd be discussing over the canapés? Might just have to crash that party, on official business, of course. Anything that Rothwell got up to was news. Put him together with Paisley's husband, Seamus and presto, a conglomeration was born.

I resumed typing at a furious pace. Finished the write-ups by seven-fifteen. I checked them quickly, left them in a pile on Teddy's desk with a note, then raced home to the flat I rented for eighteen dollars a week. Showered and changed my clothes in record time. Clean white shirt, khaki dungarees and topsiders with no socks. Glanced at the pages I'd stuck up on the wall. Drew an arrow from Norma to Blake Rothwell. Below Normal's name I wrote, baby, intoxicated, unknown chemical in her blood and added a question mark. Was it Blake's? Or could someone else be the father? Then hit the road. The light burned strong and clear, filtered by the trees in the distance. The sun wouldn't set for at least another hour yet. I loved being able to ride around in a convertible with the top down at dusk, where the temperature hovered in the low seventies and I could feel the breeze on my face ruffling my hair. Oh Lord, please don't let summer ever end, I silently prayed. And added, please don't ever let me grow old too. And keep the stories coming fast and furious.

Chapter Eight

Darlene Norris lived in a house she rented on the southern edge of town. The house itself, a split-level ranch style, sat on two wooded acres where it wasn't unusual to see deer grazing in the back or even the occasional beaver waddling along the banks of the creek snaking through the property. The owner spent a great deal of time in Europe researching Medieval painters and paintings. According to Darlene, he taught Art History.

She'd hung brass chimes above the door and they tinkled in the light air bursting with summer smells. Newly mown grass. Pine. Buttercups and a hint of manure mingled freely. All marking the onset of a soft summer evening full of sudden expectation. Beneath the resonance of the chimes, I heard the deeper but hushed rustling of the leaves in the maple trees as they swayed rhythmically.

I knocked on the door and waited, lost in my thoughts, listening to the indicators of life around me. When Darlene flung open the door I was startled. I may even have jumped a bit.

"Hi Joe."

"Darlene?" For a split-second I thought I'd come to the wrong house.

"What is it, Joe? You look lost."

I replied, "Maybe I am. But you look different. Uh, don't get me wrong, it's swell. More than swell."

Darlene's looks had softened, haloed in a way that I found startling and perplexing. Her hair, for instance. The best way to describe it would be to say that it had fallen down, collapsed around her face. The Darlene I knew wore her hair in a puffed up cloud—as if it had been spread over wire mesh, sprayed with Elmer's Glue-All and then, fitted to her scalp. The colour— often referred to as Canadian brown—a middling, nondescript tone with strips of blonde woven into it. And this evening in its collapsed state, her hair glowed with the vitality of a well-brushed mane; glossy and vibrant. I noticed she wore little make-up in direct contrast to the brassy rouge, macabre eye shadow and garish lipstick she'd normally trowel on when we'd gone out before. I hadn't really noticed her figure before but the simple cotton dress she wore was sleeveless and gathered at the waist. It buttoned down the front like a blouse and fell to just above the knee. Her legs were bare.

Darlene reached around me, closed the door and stayed there. Her arms coiled around my neck and she came in close. She smelled like honey and lemon, also a nice change from the usual—whatever it was she slathered on thick as molasses and heavily medicinal—that reminded me of my Aunt Minnie's closet. Needless to say, I was stunned at this transformation and didn't move. Then she kissed me in the tenderest, most lingering way and I could feel the swell of her breasts as she breathed deeply. She broke off abruptly, leaving me puckered.

"What are we doing tonight, Joe?"

"Burger Barn?"

Darlene shook her head.

"Drive-in?"

She shook her head again. Thus exhausted my menu of date options.

"Uh, I don't know."

Darlene stepped back crooking her finger at me and then pointed to a table in the hall. On it sat a large hamper.

"How about a picnic?" she said and slipped a light sweater over her bare shoulders, fitted a small purse under her arm and motioned me to take the hamper, which I did. She held the door for me, then marched me to the car. Darlene didn't even notice the state of my ride. Normally, she'd make a terse comment, maybe even refuse to get in because it had been damaged. She didn't say a word. Its appearance didn't matter to her. And to someone for whom appearances were very important, this seemed a strange departure—I didn't mind it a bit.

I switched on the radio and "Michelle" came on. Beatlemania swept the land. Trends in small towns like Applewood lagged about two years behind the rest of the world. As I wandered about in my daily meanderings, it appeared to me as if every kid I'd seen on the street recently had conformed—shaggy haircuts, black stovepipe pants for the boys, miniskirts for the girls, sharp-toed, polished shoes for the boys, impossibly high heels for the girls and acne everywhere. Personally, I preferred the Rolling Stones and a new band I'd just heard, The Who. But neither took anything away from John Mayall's Blues Breakers who represented the pinnacle in the British wave, as far as I was concerned. I knew I marched out of step with current fads, that I looked to the past for solace, before the dark times in my life. I liked music that screamed honest.

Darlene sat serenely beside me carried away by McCartney's endearing tenor. On our previous dates, she'd chat away the second the door opened, carrying on without drawing a breath. Her ambitions exceeded her real possibilities and she knew it. Particularly, in a small community like Applewood. But new elements appeared in town and rapid development stoked the aura of something larger in the works that seemed to satisfy her career ambitions at the bank.

"Where to?" I asked. Her reply resulted in a finger pointing westward. As I started down the long drive from her house and turned on to East Gwillimberry Road, she shook her hair free to catch the breeze. The fading embers of the sun lit her face with a soft glow flattening and smoothing her features. I still think of her that way; glowing and smooth.

"Darlene?"

"Uh-huh."

"Did you know Norma Jennings?"

And suddenly, her bare, perfect mouth drooped.

"Yes, I did," she answered dreamily.

"Did you know her well?"

"Oh, we hung out in high school. Then we kind of went our separate ways. But I'd see her around, from time to time. It was the three of us, me, Norma and Cindy Lou Fortunato. We called ourselves the tripod. We were inseparable in those long, bygone days."

"Cindy Lou?"

"That's right. She's dating a biker now."

"I know her. You still friends?"

"Uh-huh."

"What year did you graduate?"

"Let me see... 1960. Six years ago. But it seems like yesterday."

"Were you all in the same class?"

"No. I was two years ahead of Norma and Cindy Lou. We were in the squads, though."

"Squads?" I asked.

Then she laughed. "Sure Joe. You know. Cheerleading? It was fun. We had a real good time," she said peering into the pink mist of her teen years.

"You have a steady back then, Darlene?"

This time she laughed outright. Full-throated. Head back. "Sure I did."

"Who was it?"

"Larry Baker, the biker."

The penny dropped. "The Viking!" I screeched. "You went out with the Viking?"

"Why sure. He's sweet. At least he was back then. You know Larry? Why, you surprise me, Joe. I wouldn't think you two would have much in common."

"I sure do know him. He almost planted tire tracks in the middle of my face once." Plus, the guy had a rap sheet several yards long. He'd made the crime reports of *The Gazette* more than a few times.

"Oh Larry wouldn't do a thing like that. He's a pussy cat, really."

"Yeah, sure. And Hitler was just a misunderstood artist."

"Better watch the road. You're turning left up here," she said matter-of-factly. A road I'd never seen before opened up like a sprung trap. Darlene hadn't looked for it, as if she naturally sensed a change in direction. As soon as we were bouncing along, I understood why; the long grass and weeds had grown thick—there'd been little traffic to brush it back. If this was privately owned land as I suspected, then it hadn't been well tended.

I said, " You still see Cindy Lou?"

"Sometimes," she said. "At parties, barbecues, the drive-in…"

"At Furlingers?" I asked, sarcastically. A roadside dive on the outskirts of town known as a biker hang-out.

"That's right," Darlene replied, without a snort of surprise.

"When was the last time you saw Norma?"

" Stop reporting," Darlene said, remaining uncharacteristically poised as if she had a secret she wasn't sharing, keeping it all to herself. I used to do that with candy bars. She decided not to give out any more so I concentrated on the bumping of the tires gripping the splintered pavement hoping the remaining whitewall wouldn't erupt. Darlene hugged herself in an absent way, letting her hair blow around her face while she looked inward. She seemed distracted and lost in her thoughts.

"What's got into you, Darlene?"

She didn't answer directly, just looked skyward closing her eyes and smiling. It mystified me. Usually, she spewed trivial details about interest and mortgage rates, who dated who, who became engaged to who and most importantly, who married who. Hither to, Darlene was fixated on the mating game. Not the one ordered according to natural instinct, however, but directed by magazines such as Chatelaine or McCall's. Her vocabulary was punctuated with terms like "dreamy" and "dreamboat" applied liberally to anything or anyone where she'd been impressed in some positive way. But now I remained mystified. She'd become a cipher. I started going out with Darlene because she'd been a good guide, leading me through the more perplexing aspects of small town life, not to mention helping me open a chequing account. She'd been the first person I'd met in Applewood, except for Teddy, of course and I'd liked her open breeziness. She'd been fun. I didn't really have to think much with her especially about the past.

Suddenly, the road ended. I jammed on the brakes and the Chevy rocked to a halt.

"Come on," she said and quickly opened the door disappearing down a slope. I struggled with the hamper feeling a strain on my lower back. I picked my way carefully down the hill. From inside the hamper came the musical chiming of glasses and bottles. I found myself at the base of a grassy narrow that curved upward slightly. At its plateau sat Darlene, her back to me, her smooth shoulders dappled with the dying light. I set the hamper down beside her.

"What's this?" I asked, indicating the rush of boiling, molten water just below. It looked like a volcanic stream spuming out of a fissure.

"It's the top end of Buttermilk Creek," she replied, lost in the roiling currents.

"How did you find it?"

Finally she smiled upward, shading her eyes. "My parents own it. This is the back end of their property. I used to spend a lot of time here when I was a kid. It's my secret place."

"It's pretty."

"I know." She hesitated then, biting her lip. "I used to come here with someone."

"Who?"

"No one you know, Joe. Anyway, it's over now." And she flashed a weak, pain-filled smile.

We ate in silence. I uncorked the wine and poured out a glass each while Darlene unwrapped packages of cold chicken and roast beef, laid out fresh kaisers, condiments, cheese, an entire strawberry rhubarb pie and a thermos of coffee. I was impressed. We toasted and drank our wine, munched chicken and cheese and crusty bread. Darlene didn't seem to be eating but watched me while pressing the wine glass to her full lower lip, thinking to herself. I wiped the poultry grease from my hands. She'd even thought to include a wet towel.

She set the glass down, wrapped her arms around my neck and pulled my face close to hers. Kissing became an extension of our appetite and I thought Darlene, who ate little, would devour me. She'd never done that before, either. When I opened my eyes dusk had leveled completely to night. There was a moon, however. And the bluish light showed her to advantage, enlarging her spirit and sensuality until she became a breathless presence in my arms. She unbuttoned the front of her dress, then unhooked her bra while I stared in disbelief. She took my hands and placed them on her while I felt her nipples grow hard in my palms and I said, "Darlene, this isn't like you."

Holding my hands tightly to her, she replied, "I know."

"Is this a dream?"

"Yes," she breathed and lay on her back taking me with her and I kneeled over her. She traced an outline on my lips with her fingers. Then staring steadily into my eyes, drew her dress up to her hips. Electric blue light glinted in the tangled mound of her sex. "Lie with me," she said.

Slowly I pressed my body weight against her and we embraced. She held my head in her hands and trembled. She spoke softly, barely murmuring.

"For once I want to feel the true magic of love, Joe. Just this once. Just this one time and then I'll know." Her words made me fearful, that things between us had suddenly turned serious, even meaningful. Somehow it didn't feel right to me but I couldn't reply, couldn't force a sound out of my swollen throat, not wanting to say the wrong thing that might disappoint her in some way. God knows, I couldn't take the chance of letting her down—what she said seemed so important to her. Let's face it, I was confused by this turn in her behaviour.

Sometime later, after we'd made love, I looked up and Darlene had disappeared. I found her naked and shivering on the riverbank staring down at the dark water. I could hear it boiling in my ears. Gently, I said, "What are you doing, Darlene?"

"Watching the ants on the river."

"Ants? What ants?"

"When we were kids, we used to make these little rafts out of popsicle sticks. Then we'd get these ants, put them on the raft and float them down the river. Usually, they just drowned. But there was always one who'd make it downstream upright and intact. That one was the winner. Didn't you ever do that?"

"No."

She looked up at me, covering her sad face with a tragic smile.

"Don't worry, Joe. I don't expect you to marry me or anything. I just wanted this to happen, that's all. I don't want to end up like Norma. You understand, don't you?"

"What do you mean? End up like Norma how?"

She hesitated, biting her lip. "I mean, alone, that's all. That's all I meant by it."

I said, "But why..." But she pressed her finger to my lips silencing the question. She shivered and held herself.

I helped her up and it was as if she wanted to extend this last moment, something that I sensed she'd already determined may never happen again perhaps until her wedding day, if she ever had one. Then, she hugged me full out and hard, flattening her quaking body against mine like an iron pressing a linen shirt.

She said, "Kiss me one more time, Joe. It's got to last for eternity."

Chapter Nine

Item—Maisie the sow delivered an even dozen piglets the day before yesterday. Delighted parents, Jan and Evan Beatty of R.R. 2, Freedom Township, were overjoyed at the news. "Maisie's like my very own child," exclaimed Jan Beatty, 41. "We couldn't be happier. Said Evan Beatty:"The Lord has blessed us mightily on this day." The piglets were all named Maisie after the sow and weighed between 2 1/2 and 3 1/2 pounds each at birth.

Item—A coroner's jury will commence today at the Old Courthouse to determine the circumstances in and around the death of Norma Jennings, aged 22. Miss Jennings died in a boating accident three days ago. The driver of the high-powered speedboat, Blake Rothwell, 21, son of prominent developer, Phillip Rothwell, is expected to be called as a key witness. Dr. Reinhold Elgar of Toronto has been called in to conduct the hearings. The proceedings are open to the public: Room 215, Old Courthouse, eleven a.m. /30

As I finished re-reading the hollow words I'd written the day before, I thought of Lizzie Boston and her seemingly normal life and what may have happened to propel it unerringly to its gruesome and undignified conclusion. What had gone on between her and her husband Ellis, now transformed into the birdman of Applewood? How shameful and embarrassing, it seemed to me, seated at my wobbly desk, leaning back with my feet up sipping at a paper cup filled to the brim with sweet, aromatic, doughnut shop coffee. Sweat trickled down my sides collecting in the waistband of my cotton trousers. Just yesterday, to those who knew her, silver-haired Lizzie had simply been a neighbour or a friend. An unassuming woman quietly living her life in her own way and according to a set of principles she preferred. Her husband had been known as "someone

I went to high school with," or "a guy who played a mean game of baseball". Now he could be found jabbering to himself in a dank holding cell embedded in the belly of the police station, examined by squinty-eyed professionals who were attempting to determine if his sanity had exploded in a sudden beating of wings.

I hadn't slept well last night and my pattern of thinking proved it. Then there was Darlene, who wore a mask by day as she fought her way through moments of wadded dollar bills and mortgages and the relentless minutiae riddling loan applications and financial statements only to de-shell at night to become a soft, palpable organ of sensitivity. I couldn't reconcile Darlene's demeanour last night with the person I'd known her to be. She'd gone right-angled on me and left me behind. From warm but practical and chatty to soft, fuzzy and moon-glowed in a couple of days. It was as puzzling as the deaths of Norma and Lizzy Boston. She'd exposed something of herself to me and I didn't get it. The message came in coded. On the drive home, I tried to pick her behaviour apart. But I was stumped.

Before she got out of the car and I could ask her what was going on, she kissed me tenderly on the lips, touched my cheek, smiled with tears in her luminous eyes and walked briskly to her door not looking back. I knew then, it had been farewell. She would not be able to look at me without feeling pain. Although I knew this, I didn't understand why or what reasons could possibly explain it as remorse chugged away in my gut. Had I taken something from her? Something too precious and illusory to give back?

The coffee had grown cold. The chocolate-glazed doughnut, ordinarily my favourite, sat glistening and unmarked. An ache that was more than mere appetite gnawed at my innards telling me that maybe I'd missed the best part of her.

I glanced up and away. Dusty Rhodes lay asleep in Teddy's chair. His bony knees were draped over one padded arm and wedged sideways against the edge of Teddy's desk, long, stork-like legs thrust at an awkward angle. He'd been out on one of his midnight forays shooting nocturnal animals again. Then back to the darkroom to see what he'd captured. I didn't want to wake him. But judging from the angle of his head, bird-like in its posture, he'd have a helluva crick when he finally awoke. He looked like a younger version of our own local birdman, Ellis Boston.

Chapter Ten

Reinhold Elgar looked impressive. An imposing man whose seamed face and silvery hair belied dignity, purposefulness and told you in no uncertain terms it understood the gravity of its station in life. Behind the gray eyes, however, lay the faintest twinkle and those rounded, determined lips seemed perpetually on the verge of cracking a smile. Elgar knew who he was and what he had to do.

By the time I arrived around eleven-thirty on Thursday morning, the jury had already been selected and Dr. Elgar prepared to hear testimony. The room was uncharacteristically crowded. Not every day that such an event took place in Applewood, but I managed to squeeze in beside Constable Hal Bigelow who attended in his capacity as a witness. Hal looked particularly thoughtful and just raised his eyebrows up into his carroty hairline as I sat down. I knew how he felt and I wondered how he did that with his eyebrows, as if the skin of his scalp were a loose pancake of flesh he could manipulate at will. But I reminded myself, there were other matters to contemplate. Elgar was speechifying.

"And so ladies and gentlemen of the jury," Elgar said in a solemn tone that grabbed everyone's attention," I must remind you and those in the audience, as well as, the honourable members of the bar present here today," and he bowed half-mockingly, "that a coroner's jury has a special job to do. It is not up to us to lay blame or even point fingers. We are not in the business of exposing culprits, much as some of us may desire to do so," and here he smiled, drawing the tissue of his kisser back to expose the even, yellowed teeth of a habitual pipe smoker. "No. No. Our particular task is to look at circumstances, albeit tragic as they are and make recommendations so those circumstances are never repeated again. In other words, we are not a court of law although we follow its precepts and decorum. We do not lay charges nor convict criminals. That of course, may come later. Ours is a community responsibility and it is the safety of the community that is our paramount concern. In short, the jury's recommendations help ensure that similar tragedies need never again occur." And with an ironic twist of his lips added: "I usually remind members of the legal profession present there's no need to conduct themselves like Perry Mason or Hamilton Burger, for that matter." Obviously, this tepid joke made up part of his standard refrain, Perry Mason was terribly popular on television and in anticipation of a mouth-filled response, Elgar broke into a full-fledged grin. He wasn't disappointed. The modest members seated in the public gallery roared and guffawed, eager to break the tension. Rest assured, Elgar thought to himself, that the proceedings would go well for him from this point on as he now knew the measure if not the mettle of his audience. He couldn't have been more wrong.

Only Horatio Bongard, the crown counsel—a local boy made good and Freddy Oliveira, Blake Rothwell's slick retainer brought in from a big law firm in Toronto, never cracked a smile. Didn't even show a tooth in their collective taciturnity. Oliveira shook his sleek, well-oiled head while Bongard shrugged to himself whistling noiselessly through the gap in his two front teeth that resembled shutter doors fallen loose from their hinges. Blake Rothwell sat between his lawyer and father looking young and arrogant but subdued. He exuded the brooding romanticism of a dark-haired James Dean, from the ducktail to the chiseled cheekbones to the delicate, expressive features. He too, wore an expensively tailored linen suit of sombre blue—banker's blue. The gaudy rings on his fingers and the large, gleaming watch supplanted any notion of austerity or even, humility. And yet it was my utmost conviction that he remained single-handedly and carelessly responsible for the death of Norma Jennings—a girl I'd only seen around but couldn't help but notice. She'd been one of his things that had gotten damaged and then, callously, he'd thrown her away.

"I've been given a list of witnesses here," Elgar said. "They shall be summoned in turn. The lawyers will question them and I will question them and then after we're all through, the jury will retire to discuss what they've heard and then, reaching a consensus, will return with their recommendations. I trust that is satisfactory for all and simple enough to understand." Without waiting for a yea or nay, Elgar flattened his palm on the surface of the table as if he was looking for a pulse and pronounced: "Let's begin."

The first witness called was Hal Bigelow, who rose from the bench where he sat and strode purposefully to the front of the room, the wedge of his highly polished shoes pounded the wood floor like thunder claps tormenting an uncertain sky. When he finally sat, after the obligatory oath, Hal looked feverishly uncomfortable on the narrow wooden chair.

Elgar nodded and Horatio Bongard rose to his full height of five feet six inches, padded like an overheated spaniel to the witness chair and wagged his round head while wisps of his fine blond hair stiffened up in the overwrought humidity. Bongard's lips disappeared in a forced grin.

"Constable Bigelow, why don't you tell us what happened early in the morning of June 9th." His voice grated and whistled in a nasal-like tone, as uncomfortable to listen to as the high-pitched whine of a grinder on soft metal.

Hal flipped open his pad to refer to his notes. His voice resonated yet was surprisingly soft given the enormous chest cavity from which it emanated. He read haltingly.

"About three-fifteen on the morning of June 9th, a call came into the station-house. I took it at my desk. A man, who identified himself as Amos Willoughby, a local cottager, said he had been out walking late that evening along the beach at Rattlesnake Bay. Mr. Willoughby said the moon was bright and as he walked along the shoreline, he thought he saw something at the water's edge. He went up to take a closer look and saw a woman's body rolled by the surf onto the sand, washed up, he said. Mr. Willoughby drove to his cottage to use the phone. I told him to stay at home and I would contact him later in the day. After having spoken to Mr. Willoughby, I telephoned the coroner at home, Dr. James Seaton and apprised him of the news. Then I phoned the mortician, Steff Randolph. At approximately four a.m., the aforementioned and myself met at the location described by Mr. Willoughby. There, we found the partly clad body of a young woman, who appeared to have drowned. She matched the description of one Norma Jennings, aged 22, who'd been reported missing earlier by Mr. Blake Rothwell. We removed the body from the lake and Dr. Seaton undertook a brief examination. Then the deceased was transported to the town morgue to await the autopsy by Dr. Seaton." Hal flipped the notebook closed and stared straight ahead as if he were the one on trial.

"Was there anything else about the condition of the body that you noticed, Constable Bigelow?"

"Objection!" yelled Freddy Oliveira. "Calls for speculation on the part of the witness."

Elgar's face clouded. Bongard looked mildly surprised. "Just asking if the constable observed anything else. I'm not looking for a detailed forensic analysis," Bongard retorted in a miffed and hurt tone as if saying, why are you doing this to me?

Elgar pointed at Oliveira. "Obviously, Mr. Oliveira you didn't heed my little speech of a few moments ago. I will not tolerate further interruptions without cause. If this keeps up, I won't think twice about having you turfed out of here and barred from these proceedings. Now sit down, please."

Freddy grinned and bowed to the crowd then resumed his seat. Elgar turned to Horatio. "Continue then, Mr. Bongard."

"Constable Bigelow? Anything else about the body that you noticed?"

"No sir. Not that I could see. It was still pretty dark."

"All right, then. Did Mr. Willoughby state what he was doing out at that very early hour?" And Bongard glanced at Freddy Oliveira to see if the question was all right. Freddy grinned and waved at him mockingly.

Hal replied: "No sir. But I imagine Mr. Willoughby can answer that question with more certainty, Mr. Bongard."

Bongard acquiesced. "I'm certain you're correct. What happened next, after the deceased was removed from the beach?"

Hal flipped the notepad open again. "I drove out to the Jennings residence about 5:11 a.m. and spoke to Mr. Jennings. I related the events to him. He accompanied me to the morgue for the purpose of identifying the body. Which he did."

"Miss Jennings had been reported missing earlier, had she not?"

"That's correct."

"Fill in the blanks for us, please, Constable Bigelow."

With studied concentration, Hal backtracked through the tiny pages. "Yes sir. About eleven-thirty pm. on the evening of June 8th, Mr. Blake Rothwell came into the stationhouse accompanied by his attorney, Mr. Frederick Oliveira and Mr. Rothwell's father, Phillip. They came to report that Miss Norma Jennings, a close personal friend of Blake Rothwell, had disappeared while the two were riding in a speedboat earlier on the same evening. Blake Rothwell stated that Miss Jennings had slipped overboard while he was at the wheel of the boat. Against his wishes, Miss Jennings had climbed forward to the bow and sat facing the driver while kicking her heels in the water. When the boat hit a large wave, apparently Miss Jennings lost her balance and fell overboard. Mr. Rothwell stated that he momentarily lost control of the speedboat and didn't notice Miss Jenning's disappearance. After some moments, he brought the boat under control, he looked up and she'd disappeared."

"Did Mr. Rothwell attempt to locate Miss Jennings?"

"He didn't say."

"How did Mr. Rothwell appear to you, Constable?"

"Dry," Hal replied and a short-lived rash of tittering broke out. Elgar glowered at the audience and they shut up.

Then Freddy Oliveira was on his feet, gesticulating, words exploding like depth charges. "I object to Constable Bigelow's tone. I object strenuously to what he's implying. He's impugning the reputation of my client, Dr. Elgar."

"All right, Mr. Oliveira. Duly noted. Constable Bigelow. Try to refrain from any sarcastic inference. Please rephrase the question, Mr. Bongard."

Bongard gave a long doggy sigh. "All right. Constable, how was Blake Rothwell dressed at the time. What was he wearing, I mean."

"Mr. Rothwell was wearing a white polo shirt, cotton slacks and topsiders, no socks."

"And his demeanour?"

"Sorry?"

"Did Blake Rothwell appear, well, sober to you?" Oliveira jumped to his feet but before he could open his mouth, Elgar barked, "Sit down, Mr. Oliveira, this instant or I will have you removed." Freddy sat down without a word.

"I would say that Blake Rothwell appeared both subdued and sober. Quite some time had passed between Miss Jennings disappearance at approximately six forty-five pm. and Blake Rothwell's statement taken at the police station five and a half hours later. I attempted to question him about the discrepancy but Mr. Oliveira refused to let him respond."

"I see," Bongard responded thoughtfully. "Are there a lot of boating accidents in this area, Constable?"

"About a dozen or more each summer, I'd say," Hal said.

"How often would you say the over-consumption of alcohol played a part in these accidents?"

"More often that not, Mr. Bongard. People drink in boats all the time and that's a fact. Boats and cars are dangerous when operated by people who are drunk."

Bongard smiled his feline grin. "No further questions. Thank you, Constable Bigelow."

Elgar said, "Now's the time to speak, Mr. Oliveira, if you so wish." A chastened Freddy stood up and replied, "I have one question."

"Go ahead."

"Constable Bigelow, you have no evidence to prove or even suggest that Blake Rothwell had consumed alcohol while driving the boat, do you?"

Hal shrugged, "No, that's true. We don't have any evidence to that effect." Freddy sat down.

Elgar looked perturbed. He liked his hearings calm and non-confrontational.

"Thank you, Constable Bigelow. That's all for now. Please make yourself available should we need to call on you again."

Hal lurched back to his seat. He sweated heavily.

Elgar consulted his list. "Dr. James Seaton, please."

Doc Seaton waddled to the front and settled into the sternly appointed chair emitting an arthritic grunt. Doc sported his most elegant seersucker get-up and tartan bowtie. His oxfords were immaculately polished and the bright sunlight flooding the room struck the lenses of his spectacles rendering them entirely opaque. The sudden opacity transformed Doc's cherubic face. It transmitted disquieting cruelty. He looked evil in the shattering light. Even though he was venerated by virtually everyone in Applewood. Doc's capacity for evil, or anyone's, just wouldn't have surprised me. I guess that almost nothing would have surprised me then given my own family history.

Horatio Bongard began. "Dr. Seaton, you are the coroner for the town of Applewood?"

"Yes sir, that is correct. Also for the townships of Yohnapta, Broward, Lanark, Fitzroy, Medvale and Querulous too."

"Yes, thank you. Now, Dr. Seaton, you received a call from Constable Hal Bigelow early on the morning of June 9th, did you not?"

Doc nodded, as if that's all he had to do in lieu of a reply. "Without dwelling on extraneous detail, would you just summarize your findings for us, doctor?" asked the Crown Attorney.

Doc nodded. "I'd be happy too. The actual cause of death was by drowning. Of that there is no doubt. There were other factors, however..." And as he said this, the room started to buzz and I could feel virtually everyone move an inch closer to the edge of each and every seat. "…for instance, the blood alcohol level in the body was point one five."

"For the jury's edification, do you consider that high?"

"Miss Jennings was far from sober. She had more than twice the level of alcohol in her bloodstream necessary to render her thoroughly inebriated. And there was a chemical substance in the bloodstream which I have not yet identified." Again the audience started and whispered conversations commenced in earnest. The community tongues wagged in four-four time.

"Chemical substance?"

"Yes, that's correct. A sample of blood was sent to the lab at Hazelton which usually does the analysis. I received a call from them this morning stating that it would be necessary to send the sample on to the Centre for Forensic Sciences in Toronto for further testing."

"When are the results expected, Dr. Seaton?"

"In two to three weeks time."

"Do you have any notion of when the chemical was consumed by Miss Jennings and how?"

"I can't answer the first question with any accuracy. Sometime within 24 hours of her death would be my estimate. As to how the chemical was taken, I'd suggest Miss Jennings took it orally. She simply swallowed it," Doc said.

"So, it is possible that Miss Jennings consumed this chemical substance while in the company of Blake Rothwell?"

"Yes, it is certainly a possibility," Doc replied.

I glanced over at the Rothwell side. Freddy Oliveira tensed like a cobra ready to strike.

Elgar broke in. "Would you please venture an opinion, Dr. Seaton?"

"Sure. If I can with any certainty, Dr. Elgar," Doc replied.

Elgar actually looked grateful but still troubled.

"Do you think this chemical substance will have a significant and direct bearing on the findings of this jury?"

Doc hesitated, measuring his words carefully.

"I don't expect so, no. Whatever it is, I suspect it may have impaired Miss Jennings even further. It may have some relevance for the police if there is to be a subsequent criminal investigation."

Freddy Oliveira shot to his feet, spittle flying from his angry face. "This is outrageous! I object to these scurrilous remarks in the most strenuous terms," he hollered.

"Mr. Oliveira."

Freddy screamed even louder.

"This is prejudicial to my client's right to a fair trial should one be necessary. It is also a slanderous attack on his reputation which is of the highest possible standard. This is a travesty, a mockery of the jud…"

A gnarled fist crashed heavily down on wood. It became a shouting match between Elgar and Freddy and Elgar won.

"Be seated, Mr. Oliveira or I will have you ejected at once!"

Just as quickly, Freddy ran out of gas.

"All right, Dr. Elgar. I think I've made my point." And he sat down making certain to smooth out the creases in his silk pants, then crossed his legs moodily.

I jotted down a few notes. Instinct more than anything tangible indicated the sense of a pattern with Norma forming the linchpin. I found myself wanting to know her and felt again in the pocket of my jacket for the smooth, cool surface of the clam shell. Come on, Norma, give me something, I thought.

Elgar, still angered and flushed, turned to the jury," I apologize for this unconscionable outburst and trust it will not happen again." He turned back to Doc Seaton and Horatio. "Please continue."

Horatio had endured the outburst silently, standing with his arms crossed rubbing his fleshy chin with one hand and wondering, no doubt, what on earth had compelled him to become not only a lawyer but a crown counsel. He reached no obvious conclusion as he decided to continue gloomily with his questioning.

"And now Dr. Seaton, were there any other findings from the autopsy you wish to disclose to the jury?"

Doc took a deep breath. "Only one."

"And that is?"

"Norma Jennings was approximately eight weeks pregnant at the time of her death."

And for a prolonged moment, there ensued a collective hushing of breath as the room catapulted into a shocked silence, until that is, someone came to their senses. And this time, Blake Rothwell sparked to life. He jumped to his elegantly clad feet.

"No! No! That's a lie. It's a damn lie!"

His father and Oliveira took hold of him attempting to restrain the distraught but expensively clad beanpole who fought their attempts to pin him between them. He kept screaming, driving himself to the verge of manic apoplexy.

"That's a lie. A bald-faced lie. Liar. Liar. Liar," he screamed.

Aging, farm-bred bodies rose and twisted in their places, necks craned and tongues fibrillated at uncommon frequencies. The room rose to pandemonious heights. I jumped up seeking an avenue of escape but was trapped by the squeezing bodies, forced to listen to the nasal-toned jabbering around me. Cries of, " Oh, my goodness gracious, land sakes alive, what do you think of that? I knew it, I knew it, what a scandal. That's what happens when you run with the wrong crowd and it's the devil's own doing. Lord, lord, how times have changed," and other heart wrought sentimentalities commenting on the fall of the less pure around them.

Dr. Elgar hovered on the verge of losing total control of the situation. There's nothing like a secret pregnancy revealed to set fire to small-minded passions. The hubbub crescendoed like a torturously stolid tidal wave barreling its way to an unsuspecting, helpless island. Blake Rothwell continued screaming and carrying on, overwhelmed only by the greying crowd pressing in to get a better look rather than help subdue him. Dr. Elgar had no choice but to pick up the hitherto unused gavel before him and smash it repeatedly on the surface of his hapless desk.

"That's enough. That's enough, I say." Bang! went the gavel. Bang! Bang! To no avail. It began to look hopeless until I spotted a powerful current forcing bodies apart as if they were floating jetsam on the tide. Without my noticing, Hal Bigelow had cut a swathe from his seat to the front of the room where he now stood next to Dr. Elgar. He removed his pistol, pointed it upward and fired it once, twice, three times and suddenly the room, reeling from the bitter odour of cordite and puffs of smoke hanging in the air, instantly clanged silent. A lady to my left fainted, crumpled on the spot without a sound. No one gave her another thought. I stood there trying to merely absorb the wondrous goings on.

Dr. Elgar spoke, his voice cracking.

"Now then. We'll have none of this or I will close this hearing to the public. I thank you Dr. Seaton for your patience and excuse you for now. We are in recess until two o'clock this afternoon." And for good measure he banged the gavel again. It rapped sharply in the stilled room. No one dared move for the moment. Elgar quickly gathered up his things and hurried out the back entrance, to gather himself undoubtedly for what was to come and maybe grab a quick shot at the licensed bar in the Two-Tone Hotel down the street. People began to return to their senses and a slow murmur and rustling resumed as audience members began to file out, making their way up the aisle. The jury too, seemed bewildered by it all, stunned confusion etched on their serious, conscience-stricken faces. And then Hal Bigelow leaned down toward me.

He winked. "Say, do you want to get some fishing in this Saturday? I know a sweet little spot at the top end of Coca-Cola Falls."

I hated fishing but I looked at his ruddy face and shrugged.

"Sure. Why not?" I could use the time to reflect away from all this hubbub. Besides, it made as much sense as anything else.

Chapter Eleven

I rushed back to The Gazette to work on my feverishly scribbled notes hoping to beat them into shape before the afternoon session. Proceeding down Perkins Avenue, I imagined the entire town, the streets, shops, offices, salons, everyone everywhere was a-buzz with the happenings at the courthouse.

The street baked in the heat and I wilted in my drip'n dry summer suit. My stomach growled out pangs of hunger. I stopped in at Marge's Take-Out to pick something up on my way back to the office. There was a short line. All Marge had was a cool glass showcase of pre-fixed sandwiches, a couple of stove tops, coffee and juice machines and a fridge where you could select your own pop or milk.

Two places ahead of me I couldn't help but spot a piled-up outgrowth of glossy brown hair and peeking around the grease monkey in front of me, a pair of tanned, sandaled feet and long, shapely legs that set my heart a-flutter.

"Beverly?" She turned, surprised then gave me a languid smile.

"Ah, the intrepid reporter, Mr. Joe Simpson. You've been a busy boy."

"Yeah. Well, things have been pretty hectic."

"I'll say, your byline has pushed all the wire services right off the front page."

"Er right. Didn't know you read the paper that closely, Bev."

She laughed, full-throated. "Lots of things you don't know about me, Joe."

It was now her turn to order. "Tuna salad on whole wheat, please, Marge and I'll take an orange juice too."

Marge, a heavy-set woman with woolen, dyed red hair worked quickly and efficiently behind the counter.

Marge said, "There you go, doll. That's a dollar for the tuna salad and twenty cents for the juice. Thanks honey. Do something about that hair, will you? Next, please."

Beverly snorted and turned to leave. "Don't forget about tonight, Joe." And then she was out the door that rattled as it slammed along with a jumble of my thoughts.

"Come on, Joe. Snap out of it. What'll you have?" Marge asked.

"Oh. Sorry, uh, corned beef on rye with mustard, Marge. And I'll take a coke from the fridge."

Marge replied, "Now you're talking." Before I knew it, she had placed a warm package wrapped in brown oil-paper in my hands. I left her a dollar fifty-five and was out on the street clutching a cold coke in one hand and a steaming sandwich in the other.

The air hung dank and heavy. A slight breeze came in off the Bay, stirring the litter strewn in the street. There never used to be litter. Old newspapers, candy wrappers, slats of cardboard. I sniffed and smelled something sour too, like a brewery having let the hops jump out of their copper vats.

Back in the office, everything seemed perfectly normal. Paisley O'Toole sat at her desk, a fresh vase of cut flowers in front of her, looking cool and poised as she puzzled out her column. I wondered who in the town's aristocratic clique Paisley planned to zing this time. Nadine Morgan, the office manager sat huddled over a pile of disheveled papers, bills I assumed, muttering angrily to herself, the old brown sweater pulled around her tightly, ash tray overflowing with cigarette butts and her twentieth smoke of the day hanging from her withered lips. It was almost enough to make me quit just looking at her. Teddy gave Stumpy Butler his daily grilling. All I heard was the muffled yells behind the closed glass door as Stumpy stood there stoically, almost a heroic figure, his sparse head bowed hurtfully and the powerfully thick arms and smithy hands hanging at his sides. Dusty Rhodes stood in the corner of Teddy's office smirking in the way only a 19 year-old kid can who never took anything too seriously.

I sat down at my desk, hung up my jacket and unwrapped my lunch. I took a long hard pull at the coke bottle. Paisley studiously ignored me and that was just fine. As I ate, I began going through my notes. The office seemed unnaturally quiet. In the summer time, the phones barely rang as everyone dozed off leaving the news to its own design. I thought about Ellis Boston and what he was doing right now. Had they cuffed his hands together behind his back? Or shot him full of dope? Or maybe, they just stuck an electrode in his head and turned on the juice.

I rolled up my sleeves and set to work, knowing there wasn't much time to write everything up from this morning. I wanted to make the afternoon session on time since I knew that Blake Rothwell was slated to testify and I couldn't miss that. I wrote away, corned beef in one hand, pen in the other, pausing only to take a tug at the coke.

I must have been entirely engrossed in what I was doing because I didn't see or hear him come up, that is, until a pudgy hand was stuck in front of my face. Then I looked up. A heavy-set man stood sweating under a mop of curly brown hair styled in a pompadour even though he had to be middle-aged, at least. I took in the parboiled red complexion. A pair of small grey eyes sized me up. He wore flip-up sunshades on his glasses, a plaid jacket, cream shirt and tie and banana yellow slacks. I knew that his shoes were white and had tassels even without bothering to look.

"You must be Joe Simpson," he said.

"Who wants to know?"

The big man grinned. "Barrett Thompkins, national editor of the Toronto Herald-Dispatch." So I shook his fleshy hand. "That was some scene in the courtroom, huh? Never seen anything quite like it," and shook his preened head and guffawed to himself.

"What brings you to Applewood, Mr. Thompkins?"

"Well, two things, I guess. I came to cover the coroner's jury and also, I wanted to meet you, Joe. I've heard good things about you."

"Really?" I thought he darted a quick glance in Paisley's direction but she remained impassively still so I knew she strained to hear every syllable.

"So one of the top papers in the country sends its senior editor here, to Applewood?" I asked.

Thompkins expression became a caricature of seriousness. "The top paper, Joe. The top paper in the country. And anything that involves Phillip Rothwell interests me greatly. He's an extremely influential man. I've been following his career for years now. This is big news, son. Very big news. I was sent here to get the story right. That's how it works in the city. Even editors don't forget where they've come from or what they do best. We get our hands dirty. It keeps us sharp, on our toes." I didn't really know what to make of this so I said nothing. It seemed to me there was some implied criticism of Teddy in his remarks.

I said, "That's good. It wouldn't do to get too rusty, would it?"

"I just wanted to pop in and say hello. I'm sure we'll be running into each other again soon. While I'm here, I think I'll pay a courtesy call on your editor."

"Sure," I said. The beefy banana man nodded and sauntered to Teddy's office where the verbal onslaught of Stumpy Butler had just subsided. I looked at his feet. I was right. Tassels. I shot a quick look at Paisely but she feigned busyness writing in her languid manner undisturbed by the commonness of the world around her. She moved in an envelope of serenity. It traveled everywhere with her. It fit neatly into her suede purse. She could take it out whenever she wanted. It did tricks for her. Ah, nuts. This seemed more than curious. But then again I had no complaints, life was full. Nuts again.

When I returned to the courthouse, the trial room buzzed with expectation. People hankered after more fireworks, I figured, more bombshells. The room burst at the seams, heaving with people as it appeared most folks had told a neighbour who'd told a relative who'd dragged along a friend. All the seats vanished and leathery-faced spectators lined the walls two and three deep. Applewood didn't have a bona fide press gallery, so I jostled my way along the side up to the front where I could get a clear view of the action. Just as I squeezed between a rawboned young farm hand in overalls and his similarly outfitted cousin, both emanating that vinegary, outdoor smell on them, I heard something like a snake hissing.

"PPsst! Joe. Over here." I searched the crowd. In the front row of seats, a pudgy hand went up. It was my newfound friend, Barrett Thompkins.

"Hey Joe! I've got you a seat. Come on."

What the hell, I shrugged, if the man wanted to save me a seat, I wasn't going to argue any, particularly if it gave my nostrils a break. Leaving the farm hands to their own company and not regretting it, I jostled my way across to the front row.

"There you go, front row centre," said a beaming Thompkins.

I sat down. "Thanks. But I don't mind standing."

"Well, when you get a few years and maybe," and he patted his ample girth, "a few pounds on you, Joe, you'll appreciate the use of a chair, even a sharp-edged one like this."

"Yeah, well. Thanks again, Mr. Thompkins."

"Barrett please. Call me, Barrett."

"Yeah, sure...Barrett." I had my stuff all ready to go and made a few notes detailing the size and mood of the crowd, the atmosphere in the room, for background colour. A stir burbled up as Freddy Oliveira, Phillip and Blake Rothwell entered the courtroom. The crowd watched collectively as they took their places with an auspicious sense of decorum. No sooner had they settled and the murmurings began to hum than Dr. Elgar, looking decidedly less self-assured and tight-lipped, entered too, surveying the room sternly. The murmurings subsided momentarily as he set his papers down with a thump and bowed his head to review a document, then the sound increased in pitch a full notch. Elgar looked up sharply and the mutterers cut back instantly as if he'd threatened to penalize them for talking; take away their pension or pogey cheques. Elgar cleared his throat, poured a glass of water and took a sip, then proceeded to sit.

"Jesus," said Thompkins, "What's he waiting for? The beginning of a new millennium?" But not much else as it happened. Almost as if that were his cue, Elgar spoke. His voice dribbled out subdued enough making us strain to hear causing the room to fall completely silent apart from the rustling of starched denim and shuffling of a dozen pair of clodhoppers. It was an old actor's trick but effective. Elgar's tone, however, had a palpable edge. You could feel it.

"Before we hear testimony this afternoon, ladies and gentlemen, I want to caution everyone in this room. If there is a hint or even the beginning of a hint of a repeat of this morning's despicably unruly goings-on, I will clear this room without hesitation. Then everyone apart from the direct participants will be barred from these proceedings. I hope that is clearly understood by everyone including legal counsel and witnesses. Make no mistake about it. Now then, you've all been warned. Let's carry on with the business at hand...and absolutely no shenanigans. The last witness to be called is Blake Rothwell."

The younger Mr. Rothwell stood up and moved his lanky frame to the witness chair with what I can only describe as a strut. As a parent or teacher, a walk like that would make me want to haul off and kick him in the butt.

The court clerk swore Blake in. Once again, Horatio Bongard edged his way gingerly to the front, nodding his fly-away head in a bobbing fashion. Bongard didn't live in Applewood but I'd run into him on more than a few occasions, since he was the only crown counsel hereabouts. I'd say we had something more than a how-do-you-do type acquaintance. I reminded myself to get quotes from him, Elgar, Freddy and the Rothwells after the session today. Horatio didn't waste any time.

"Mr. Rothwell, were you drinking alcoholic spirits the night of Miss Jennings unfortunate disappearance?" Just as he concluded, two things occurred in simultaneous action. Freddy Oliveira jumped up with his mouth open and Dr. Elgar pointed his gavel directly at him as if it were a weapon. They both froze without either getting a word out. Horatio blinked at one, then the other and sighed. Ever so slowly, Freddy dissolved into movement easing back gradually into his seat and Elgar, like ticks of the clock, lowered the gavel to the desk ready to pick it up again at a second's notice should it be necessary. The first stand-off dissolved. Horatio continued.

"I repeat. Were you drunk that night?"

Blake said, "No."

Horatio threw up his hands in disbelief. "Oh come on, Mr. Rothwell. You are aware are you not that part of a mickey of Jack Daniels, the label intact, was found embedded in the hull of your boat and presumably Miss Jennings was in possession of it prior to falling overboard, as it happened, to her death?"

The heads of the crowd swiveled collectively between Elgar and Oliveira to see what reaction might be forthcoming but the temporary truce was still in effect although Freddie twitched in irritation.

"I don't drink and I can prove it," Blake complained peevishly.

"Please do," replied Horatio.

"I have a physical intolerance to alcohol. Every time I try to drink I become violently ill. And Mr. Oliveira has a doctor's certificate to back me up."

Elgar looked up then. "Mr. Oliveira?"

Freddy held the paper aloft as if it were a flag blowing on the rampart of battle for all to see and from it, take courage.

"Right here, Dr. Elgar." He sprang up like a cougar and moving swiftly placed it in Elgar's outstretched fingers. Elgar unfolded the paper in dramatic fashion, crinkling it loudly in the deathly silent room. He examined it for a long moment, then grunted.

"Looks legitimate," he said and held it out to Horatio who also spent a long time poring over it, probing for some fakery-quakery fallacy. Horatio sighed again, the world on his shoulders, and passed it back to Elgar.

"You can't deny then, Mr. Rothwell that Miss Jennings was drinking heavily that evening?"

"No. I can't deny that."

"What was the nature of your relationship with Miss Jennings?"

"We were friends."

"Friends," Horatio repeated layered with sarcasm. "Friends. If you were friends as you say, then why did you act in such a callous and reckless manner, Mr. Rothwell? The fact that you were sober, as you claim, makes your actions even more reprehensible."

Elgar broke in. "Stop badgering Mr. Bongard and ask a question, if you will." Then he shot a glance at Freddy, who bowed slightly in Elgar's direction as if acknowledging a favour. Horatio accepted the rebuke but continued unperturbed.

"Why didn't you stop her when she crawled to the front of the boat?"

"At first, I didn't realize what she was doing and then when I did, it was too late."

"Did you call to her, ask her to come back in?"

"Yes, I did but she wouldn't listen."

"How fast were you going at the time?"

"Pretty fast."

"Precisely how fast?"

"About 22 miles an hour, I'd guess."

"That's just about top speed for a boat of that type, isn't it? It's a Shark with twin engines—about 150 horsepower, I believe?"

"Yeah. That's right."

"How long was Miss Jennings seated at the bow?"

"I don't remember exactly. Maybe a minute or two at the most."

"Whose idea was it to take the boat out?"

"Norma's. I didn't want to go."

"Had she been drinking earlier in the evening?"

"Yes."

"And you took the suggestion of an intoxicated young lady, seriously?"

"I thought it would be okay," replied Blake uncomfortably, a note of misery creeping into his voice, rather neatly, I thought.

"Were you aware of the weather conditions that evening, Mr. Rothwell?"

"Well, I knew it was windy and there'd be some chop on the Bay. But you can't always tell from the shore."

"So Norma Jennings climbed out on the bow and faced you, a mickey of Jack Daniels in her right hand, laughing presumably, having a good time?"

"Yeah."

"And then what happened?"

"It's hard to remember clearly, it was so fast. The boat suddenly hit a deep trough and the nose sort of dove down and then a big wave came right behind it and caught us square. The next thing I knew my side came up almost vertical. I thought we were going to flip. I think I yelled to Norma to hold on, something like that. I panicked too, I guess. Then, I cut the engine and it passed. We leveled out with a big whump smacking the water so hard I was jolted right up my back. By then Norma had gone over."

"What did you do then?"

"I, uh, I called out to her, you know but she didn't answer. I was scared. Really scared, man. Then I began to search around but the water there is very dark and dusk was coming on fast and I just couldn't see anything. I mean I just couldn't see, you know?"

"You never thought of going after her?"

"No."

"Why is that?"

And finally, Blake Rothwell wrung his small hands and crossed his skinny legs like a kid needing to go to the bathroom. His handsome face contorted into shame and embarrassment.

"Uh, I can't swim. I never learned how," he rasped.

Horatio looked to the heavens for guidance or out of exasperation.

"Let's get this straight, Mr. Rothwell. If you had asked your father's permission to take the speedboat out that night, what do you think his answer would have been?"

"Well. He probably would have said no, I guess."

Horatio went into the nodding routine again. "Were you wearing a life jacket, Mr. Rothwell?"

Blake shook his head. "No, I wasn't."

"Let's recap, shall we? We have a non swimmer not wearing a life jacket and an intoxicated young woman also not wearing a life jacket taking out a speedboat against the rightful owner's permission in all likelihood in rough weather. Rough enough that you couldn't handle the boat or the girl, could you Mr. Rothwell?"

"All right. That's enough of that Mr. Bongard," ordered Dr. Elgar. Horatio's complexion had reddened from the exertion of his questioning. He had worked himself up into a lather, something all respectable crown attorneys do on demand.

Horatio said, "One more thing, Mr. Rothwell. Would you say you acted responsibly that evening?"

Blake stared straight at Horatio. "I didn't want her to get hurt. I never wanted that to happen. It was all a mistake. A terrible mistake."

Horatio appeared thoughtful. "Perhaps, Mr. Rothwell. Try telling that to Miss Jennings' family. You were both reckless and careless that fateful night. No further questions." And he strode to his seat and sat rigidly looking down at the floor.

Thompkins butted me in the ribs with his elbow. "Hey! He really took the kid apart, didn't he? But he didn't ask him about the girl's pregnancy, did he? Now that's an angle I'd like to see followed up."

"Uh-huh. Well, Mr. Thompkins, the question of Norma's pregnancy is somewhat beyond the interests of a coroner's inquest, don't you think?" I replied.

"Well, it's news son and that's what I'm interested in. News. Plain and simple."

Elgar asked, "Any questions, Mr. Oliveira?"

"Just a couple," Freddy said, ever the professional and still confident after the drubbing Blake just took from Horatio. He went up to Blake and his manner was in direct contrast to Horatio's. He spoke with utmost gentility.

"Blake. Are you sorry for what has happened?"

"Yes. Very sorry. I cared for Norma. I, uh, I was thinking even of asking her to marry me."

"Yes. And then we can assume you would never even think of doing something like this ever again, would you?"

"Never. I've learned my lesson the hard way. And now I've got to live with it the rest of my life. I'll never forget her, I swear. Never."

Freddy nodded and patted the boy on the hand. "All right. That's all I have, Dr. Elgar."

Elgar nodded gratefully, visibly relieved, expecting, I imagine, for it to be far worse than it turned out to be. All that was remained was his summation and address to the jury. Since I wasn't particularly interested in what Elgar had to say, I stood up to go because I could guess the outcome having attended quite a few of these juries in the past. The jury would be awhile deliberating but not too long and I already knew what the recommendations would be. I'd bet on it. So, my predictions were as follows: Stricter enforcement of the use of life jackets in all marine vehicles at all times and higher fines too. Increased vigilance and laying of charges by the Ontario Provincial Police's Lake Patrol Division where alcohol is found open and available while operating a boat of any kind. Licenses should be revoked from boat owners who fail to comply. And last, the posting of even more signs in dangerous areas along the shore be it warning against swimming or boating and listing the potentially hazardous conditions for each. As it turned out when the jury did release its findings, my hunches were just about on the money. Believe me, I knew my audience.

"What's your rush?" Thompkins asked me. He blocked my path and all I could think about was writing up the articles for tomorrow's edition. Besides, I promised Wishbone and Beverly I'd show up to Wish's party that evening.

"Gotta go, Mr. Thompkins. I'll see you around. Thanks for the chair." I started to leave but Thompkins grabbed hold of my jacket.

"Say listen, kid. Maybe you're free for dinner tonight? Maybe we can talk about some things? Whaddaya say?"

"I'm busy tonight. But thanks anyway."

Thompkins persisted. "Come on, kid. I'd like to talk about a trivial little thing like your future. And I'm gone first thing in the morning. It's on me," he said and gave me a wink that indicated this constituted an extremely rare and precious offer. Ah, I thought, what the hell. I guess I could listen to what this goofball had to say as long as he paid for a decent meal. Shoddy, I know, but there you are.

"Is an early dinner okay, say 5:30? I've got to be somewhere around seven."

Thompkins indicated his agreement by releasing my jacket. "Fine. Meet me at The Round Table. I'll be in the bar."

I nodded. "See you then." The Round Table happened to be the classiest restaurant in Applewood frequented by the likes of Paisley O'Toole, her husband, Seamus and their crowd. If Thompkins wanted to impress me, then maybe I was impressed the littlest bit.

Outside on the courthouse steps I drifted with the crowd, flowing on the tide of gossiping humanity. The sun still climbed in the sky and it felt good to get out into the air. After the clenched fist of the inquest, there was room to let your ribs go without rubbing up against your neighbour. But I didn't dwell on any of that. There was work to do.

A massive hand slid over my left bicep and squeezed so hard I yelped. I felt myself pulled sideways against the moving current. Sharp cries of annoyance pricked my ears.

"Jesus, Bigelow, you don't have to flatten it, you know," I shouted, rubbing what little was left.

"Yeah," he said briskly. "Sorry about that." But then I noticed something else in his eyes, something that made me ask a question.

"So, why the strong arm, anyway?"

"Come on over here," he said, beckoning me to an alcove deep in shadow, off the main steps and isolated from the steady stream of foot traffic. "Cigarette?"

"Thanks," I replied. We lit up. "This is uncharacteristic generosity," I said, watching the town folk shove their way about their business.

Hal blew smoke up to the sky. I waited. Then he came to it.

"You know Darlene Norris, don't you?"

"You know I do. What about it?"

"We found her car. Looks like it was abandoned. She didn't report back to work after lunch. Didn't call. The manager called her folks. They didn't know anything."

I felt a thud in my gut. "Where was the car?"

"Up by Buttermilk Creek. Found a pile of clothes by the riverbank, folded in a nice neat pile and footprints going in. That's at the top end where the current's pretty quick and strong. The Chief's got a diving crew up there now."

I swallowed hard. The pavement jumped. My head reeled. Hal steadied me. A wave of nausea surged up my gut. "Any note?"

Hal shook his head, no. "Anything you want to tell me, Joe?"

"Meaning what?"

Hal took a drag, then let his hand drop away from his face and rest on the butt of his police issue .38. It looked like a toy pistol swallowed up in his big mitt.

"Meaning don't get shirty on me, Joe. I'm just asking a question. Like do you know anything? Maybe you can help us. Did she say anything to you recently?"

I could feel my hands starting to shake and the Sweet Cap dropped out of my fingers and rolled down the steps. To stop the trembling, I locked my fingers together and squeezed hard. A man in the floating crowd guffawed loudly. It was a harsh sound and I flinched.

Selfish bastard," I muttered.

"You wanna give it to me at the station or just sit in the car?" he asked politely.

"Let's go to the car."

Hal nodded his peaked head, the brim of his cap throwing a shadow over his eyes, sharpening the ruddy cheeks and fleshy nose. Although the sun was doing its level best, I shivered in my summer suit feeling cold sweat trickling down my sides, slithering like a sidewinder along my spine.

We got into Hal's patrol car. It was a '64 Plymouth and had taken its share of licks. A rebuilt job that had been painted so many times, it looked like pieces of different cars stuck together. He kicked the starter and pulled away from the curb. I rolled down the window, fumbled for another Sweet Cap, punched the lighter on the dash, waited for it to pop up, then lit the cigarette. We seemed to be moving fast. I just felt the motion and things sliding by. When I looked up, the county road south of town rolled by. Hal pulled in under a stand of maple trees.

He reached under the seat and handed me a flat bottle.

"Here, take a pull. It'll help settle you."

"Thanks." I poured some down my throat hoping it would burn away this cloud of misery. Instead, it just burned like hell. But it woke me up. I handed it back. Hal shook his head. I took another pull. Then, I left it in my lap.

I said, "We had a date last night. She'd made up a picnic. We ate it. On the banks of Buttermilk Creek."

"Maybe that's how she got the notion," he said.

I thought about that. "I don't know. But I don't think so."

Hal tapped his fingers on the steering wheel. He'd taken his cap off and wiped out the sweatband with a soiled handkerchief.

"Why do you say that, Joe?" His voice stayed flat. He could have been checking the box scores.

I shrugged. "Just a hunch is all. No reason, really."

Hal nodded thoughtfully, without speaking. Then he looked up.

"You know her folks?" I shook my head. "Doc Seaton's with them now. He's known them for years. Hell, he's known everyone for years. Took it pretty hard. She was an only child."

"All I can tell you is that she seemed different."

"How different?"

I was still clutching the bottle. Some dust blew in the window and speckled the crystal of my wristwatch. Although I'm not left-handed, I wear it on my right arm.

"Just subdued. Quiet and introspective. Different. Normally, she'd talk your ear off. But not last night. Like she had something on her mind but..."

"But what?"

"Couldn't say what it was."

"Anything else?"

A fragment came back to me. "Yeah, she said she used to go up there with somebody."

"Who?"

"Dunno. She wouldn't say but I got the impression that it ended badly."

Hal sat back rubbing his big jaw. Then he yawned.

"McKie's wasting his time with those divers. It's too fast and deep up there at the Creek, especially with the water so high this year. Either she'll snag on a rock or branch downstream, or she'll surface in the Bay sometime. Just like Norma."

"Just like Norma," I repeated. "They were friends in high school."

Hal crinkled his brow. "That so?"

"Funny," I said. "When I kissed her before taking her home, she said it would have to last an eternity." Hal gave me a funny look—a little bit of pity, maybe, but said nothing. After a moment, he started up the cruiser and drove back to town. He dropped me at The Gazette. Darlene's body was never found.

Chapter Twelve

Item—June 12, 1966

Pandemonium broke out in the Old Courthouse this morning during the coroner's inquest into the death of Miss Norma Jennings, aged 22. Under questioning by crown counsel, Horatio Bongard, Dr. Seaton revealed a mysterious chemical substance had been found in Miss Jennings' bloodstream—a substance hitherto unidentified. Blood samples have been sent on to the Centre for Forensic Sciences in Toronto for further testing.

Dr. Seaton revealed that Miss Jennings was approximately eight weeks pregnant, whereupon, Mr. Blake Rothwell leapt to his feet, screaming, "Liar. Liar. That's a bald-faced lie." The room erupted into such disarray that Constable Bigelow was compelled to fire his pistol three times in the air to regain order. Miss Violet Ferguson, 53, a spinster, of RR2, Hagersville, fainted dead away. And so the morning session ended.

The afternoon session, that began at 2 PM., unfolded as a far more subdued affair. The last witness called was Mr. Blake Rothwell. Under firm questioning from Mr. Bongard, Mr. Rothwell admitted that Norma Jennings had been drinking that evening but he had not, claiming a physical intolerance to alcohol. He also stated that neither he nor Miss Jennings wore life jackets in the boat and that weather conditions were rough and uncertain.

Mr. Rothwell said he had been unable to prevent Miss Jennings from climbing onto the bow of the boat. After her disappearance, Mr. Rothwell searched the vicinity but found no sign, citing the darkness of the water and that dusk fell rapidly. When asked by Mr. Bongard if he would have gone into the Bay after her, Mr. Rothwell admitted that he couldn't swim.

After Mr. Rothwell had been dismissed from the witness stand, Dr. Elgar addressed the jury, summarizing the findings and then they retired to discuss their recommendations.

30

Privately, I'd heard that Mr. Rothwell Sr. had offered to compensate the Jennings family generously. He'd already picked up the tab for the funeral that was to take place tomorrow morning at ten a.m. I'd heard the so-called compensation represented a big number, something in the area of $100,000, but then it was just a rumour and I dealt in the business of facts. I wondered who'd pick up the tab for Darlene.

All in all, in a time of incredulity, the inquest had been a most incredulous event even for Applewood. In parlours across the land, tongues wagged of nothing else. Forget all the usual stuff of these serious-minded discussions—the crazy new music, the way boys wore their hair, the shockingly short skirts on young girls and even, the bloodiness of a far-off war in a distant place called Vietnam beginning to appear in our newspapers and on our TV sets. It was all a gauzy dream involving characters of someone else's imagination.

A thought based on the faintest notion had been nagging at me and now that I had a bit of a breather, it was time to act on it. I kept telling myself I'd been a victim of crime as a boy and that's why I could sniff it out, even way out here in a hick place like Applewood. Something stunk up the joint. And my nose was the prime sniffer. I picked up the phone.

"Hello Doc? It's Joe Simpson, here."

"Hi Joe. Quite a commotion this morning, wasn't it?"

"No thanks to you, of course. You know better than me that folks hereabouts live for scandal-mongering and you gave them more in a minute than they've had in the last decade."

Doc chuckled. "Well, Joe. I guess I underestimated our fair citizens somewhat. I was merely reporting scientifically derived evidence, that's all."

"Yeah, sure Doc. Listen, speaking of scientifically derived evidence, a thought occurred to me and I have to ask you something."

" You've never been squeamish before."

"It's that chemical thing. Bothers me no end. I was wondering if you took blood from Ellis and Lizzie Boston and ran an analysis on them too."

Doc chuckled again. "Why Joe, you know I think you'd make a fine detective. My business too, involves looking for clues of a particular kind."

I became excited now. "Let me guess. Tell me you found the same chemical in Ellis and Lizzie, as in Norma? Tell me I'm right, Doc."

Doc paused for effect and I could hear his quiet wheeze crackling over the wire. "You're 100 percent correct, Joe. But Joe, I don't have to remind you that this is not for public consumption. I don't know what the implications of these findings might be but it's very curious, nonetheless, wouldn't you agree?"

I replied, "I'll say. By the way, how's Ellis doing? Is he still making like a bird?"

Doc sighed and I pictured him taking off his spectacles and rubbing them clean with his handkerchief.

"Sad. Very sad. To tell the truth, I don't know, Joe. He may be a bird, he may not. He's subsided into a kind of catatonic state, or so the psychiatrists say. Anyway, he doesn't belong in a jail cell and I doubt he'll ever come to trial, either, if it came to that. Ellis has been moved to Beech Mental Hospital in Brigsby and as you know, once you're in, chances are, you'll never see the light of day. Not with that cockamamie crowd running things over there. It's a wonder they get let out themselves."

"I'd like to see him, Doc. Do you think that's possible?" I wanted to explore the connection between Norma and Ellis but for the life of me, I couldn't see it. Not yet.

Doc grunted. "I can't say. But I'll see what I can do. In the meantime, until we find out from Toronto about that chemical, you'd best keep it to yourself, you hear now, Joe? I don't want to read about it in the Gazette, not until I say so. Okay?"

I said. "I got you, Doc. Do the cops know about this?"

Doc replied, "No. But you can tell Hal Bigelow if you like. He's the only one with any smarts. The rest of 'em share one brain between them. Not that I'd admit that in public, either. I gotta go. I'll talk to you later, Joe."

I didn't want to think about what Doc needed to attend to.

"Bye. And thanks, Doc. I'll be speaking to you."

The Round Table lay situated almost in back of the Old Courthouse across the street from the Two-Tone Hotel. That's not really its name, of course, I just call it that because its facade is constructed of white and black stone—locally mined quartz and obsidian. Outsiders refer to it formally as The Ambassador

Churchill Hotel where all distinguished visitors temporarily reside. Apparently, Lord Churchill did actually spend one night there just after the war, on his way to visit a nephew at St. Andrews school for boys, in nearby Grafton. St. Andrews was a very fine private boys school and ideal for the British upper classes, including royalty. It had all the amenities of snotty public schools in Britain but happened to be conveniently located across the Atlantic. It is now a bottling plant. The room rates at the Two-Tone were uncommonly expensive, ranging from $27.50 for a single to the deluxe suite for $55.00 a night. Meanwhile, the old Tranquillity Inn on the edge of town had been good enough for me. Six bucks got you a clean room and private bath and if you were really lucky...a black and white TV. I'd spent six weeks there when I first moved to Applewood. Otherwise, the rooms came equipped with radio sets. And guess who recently purchased the Two-Tone Hotel? That's right. Phillip Rothwell himself.

Rumours currently circulating had Rothwell trying to wrest control of The Round Table from its owners—Mickey (she) and Delaney (he) Truscott who liked to live well and often neglected the means to pay for it. And although they operated the most successful restaurant in four counties, they seemed perpetually one step away from insolvency.

Delaney—a handsome man in his fifties with dark, slicked-back hair, a gruff manner and a Hollywood grin. Old-timers whispered that he'd been mixed up in a bootlegging operation during the Depression, a piece of gossip I'm sure he encouraged. It didn't seem to hurt business any. At the lunch and dinner hours, Delaney patrolled the front door attired in a double-breasted blue suit by daylight and a formal tuxedo by night. At eleven-thirty a.m. on the button, Delaney descended the stairs, adjusting his tie in the mirror on the landing, a cigarette hanging from his movie star lips. I guess you'd say the two of them personified something no one else had then or have had since; Glamour with a capital Gee.

Mickey had the brains and Delaney the muscle. She had a quick laugh and playful manner but a mind like a steel trap. She never said no to Delaney, never denied him anything. So, when he wanted a new sports car, she bought him a bright red Jaguar XKE convertible—a car I'd personally pawn my soul for. When Delaney decided to try his hand at horse breeding, she set him up on a farm complete with stock and stables. When he wanted to get away for a while, they cruised the Caribbean in a private yacht. Delaney had charm and style and because of his masculine allure, women virtually swooned in his muscular arms. Mickey and Delaney enjoyed good times largely due to the boom in development and Applewood's growing reputation as a year-round tourist resort. But I suspected that the times would catch up to them someday. Only the Phillip Rothwells of the world prevailed. People like Mickey and Delaney would cease to be relevant and those deemed relevant would take over. We all have our day. But for some it comes and goes a little faster than others.

Chapter Thirteen

I entered The Round Table bar at precisely 5:32 p.m. The wooden bar itself never failed to make me whistle. Simply put, it was a beauty. Delaney stumbled across it by accident in a half-demolished hotel in Toronto. The hotel bar—The Silver Rail—the first to re-open in the city after Prohibition had been repudiated. The bar dated from the late 1800's. Carved out of the deepest, most burnished mahogany and shaped in a sweeping arc some eighty feet long. The foot rail was made of pure, beaten silver. All the fixtures, taps and settings, even the huge mirror frame behind it were also pure silver polished to a high sheen. Delaney bought it on the spot, then had the entire structure ripped out of its moorings in sections and hauled by truck to Applewood. Delaney brought in craftsmen from all over the region where the bar was lovingly and imperiously, restored making it the prized headpiece of the Truscott's fine establishment.

Not much of a social drinker by nature, I preferred to drink my liquor in private. Still, I liked to go in and sip a rye whiskey on the rocks and feel the aura of the place. And I felt the need, from time to time, to be part of something that had a history, something that had lasted. Generally, I liked older things; they had a substance and solidity that the new missed by a mile. It gave me a sense of place and comfort. Maybe it was something I associated with my father before he became a violent drunk. I knew him as a young man mainly from the photographs my mother kept in her hope chest. He'd been a tail gunner in the RCAF. He came back from the War a maniac. He drank. He fought. He beat my mother senseless. So, one night she couldn't take it anymore and stabbed him to death. I saw her slapped down by powerful men. They didn't take into account all the pain and beatings she'd endured. None of that came out at the trial. As far as the lawyers and the judge and the men on the jury were concerned, she'd committed murder, plain and simple. Home for her now remained a six by six cell in the Prison for Women down by Kingston. I was only twelve and left on my own, didn't have any other living relations. Hell, you can't waste time crying about it. I was lucky though. Out of all that misery, something smiled on me when a family took me in. Gus Sperkados had been the assistant city editor at the Toronto Mercury where my father worked. A straight family man with four kids of his own. Never a quiet household but you could feel the love in it. It took me a while, a long while but finally I began to feel a little of it too. Bullies picked on me at school. Not many kids had a murderer for a mom. I got into a lot of scrapes, coming home to the Sperkados household with black eyes and split lips every other day, it seemed. Gus hauled me down to Sully's gym on King Street. A barebones place with a single, canvas ring but Sully, an old-time fighter with fists as hard as dumbbells, taught me how to box and more, how to street fight. As I progressed through school, I gave as good as I got but most of the scarring formed on the inside. Finally, after graduating high school, Gus got me on as a messenger at the paper where I worked my way up to junior reporter. Then I saw Teddy's ad and thought I could make a fresh start in a town where my history didn't matter.

Thompkins hadn't changed his clothes and stood out like a sideshow in a cathedral. I slid on to the leather stool beside him.

"What're you having, Joe?" he drawled. It was clear he'd been holding up the bar for quite some time. Delaney worked the taps. I guessed the regular barman had taken a break.

"Canadian Club on the rocks, please Delaney," I said.

"Coming right up, Joe." Delaney poured without looking and didn't spill a drop. He set the glass down then wiped the bar with a pristine towel. Glancing in the mirror, I spotted a girl who looked a lot like Darlene, the brassy version of Darlene, seated at a booth talking briskly to a stylish young man in grey. The girl glanced over in my direction, then just as quickly looked away, halting her conversation momentarily. After a beat, she picked it up again as if nothing had happened. But my, oh my, how a life's history is communicated in a single look and it saddened me all of a sudden. That look made me think that I might have been able to do something for Darlene, say something that might have changed her mind. I missed it and felt badly I couldn't help her somehow. Not even the comforting smell of leather and cigars helped. I really wanted that drink. No sooner had I downed it, Delaney poured me another.

"It'll do you good, kid," he said.

Thompkins' eyes narrowed shrewdly.

"You know that little gal?" he asked.

"No. I used to know somebody like her."

"Pretty little thing. Maybe you should have grabbed your gal while you had the chance, Joe."

The last person I needed as a Miss Lonely Heart was Barrett Thompkins. His fat, patronizing face began to irk me.

"Let's move on to something else, okay, Barrett?"

He chortled into his rye and ginger ale.

" No problem, Joe, if that's the way you want it. Why don't we drink up anyhow and move in for dinner? Reservations for 5:45 pm., which is now." And that's what we did, although I regretted leaving the warmth of the bar. I wasn't making sense. Eighty-two degrees outside and I fretted about warmth? But I wasn't referring to the temperature. Delaney nodded to us as we left and gave me a wink.

The dining room began to fill up but it was early yet. In the summer time, only those over the age of seventy ate at The Round Table before eight o'clock and people like me, of course, who had urgent prior commitments. At 6 pm., it felt like lunchtime except that I felt tired and sweaty and just wanted to go home and sit under a cool shower for a week.

Barrett said, "Since we're on a tight schedule, I took the liberty of ordering ahead. I hope you don't mind. It's not something I'd do ordinarily but in the so-called interests of elegant dining, I didn't want you to feel pressured or anything."

"Fine, Barrett. That's considerate of you."

Thompkins shot his cuffs like a magician about to pull a bull elephant out of his sleeve.

"Here's the menu. Hope you like it. In order then..." And he ticked them off with his fingers. "...Shrimp cocktail. Caesar salad, light on the garlic. Never know who'll you'll be kissing, right? Rack of lamb with spring potatoes and fresh-shelled peas. French stick. Pecan pie and coffee. And any alcoholic beverages you care to imbibe along the way. Now, how does that sound?"

"It sounds like a lot to eat. But I think I can manage and talk a little at the same time." Jeez. No wonder he weighed about six hundred pounds.

As the shrimp cocktail arrived, I said, "Okay Barrett. You start. What's on your mind?"

"Spoken like a true newspaperman, Joe. I like that."

"Sure. Hit it."

"I've been reading your stuff, Joe. It may surprise you to know that I read a lot of the regional papers, particularly the dailies, as often as I can. And I've been perusing The Gazette pretty regularly for the past six months or so. In addition to my senior responsibilities as national editor, I'm also a bit of a talent spotter. I pride myself on that. Without sounding too immodest, I hope. A great newspaper doesn't stay great without great reporters and I'm happy to say I've recruited my fair share. Let's see, now, Grant Neilson, for one. Lydia Kelley. Valerie Bruno, Bob Panatella and Victor Carlos. All top-notch talent. And I found'em all. Valerie and Bob, as you may know, still work for me and the others have gone on to television except for Victor, who is writing a book. But they formed the nucleus of a terrific staff at one time."

"You offering me a job, Barrett?" I asked through the garlic haze of the Caesar salad.

"Heh-heh. Joe, you've got qualities I admire. I like your work. It's clean. It's crisp and it's got style. Here's what I've got in mind. It seems to me that Applewood is a happening little place, suddenly. There's a lot going on here."

"Especially with Phillip Rothwell and company happily parked here, right Barrett?"

He nodded vigorously. I thought he'd wrench his neck.

"That's right, Joe. Dead bang right. Not to mention some other interesting occurrences, of course. Here's what I've got in mind. I'd like you to work as our stringer out here, Joe. You feed me interesting stories from the area and I make sure they're published in Toronto. You'll get national exposure and decent pay. What do you make now, Joe? I'd say in the neighbourhood of 100-150 bucks a week. A top reporter in the city makes 350, sometimes 400 for the best. Every story you file for me, I'll pay you an extra 25 bucks and if it's really good, 50 for a feature. And if you're worried about Teddy Graff, don't be. I've already spoken to him about it and he said it's up to you. As long as it doesn't interfere with your work at The Gazette, he doesn't mind if you string for us. It's a good opportunity, Joe. And eventually, say, after the summer, if you wanted to move to the city and it all works out, I think we can find a spot for you. Wouldn't be anything glamourous at first, maybe copy editing, something like that. But it'd be a helluva start for you. So, what do you think?"

As he blathered, I ploughed through the rack of lamb like nobody's business. Barrett had barely touched a thing. I decided to be cagey. After all, it could very well be a good opportunity yet a sneaky part of me remained suspicious. It seemed almost too good and his description of Teddy's response didn't sound like him at all. More likely, Teddy would have aimed a kick at his big fat, banana yellow butt.

"Sounds very interesting, Barrett. And like you said, it could be a very good opportunity. But if you don't mind, I'd like to sleep on it and give you a call in a couple of days. I hope that's amenable to you?"

Barrett seemed uncertain. I suppose he expected me to jump at it thinking I was some hick reporter lying around dreaming of my big break. Well there might be some truth in that but I didn't want to seem too anxious, either. And I did want to shoot it by Teddy if only as a courtesy.

"Fine," he replied. "Fine. Here's my card. Give me a call in Toronto beginning of next week and we'll finalize the details. You're a fine young man. I see some national newspaper awards in your future. And who knows? Maybe even my job one day." Barrett nodded and smiled but it was now time for him to get down to the serious business of eating since I'd prevented him from doing that until now. And he did get serious mighty fast. After a while, he looked up. "Did I mention that I knew your father?"

"Jesus. I mean, no, you didn't." Shot between the eyes. Barrett had the killer instinct and maybe that's how he climbed so far in the newspaper scene.

"Helluva newspaperman," he said. "Damned shame what happened."

And that's how he summed it all up. Just like a badly written obit stuffed in the back pages. I felt a rage rise within me and had to work damn hard to keep it from shooting out my ears. I put on a cool smile instead. Thompkins narrowed his eyes as he chewed a lump of red meat.

I shook hands with Barrett Thompkins at the front door of The Round Table under the discreet but watchful eye of Delaney, who gave me a friendly wink. Barrett then headed back to the bar. After he'd waddled off and I turned to take my leave, Delaney held the door for me, then stepped outside, put a cigarette to his lips and said, "Got a light, Joe?" I knew he always carried an engraved gold lighter in his right hand pocket and he knew that I knew it too.

"Sure Delaney. There you go." He offered me one of his Dunhills and I lit them both with my Zippo. Delaney blew some smoke into the humid air and I waited for him. That tux must have been terribly uncomfortable on such a close night.

"You know that fellah well?" he asked suddenly.

"Barrett Thompkins? Just met him today, actually. He came around to The Gazette this afternoon."

Delaney smirked. "I can't stand those trousers. Makes a man look like a buffoon. Did he offer you a job, Joe?"

"Yeah. He did. You know something, Del?"

He let me have the full impact of his devil-may-care Irish charm and showed his pearly white teeth.

"Do fish fly, kid? Thompkins is hooked in with O'Toole, Rothwell and that crowd, Joe. If he wants something from you, you'd best know what you're getting into. They're in tight. But then, you never heard it from me. They're good customers of course but I like you, Joe. So I figured I'd just wise you up a little. Now it's your choice. You're all on the same level. I don't like to see people walking down blind alleys without knowing what's on the other side."

"Thanks Delaney. Considering I'm not such a great customer of yours, that is."

"Well you did us a favour last summer and I want you to know I appreciate it and I don't forget those things," he said. I'd written a heritage piece on the bar that had won a regional writing award and also brought in a lot of curious tourists too.

"I sensed that Thompkins had an angle. Thanks."

Delaney nodded and flicked the cigarette into the gutter.

"Sure kid. Drop by anytime and I'll stand you to a drink at the bar. We can swap stories, okay?"

"Okay."

"I'll see you. I've got to get back in. Mickey'll be all over me if she thinks I'm letting things slide." He patted my shoulder then walked gracefully up the stairs and entered the restaurant to resume his role as the elegant cigar store Indian. He squared his shoulders before disappearing into the plush corridor.

Chapter Fourteen

Rushing home felt more than familiar. I spent barely a few milliseconds there daily, mainly to shower and change. I grabbed a pair of jeans, polo shirt and topsiders—no socks. I paused, glancing up at the sheets of paper stuck to the wall hoping a pattern might emerge. So far, just sheets of paper with names and a couple of arrows. Since the air had felt laden with moisture, rain was hovering on the Bay side, I grabbed my jean jacket before heading out the door.

I wasted a further seven minutes putting the top up on the car. Fortunately, it never took more than three to five minutes to drive anywhere in Applewood. My glow-in-the-dark Timex told me it had just ticked past seven o'clock. I struggled with the damn top. In about 90 seconds, I sweated like a pig, dirty from the grimy vinyl. I didn't even stop to think about what I planned to do, where I headed or what might happen. I should have. It would have been a lot safer.

Furlingers lay like a blot on an already desolate outcrop. A beat-up roadhouse plunked down in the middle of a gravel pit, just off Highway 28 and County Road 6. The beginnings of a parking lot had been dug up around the building but hadn't been finished. When the air turned arid, the dust flew and when it rained, you sank into a quagmire. The roadhouse stood low and flat-topped with four rectangular, dirty windows set into stucco walls and dirtier curtains drawn across them. Over time, rain, dust and the elements had coloured the stucco a mealy gray. A neon sign fastened to a rusted metal pole that hadn't been oiled since Queen Victoria's coronation creaked in the breeze. The "G" and "R" had burnt out—ghost images on a metal landscape.

A brace of motorcycles—big nasty machines and well-traveled—stood end-to-end like a rugby scrum down the length of the half-dug lot. I parked on the opposite side, close to the road, front facing out. Just in case. I may want my tires to grab the tarmac fast.

The wooden entrance had been used for knife practice. Or some drunk had mistaken it for a stand of firewood of a chilly evening. Half the lower panel had disappeared. I paused. A cloud rolled in overhead and I shook off a shiver. The wind blew up and the drainpipes rattled hard. Like an old sailor's teeth.

Inside— an interior decorator's nightmare. Essentially, one large, open space, a formica bar stood off to the right. It may have been plastic once. A small bandstand slept at the very back. You could clear a spot for dancing if you wore a size two. Along the far wall to the left, spooled a line of velvet-clad booths. The upholstery complemented the fake Chinese lanterns growing out of the ceiling. They glowed faintly orange. The joint had all the charm of a dental lab. To the right of the bandstand stood a lonely pool table. Two of the bikers gripped cues. They looked for the switch to turn them on. Just beyond the cue balls, four more, two of each variety, sat all over each other, drinking and laughing loudly. Nothing else breathed. You could have died in a corner and lain there a week.

I took a stool at the bar. The seat was cracked and cold. The barman appeared terribly preoccupied cleaning his cuticles with a paring knife. A lean buzzard, strung out like a whipcord. A thin, badly pock-marked face and hooded eyes. His wore his reddish hair slicked back from a high forehead into a pronounced widow's peak. In keeping with the place, he sported a filthy T-shirt over a filthier apron. He whistled tunelessly through his front tooth.

I tapped the bar. About an hour later he looked up.

"Draft," I said. For a long time he didn't move. It was an important decision.

"Your funeral," he replied, reaching down to snag a glass. He drew the draft from the tap, then set it down and shoveled it down the bar top effortlessly. A splash slopped over the rim of the glass.

I said, "What, no peanuts?"

"Fresh out," he replied and smiled nastily. I saw nothing in his eyes.

I took a sip. Warm and tasted like drool. I smacked my lips.

"Good beer," I said. "Must be a local brew."

"You got it," replied the bartender, still smirking but anxious to get back to those grimy fingernails.

I threw a tough one at him. "You know the Viking?"

He shook once, like a dog stepping out of the water. "Never heard of him."

"Know where I can find him?"

He cracked a real smile then, teeth, gums and everything. "You don't hear so good."

"I heard he hangs out here. Can't miss him. Big guy. Albino. Rides a Harley."

"Sounds like a lot of guys," he said, moving down the bar to take up his craftsmanship. He'd been away too long.

By their smell—oiled leather, monkey grease and sweat—I could tell they were close. One of them poked me with a cue. I turned around to face them. I wasn't afraid of trouble. Rarely did I look for it but if it came at me in the shape of a roadblock, I'd drive right through. They smiled too. Everybody seemed happy and relaxed. They'd had a nice big dinner. And liqueurs after. I was so calm that my gut turned to a lump of iron. My pulse couldn't even break 180.

The one on my left came in short. He had a paunch the size of a watermelon, an open guileless face, tightly curled black hair and a goatee shading his pudgy chin. He looked like a boy who'd enjoy wrestling with bears. One of them bit half his right ear off. Half-ear rocked back on his heels, forward and back, like a tub listing in the harbour. No go, I thought. He'd go over like a ton of bricks. Those boys usually do. His rangy sidekick was another story. He had the face of a weasel and the fangs to match. Must be related to the bartender. His shoulders were no wider than a coat hanger and long, lasso-like arms hung down to his skinny shanks. Arms that could wrap themselves around you like a python and squeeze. Squeeze plenty. He had ginger hair, the colour of a frisky cocker spaniel, lovingly sculpted into a ducktail. Long narrow sideburns cut the lines of his face like scars. I relaxed. They made me feel at home.

"You boys know the Viking?"

The fat one sniggered. Weasel face tapped me with the cue.

He said, "You wanna dance, fella?"

I said, "Joe."

He shrugged. "You wanna dance, Joe?"

I said, "He rides a Harley, like you. He's big, white and over twenty-one."

"Does that mean you don't wanna dance with me?" Weasel face said in a simpering tone.

My elbows remained propped on the bar.

I said, "Hell, I'll even kiss you if you'll give me a straight answer, honey."

Fatso put his head back and roared. Weasel face didn't take it too well. His pride or whatever he called it, teetered. And if a guy could rile that easily, then you knew he didn't think too clearly even when the puzzle was simple. More often than not he'd make a stupid move.

Like now. It had to be the stick. He just wouldn't think to let go of it. And I didn't want those arms coming around me. Giving me the squeeze. I blocked the cue with my left forearm just as he moved to bring it down across my scalp. Rising up off the stool, I gave him two good shots in the ribs which sucked his breath out, then snapped his head back with a right cross. Weasel face went up on his booted toes, then sprawled back against the lame pool table. By then, of course, Fatso hugged me. He moved fast for a guy carrying so much blubber. The barkeep looked very happy. Almost delirious. Still picked away though. I took most of Fatso's weight on my left shoulder and it went numb. Then he climbed up on my back, riding me hard and I buckled. His right forearm worked its way neatly under my chin toward my throat. I heard the sound of wood scraping on wood. Something hit the back of my knee and we both went down. By then, Weasel face rolled his head around, probing with his bony fingers for any soft spots along his jaw line.

I looked up from the floor and saw six and a half feet of human, white marble towering above me. He prodded me with a size 14 motorcycle boot.

"Jump up, Bud," he said quietly. Then he turned and stomped as quietly as a caterpillar tractor to a booth. By the time I got there, he sat spread across the seat chewing thoughtfully on a wooden match. He was used to this. Guys got busted up all the time. His hair had the consistency of shiny cotton. Long and parted in the middle. He'd managed to grow a wispy beard. It looked like the fuzz off a cashmere sweater. You could rub his eyebrows away with your thumb. Each bleached eye had a pink rim encircling it like you see on some snow bunnies or cokeheads. He showed a big calloused palm. I took it as my cue to sit. He continued to chew the match, then spat a sliver on the table.

"So, you're willing to get your face bent just to talk to me?"

I grinned. "I guess I can be a little rash at times."

He said, " Next time, I'll let them take you out back and tie you to a pole."

"I'll keep that in mind."

He lifted his head. "Step it up."

"I'm Joe Simpson. I write for The Gazette."

"Yeah, I know who you are. Tell me you're doing an exposé on street crime."

"I'm just doing background. You know, soaking up the local colour, getting in the groove." I pause. "You heard about Norma Jennings?"

"Don't play dumb, man. I gotta know everything that goes on around here. That's my business."

"Okay. So, you knew her."

He sat back and looked pensive, the broad planes of his face softened.

"Yeah sure. I liked Norma. She was good for a laugh. She went with the wrong kind, though."

"You mean, Blake Rothwell?"

The Viking ground the entire match between his teeth, sulphur tip and all, then swallowed it.

"Guy doesn't stand for nothin'. He's got a few bucks in his fancy pants, that's all."

This was funny. More than funny. Practically comical. Character analysis from a biker. "Unlike bikers you mean?"

He nodded emphatically. "She shoulda hung out with us. She'd still be alive, that's for damn sure."

"You know where she liked to go?"

He shrugged his shoulders. "Just around like everybody else."

"I guess you knew she was pregnant."

The pink irises widened for a scant second. The flanges of his nostrils flared. "Rothwell?"

I shook my head. "Don't think so. Another party. You wouldn't happen to have any ideas, would you?"

He shrugged. "Everybody moves around. It's hard to keep track. There's a lot of shacking up."

Carefully, I said, "And then there's you and Cindy Lou."

His eyes widened. They looked like pale stones. The corners of his mouth went down. He leaned in. "What about us?"

"Keep your shirt on. She was friends with Norma."

"Where'd you get that, Jack?"

I sat back and smiled at him. At his white hair and pink skin and pink-rimmed rabbit's eyes. "It's common knowledge. They were cheerleaders together. You were on the football team."

"Until they kicked me out for punching the coach."

"And then there was someone else too."

The Viking knit his brow. An eagle could have built a nest on it.

" Who was that?"

"Darlene Norris."

He let out a whoosh of breath. "Darlene. Yeah, Darlene," he almost whispered.

"She's disappeared."

He grabbed my right forearm and squeezed it like a rotten lemon. Squeezed until I though the ulna would split.

"Whaddaya mean disappeared," he growled.

I tried to shake my arm free.

"Let go, dammit. I mean exactly that. Her car and some clothes were found up by Buttermilk Creek. The cops have got divers dragging for her body right now."

The Viking dropped my arm and sat back on the bench running his thick, nicotine stained fingers through his scalp. It made the sound of a rake on crab grass.

I said, "It's kind of a coincidence, isn't it? Norma goes in the drink. Darlene disappears and that leaves Cindy Lou. And the three of them connected."

"You leave Cindy Lou out of this or I'll break your back." But he said it without conviction or malice. Just habit. "I didn't hear about Darlene. We dated in high school."

"I believe you. But then I'm not the one pulling the strings. I'm just trying to find them. Get some answers. That's my scene. Just before she disappeared, Darlene told me she was seeing somebody but they'd broken it off. It sounded like somebody important. Any ideas?"

The Viking shook his head. "I'm no matchmaker. I don't track who's seeing who."

"You never saw her with anyone?"

"Nope."

"But you were friends in high school."

The Viking sighed. "That was a long time ago, Bud."

I glanced down at my watch. It was time to split. "We'll have to pick this up later. I'm late. Listen, if you hear anything about Darlene or Norma, will you let me know?"

"Why should I?"

"Because I think you cared about them. The funny thing is, so did I. Think about it. I just want to know what happened, nothing more." I slid out of the booth.

He stopped me.

"Listen, Simpson. There's things happening out there. But it's not us, you get it? It's not the High Riders, beyond the usual stuff."

I wondered what that meant. Hot cars? Theft? Robbery? Or worse?

"Maybe you'll hear from me. Maybe not. But it's anonymous sources, right? Or you got tire tracks up your back."

I grinned at him. "If that's the word, that's the word."

I left him sitting there pulling at his big, pink lips and walked out under the faded Chinese lanterns, past the rickety tables, beyond the scuffed bar and sulking bartender, out into the dust clotted night air. Speaking of tracks, I had to make fast tracks back to town.

Chapter Fifteen

I left the car across the street from the record store, and loitered in front of the window with the blazing peace emblem waiting for someone to show up. I lit a Sweet Cap and peered inside to see if anyone might be there. I wanted to get the cruddy taste of Furlingers out of my palate. Lit by a string of single streetlamps and the odd bulb placed over a doorway here and there the street seemed abandoned and forlorn. I could have been standing on the main strip of a ghost town. All I needed to see was the tumbleweed and bramble bush blowing down the street. Norma. Darlene. Cindy Lou. Ellis and Lizzie Boston. I was lost in thought when Beverly came up from behind and touched me on the shoulder.

She said, "Hi Joe."

"Hi Bev."

"I'm glad you could come."

"Yeah. Me too." I sure knew how to make intelligent conversation. Two syllable words had suddenly become a challenge. Beverly took my arm and we began to stroll side by side.

"Wish is around the back." Her bare arms felt warm against mine. I felt the heat that began at the bottom of my feet and percolated upward like a lava flow in reverse igniting each part, as the flow burned everything in its path until finally, the volatile heat surged up into my face, engulfing the roots of my hair in flames.

"Warm night," she remarked.

"Yeah." It hadn't been five minutes ago.

Just as we rounded the corner of the building, Beverly stopped abruptly and faced me square. "Joe. I don't want you think this is a date or anything, okay?

We can be together or not, all right? If you're worried, Wish is fine with it," she said. "But I do like you, you know."

I was taken aback. Now if I were a smooth operator like Wishbone, I would have gazed back at her and said something cool.

Instead, I said, "Okay."

I guess it had the desired effect, because she smiled then and said, "Cool." And flung her arms around me in a crushing embrace. Her full-bodied form clung to me and that lava flow began to quake to the beat of my racing heart. For a moment, I felt like I was going to swoon, something I'd done only once in my life—at a rock concert in a packed gymnasium.

After releasing me, she said, "I just wanted things to be clear, that's all."

Rubbing my neck, I replied, "You've got a helluva grip, Bev."

"I'm strong, Joe. You've no idea."

We finished rounding the corner and my jaw dropped. A pair of jugglers threw pins at each other with lightening speed, each pin a whirring blur as it traveled, then smacked crisply into the palm of the other and instantly back again. The air buzzed, full of flying, spinning wooden objects. A young man and woman, both with equally long hair, walked casually on their hands carrying on a conversation. They walked toward each other, then kissed, and back-pedaled a bit then repeated the sequence. Another young man put a mid-sized German shepherd through a series of tricks—it rolled over, barked on command, walked on its hind legs and found a biscuit hidden in the pocket of his vest. A man in white face busied himself riding a unicycle with an extended seat. He rode it with one foot, balanced across the seat on his abdomen, used his hands to pedal, stood on his head, all without missing a beat or losing the rhythm.

"What's going on?" I asked Beverly.

She shrugged as if it were the most normal thing in the world. But you must remember this was 1966…in Applewood.

She said, "Oh, they're a bunch of Wish's friends from the States. They've been staying with him awhile."

I pointed. "What's that?"

The motorized piece de resistance, if you will—a bus unlike any I'd ever seen. Formerly, an old Greyhound but had been transformed with a display of colours and designs that I can only describe as having been painted by an artist who'd gone happily mad. There were rainbows, mandalas, peace symbols, birds a-wing, constellations and astrological signs of the universe rendered in fire-breathing colours of contrasting hue and intensity. The bus radiated in glowing, fluorescent waves. Not an eyesore exactly, it went far beyond that. It existed as a dream and nightmare intertwined then set down on the planet for the ordinary among us to gawp at. The performers dressed in various forms of costume and their garishly painted faces made me think I'd stepped into Renaissance Italy.

Who were these people? As we approached, various shapes emerged out of the shadows; kids I'd seen about town having stolen away from home. I wondered what stories they'd made up. All these kids just wanted to fit in somewhere and for some reason didn't, mostly hanging out at the record store. They looked up to, even idolized, Wishbone Jones.

Wishbone Jones, resplendent in buckskins from head to toe, sat behind the wheel of the wild bus talking to a large, muscular man wearing a sleeveless leather jerkin and blue jeans. The man's head had been shaved smooth and painted in a rainbow of colours and celestial designs. On the back of his head an American flag was etched into the skin. I took in a broad face with sharply angled cheekbones. An aquiline nose sniffed in the world. Grey eyes saw out but revealed no emotion. The mouth showed cruelty.

Wishbone said, "Joe Blow. What's shaking?" And we did our hand slap thing.

"Not much, Wish. Thought I was in 17th century Florence for a second." Wishbone threw back his head and laughed outright.

"No," he said. "But you're pretty damn close, Joe." And turned to the large, strange man who'd remained silent. "See what a little education can do for you, Damo?"

The man nodded politely and said, "I do indeed."

Then Wishbone introduced us.

"Johnny D'Amato—Circus strongman, sculptor, psychologist, escape artist, philosopher, lover of women, fugitive from the law and finally, trickster, meet Joe Simpson, our local excuse for a newspaper man." D'Amato took my hand in a grip that, if he wanted, could have turned my fingers into mush.

"Nice to meet you, Joe. Call me Damo. Wishbone says you're a good head," he said in a voice that rumbled like thunder out of a storm cloud.

"Thanks," I replied. "You performing in the area?" Wishbone and Damo both roared at that one. You'd have thought I'd told the funniest joke in the world.

"In a manner of speaking," Damo said, actually flicking tears from his eyes, while Wishbone kept snorting into his moustaches.

"I guess you'd say we're a performance troupe. We call ourselves The Flying New Jersey Jokesters—Jersey Jokers for short."

"Is that where you're from? New Jersey?"

"Nope. You ever been to Jersey?" answered Damo, showing the fine edge of his teeth. I couldn't help but speculate as to why a man in his thirties, a mature male, educated it seemed and well-spoken, would transform himself into something resembling a carny actor verging on the edge of the grotesque.

I said, "Maybe later we'll shoot the breeze."

Damo shrugged. "Maybe."

"But you've got a philosophy, am I right?"

"You know, Joe Blow, a little education can be a dangerous thing."

"I'll take my chances."

"Maybe we'll talk. And maybe we won't," he said, mysteriously. Damo seemed to be laughing at me. He moved off to round up his painted companions.

Wishbone suddenly piped up.

"Joe. Whyn't you and Bev grab a seat somewhere. We're going to head out in a second."

"Strange guy," I said to Bev as we took our seats. That put it mildly. Dusk had crept in quickly. I noticed the bus windows had been blacked out. I didn't see any conventional seats but a leather sofa, a love seat, a couple of wingback chairs, a bed and half a dozen stools. Most of the kids who'd skulked in while Damo and I talked chose to sit on the floor. Beverly and I sat on the couch beside a couple who sat upright with their legs crossed and eyes closed.

"Meditating," confirmed Beverly.

"On what?" I asked.

"On anything. Life. Love. Nature. You know, the usual things, Joe," she said as if I should have known precisely.

Meanwhile, members of the Jersey Jokers began piling on board. The hand standing couple did exactly that, walked down the aisle on their hands. One of the unicyclists rode on, all flush with the excitement of being out in the fresh air and of exercise. By the time all the Jokers and their various pieces of equipment were stowed, the bus was crowded. Bev and I pressed up against each other. Damo sat up front with Wish.

"All aboard," Wish yelled, hit the ignition, kicked the gears in and the bus lurched off into the darkness; destination, moon. As soon as we began to move, from literally everywhere came this soaring, pounding, nerve-wrenching, ear-piercing music. I turned to Beverly in mild shock and confusion.

"Electric Dream," she said, matter-of-factly. "Wish's current favourite."

After some twenty-five minutes of the musical assault and battery coupled with the heaves and groans of the bus, I'd just about reached my limit. Give me the town morgue any day. As soon as we headed out, matches flared around us, butt ends glowed in the dark but the aroma smelled unlike any tobacco bought at the corner store—sweet and pungent. Reefers on the move. The odour wasn't unpleasant but on top of the brain splattering music and the warm, sweating bodies, I began to feel a little disoriented just from inhaling the local air. I heaved a sigh of relief when the bus slammed to a stop.

"Party time!" yelled Wish to whoops and hollers of the intrepid travelers. "Everybody off the bus!!" I witnessed an Olympic start in slow motion, everyone sprang to action languidly, rolling loose-limbed down the aisle to pour themselves off and down the steps to freedom. I stood up, rubbery-legged and leaned on Beverly.

"You okay, Joe?"

"Sure. It's just stuffy in here. I need some fresh air then I'll be perfectly fine, Bev. Just perfectly fine."

As soon as we stepped off, I sucked in the moisture-laden, pine-scented country air with humble gratitude. A huge bonfire crackled and roared in a dug out pit around which, half a dozen young people sat in a virtually frozen state, transfixed by the leaping and dancing of the orange-blue flames.

Through the trees at a distance of about 100 yards, I saw a clearing and in it stood a white, clapboard farmhouse. Crude torches of straw bound in kerosene-soaked burlap had been mounted on thick wooden stakes pounded into the ground. Light standards. I pictured the woods ablaze. Meanwhile, the Jersey Jokers continued their playful antics—juggling, balancing, cycling and other gymnastic gyrations in total concentrated silence. I kept looking for the dwarf and the Fool to come tumbling out singing rude ditties accompanied by a minstrel on a mandolin. Wrong era and form, I supposed. Wishbone clapped me on the back.

"There's beer and wine in the tub over there, Joe. Or if you like, catch some of the grass that's bound to be floating around anytime now. Music'll be on soon. The band's just setting up in front of the house."

"The band?"

Wishbone stared at me as if I'd lost my senses. "Well, sure Joe. You can't have a good party without a band, now can you?" Then he walked off with Damo shaking his shaggy head.

"Wish always has a band at his parties," Beverly said.

"Where does he get them from?" I asked.

Beverly shrugged. "Various places."

"Isn't that expensive?"

Beverly laughed and punched me sharply in the shoulder.

"Boy. You're an odd one, Joe. They don't charge anything. They play for free because they like to. Want a drink?"

"Are you old enough to drink?"

"Oh Joe. You're a scream. Really you are."

"Just kidding, Bev."

I began to wonder about this Damo character. To look at, he was impressive, I'll admit. He WAS built like the strong man in the circus and I wondered if he bent iron bars with his teeth or lifted elephants on his back. Over six feet tall with a physique that wouldn't have embarrassed Steve Reeves—the current muscle bound film hero starring in Hercules. The tattoos really started me thinking—snakes coiled up each forearm, a heart on the right bicep and the planet Saturn complete with rings and moons on the left looking as if it might hurl itself into orbit at any moment. Where the thongs of his leather jerkin had loosened I could see glimpses of another etched across his ridged abdomen—a forge hammer encircled by a ring of fire. Only two places I could think of where men got tattoos like that—prison or the military.

Bev returned handing me a Black Label.

"That's all there is," she said.

"That's fine. My favourite brand."

She took my arm again. "The music'll start soon."

"Do you live out here, Bev?"

"Sometimes."

"What about your folks?"

"Oh. We don't get along so well. We haven't for awhile."

"Why's that? If you don't mind me asking."

Beverly smiled in an embarrassed way.

"There you go, asking questions again. Questions that do more than just need an answer, Joe. I guess it comes naturally to you."

"It may be the only thing. But you don't have to answer any, Bev. Nobody does. But they usually do."

"Oh well. My Dad's kind of scary, you know. He's got a mean temper. And he drinks too much. My Mom is afraid of him. My Dad and I just end up screaming at each other all the time. It's not very pleasant. It's not a good place for me to be right now. I think it's better for everybody when I'm not there."

I gestured to our surroundings. "And this is?"

"Sure. I can laugh and be free. Be myself without worrying about anybody getting angry or yelling. I can just be me."

"And then what Bev? What do you do after these people take off or you decide this isn't what you want?"

"I can't think that far ahead, Joe. I'm just living for now, that's all and it's good enough for me... right now. We'll see about the rest."

"Are there other kids in your family?"

Bev nodded slowly.

"I've got two younger sisters—Maude is fourteen and wants to run away and live with me. Isabelle is eight and she doesn't know what to think but she's pretty young yet. But it hurts me when I think about them. That I left them behind there. That maybe I ran out on them. But I was suffocating there, Joe."

"I get it. And sorry it's been so tough."

She shrugged. "It's nobody's fault. Just the way it is."

"How do you feel now, Bev?"

"Like I can do anything I want. Go anywhere I want."

"Because of Wish?"

She took a long swig from the Black Label, then wiped the back of her hand across her full lips. "He's been supportive."

" So, what do you want to do now that you've got choices?"

"I don't know yet for sure. Just as long as it's something important. Oh, now you're laughing at me. You're thinking I'm simple-minded."

"No, I'm not. I wasn't laughing. Really. Tell me."

"I think I'd like to write. Maybe even do what you do. You know, start somewhere like The Gazette."

I thought about that. "Why not? You're a smart girl, Bev. And you actually read which seems to be a pretty rare phenomenon these days. But you know, it's not a bad idea to think about going to school. To university, I mean."

Beverly cocked her head to the side and a hank of glossy hair fell across her face. "University? I hadn't even thought that was possible. I just figured you learned on the job, sort of like being an apprentice. Is that what you did, Joe?"

I nodded. "Pretty much. But it's not the only way."

Her eyes lit up. "Hey, let me ask you some reporter questions, okay?"

"Uh sure, okay."

She cleared her throat. "What do you think is going to happen after the inquest? Do you think Blake Rothwell is going to be charged and if so, what do you think the charges will be?"

I laughed nervously. "Good questions. But we'll have to wait and see. It's up to the Crown to decide if he's going to be charged or not."

"Any idea who the father of Norma Jennings' baby is?"

"Er, no, no idea really."

"Could it be Blake Rothwell?" Beverly asked.

"It could be, I suppose."

"Do you think any of this negative publicity will affect the new Applewood resort development being built by Blake's father, Phillip?"

"Well, I'm not sure it's going to help the development if that's what you're asking," I replied.

Bev swayed and hummed to herself. Her brow furrowed.

"So, how did I do ?" she asked.

"Actually, they were very good questions."

She took a sip from the bottle, smiled and wrapped her arms around my neck touching her forehead to mine. I smelled the beer on her breath.

"I do like you, Joe Simpson. You're different from most of they guys I meet."

I looked into her eyes and thought about my early life.

" I know what it's like to want something and to have things hold you back." I replied.

"I sensed that about you, Joe. Deep, dark secrets hidden away."

When she said that, I wanted to pull away but she held me firm. I laughed instead but it came out like a high-pitched whinny. "We've all got secrets," I said.

"I know and I'm going to excavate yours, Joe Simpson and that's a promise," she said. A sudden chill streaked up my spine.

Chapter Sixteen

And suddenly, I remembered in vivid detail a dream I'd had the night before. *I was driving a lone, dusty country road and the car suddenly stopped. Pulled itself over to the side of the road.*

As I watched the dust settle around the car, I felt great anticipation. I felt quite extraordinary, as if a powerful, external force had taken control of my hands and spun the steering wheel at a preconceived moment stopping the Chevy at an appointed place. I took a blanket from the trunk, spread it on the grass and settled on my back looking up at the iridescent sky through shuttered lids. So peaceful, slowly melting into the ground. Delicious.

The grass felt soft, the air warm and buzzing with insect life. I slid into a reverie, padded against the outside, now muffled and far away. In a series of abstract mind clicks, images flashed on a dark membranous screen. I saw Norma bobbing like a gutted fish on a secretive current, her blonde hair twisting slowly about the underbelly whiteness of her face. Doc Seaton made deft cuts with a gleaming scalpel. I heard the sterile ripping of flesh. Hal Bigelow stared at a darkening sky challenging the heavens to open up. Steff Randolph and his assistant Alistair laboriously covered a newly made corpse in gift wrapping. I saw Lizzy Boston bent over, planting tomatoes in neat rows. An expression of wide-eyed horror transformed her face. She stood up and screamed, as, out of nowhere, a garden hoe grew out of her back and slowly, Lizzy rose to full height on the tips of her sneakered toes, then like an ant hill crumbling, she fell face forward into the dark humus of her garden. Teddy Graff shook his thick head waggling a finger under my nose, rebuking me for something I hadn't done. Cindy Lou blew a massive bubble, that freed itself from her pouty lips. It floated upward then descended like a cannon ball shattering the earth. Through a pool of water came Wishbone Jones, riding a broomstick, dis-

mounted then tied it to the knob of a cupboard door where it awaited in readiness, quivering for his return.

I fluttered for what seemed a long time until a rustling sound somewhere out beyond caused me to stir. How long had I been out, I wondered? Not more than ten minutes but even as my eyes opened, I still felt adrift, the ground undulating softly beneath me.

Once more the rustling came and this time it was loud enough that I opened my eyes. I looked up. Wild hair haloed by the sun; features blunted by shadow. Beverly. I realized I didn't know her last name as she gazed down at me. She looked enormous as I glanced at her brown toes wriggling freely on the blanket. I wandered up limbs the length of Douglas Firs to a sharp chin jutting over a pair of billowing breasts, packaged loosely in a peasant blouse of startling white.

"Hi Joe," she said, her nutty brown face expanding into a rubbery grin.

"Beverly. What are you doing here?" She reached a hand down and pulled me up. I could feel her tensile strength. "Thanks."

She replied," I come here a lot. This is near Wish's place, you know."

"No. I didn't know."

We stood for a moment and again I felt both awkward and foolish. She smiled and held out her hand to me.

"Come on,"she said. "I want to show you something." Our hands clasped and I could feel a bolt of heat surging along my arm, through my torso and down to my toes.

I gulped, "Okay."

She tugged on my hand and I followed her toward the woods like a contented mongrel heeding its master. Top honours in obedience school.

Instantly, the world turned from bright to inky dark as soaring oak, fan-like maple and stout jack pines blotted the sun from view. Sudden, surprising shafts of light penetrated the foliage. The atmosphere grew eerily close and damp, as if suddenly we wandered aimlessly in an enchanted forest. A thunderous beating of paws on packed earth drummed through the tangled growth. I jumped about half a mile. Beverly followed a prehistoric trail tramped down over an eon or two. It was impossible to make out if you didn't know it was there. She seemed to follow it by some internal radar. A branch whipped into my face. I began to feel just a little bit humiliated.

"Sorry about that," she giggled.

I asked, "How much further?"

"Not far." And then she whistled a tune in a register that soared beyond the normal range of humans. I marveled that a person could whistle like that and still sound melodic. I recognized the tune, Greensleeves, but it was the weirdest version I'd ever heard and seemed to come at me from everywhere at once.

Beverly followed the etchings of the path easily, although she wore open-toed sandals, not once did she stumble or snag her loose skirt on any of the brambles. I wasn't as adept and tripped clumsily behind her, laboring badly. It was embarrassing. Raggedy gasps of air.

"Almost there," she called.

Up ahead stood an imposing wall of leafy green. Beverly simply disappeared into it. I stopped at its feathery edge reaching out tentatively to touch the same spot. Leaves trembled in her wake. I gathered myself up, closed my eyes, held my breath and burst through the verdurous blanket fully expecting to plunge into some noxious bog hole.

What I saw and felt startled me. The air looked clear and smelled fresh as if we'd scaled a mountain. The atmosphere remained so hushed that every footfall, every breath sounded unnaturally sharp. We'd landed in a clearing resplendent with daffodils, marigolds and daisies surrounding a shimmering pond.

"Isn't it beautiful?" Beverly exclaimed, her face lit up with joy and mischievousness. I was dumbfounded. All I could manage in response was a nod. After some moments, my voice rebounded from its rusty prison.

"What is this place?" I croaked.

"It's called the Wishing Well," she said. "If you make a wish here, the legend says it will come true."

"Really?" Normally, I didn't believe in legends or myths but the preternatural quality of the place could turn even a cynic into something else, into some mystic presence maybe.

She nodded emphatically. "Uh-huh."

Again I felt a sense of expectancy and it came through me like a hot flash; dry mouth, pounding in my ears, blood rushing from my face and a lack of will in my limbs. I noticed a blanket, towel, book and some fruit on the ground near the edge of the shimmering pool of water. Water that looked so inviting it could have been temptation itself. Water that bedazzled and beckoned a thirsty visitor who'd chanced upon this hidden oasis from a soulless desert. Light on the water danced and sparkled with such intensity that I became mesmerized by it. The twinkling *captivated me in a totally delightful way and my dry lips cracked into a grin. From somewhere her voice came.*

"Why don't you make a wish?" she said.

I nodded. "Okay."

"Close your eyes." I closed them.

Self-conscious feelings dropped away within a scant second. I stood there swaying like a blind ass for a moment not really thinking anything but waiting for something to come to me not knowing what it might be. Then I opened my eyes. Beverly stood with her back to me by the shore some fifteen yards off, her clothes in a crumpled heap by her feet. Her smooth skin was caramel coloured from top to bottom.

"Guess what?" she called back.

"What?"

"You just fished your wish."

And then with all the supple grace of a gymnast, she bent her knees spreading rounded buttocks slightly as a pair of sinewy thighs tensed, swung her arms upward and sailed in a perfect arc up and out slicing the water with only the slightest rip. She surfaced, swam a few powerful strokes to the middle of the pool and gestured while flinging slick hair out of her eyes.

And what I remember is a Morse code full of pulsing sensations. Pleasure vibrated up and down millions of times like little jolts of electricity starting at my toes and shooting farther and farther up my joints hitting every erogenous zone making me sigh and wince and best of all, smile as each genuine second ticked off in what I hoped from the depths of my soul, from the deepest region of my heart, would be an eon.

I grabbed at my clothes in haste to strip down, hopping on one foot, then the other. I tripped and ended up sprawled chin down in the grass. Beverly choked herself with laughter. She went down for a full count before re-surfacing spitting up water like a convulsed porpoise. With a triumphant tug, I yanked free the twisted debris of my trousers and cockily flicked off my briefs. Beverly applauded with whistles and whoops of appreciation.

In that supercharged moment, I summoned all the energy I had and flung myself far out into the sparkling depths. The water was colder than it looked, cold enough to take my breath away for an instant. My skin tingled as I swam out to her.

"Took you long enough," Beverly snorted. "I'm not the type of girl who treads water for just anyone, you know."

"I've come to realize that," I replied.

We pressed our palms together while kicking to keep upright. The water was clear enough that I could see the shimmering image of her body, her long legs and the dark triangle between her thighs. I was just as visible and as we kissed, she smiled. Her lips were cold with a bluish tinge and tasted sweet, of the water itself. We came together in a tighter embrace and her belly brushed my hard phallus.

"Ooohh. What's that?" she said archly. "I thought they shriveled in the cold."

"That shows how much you know."

Beverly kicked upward and swung on to her back away from me and not incidentally splashed water in my face. I chased her and it became a race. She crawled up onto a hidden sandbar, stretched out langourously on her back and watched me through slitted eyes. She didn't have to wait long. In an instant I was beside her and we both smiled at each other foolishly in the expectation of something more serious about to take place.

I ran my hands over her and under her and felt her limbs shudder, even as we embraced and her stiff nipples pressed my chest and our mouths cleaved to the other, fragments of the commonality of life continued to emerge.

In a heated rush Beverly pulled me on to her, lifting her hips reaching to my groin and suddenly before I could blink, I was inside her, feeling the shock of her heat and the motion of her pelvis and the tightening of her round buttocks as we mis-stepped at first but then gradually found a mutual rhythm. We were so very close and I watched her as her hazel eyes closed, then opened and fluttered, then closed again, her slender nostrils flared with each charge of breath, the friction of our bodies bringing out sweat and her smooth skin turning slick as we kept moving higher and higher still. I was above her watching her steadily as she seemed on the edge of great pain and held me off with her arms held straight, elbows locked. The more I lifted her with my hands, the more pained and fearful she became pressing her lips hard and finally then, her breath exploded in a mother birth cry and her limbs went rigid but she was smiling and her eyes shone as we closed the gap between us and I kissed her heaving breasts. We held each other for a long time rocking slowly from side to side and I became aware of the strength of the sun on my back and understood how tan lines could disappear without your knowing it. She held my face between her hands and looked directly into my eyes.

She said, "It was exactly how I thought it would be."

Which made me realize she had been thinking about this all along, that is something else people in different places have in common... thinking about other people and wondering about their chances together.

I said, "I'm glad."

And for such a simple thing, an expression of joy sprang on to her face and she covered me in kisses with renewed passion insisting we stay exactly as we were until I grew into her again.

Chapter Seventeen

In the midst of that spine-tingling, salubrious moment punctuated by the heady feeling of Bev's embrace— flashback to that previous vision— the cacophonic scream of machines filled the air and through the woods they came in a long column, crashing through briar and twigs and early summer hay. We broke apart startled by the noise of throbbing engines. Night blanketed the heavens in its fullest, deepest sense. The bikers, hair streaming back, eyes coated in coal black shades, careened and thundered in a circle around the fire, around us as we stood together, coughing out dust and thick smoke as each machine vied to out-roar the next. After completing its ring, each bike bounced off through the trees where the leader stopped in the clearing, scattering people, bottles and blankets from his path. Wishbone and Damo emerged from the house. They slapped hands with the leader of the motorcycle pack and Damo gave the other man a wraparound squeeze that lifted him off his feet—no easy feat since the biker looked as if he came in at about 250 lbs. with a sagging gut spilling over his jeans. The rest of the pack, including half a dozen women, gathered around the three in the manner of women through the ages standing on the periphery of men in power, hanging back until summoned.

Beverly shuddered against me. "I don't like those people."

"Who are they?"

"The Devil Riders. The big fat one is Bobby Ross—he's the leader. Sometimes, I just don't know what Wish sees in certain people," she said.

I wondered about that too, as Bobby Ross slung a meaty arm each around Wish and Damo and they marched off to the house with the gang laughing it up behind them. The men wore denim vests without shirts. The women were costumed in tight jeans, leather chaps and white T-shirts. All of them wore boots girded in jangling chains with gleaming metal toecaps. The raucous interruption by the bikers barely raised a stir among the others. The jugglers tossed their pins, the dog trainer played with his dog, the hand standers walked a fallen log stripped of its bark. Only the unicyclist had stopped and appeared to be asleep under a tree.

Beverly pulled me away from the rest and we strolled down a slope and came upon a large flat boulder. Beverly scrambled up and beckoned me to follow, which I did with some difficulty, my topsiders slipping on the cool smooth surface. Beverly had wisely removed her shoes, dropping them at the base. Sounds from the encampment reverberated off at a long distance.

Then Beverly began fishing down the front of her leotard, moving her fingers between her ample cleavage and yanked out what I thought was a hand-rolled cigarette, stuck it in her mouth after wetting it down with her tongue licking it elaborately, struck a match and lit it, then drew down deeply. After a long moment, she blew all the smoke out in a rush practically choking.

"Want some," she gasped.

I nodded and took a long drag. It went down well with the Black Label as a chaser. I took another drag holding the smoke in my lungs then blew it out and handed it back to her.

Bev smiled. "For a moment, I thought you were going to finish it but then you didn't. Guess that says something about you, Joe."

"Like what?"

Beverly took the reefer and drew on it, then handed it back to me. "You're considerate."

I took a drag. Then another. My lungs went into meltdown. But the sensation. Tingling and nauseating both. Whew. Beverly fished out two more joints from that lovely spot and we smoked them both.

Some moments later, I found myself floating on my back gazing up at the star-lit sky barely aware of the cold rock seeping into my bones. It was somebody else's body. Someone, perhaps who lived in Moose Jaw or Cincinnati.

"Isn't it beautiful, Joe?"

"Isn't what beautiful?"

"The sky?"

"What sky?"

Beverly giggled. "Joe," she said in a tone that said, get serious, will ya? "Joe?"

"Yeah."

"Have you ever made love this way?"

"Lying on a rock?"

"No. I mean, this way. You know, high."

I thought about it. "No."

" Do you want to? "

"Sure," I replied, not certain how I was going to get my body to move exactly, as it seemed my limbs had become disengaged, responsive only to distant commands. Beverly slid her hands under my shirt. "Your hands are cold."

"I know. You're supposed to warm them up."

"Ah." As it turned out I didn't have to, Beverly crawled on top of me with her full weight, which wasn't inconsiderable. She kissed me but it felt like she touched someone else's lips and then I thought, whose? They were mine but not mine, exactly. I felt her breath, it blew warm on my cheek and the pressing of her pelvis became rhythmic. Yes, things began to stir. Suddenly, she seemed in a hurry and began pulling at me, pushing my arms above my head, lifting my hips, tugging at my ankles and cool air drifted over me but it was quite pleasant. Beverly then slid away and I listened to the rustling of her clothes and the music of her nimble fingers on buttons, snaps and zippers. For some reason, I don't know why and probably never will, I decided I could move, that I'd regained control of my limbs and it seemed such an exhilarating discovery that I surged up, feeling a rush of power. Maybe I wanted to get away? At least for a second. Then came the numbness. There was a crashing in my ears.

"Joe? Joe? Are you there? Where are you?"

"UUnnnhhh…"

"Joe? Are you all right?"

"Uuunnnhh…yeah…no…I…uh, sort of…flew…but very badly…"

Beverly scrabbled down the rock face descending to where I lay sprawled at the base. I saw stars now, the entire galaxy, in fact. I didn't feel pain exactly, just a pounding, throbbing sensation slowly spreading outward like a fan. Beverly's hands were on me, probing for gaping wounds.

"Is anything broken? Can you stand up?"

"I don't know. And yeah, I think so." For some reason, I giggled.

"Let me help you." She reached down under my arms and scooped me up, the way a fireman might during a rescue. Beverly then backed me up to the side of the boulder for support, pressing me with her ample bosom. It dawned on me then she was entirely, deliciously naked. She reached down.

"What's this?" she asked. I didn't answer because I felt a twinge of embarrassment. "Well, it's nice to know that some things still work in a pinch."

"Where there's a will," I replied weakly. "I'm sorry. I don't know what got into me."

"That's okay, Joe. As long as you're not hurt. Can you stand by yourself for a minute?"

"If I have to."

"I'm going to get our clothes." I felt like a jointless skeleton. Beverly moved away and I saw a flash of white skin, the bottoms of her feet, actually, then just as quickly she came down again.

"Here," she said. "Let me get these on you. You know, you're a real nut, Joe Simpson."

Beverly's strong hands did all the work for me but I still had to lift each leg not once but twice, hold out my arms and I think I even wriggled my toes. Anyhow, there was this ticklish feeling of shoes sliding on to my feet. The air hummed and bristled with life, everything had become animated, even the crickets' cries had an able-bodied fullness. Beverly shimmied into her clothes in a flash. I watched her with a mixture of pleasure and profound regret.

A single, soaring note plucked from an electric guitar took wing, cutting the still air with the intensity of molten steel liquefying butter.

I said, "Wow. What's that?" And it seemed almost terrifying, lingering for an eon. Beverly jumped up and down clapping her hands. "It's the band! They're ready. Come on." And without further thought or care for my precarious condition, Beverly grabbed my hand and yanked me off uphill into the darkness.

What happened after is a blur revolving around a community of sights, sounds, sensations, and feelings massaged through the pores of my skin. I recall a jumble of detail in no particular order of significance or meaning. Here's what I do recall: Beverly half-dragging, half-carrying me through the woods. Me tripping over buried logs, hidden stumps, treacherous rocks leaping into my path. But we made it just as the band surged into its first number. Four skinny, formless guys in jeans and T-shirts and a girl with the longest blonde hair I've ever seen rattling a tambourine off her slim hips and singing with the grace and power of a hepped up gospel choir. They really turned it on. To this day, I cannot remember a single song they played but recall the feeling of being picked up and carried on an electronic wave into a weirdly peaceful musical heaven.

When Beverly and I finally arrived, the clearing was jammed with twitching, jerking, jumping bodies moving in ways that evolution never prepared homo sapiens for over the millennia of time. But no matter—you waded into the core of movement and simply became the movement itself. We became pure beauty in stark and utter simplicity. In fact, that may have been the most purely happy moment of my entire life where mind and body seamlessly separated. A body full of the exquisite pleasure of vigorous natural dance while the mind eased into complete peace—no conflicting thoughts or worries or menial choices to bother about. All of the pleasure points had been pressed. Doubts, concerns and anxieties evaporated, instantly nullified.

As things came my way, I grabbed them. Bottles of beer appeared in my hand, glasses of wine, a hamburger too, firefly ends of reefers landed in my direction where I inhaled the fragrance until I thought I would breathe no more. And all the time, wavering before me was Beverly's soulful, thoughtful face, the glossed hair, her caramel skin and the tint of holy light on her glasses. Yet dark thoughts intruded. I thought I saw my mother holding a steak knife, poised to strike; the old man moved through the yard away from the house, his fists swollen and bloodied after a delivering a beating. I tried to blow all of that away.

Between each singular musical undulation, we talked.

From out there somewhere, Damo said, "You're looking a little tense, Joe Blow."

"Yeah."

"You're feeling the sky, reaching to the heavens?"

"Trying to."

He leaned his bestriped head in and whispered conspiratorially, "Let me tell you, that little girlie can take you there. Count on it."

Damo and I sat on a downed log, the bark had been stripped off by predators and the weather, our legs sprawled in the dirt. Damo passed a reefer between himself and another man. The other guy had a wiry build and very fine hair, the colour of flax. He too, wore no shirt and his body bunched, sinew taut with motion, muscles jerking up his chest and arms, head bobbing, legs jumping to the music. He told me his name— Neal and he lived for speed. Whatever he did, he did fast. Neal was the same age as Damo and wore a toothbrush around his neck attached by a leather thong. It struck me, that the toothbrush could be a religious icon; it dangled and danced, thumping off the surface of his smooth chest.

Again I said, "Yeah." But I returned to my senses as the effects of the drug receded. Neal spoke in a rhythmic scat, be-bop kind of pitter-patter.

"Joe Blow. Joe Blow. Gotta get up and go. Pick your ass up and head to Kokomo. Whaddya say, Joe Blow? The rest is fine. The cat's got chimes. All he's losing is god's own time. Joe Blow."

Damo said, "Neal's a poet. He's exploring spontaneous syncopated rhythms in natural speech. Which when you really sit down and think about it, is all nonsense, you know?"

"Sure."

Neal sang, "Nonsense is nonsense is goodsense gone poor. What's the sense of good sense when you got none? All that's left of good sense is sense without the no. And you gotta know sense to have any good sense at all."

I said, "Neal?"

"Joe Blow?"

"I said, Neal?"

"Joe Blow?"

"You ever write this stuff down?"

Damo said, "Neal's a sound poet, Joe. Sound poetry is sounded and shouldn't be grounded. It belongs to Nature, to the trees and the sky. We remember good sound poetry forever."

"But no one will learn it. No one will benefit if it isn't written down."

"They'll benefit from Nature. They'll listen to Nature," said Damo.

"Is that what you do? Elevate Nature?"

"It elevates us."

Neal, obviously listening, sang, "Elevate. Relegate. Be the earth's delegate. Walking to the sun, handing me the gun, cosmic sky don't be shy, the heavens'll have to wait. You dig it, Joe Blow?"

I nodded. "Maybe." Neal laughed and slapped my knee.

"That's a start. Take my part, sound sense of Nature's art," he said and flung his arms open wide embracing the air and smells and music around him. Neal leapt to his feet and commenced a jitterbugging, spastic-elastic head wagging, limb churning, whirligig-like version of a demon dance, his face, body and even, persona blurring before my eyes.

"What's your thing, Damo?"

His thick linebacker's neck corded up as he showed me his immaculate teeth.

"Getting high. Making love. Looking at and living life as if it was Art. Kicking the legs out from anyone who stands in my way. Having fun. Communicating with people who think and act the same way."

"Who are you for?"

"I am for outlaws, lovers, dancers, artists, musicians—anybody with an open mind who lives their life as if each breath could be their last, who appreciates the good earth and all we've been given at no charge."

"Who are you against?"

"Cops. The government—anyone or anything that represents a repressive, small-minded institution."

"Where'd you come by those tattoos?"

He held up his left forearm. "This one I had done while I was in the navy in '56." He held up the right forearm. "I had it matched while visiting a nice, tranquil place called Attica. The rest I had done after they declared me a cuckoo son of a bitch and sent me off to the Meadowlark Mental Health Hospital in upstate New York where I became the subject of some interesting experiments. They let me go finally because the program collapsed and they realized I had a few of my marbles left, see?"

"What kind of experiments?"

"CIA, FBI-induced stuff, techniques for brain-washing, getting enemies of the state to admit to heinous crimes through the use of what I call mind-altering substances. But they didn't understand what they had, see Joe Blow? They'd created a missile and didn't even know it. The missile of good born out of evil. And I took that away with me and because of my own superior psychological know-how, I conquered. They lost."

Although my fuzzy brain struggled with this, trying to make sense of what he was saying, separating the truth from exaggeration, I wanted to ask more questions. But then Beverly appeared and pulled me away and I remember Damo's face, disembodied and magical, looming in the darkness like a nightmare.

The rest of the night melded into a blend of sensation, of movement, of heat, sweat, fatigue and finally, love. At least I think so.

Chapter Eighteen

I awoke at some distant point in time in some faraway place. The mind is a subtle and powerful instrument, I thought. My sensory apparatus sniffed the wind for a few dissoluble seconds and indicated, that, yes, night had passed into cool, grey day. Last night I'd experienced something vivid enough to be real yet set at such a shimmering distance that it could have been a raspberry technicolor dream. On the purely physical side of things, the inside of my mouth felt like the welcome mat outside the local Holiday Inn. Some bastard had wrapped my head in cellophane while I slept. I distinctly heard a peculiar crackling sound in my ears when I tilted either way.

I lay in my very own bed and could not begin to recall how I ended up here. The sheets felt dank and were terribly rumpled. I'd been restless. And then, finally, further sensory clues wafted in as I drew some deep breaths. Filling tender lungs with air. I sniffed an earthy aroma, honey and pine and the meaty smell of fertile loam mingled together. I listened. All appeared to be still. I glanced at my watch—5:43 am.

"Beverly?"

No answer. Yet I knew she'd been here. No indication I hadn't been alone. I had to wonder if it had all been a dream. Or at least one where I could remember most of the details. I crept to the window and gazed out. My car sat parked placidly in front, speckled with glutinous tears of dew. As I turned away from the window to ready myself for the day, what brought me sharply to my senses was the sudden, bellicose scream of a motorcycle racing up Nottawasaga road, some two miles distant.

I dragged myself into the shower and turned it on full blast cold. Then, I got dressed and drank three cups of coffee. After which, I sat staring at the pages on the wall and decided to add some more. I stuck up a new page headlined Damo and the Jersey Jokers and wrote down what I could remember of the night before and our conversation. They came out of nowhere and suddenly, strange things happened in town. Could be a coincidence—maybe. I put Beverly and Wish on that page too, just to complete the picture. Part of the same circle. The next page headlined The Viking and I put Bobby Ross's name along side. Bikers caused trouble and trouble found them and this community had its share of trouble suddenly. I stared at the wall, read the names I'd written and tried to stop the tingling in the back of my neck. I drew more arrows between the names that seemed to go together. The Viking and Bobby Ross. Damo and Wishbone. I stared at this primitive collage until my head started to throb again.

One hour later and I hadn't perforated the pocket of feeling that gathered closed pulling on some invisible drawstring around me. Friday. It had been a tumultuous week and there was the rest of today to get through yet. More had happened this week, it seemed, than in the previous three years I'd spent in Applewood. My perception of the town had shifted radically. It veered to the right and down. Deep down.

I let the car steer itself into town, riding the blood highway. When the road had been cut into the hills some years back, the crew mixed some local red clay into the concrete. The result revealed a diluted, blood-like colour with darker flecks of red laid down in patches. Locals said that careless drivers spent too much time looking at the road and not paying attention to their driving. Accidents piled up. Cynics named the road because it seemed that, at least once a week, some clean-up team swabbed it down after a car wreck late at night. Kids usually. Liquored up and out for a wild time.

Before heading out the door, I downed two more cups of scalding black coffee and managed to scrape some of the scum from inside my brain. My tongue still felt thick and coated with road tar. My temples throbbed to the distant echo of rock music, some band called Led Zeppelin. Music that carried through the night. It wound itself around your head like wet rawhide left to dry in the desert sun come morning. That's why I didn't notice or particularly pay attention to them.

Two statues on black Harleys coming up fast in the rearview mirror. White skin, arm tattoos and leather. So fast, they'd end up in my back seat any second. One of them tried being cute. He reached out and touched my rear bumper, patted it actually. Then scowled at me. The other one slid up and because he had nothing better to do, tried twisting off the side view mirror. I edged the car over the line. He didn't like that. The other one nudged the bumper. To show him how brave I was, I stepped on the brake and he dropped back fast. Number two veered over again to play some more patty cake. I swerved, squealing the tires to move him off. We continued to play this instructive little game three or four more times. Then, almost on cue, they dropped away, kicked the bikes into high gear and roared down the highway ahead of me, quickly disappearing around a bend. I didn't have to keep my curiosity in check very long.

Just beyond the curve, the road flared. And there, like a metallic wall glinting in the early morning sun stretched a line of motorcycles. They were fully occupied. I had a couple of seconds to react. The centre of gravity swung out hard as I felt the screaming momentum come from the rear. The back end of the Chevy lifted and shot out and away, sliding like an eel. I spun the wheel and pulled on the handbrake. The right side tires caught with a jolt. The car wobbled a bit, then, swung back the other way and wrenched to a stop. The hood lay not more than five feet from the lead biker, the one with the sagging gut I'd seen the night before. The set up formed a delicate Vee with Bobby Ross at the fulcrum.

He bared his teeth to show me how nasty he was. Biker's primp. I didn't think bikers got out and about this early. They seemed conscious.

"I hear you been talking to the Viking," Bobby Ross snarled.

Nothing in that for me, so I remained clammed. Maybe he thought I should be quivering and blubbing by now. I could see about three days growth on his cheeks and he lowered his shaggy head to peak over the mirrored aviator glasses. That made him look tougher, I guess.

"You're gonna give him a message for me," he said, making with his finger like an "Uncle Sam Wants You" recruiting poster.

"The hell I am," I snapped back. I just wasn't in the mood for it.

Bobby Ross sat back on his bike looking perplexed. Then he let out a bark of laughter. It reverberated around the group until they yelped like a pack of hyenas. Then he said," You will if you wanna live." And laughed some more.

"Then you'll have to take him the message yourself. Or send one of your soldier boys if they're man enough," I said.

Bobby Ross shook his head in mock disbelief, then spoke to the rider on his left. "This guy wants us to put the drag on 'im." His compadre worked his thin lips into something like a smile and rubbed his gloved hands together. Bobby glanced back at me as if I'd just happened by.

"Tell you what. Since you're a friend of Wishbone's and I ain't go not partic-ular beef with you, for now, I'll just give you the message anyway. How's that?"

"Sounds swell. I'll do you a favour if you do me one."

"What?"

'You heard me."

"Jesus. I'm about two seconds away from running over your face."

I said, "So was the Viking."

All things being equal, Bobby Ross nodded.

" This here's the message, newsboy. You tell him from me to stay clear of the Meadows. You got that? And if he don't, there's gonna be fireworks like he's never seen."

Marlon Brando did it better but who else would this guy use as a role model? " Fair enough. Tell me about Norma Jennings. Who was she hanging out with, beside the Viking from time to time?" At that Ross shook himself all over like a dog jumping with fleas. He pulled his chin in, opened his rubber lips and blew out. I could see one of his front teeth had cracked off. It gave his jaw a cockeyed line.

"You don't wanna know too much, do you?" he groused.

"I want to know that."

"Knowing that can get you dead," he replied, then kicked the engine of his bike alive, revving it full throttle. The others kicked theirs into action too. The line of motors growled like hungry animals. They wheeled out of formation turning themselves awkwardly around. As he circled, Bobby Ross gave me one more glass-eyed, drop-dead stare. And for good measure, one of his pleasure seekers heaved a rock at my windshield, striking the passenger side. The glass flowered with cracks but didn't shatter. The whine of disappearing engines hung in the air like an insult. I felt clear-headed now. That shook me awake plenty.

Nadine had been at her desk since eight, as was her habit. She popped her head up as I swung in and smiled through the ever-present cloud of cigarette smoke.

"Not even nine o'clock in the morning and already the most popular guy in town. Here," she said and held out her bony hand, "already, I got a personal note, a card of some kind and three phone messages for you."

"Thanks Nadine," I said, rather grimly. She looked at me curiously.

"Don't mention it. What else am I here for? I'm just a receptacle where the refuse of everyone's life is deposited," she replied, still giving me the eyeball.

"Why, that's very profound," I answered, not looking at her.

"I know. That's why I said it," and then she dropped her head back to continue her work as each sworl of smoke haloed her frizzled hair.

I parked myself weakly at my desk and let the squeaky chair spin me around for a while. I glanced at the messages. One from Doc Seaton saying he got the okay for me to visit Ellis Boston up in Brigsby. The second call came from Barrett Thompkins thanking me for keeping him company at dinner and the last informed me that Hal Bigelow would be pounding at my door no later than 6 am. tomorrow so we could take advantage of the best fishing up at Coca Cola falls. Good god. I hoped it would be a pleasant day. The thought of slimy worms and smelly fish first thing in the morning made my stomach leap like Nijinsky. Not to mention, what an unholy hour to be up and about on a Saturday. I reached for the coffee I'd brought with me and took a long, noisy slurp. But I needed to talk to Hal, lay out all of these thoughts percolating in my head. Hal wouldn't laugh at me out of his sleeve. He'd listen. Somewhere in that gargantuan skull lay a capable brain.

I passed Paisley's work area and inhaled a whiff of lavender. That reminded me that I planned to gate crash the dinner party and a flutter went through me. After last night, I didn't know if I had the steel for it, barging in uninvited on a prominent figure in the community. I told myself it was a good opportunity, in the best interests of the town to learn about the new development plans in town straight from the horse's mouth and I was just doing my job. They'd understand. Uh-huh. The O'Tooles lived on what might be called the closest thing to an estate—five rolling acres and an imposing castle-like edifice over-looking Rattlesnake Bay. In fact, the O'Tooles owned a strip of private beach adjoining their property that ran adjacent to the spot where Norma Jennings had washed up in what seemed an eon ago. I flinched. The tangled blond hair. Swollen features. Half a translucent clamshell trapped in a bone-white hand. Newsreel images I couldn't wipe away. I felt I owed it to Norma to get at the truth and maybe I could put the curse of my old man behind me by cracking this story wide open. The tingling in my neck continued to plague me, telling me I hadn't dug the facts of the story out yet. Jack Simpson sneered from the grave.

And then I thought of Beverly and I looked at her note, whose handwriting was bold and crisp. She had written; Joe, I had a wonderful time last night. Thanks for letting me drive your car. It was a fun night for me, especially when you tried to fly off the boulder. Love, Bev.

The last message formed a mystery. When I ripped open the small, square envelope, the contents consisted of a single piece of crumpled paper. A message had been spelled out or rather, cut out using the pages of the Gazette. I recognized the type. Crooked, of course. Here's what it said: The Meadows. Sunday. Midnight. And that was it. Now what was that all about? I examined the envelope. Nothing revealing, just my name written in simple, block letters. The printing of a child. Who could have sent it and what did it mean?

Teddy Graff kicked me out of my revery, almost literally. He came banging and clattering into the office, the week old stogy jammed into his lips barely disguising a huge grin. His small eyes, usually marred by anger or frustration, sparked with light and mirth. He clapped me on the back heartily.

"Great write-up, Joe. That inquest piece was beautiful. First-rate stuff. Come into my office and let's talk. Bring your coffee."

I flowed along on Teddy's uncharacteristic exuberance and good cheer, the bounce in his walk enlivening the stocky frame. Teddy actually held the door for me, indicated a chair politely, then kicked the door closed with his back heel as he turned, mimicking a move I'd seen Elvis Presley do in Viva Las Vegas, then jounced over to his desk. After sweeping aside a shambling tower of papers to create a small clearing, he sat propping his chin in his hands and grinned like a leprechaun who'd just gotten lucky. All the same, I lit a Sweet Cap. My fingers shook a little. I didn't think he noticed.

"So, what'd you think of that fat ass, Thompkins?" he asked.

Thus, the reason for the smiles, the perkiness and the unusual elevation in spirits. Teddy thought I must have given Thompkins the bum's rush without a moment's hesitation.

"Well, uh, I…" And for some reason, I held back from telling Teddy about the hijack on blood highway. Biker doings. Instinct just whispered that now was not the right time. Plus, I didn't want to get Teddy personally involved or expose the paper to something that might turn ugly and violent.

"Just a minute, Joe," he said, voice rising and leaping to his feet, poked his head out the door and yelled, "Stumpy! Get in here. I want to talk to you."

No sooner had he called than a despondent Stumpy Butler shuffled out from the back with Dusty Rhodes trotting on his heels. I could see Stumpy sigh and then pluck himself up to receive the verbal drubbing he anticipated as coming his way. As it did virtually every morning the past two weeks since the typesetter had mysteriously disintegrated. We'd been informed by the manufacturer that repair was now out of the question and a replacement wouldn't be shipped for a further three weeks meaning Stumpy would be shelled by Teddy daily until it arrived. Dusty wore his normal cocky grin. I spotted a grease smudge on his left cheek. He sported a cigarette behind each ear.

"Yes Teddy...?" said Stumpy in his own shaky way but showed no more surprise than I when Teddy grasped his hand firmly pumping it up and down like a runaway piston. Dusty's mouth dropped so far he lost his gum. It bounced off his sneakered toe and rolled under Teddy's desk.

"A capital job, Stumpy. Absolutely capital. The edition looks terrific. I want you to know I appreciate all the effort you've put in, Stumpy. And I've got a surprise for you." He whipped an envelope out of his top pocket. "Movie passes for the Centaur theatre. Take the missus and enjoy yourself. You like war pictures? Well, The Longest Day is playing next week and I hear it's a doozer. Enjoy."

Stumpy stared at the envelope in his hand almost fearfully, as if it might blow up. "Golly Teddy. Thanks. I love war pictures. Sergeant York is my favourite. Then there's Four Feathers and Hell is for Heros." Stumpy held out three fingers. As this exchange unfolded somewhere in front of me, I couldn't help thinking about Cindy Lou Fortunato. One of three. The only one of three left.

"Good. And I haven't forgotten you, Dusty. Those were great pics you took of Ellis Boston and Chief McKie. Award-winning stuff, if I'm not mistaken. So, I've got a pair of tickets for you too. Take your favourite girl. I'm sure you've got two or three to choose from."

Dusty was rarely at a loss for words but like Tommy, could only stammer out in monosyllabic tones.

"Thanks, Mr. Graff." Dusty shot me a look that said, what's got into him? I shrugged, as much at a loss as anyone.

"Well, boys. That's all I wanted to say. Just enjoy the show," Teddy said and ushered them out as quickly as he brought them in, slamming the door on their astonished backs. I could see Stumpy and Dusty clutching their envelopes and talking excitedly to each other. Not many could communicate effectively with Stumpy but Dusty appeared to have cracked the code.

I said, "That was nice of you Teddy."

Teddy beamed. "Ah well. The Centaur's an advertiser so I got them for free. Besides, I've been awfully hard on Stumpy, lately. He deserves a break. And we both know that Dusty's a great shooter. So," he said settling himself behind his desk once again, "we were talking about Barrett Thompkins."

"Right," and I said no more, as Teddy waited for me to elaborate.

Finally, Teddy said, "So, you told him to go to hell, right?"

I cleared my throat. "Well, no actually, I didn't." Teddy half-rose, his face resuming its natural purplish hue. I put up the stop sign. "Now hold on, Teddy, just a second. Thompkins said he talked to you about the offer and you said it was okay as long as it didn't interfere with anything here."

"Well, of course I said that, Joe. I wouldn't give that banana brain the satisfaction of me answering for you, now, would I? Does this mean you accepted? I get it, stabbed in the back by an ingrate..."

"Now hold it, Teddy. And spare me the soap opera, will ya? I owe my soul to you, okay? But there's another angle to this thing that you don't know anything about."

Teddy stopped bringing his bushy brows together narrowing his already pin-sized peepers. He thought I was pulling a fast one. "What angle?"

"I've got to admit, the offer is tempting, you know, especially the extra dough," I said and held up my hand again for silence as Teddy was about to slide into his fuming, blustering routine where he lay on his back and spouted steam like a whale through a hole in the top of his head. "It's not every day a reporter on a hick paper, even a good one like The Gazette, gets national coverage on the largest daily in Canada. Thompkins makes this big deal about being interested in Phillip Rothwell and RSC Developments, but I'm not buying it. I've been told they were connected somehow. Maybe that's how RSC has avoided any embarrassing press, if there's any to be found, because they've got Thompkins in their pocket? So I think Thompkins wants to use me to alert him to anything going on that might hurt RSC. Now you get it?"

"Who told you this?" Teddy demanded.

"A well-connected source."

"Okay. Okay. Protect your source, that's fine. I'm not going to beat that one to the ground. So, let's see. You're going to tell Thompkins you'll take it and feed him information, Joe? Is that what you're planning?"

"No Teddy. I thought about that. I'm going to just turn him down flat. If Thompkins wants info, let him get it on his own or read it in The Gazette. I'm not going to play that kind of game."

"It might hurt your career, Joe. Thompkins has got a lot of influence. He knows powerful people."

"I know. I'll just tell him I don't think I'm ready yet. I'll make it play, you'll see. Besides Teddy, no one lasts forever at the top of the heap. One day, Thompkins will be history and if there's an opening then, maybe I can take advantage of it. Right now, I'm going to do a good job right here. The opportunities will come. Besides, there's lots of regional writing awards I haven't won yet. And when I do, I'll be knocking on your door for a bigger, fatter raise. So be prepared." The tingling in the back of my neck already told me we had a doozey of a story right here in Applewood. Just Thompkins' presence in town confirmed that much.

Teddy clasped his gnarled hands behind his head and chewed on the cigar.

"Okay Joe. I'm glad you feel that way but you may not have to worry about waiting for that break. Canadian Press has picked up the inquest piece and they're running it coast-to-coast. How do you like that?" and he stuck out his hand and shook mine enthusiastically while I sat there. "And another thing. I won't be around forever, either, you know. And when I shuffle off or retire, I don't mind telling you, you'd be top of the list for this job."

"Well thanks, Teddy, I really appreciate that. Now that we've formed this mutual admiration society, I don't mind telling you that I don't think I can wait thirty years for that to happen. But I like it here and that's a fact. I'm not going anywhere for now."

"Good."

I told Teddy I was going up to Brigsby to visit Ellis Boston and do a follow-up to Lizzie's murder. Teddy thought that was a capital idea. And when he said that, he meant it. Teddy wasn't deceitful; bullying, badgering and irritating yes, but deceitful? No. I told him I'd be back around mid-afternoon. Just before I left I turned to him and said, "Oh yeah. Don't look for me tomorrow. I'm going fishing with Hal Bigelow."

"Fishing? You hate fishing."

"I know." And closed the door behind me.

Chapter Nineteen

The coroner's jury readied to march in with its recommendations in a few hours time. Teddy assured me that he and Dusty would cover for me if they broke before I returned from Brigsby. Having a small reporting staff limited the amount of ground you could cover and I appreciated Teddy letting me go off on my own course for an afternoon.

The clouds and humidity of the day before had instantly dried up as if god had lowered a vast nozzle from the sky and turned it on maximum, vacuuming the wet into the heavens. The air swirled dry as a bone with that brittle kind of light that flattered no one. The kind of day where all is revealed.

I drove by the record store to see if I could catch a glimpse of Bev before heading out of town but it remained closed, not due to open for an hour even though a couple of scraggly-looking kids hung around the door. Inside looked dark and gloomy. I wondered if Wish would even make it if the party carried on as late as I thought or if he felt as exhausted as I did.

I continued on my way. A lone civic employee in white coveralls forlornly rode a small street cleaner. I inhaled a whiff of detergent as he dispensed its cleansing suds to the needy streets. The acrid odour brought me back to an incident from the night before. I'd stumbled into Wish's house looking for Beverly. No one in the front room but I heard voices coming from the back. I saw Wish, Damo, Neal and that beefcake on wheels, Bobby Ross, huddled around a table. They stirred as I walked in but Wish stayed cool and sauntered over grinning, asking me what was up. Although I don't recall the exact substance of our conversation, I do recall a strong and bitter chemical smell pervading the room. I remember asking about it. Wish just shucked, saying that somebody had knocked over a bucket of industrial detergent they used for cleaning things—everything from clothes to washing the floors. He bought it by the drum, he said. Not thinking anything more of it, I staggered back out and subsequently found Beverly who searched for me outside. Later that night, I remember Bev and Wish speaking heatedly. Wish grabbed her arm but she pulled away, said something stinging and left him standing there on his own. I'd forgotten all about it until I'd driven by the street cleaner in his crisp uniform intent on keeping the modest streets of our fair town absolutely pristine. It made me wonder if Wish was a little bit jealous of me being with Bev, after all. Nothing like a triangle to stoke the fires of anger.

I drove by the silent facade of the Two-Tone Hotel and the veiled elegance of The Round Table. Instinctively, I looked up at Mickey and Delaney's apartment above searching for signs of life. While pre-occupied, I almost ploughed into a burbling, angry crowd gathered at the intersection of Geraint and Sycamore, the last intersection leading out of town. I stopped the car and observed from across the street.

My good friend, Evan Beatty, led the zealous throng of what I can describe only as country folk, people out of another time and place, his face dark with fervour. Several members carried signs with inscriptions. One read; God is Mortified without Man's Appeasement. Let's Stop Our Wicked, Wicked Ways. Live the Divine Life Now—Halt Decadence and Filth in Our Midst.

I had no inkling as to what the slogans meant or condemned beyond the usual vagueness of sin and sinning. And that had been going on forever. But as the pack broke ranks for a moment, I glimpsed the inner circle and several of their number, Holy Rollers by the look of them, had lapsed into an epileptic-like state, no control of their limbs, jerking spasmodically, foaming at the mouth. The others called out words of encouragement. Rah-rahing the zealots. Evan himself, roared and spewed his bitter invective with all the demonic tenacity of an Ahab seeking the white whale. He spoke in tongues. Spittle flew from his blood-red lips and I saw the whites of his demonic eyes roll up in their pious sockets. The fringes of the crowd grew larger and denser and moved and swayed and moaned in an elongated sigh. Their haunting cries carried upward above the sound of the wind. It sounded like the town itself, crying out in pain. As I slowly started up again, however, I thought I saw a familiar figure near the back of the crowd, showing immaculate white teeth at the amusingly garish sight, broad-shouldered, thick-armed but wearing a hat to cloak an all too obvious distinguishing feature. Damo. In the flesh. Lurking. Mocking the proceedings I imagined.

Instead of turning right at the Tecumseh side road for Highway 26, I spun the wheel left submitting to the pull of intuition. I headed toward a trailer park and an address on Oak Lane. The road turned inland away from the reassuring breeze of the Bay. The air was settled and drier. I inhaled the smell of dust and heat. The rolling hills pressing up to the water flattened out on this side of town and the spaces between the trees opened up. A door left ajar to poverty and despair. As I passed the pumping station, I heard the pistons grinding. A lonely, sad sound.

A rusted pick-up sat outside with the tailgate flat. No motorcycle boots. So much paint had peeled off the surface of the trailer, leaving the metal slats underneath to begin the race to decay. When I banged on the screen door, it rattled so hard I thought it was going to fall off the hinges at my feet. There came the rustle of movement, a quiet murmur and quick, angry steps to the entrance. She pulled the door sharply open. Her hair sprouted curlers. She wore seamless jeans, a blue cotton blouse cut off at the arms and partially unbuttoned. Baby puke decorated the front.

"Oh, it's you," she said. "Newshound. Still driving that stupid car, I see."

"Is the Viking home?" I'd tried to interview the Viking the year before when he'd been brought up on assault and battery charges. In typical fashion, he slammed the door in my face, just after I'd stepped out of the way, fortunately. The hearing for that incident was still pending. Miraculously, each of the witnesses had recanted their testimony.

She pulled a cigarette from behind her back. "No he isn't, the son of a bitch."

"Can I talk to you for a minute?"

Cindy Lou took a drag off her cigarette, shifted her weight from one foot to the other, looked quickly back over her shoulder, then, having made a decision said,

"You'd better come in. I'm feeding the kid." I followed her back. Her jeans were tight bunching up the flesh at her waist. She strode purposefully on long, cheerleader-honed legs. A straw bassinet perched full length on the horsehair sofa. Gurgling sounds came from it. She plopped herself down after scattering some tabloids with lurid headlines. None from the Gazette, I noticed. She waved an arm at me.

"Have a seat. Hope you don't mind."

She picked the child up, unbuttoned her blouse, lifted out a round, swollen breast and fastened the child's lips onto a thick brown nipple. She glanced up at me, blew her thick bangs out of her eyes and said, "Some men find this sexy." Flashed me the pouty smile, as the baby's tiny jaws worked steadily away like a pump draining water from the bilge.

"You look like the Madonna," I said, as cradling the child's black-fringed head with her right hand, she took a long drag with her left. She let out a squeal.

"Ouch. That smarts, you little, sucker," she said.

"I've got a message for the Viking from Bobby Ross."

She looked up sharply in surprise. "Oh yeah? What does that fat slob want? And since when are you gophering for bikers, anyway?"

"What's the Meadows?" I asked, blowing by her repartee.

She shrugged. "It's just a place where bikers hang out, to party, you know. It's to the north of the Bay and a mile west of 26 along a gravel road. Who wants to know?"

I thought about that a bit. "Seems hardly worth the trouble, then."

"What does?"

"Warning him off the place. Ross said there'd be real fireworks if the Viking showed up there. Sounds a little more serious than a turf war over a picnic spot."

Cindy Lou focused her brown eyes inward, mashed her cigarette into an ashtray and turned her attention to the kid. "I'm sure I wouldn't know," she said with all the sincerity of a quack medium raising your mother from the dead.

"You know she was pregnant," I said.

Her head jerked up. "Who?"

"Norma. Seven or eight weeks when she went in the drink."

Cindy Lou bit her lower, pouting lip. "I didn't know that," she said slowly, her voice tightening up.

I said, "You should read the paper more often. You know the father?"

She shook her head. "Haven't a clue," she replied.

Well, I thought, here goes. "Suppose I say, I think you do know. Suppose I say you know the guy. What do you think of that?" I fished for a reaction and got it.

Cindy Lou swallowed hard, then her upper lip drew back from her teeth in a snarl. "Then I'd say you were a lying bastard. And I'd say get the hell out of my house. I should never have let you in here. I'm saying it now. Get the hell out of my house." The baby started to wail as she'd pulled the nipple out of its groping mouth. She bent over it. "Oh baby, I'm so sorry. I'm so sorry." Then she placed it on her shoulder, cradling its head against her cheek and rocked back and forth. "It's okay little baby. Mama's here. Mama's here." Then her eyes, dark and flashing, flicked out at me.

"I thought I told you to scram."

"Listen, Cindy Lou, I'm just trying to find out what happened here, okay? I didn't know Norma really but I liked Darlene a lot. What can you tell me? This isn't for the paper, okay, it's personal."

"Will you get the hell outta here if I tell you what I know?"

"Yes."

"This is it, okay." She gave me a piercing look. I nodded. "The guy Norma was seeing was older, some guy with money, some business guy. She refused to say anything else. I'd ask and she'd clam up." She pointed at the door.

"Okay. Thanks." I had no reason to linger. " So long, Cindy Lou." I paused. "If you happen to remember anything else, give me a call at The Gazette. And think about this—Norma's gone and so is Darlene. You're the only one left. And maybe you know something you shouldn't. And I'm not talking about the Viking and his shenanigans, either."

"Yeah sure. I'd call you when hell freezes over," she sneered. But a worried look squirmed itself onto her face, just the same.

Damn. She knew more than she was telling but the last thing I needed was another personal encounter with the Viking. If Cindy Lou told him to, he'd rip my head off and probably laugh while he was doing it. I slid into the Chevy, banged the steering wheel with the meaty part of my palm and drove slowly back the way I came, wondering if any of it was important at all. I just didn't know. I was hoping she could tell me who Darlene had been dating. The mystery man. But I did know that I'd had my fill of bikers and bikers' girls to last me a long, long time.

As soon as I reached Highway 26, I gunned the engine and let the Chevy sail. The sky opened up. The dry breeze had cleared off some of the clouds. I slipped on my Ray-Bans to protect my eyes from the withering light and dust spun up by the car's wheels.

* * *

Brigsby was a small town, smaller than Applewood, about 4500 souls and just a forty-five minute journey to the north-west. Its reputation boasted two things; the magnificent sweep of its apple orchards that yielded the succulent Brigsby

Red—a fruit that gave good eating and baking too—and the Beech Mental Hospital, perhaps the livelier of the two. The province administered the facility and as Doc Seaton said, once you got in, you rarely got out. Only the ones who voluntarily signed up for specific programs could walk away. Those declared mentally incompetent by the courts or a single psychiatrist, had committed a criminal act and were deemed incapable of comprehending the consequences of their actions or were committed by a family member, stayed incarcerated at the infamous Beech, sometimes forever.

Technically speaking, Ellis Boston remained at Beech for a period of assessment normally lasting ninety days but could be extended if the presiding psychiatrists so wished. I told myself this was a human interest story. Killing wives didn't happen that often in Applewood and Ellis' standing in the community as a God-fearing, upstanding citizen meant the incident kept tongues wagging. Ellis had been known as practically minded and down-to-earth. I wanted to see if I could figure out what happened to him. Why did he act so uncharacteristically and did his bizarre behavior have any connection to the other strange events that had taken place? Meanwhile, Chief McKie and his crack troops continued to gather evidence. If the evidence stuck, the shrinks would then put forward a recommendation as to whether Ellis possessed the mental acuity to stand trial. A double-edged sword and difficult to determine the better route. If Ellis gets charged with Lizzie's murder and found guilty, he could spend at least ten to fifteen years in prison without parole. If the doctors reached a consensus that nullified his mental bearing, Ellis might spend the rest of his life in limbo without the police ever charging him with anything so much as littering. I believed the chances were better than even that the latter would occur even if Ellis aced the mental assessment. They just hated letting people out of Beech. An admission of defeat, I guess. Frankly, I'd rather take my chances with the courts. With a prison sentence, you knew it came to an end point eventually. Not so at Beech, that was the sad truth of it.

I turned west from 26 onto county road 16 that led straight to the heart of that bustling metropolis, Brigsby. It had been named after a British émigré, a would-be farmer who travelled to the Prairies in 1857, and before reaching his destination, fell down dead of a heart attack. John Brigsby lay buried under what is now the town square. The family, not knowing what else to do after their leader's abrupt demise, simply stayed put, and that is how Brigsby, rather ignobly, came into being. Not much to commend it, so building a mental hospital as a kind of monument, made sense. Beech Mental Hospital went up in the 1930's, designed by an architect inspired by Gothic romance. The project came about as a patronage contract awarded to a newly elected member of parliament, a descendant of the original Brigsby, one John Brigsby Holmes, who supported a controversial labour bill in the provincial legislature. The bill prevented more than six labour organizers from congregating in the same public place at a time thus limiting the capacity to mount violent strikes. At any rate, it took place during the Depression and any patronage contract gained appreciation whether the work delivered anything remotely meaningful or not and resulted in the embarrassing blight now known as Beech. Because of the hospital's ominous reputation, Brigsby didn't rank highly as a tourist spot. In May 1947, a mad killer by the name of Remo Rogers escaped from Beech and wreaked havoc and mayhem for ten days. He held a family hostage terrorizing them until a police marksman shot him through a lit window at the stroke of midnight. At any rate, tourists have long memories and Remo effectively axed the tourist trade, the fear being another celebrated escape. So, no cottages or resort developments, nor sailing clubs or golf courses planned. No flashy restaurants. Or nightclubs. No families in funny clothes wobbling bicycles along quaint streets. No chic cafes. No cool people. Brigsby remained a dour community that just happened to produce the best damn apples in the entire province through geographic happenstance rather than expert cultivation and farming techniques. Lately though, some enterprising locals had branched out to include apple pies, cider and apple butter in addition to the crop they exported to market.

Driving through the gentle curves and staggered rises I had the feeling of being on the verge of something exciting, something important without knowing what I would find or where it would end up.

Beech Mental Hospital embodied the most forbidding place I'd ever seen; an appropriate set for Gotterdamerung. I expected the Valkyries to buzz the car at any moment. An architectural hell-on-earth that ensnared the body and tortured the mind. Brigsby's architect descendant cornered the market in cinder block and barbed wire. Apart from deeply tinted mesh windows framed in wood and criss-crossed by iron bars, not a speck of natural material appeared in the construction of the complex. It rose, sombre, and menacing at the pinnacle of a meandering road cresting into a plateau. From the massive gates one could see the sleepy community of Brigsby sprawled at its feet as if Beech, the nasty giant, menaced its cowering prey.

A guard standing at least seven feet tall and weighing 300 pounds—Mr. Potato Head on stilts—came over to my side of the car and eyed me suspiciously out of a doughy face. He looked like he'd been bred in a lab dish, then flung into a canoe. I quickly handed him some identification. He continued to eye me maliciously making my flesh crawl while I attempted to smile disarmingly. Nice monster. Good monster. I prayed he wouldn't slip and fall and crush me under his outstanding girth. After poring over every punctuation mark in my press card, he handed it back to me, then clomped over to the gatehouse and flicked a switch. Doc Seaton had made certain my name appeared on the guest list. I saw a green light flash on the control panel. Then I heard a bright humming sound and the gates lurched apart. As I drove through, I wondered fearfully if I'd be let back out. I knew also, that everyone who entered thought exactly the same thing.

Behold the polyester version of the Magic Kingdom. Proportion went AWOL; the guard, the gate, the scale of the building that soared in all directions and the expanse of the parking lot standing virtually empty even though it could hold enough tanks to provide ground cover for a battalion.

In the excessively bright foyer of the main building, a man appeared in a sparkling white lab coat. He had a fringe of white hair ringing his skull, a bulbous nose and a bristly white moustache but was solid and forceful looking. His complexion radiated the hue and texture of grey pudding. A frozen smile hinged on his face. I'd seen a ventriloquist's dummy look less wooden. I started to walk around but the guy blocked my way.

"Mr. Simpson? I'm Dr. Rumplemeyer, in charge of the facility's public affairs." We shook hands briskly but it was like touching the dead.

I said, "Nice to meet you, Doc."

Rumplemeyer said, "Dr. Seaton asked me to expect you. I'm at your disposal, Mr. Simpson. We're a friend of the press and always have been. This is a very scientifically-based institution here, Mr. Simpson. The level of research is comparable to that of any in the world."

"Yes. I'm sure it is," I replied, thinking, that, for mausoleums, perhaps.

He went on. "Some of our staff have conducted pioneering experiments with the criminally insane. The results have been astounding."

"I don't doubt it for a minute."

"What can I do for you today?" asked Rumplemeyer.

"I'm here to see a patient. A new patient by the name of Ellis Boston."

Rumplemeyer lapsed into silence as if he'd been switched off.

Then he said, "Mr. Boston is catatonic, you know. Won't get anything out of him. It's a waste of your time. Perhaps you'd like a tour or a chat with some of our capable staff instead."

"Nonetheless, I'd like to see Ellis Boston," I said more firmly.

"Just what is your interest in Mr. Boston?" Rumplemeyer asked.

"Well. He's a citizen from the town of Applewood who has become enmeshed in tragic circumstances. In other words, he's still news for the present. That's why."

Rumplemeyer said, "As long as you are aware that Mr. Boston is receiving the most humane, individual and advanced care possible, then I have no objection to you seeing him, Mr. Simpson. I would be happy to escort you."

"Swell. Ready when you are."

"This way, Mr. Simpson," and Rumplemeyer, Ron according to the badge pinned on his crisp lapel, indicated a corridor with his arm outstretched as if some hidden puppeteer had pulled an invisible wire.

I clicked my heels and bowed crisply. "I await your orders."

Rumpy nodded without saying anything not quite sure of my manners or motives. As we marched down the long corridor cut off by a steel reinforced door, me in front, I felt his shrewd eyes boring into my back. Rumpy pressed a button with his forefinger and the steel door lurched open to reveal a holding area where two guards even larger than the first I'd seen, were seated at a bare table.

Rumplemeyer turned to me and smiled.

"I'm afraid you're going to have to empty your pockets, remove your belt, pants and shoes, please." I registered surprise. "Mr. Simpson, this is an institution housing the criminally insane. We just can't take any chances. The most mundane item can, in their hands, become a lethal weapon."

"I see."

One of the guards placed a small metal locker on the table. Which I did while being scrutinized silently by the three. "I'd like to take my notebook and pen, if that's okay?"

Rumplemeyer and the guard exchanged looks.

"I think that will be all right," Rumpy replied. "As a matter of fact, I'll leave you here. Lawrence will take you to Mr. Boston where you can spend as much time with him as you like."

"I'd like to see Mr. Boston alone, if I may."

Rumplemeyer nodded. "Certainly. He's in isolation. Lawrence will be immediately available to you. Stop by on your way out, Mr. Simpson and let me know how it went." We shook hands and the feel of his palm against mine reminded me of my fishing trip with Hal Bigelow in the morning. Slimy and wet.

"Will do."

Meanwhile, the genial Lawrence gingerly probed through the pockets of my trousers and examined my shoes for hidden weapons, I presumed. Finally he sniffed, then handed the lot back to me, minus the belt. "You gotta leave the belt here," he said. I wasn't going to argue.

Lawrence said, "Follow me," and nodded to his cohort who released the lock on the portal to the wing where the patients, the crazies lived. I don't know what I was expecting exactly but my alarm subsided when I realized this part of the building resembled a hospital rather than a depraved scene out of Marat/Sade, with the exception of bars on the windows and robust locks on the doors. No jabbering inmates writhing on the floor, no wails or piercing cries, no hands grasping at freedom through the bars of their cells. In fact, it seemed all too quiet. Lawrence appeared an amiable brute and sauntered along casually. His polished leather boots squeaked as he trod the polished floor.

"Worked here long, Lawrence?" I asked.

"'Bout ten years," he drawled.

"You like it?"

"It's a pay cheque," he laughed. "Ain't much else to do around here. I'm not part of the apple farmer's association and if you don't belong, you haven't got a hope in hell of growing apples in these parts. The land is passed from generation to generation like a sacred trust, you know? My wife's uncle is an apple farmer but he's passing it on to his own kids. After apple farming, there's just Beech or move, and the wife wanted to stay close to the rest of her family."

"I see. Is it dangerous working here?"

Lawrence stopped, put a meaty fist to his fleshy chin and pondered. "Could be at that. We've had some real loonies in here. Between you and me though, they keep 'em so doped up, they don't know if they're coming or going. They're pathetic creatures. They don't know what they've done, who they are, can't even tie their own shoelaces. And at the end of the day, I get to walk out of here and go home to my family. They can't do that. No sir. And likely, ninety-nine percent of 'em never will."

"You mean they'll never be cured?"

For some reason, Lawrence thought I'd made a joke and gave me a playful shove that sent me reeling half way down the corridor.

"Cured? That's a good one. How can you cure somebody when you only see a doctor maybe once every two weeks, if that? The only therapy they get here is the pharmaceutical form, if you get me. But you didn't hear that from me, okay? If it gets in the paper, I could get fired. Forget I said it. I gotta watch my mouth sometimes. I'm only a few years from qualifying for a pension and then I can do what I really want."

"What's that?"

"Nuts."

"Nuts?"

"Yup. I'm going to grow nuts. I figured I've been surrounded by 'em for so long I'll kind of miss 'em when I leave here. But the climate here in Brigsby is perfect for certain varieties and I figured it's an untapped market. Yes sir, you've got your brazils, pecans, walnuts, lichees—I've got it all worked out. Plus, you can harvest two crops a growing season. So, you won't say anything, right?"

"Don't worry. Your secret's safe with me. Mum's the word on the nuts, Lawrence."

Lawrence seemed satisfied with my response and I had no desire to antagonize him since my safety depended on it. He looked conspiratorially up, then down the corridor, took hold of my lapels and drew me toward him. I felt my toes dragging on the floor.

"There's other things too," he whispered, loud enough to be heard on the other side of a crowded room during a cocktail party.

"What things?"

"Experiments. Dr Gleason's got some kind of research grant and they use some of the patients here as guinea pigs without telling them what's going on. Not even the families know."

"What kind of experiments?"

He released me suddenly and I fell on my backside. "I've said too much already."

I picked myself up off the floor and dusted the seat of my pants instinctively. The linoleum shone brighter than one of those famous polished Brigsby apples. "C'mon, Lawrence, you can't just tantalize me with some info and drop it."

He shook his enormous head. "I'll lose my job."

"Look Lawrence, just a few days ago, Ellis Boston was an ordinary guy leading a pretty normal life. Suddenly, that's all turned upside down. In the blink of an eye. One day, he's a farmer and now he's a mental patient and his wife is dead on a slab in the morgue. This sort of thing should not be happening. If it could happen to a paragon like Ellis what about regular schmoes like you and me?" Lawrence looked at me warily. "Look, if it makes you feel better, it'll be off the record. I won't say or write a thing about it. What do you say?"

"Off the record?"

I nodded reluctantly. The phrase every reporter loathes. "Yeah. Off the record. Not a peep."

Lawrence thought long and hard. I heard the wheels of his brain clanking but after some deliberation, he made up his mind. "I dunno about the experiments exactly. Behavioural kinds of things. They use drugs and sleep deprivation, you see, then plant suggestions in the patient's heads to see if they take. Make 'em do things by giving a signal or repeating a phrase. It seems like pretty kooky stuff to me but nobody cares about the people here, so it's perfect for them. The money's from the feds. Department of Defense."

"How do you know all this, Lawrence?"

He gave me a look. "What do you think, Mr. Simpson, that because I'm a guard here I'm a dummy? Let me tell you, I've got two years of community college and I studied biology, botany and chemistry. I do a lot of reading in the library too, psychology books mostly. Believe me, we hear a lot of things. We get around. I heard talk that your party, Mr. Boston, is the next guy in the chain."

"What?"

"Yeah. You see. He's perfect. Because he's catatonic, at least for now anyway, it's like he's got no personality left or it's hidden and for what they're doing makes him a good subject. It's like he's a blank slate. And the docs want to fill in the blanks… get it?"

"Can they do that?"

Lawrence nodded ominously. "Can and are. With the okay from those guys you and me put in Ottawa. It's spooky stuff, let me tell you."

"Well, thanks for spilling. Couldn't have been easy."

The big man looked sad and pensive. "I had a cousin, Brent. We were close and he took me under his wing when I was a kid. Anyway, he had a lot of stress in his life. One day, he blew his top and attacked a neighbour. Beat him pretty bad. He was booked and committed here. My uncle had a choice, Beech or hard jail time. So they chose Beech. He came out of here a zombie. A year later, he jumped off Dead Man's Plank and never surfaced. They found his body on the other side of the bay."

"Geez, that's tough, Lawrence but I'm not sure what I can do for Ellis, to be honest about it."

He nodded glumly. "Sure. I understand. I guess I just feel sorry for these guys, sometimes and they remind me of my cousin." We halted outside a door marked 1310-B. "He's in there. It's an isolation cell. You go on in. I'll be right outside. Take your time. If you need something, just holler and I'll be in like a flash," Lawrence said, drawing out an enormous ring of keys and fitted one into the lock swinging the door open and motioning me in like a convivial host. I nodded with compressed lips, thudding heart and fighting the most excruciating sense of trepidation, stepped inside.

The room was painted avocado green—a soothing colour if you're a salad lover. A single, low-wattage bulb set high in the ceiling enclosed in wire mesh—the only light source. A particularly enterprising inmate might, I suppose, fashion a pair of stilts out of the various wood shavings left by the cleaners in the corners, then vault repeatedly into the light, smashing their brains into oblivion after thirty or forty attempts. I guess they just didn't want to take the chance. A sad, narrow cot had been bolted into the wall. I spotted one wooden chair. On it sat Ellis Boston. I stared at him, shocked at the radical change in his appearance.

To put it simply, Ellis had transformed from a robust, ruddy-faced farmer in his 50's into a creature, a pathetic, elongated gnome in a tatty bathrobe and pajamas, the bony knobs of his feet sticking out of the paper slippers he wore. Physically, he'd dried out, as if hung upside down from a twig in a killer drought, his skin translucent through which veins, arteries and bone showed through. He made no sign when I came in, his head tilted, looking absently at the floor. His large farmer's hands lay folded serenely in his lap. He remained absolutely motionless. I couldn't even tell if he was breathing. His mouth hung open slightly. I stood there for a minute or two. And again, I detected no movement except for the pulse of my beating heart.

"Mr. Boston? Ellis? Can you hear me?" No response. "Ellis? I'm Joe Simpson from the Applewood Gazette. I hope you can hear me and maybe we can talk a little? You must be wondering what happened. One day, you're a successful farmer growing corn and beets and tomatoes, married to your high school sweetheart and then suddenly, your world is tossed around and you don't know where you are. Can't figure it out. Nothing seems to make any sense, does it? You know, one of the things I like best about Applewood is its tranquility—being close to the countryside. You see, Mr. Boston, I grew up in the city and barely saw any open spaces or greenery. It certainly does ease a man's pain, if he's prone to it. The city is noisy and dirty. But the countryside. You can breathe the air, enjoy the open spaces." Again, no response. I inched closer until we were about three feet apart. I watched him closely to see if he blinked. He did but very infrequently. Well, something was moving. I tried again. "Ellis. You may not remember but I've stopped by your stall at the farmer's market and bought some of your produce. Sweet tasting tomatoes and that peaches and cream corn? Delicious. Listen, Ellis, I just want to hear your story. Your side of it. Can you tell me what happened on the day Lizzie died?" More terrifying silence. Not even a breath whistled through his pinched nostrils.

My spirits sank like a lead weight. The green room became oppressive, even nauseating. Without knowing why exactly, I slumped to the floor, my back against the nearest wall and waited. What for, I didn't know. Some ten minutes passed in the most rounded silence I'd ever experienced. Like being shut up in a water tank and floating on gentle waves. Rather than being soothed I felt suffocating terror. The few minutes passed slowly. Finally, I sighed and could stand no more. Ellis hadn't budged a millimetre. The trip down here had been a waste of time. I stood up to leave moving to the door so Lawrence, the friendly giant, could let me out.

Then a voice belonging to a scarecrow scratched its way out: "You're the one who found me, ain't you?" I froze. As soon as I dared, I turned to find his lifeless eyes, with the merest spark flickering behind them, focused on me.

"Yes, Mr. Boston. I'm the one who found you," I answered softly.

"How did I get here?" he asked genuinely curious. "I can't remember, exactly. I imagined I flew but that sounds crazy, don't it?"

I moved closer. "Yes, I guess it does. Do you remember anything at all, Mr. Boston? Like what happened to Lizzie, for instance?"

He wet his lips with his tongue. "I'm so damn thirsty and they won't let me have anything to drink."

"Do you know where you are, Ellis?"

"The hospital. I'm a sick man. I know that."

"What happened to make you sick, Ellis?"

He twisted his head, stretching the scrawny tendons in his neck while he thought. "It was most peculiar," he replied.

"What was?"

"Me and Lizzie both. It'd been carrying on for a few days. Weird things. I'd be out in the fields and suddenly the cornstalks would rise up and attack me. I'd run but never get away. My tractor tried to poison me with a cloud of purple smoke. It sounds strange, I know but I swear it's true. And then finally, they got Lizzie out in the garden."

"Who did?"

"I don't know. Something tall. Big. As high and wide as a…"

"…a tabernacle?"

Ellis nodded, his mouth gaping forcing his eyes wider. "You seen it too. Oh thank the lord, I thought I was the only one…" And tears rolled out of the corners of his eyes and flowed onto his trembling lips.

"Go on, Ellis. What happened next?"

"It came up, see and spread out its hands like this," he said, spreading his fingers wide like a fan.

"And they were on fire?"

He nodded as vigorously as a skeleton could. "Yes. Yes. Oh, thank the lord. I seen it. They were on fire and it reached down to Lizzie. She didn't see. She didn't know. I had to save her. So I come running and running and I never seemed to go nowhere but finally just as it was about to touch her, send her up in flames, a weapon appeared to me and I slew it like St. George slew the dragon, yes sir. But it was too late, it got to her first. My precious Lizzie was taken. Then I saw her soul fly up and out of her body and I just knew I had to get it back. So I took off and flew after it. At least I think so."

"And then I found you."

Ellis again nodded his head weakly.

He tired from the effort of talking. "Uh-huh." His body hadn't flickered in the slightest, as if his mind had come unfrozen and in the few precious moments of life left, I could see the beginnings of a retreat.

Ellis said, "I've got to go now."

"Where Ellis? Where are you going?"

"To the tabernacle. They got me too. That's where they're keeping Lizzie. I've been away too long. She's missing me. Thanks for stopping by, I owe you one. Maybe we'll talk again." And suddenly, he was gone, sunk into his frozen state unredeemable in its isolation.

"Ellis? Ellis? Come back. Come back," I called, but it was little use. I might as well have talked to the chair or the wall. Ellis had vanished.

When Lawrence opened the door, he said, "What happened? You look like you have seen a ghost."

"I have Lawrence. And he's in there somewhere," I replied, indicating Ellis Boston or rather the poor, lost soul we called by that name.

As I belted my pants and returned the personal effects to my pockets, I shook Lawrence's hand. "Thanks for everything, Lawrence. Maybe I'll see you again."

He gave me a two-fingered salute. "Sure thing."

"Oh and I'd like some of those nuts when you get around to growing some."

"You'll be my first customer," he said. The other guard just blinked at the two of us not sure if we were joshing or not.

Rumplemeyer hovered by the door outside the holding area. I tried to walk briskly past him.

"How was your visit?" he asked.

I looked at him. "Sad. Very sad."

I spun on my heel and walked quickly toward the main exit while he trailed after me. At the door, I shook his hand briskly, thanked him for his kindness. Rumplemeyer shoved a press kit into my hands and then I left him with this hinged, puzzled smile hanging on his strange face.

When I said sad, I meant it from the very core of my being. My heart went out to Ellis Boston who'd withdrawn to a place where he wouldn't be touched. I'm no Sigmund Freud but it seemed to me that Ellis had been hallucinating. The real issue is what caused it in the first place? I said to myself but riposted sternly, Ellis doesn't deserve this. Beech will bolster that guilt if Ellis ever comes out of his hiding place long enough. I felt pressed by a great weight that only lifted gradually the further I drove from Brigsby. Screw their stupid apples too.

I forced myself to look at the green leafery, to feel the healing warmth of the sun, to hear the teeming insect life buzzing in the woods and resolved if I could help that poor man, I'd sure as hell try. It was one thing for Lawrence to whisper secretly about the clandestine goings-on and another to prove it. I knew that. Further to that, what caused Ellis to become a loony?

Chapter Twenty

Applewood hadn't changed a jot since I'd left but now it seemed sprightlier and I felt true affection for it. Friday afternoon in the summer and people pined for the weekend, barbecuing in the backyard, frolicking on the beach and generally, weathering the influx of weekenders who descended on the community. We pretended that the precious time wasn't spoiled by the noisy invasion. I passed the RSC Developments project in the works on the edge of town. It was a new concept; a complex of something called townhouses, the concept adapted originally from Britain where row houses have been in existence for centuries.

This particular development, called Applewood Manor and Marina took the idea even further. Built for convenience, Rothwell wanted to construct a self-contained community with its own shops, amenities, marina for boats, docks, beach, you name it. Older, retired folks would spend the summer without any of the fuss associated with their own cottage. No more septic tanks, cutting the grass or weeding the garden. All taken care of for them by Rothwell...for a fee, of course. And they spent time with people like themselves, boring people mostly, I thought, so maybe it was better to have them all corralled together. But Rothwell had glommed on to something. He'd sold out the entire stock of 105 units before an inch of ground had been broken. And at an average price of $37,000 each, he wasn't doing badly at all. I, personally, deplored the lack of privacy and felt these new developments represented blights on the country-side. I'd rather see an overgrown, rancid swamp in its place. Applewood and a number of other communities blessed with the beauty of natural settings felt the impact of rapid changes, many of which had been approved by the original citizens. Money poured in. People jabbered that Applewood could become the next Atlantic City with its boardwalk and resort hotels and beach. And I thought, sure, add the white fleshy bodies boiled red in the sun, women in too tight bathing suits and men who spoke vulgarly about them, snickering among themselves. To me, Atlantic City lived its life like a cheap, smelly cigar. The powerful few would walk away with their pockets bulging.

Last week, just before Norma drowned and Darlene disappeared, I'd been out to the Applewood Manor construction site. Hal Bigelow investigated an act of vandalism. When I pulled up, I saw Rothwell screaming at Hal. Hal's face had clamped down hard but he wasn't saying anything back. When I strolled up, Rothwell turned on me.

"What the hell do you want here, Simpson? This is private property and closed to the press."

"I'm standing on this side of the property line, Rothwell, where it's public. Heard about some equipment being damaged and came to check it out."

Rothwell wore a hard hat, a white shirt rolled up over tanned forearms and carried a scroll of plans that he waved around. "It's getting out of control, these criminal acts and the police," he shot a missile of loathing at Hal, "are doing absolutely nothing to stop it. Why do I pay taxes? What's the point?"

I pulled out my notebook and pen. "What was damaged?"

Rothwell pointed to a trench where a backhoe stood frozen. "Sand in the tank. Second one this month. It's costing me thousands and delaying the work. We're behind schedule as it is."

"Anything else?"

"Plenty," Rothwell spat. "Supplies have disappeared. We've lost 50 bags of cement, truck tires flattened, windows broken…it goes on and on. I've got my own men here watching the place at night. But there's been no progress at all when it comes to apprehending these criminals."

A siren blasted behind us. I turned to look as the Chief's pick-up bounced along the dirt track leading to the development site. Then it plowed to a stop in the sand, the doors were flung open and Chief McKie and his deputy, Arne Guenther stepped out. The Chief cursed as some dust flecked his highly polished boots. The two stomped over.

"About time," Rothwell spat.

"Now, don't you worry, Mr. Rothwell, my deputy and I are here to take personal charge of this here investigation. You're in the best of hands."

"You'll forgive me if I don't clap and cheer."

"I understand you're upset," the Chief said, moving his Stetson around on his pin-sized head, "but I guarantee we'll catch these hoodlums and put a stop to these shenanigans so you can get on with your important work."

Hal and I exchanged looks. I thought it best to check out the limitless sky before I puked.

"Now look here, McKie..."

Arne Guenther stepped in, the chief's enforcer. A cunning guy with shrewd instincts attuned to opportunities for personal advancement. He stood tall, rangy and mean. "Mr. Rothwell...why don't we discuss this where we have a little more privacy?" He flicked his right hand toward me. The left rested on the butt end of the gun riding his slim hips.

Rothwell hesitated, then nodded. "Let's go to my private trailer. It's down by the water in the shade."

McKie smirked and turned to Hal. "Constable. You can resume your duties now. We'll take over here."

Hal worked something distasteful around in his mouth, then said, "Chief." I pretended to be invisible and jotted notes in my pad. I saw Guenther start toward me.

"Well, I guess I've got everything I need. See you around, gentlemen." And headed to my car. As I glanced back, Hal, massive hands rigidly on his hips, strode to his cruiser. He wrenched open the door, swept his cap off his head and whipped it inside the cab while McKie, Guenther and Rothwell strolled leisurely toward the shade. To serve and protect. But whose interests were being served and whose were being protected? Someone or some group seemed determine to throw a spanner in Rothwell's development plans.

Cruising by the town square, I noticed the Jersey Jokers had come out of hiding. They were giving an impromptu performance and a sizeable crowd had gathered. The Jokers jumped and leapt and juggled their flamboyant little hearts out. I noticed a young girl with frazzled hair moving through the crowd of sixty or so, discreetly seeking donations. No one refused her. Cheaper than the circus. And no sad looking animals, either. It seemed the Jokers might have a prosperous summer too.

I parked the car at an expired meter leaving my PRESS sign conspicuously on the dashboard and strolled over to the square. I came up from behind and placed my hands on her shoulders. She turned.

"Hey Joe." She threw an arm around me. " Did you get my note?"

"Sure did. I stopped by the store this morning but it was closed. I just got back from Brigsby."

"Well. Wish was late which isn't surprising considering last night. I had to call for over an hour just to wake him up."

"Well, I was a little groggy myself."

Beverly thumped me on the chest. "I know."

I frowned. "Funny, but I don't remember you driving my car."

Beverly crossed her arms. She was wearing a grey and black plaid sleeveless bag dress, gathered under the bosom. "I'm not surprised. You were asleep in the back seat."

Now I was confused. "Bev. I'm not sure how to ask this but, uh…"

Her brown eyes widened. "Uh-huh?"

"Well. I don't remember what happened. I must have passed out. I thought I dreamed you were at my place."

"No, that wasn't your imagination, Joe. I was at your place."

"Ah."

"And it was sweet, really, it was. You lay in my arms and sort of snored with your mouth open. But I got up early and left."

"Then nothing happened?"

"Not really. But that's okay. Like I said, it was sweet. You seemed so innocent, lying there, kind of like a hairy, newborn baby."

"I feel like a sap. No check that. A complete nincompoop."

She brushed my face with a smooth, cool palm. "Don't worry, Joe. There'll be plenty of time for us." Gave me the shivers.

"That's the trouble, kid. I do worry. I worry all the time. I'm just a natural born worrier. I've got it bad. Tattooed on my soul. I've been in too many dark places lately."

She caressed my cheek. "Poor baby."

I took her strong hands in mine. "Say listen…you interested in having an ice cream? I haven't had lunch yet." We strolled off the grassy square, away from the kids with their mouths hanging open, away from the antics of the mischievous performers, hand-in-hand and I felt her uncompromising warmth flow into me. The chill I'd felt in Brigsby melted away.

Beverly demolished her cone in a minute flat then declared she had to get back to the shop. "Wish'll be looking for me," she said. She gave me a smack on the cheek and strode off.

I walked back to The Gazette feeling puzzled.

Teddy was out when I showed up. Nadine worked quietly away. I listened to the scratching of pencil on paper as she added columns of figures and the frequent hacking spasms that wracked her emaciated frame. I could hear Stumpy Butler pounding type in the back room and cursing his bad luck. In short, all was normal.

"Doc Seaton and Hal Bigelow called, Joe. Have a nice trip?"

"It was ghastly, Nadine. Perfectly ghastly. But I got some interesting stuff."

"Jury came back by the way. Around eleven this morning. Teddy covered for you. They'd been deliberating since eight. Teddy left you a couple of movie passes. You were right on the money. The jury recommended a crack down on drinking and driving in boats, mandatory wearing of life preservers and warning signs on the beach about boating at night."

"I'm not interested in seeing The Longest Day."

"Well, I hear a new movie with Shirley Maclaine is coming next week. Sweet Charity? You like musicals? I do."

"I guess so. I don't know."

"What's the matter, Joe?"

"Ah, I don't know."

"You got girl trouble?"

"Oh, I guess so, in a manner of speaking," I said, thinking of two dead girls, who'd been young less than a week ago.

"Well, if you did, it'd only make you even with about half the world's population, that's all," she said.

"I guess that's true enough," I replied.

"I know I'm right on that one," Nadine said. "Have a cup of coffee and relax for a minute. Then, when you're ready, get to work. That's what I do."

I laughed. "Okay. I've only had ten cups of coffee today."

Nadine had made a fresh pot of coffee and it wasn't half-bad. I sat at my desk sorting my hastily scribbled notes taken at Beech. Thoughts spilled around in my mind. Strange doctors. Spooky hospitals. Big business in small, quiet communities. Land development. And not the least—money. How the smell of it floated on the air. All you had to do was sniff, brother, and you'd get a wad of the stuff. Hopefully, I'd get a better idea when I stopped in at the O'Tooles unexpectedly.

Editorial—June 14, 1966—Beech Mental Hospital, Brigsby.

Beech Mental Hospital in nearby Brigsby is a forbidding place. Its massive gates rise ominously above the landscape where it is frighteningly situated at the top of a rise overlooking this benign farming community.

Several days ago, the unfortunate Ellis Boston, who is suspected of killing his wife, Lizzie, was removed suddenly to Beech Mental Hospital for what authorities call a "period of assessment". Mr. Boston sits in a stark room devoid of furniture; a cot bolted to the wall and a single wooden chair, upon which, he sits, motionless and alone. Treatment is sporadic. According to hospital records, patients are visited an average of once every two weeks by a practicing psychiatrist. The miserable inmates rise at 6 am. and are put to bed at 7:15 pm. sharp with no exceptions. Most are sedated much of the time.

Ellis Boston has retreated into himself. On the outside, he is a shell. But his personality is there, hidden away. That frightened self emerged for a few scant moments and we spoke together. In his own mind, Ellis Boston was not responsible for his wife's killing. He tried to protect her. Ellis claimed a demonic being rose up with hands afire and attacked his wife, Lizzie. He picked up a hoe, the only weapon available to him and ran to save her. We know the tragic result.

Something very disturbing happened to Ellis Boston, a man who had lived quietly and responsibly in this community his entire life. There seemed to be no clear or apparent motive for him to have snapped, if that's what happened. His finances were in order, his health excellent and according to friends and relatives, the Bostons were a happy and contented couple married for 29 years. How do we explain what happened? It may not be possible. As long as Ellis Boston is penned up at Beech Mental Hospital, we'll never know.

Mr. Boston deserves better. He deserves to have the opportunity to comprehend what caused him to act this way. The community of Applewood deserves better too. As long as the laws of this province give doctors and bureaucrats such immense control over the lives of those who are helpless to speak for themselves, our rights are violated. Say a prayer for Ellis Boston and those like him where in a single moment their lives changed forever. It may be the only solace he'll ever receive from now until the hereafter.

30

I know this piece constituted an emotional outpouring but I'd let my instincts carry me on this one. I felt ashamed that I hadn't done the same for my mother. Taken up her cause. I hadn't lifted a finger to help and I hadn't seen her in over eight years. I let Ellis make me feel guilty. Writing it left me exhausted. I glanced at my watch, 5:15 pm., time to return home, shower and change. I left the column on Teddy's desk with a note, a plea really, to let it run as an editorial piece in Monday's issue. I wondered if he wouldn't fire me come Monday and hire one of those eager hopefuls waiting in the wings he referred to so often. Nadine and Stumpy had left. I locked the offices behind me. As I raced to the car, I noticed the empty, forlorn town square. The holy rollers and the Jersey Jokers had gone home for the day.

Chapter Twenty-One

I rode down Vine street and then turned left on to Birch avenue and left again on to the appropriately named, Manor road. It climbed up from the bay and ended literally at the O'Toole's brick drive.

It was a beautiful time of day, my favourite, next to early morning when only the crickets and dew were up and about. The light softened, the earth stilled and became tranquil as the world sat down to its supper. My heart felt light. And curiously determined.

I stopped outside the gates to the O'Toole estate, lit a Sweet Cap and sat in the car. I sucked in the solitude and tranquility, wondering how many more summers there'd be like this? Not too many, I ventured.

I smoked the cigarette down, then flicked it on the road where it erupted into a shower of sparks bouncing along the pavement. Checking my face in the rearview mirror, I hoped I hadn't gone overboard on the Old Spice. One thing to smell like the sea and another to reek of it.

I drove on up the hill and parked between a 1956 Rolls Royce Silver Cloud on my left and a black Cadillac Coup de Ville on my right. I trod a sweeping path punctuated by marble slabs set into the earth. The house sang updated Tudor with a stone foundation extending up to the second floor. Tall windows set off the front and a slate balcony jutted from each enclosed by rod iron piping. To the right, they'd added a glass solarium with a domed roof. To my left, sat a pair of French doors opening onto a ballroom. Further on, another set of doors led out to a wrap-around patio covering the far end of the house front and back. The grounds were immaculately groomed and golf course green. You could putt without fear on this piece of property. Seamus O'Toole must own a fertilizer company or keep horses, I concluded, admiring the blooms on the rose bushes whose buds exploded vibrantly into red, yellow, white and sweetheart. They were lovely. I wanted to pluck one and stick it in my lapel.

Figured a reconnaissance was in order and hoped Paisley didn't employ a brace of snarling wolfhounds to patrol the grounds. I ventured around the side creeping through the late blooming tulip and sprouting daffodil beds that had been recently watered. Hence the sucking ooze at my feet. Glancing down, I lifted my right topsider and grimaced at the layer of mud. "Geez." Undeterred, however, I slogged through carefully avoiding the flowers. Didn't want to bend any petals in Paisley's lovely garden. Just above the stone casement, I spotted windows and the curtains pulled open. Perfect. I slurped over and peered around finding the elegant back of a blonde woman in a Chanel suit holding a cigarette in her left hand and a martini in her right. She blew a plume of smoke to the impossibly high ceiling. I spied in on a spacious and elegantly appointed room. Low-lying settees covered in brocade, leather wingback chairs sturdily set in formation and floor-to-ceiling bookcases lined the walls. Must be the library, I deduced. Brilliant. The centre of the room had been cleared and some kind of display encased in glass occupied the attention of three men huddled over it. I tried boosting myself up a bit on the casement to get a better look but my feet slid down the brick facing. Hearing the slight commotion, the woman at the window turned her head. She spotted me. I waved at her and she arched an eyebrow in response. I smiled. She smiled then turned back to the three men and said something.

"I think there's an intruder in the shrubbery," she said. "But I wouldn't worry about it. He seems harmless."

Phillip Rothwell replied. "In that case, have another martini, darling. We're busy." Seamus O'Toole looked up sharply and strode toward the window. Red O'Brien merely guffawed at Rothwell's remark.

I crouched down flattening myself to the wall. I heard the window being winched open and glanced up to see the craggy profile and bleached gingery beard of Paisley's husband jut his head out to take a look. His crinkly blue eyes swept the perimeter.

"I don't see anyone," he said gruffly. His head disappeared. "You must have been mistaken, Roberta."

"Yes," Roberta slurred. "Must have been."

Nothing for it now but to crash the gathering. I slogged back around to the front and figured peeking in the rest of the windows wouldn't get me anywhere.

I scraped the soles of my shoes on the sharp creases of the limestone steps leaving blodges of wet mud.

I stepped up to a front door they'd stolen from a small cathedral and rang the bell. After some moments, it was heaved open by a withered maid in full uniform. She stared at me sourly but considered letting me in though she hesitated, thinking I could be a waiter or a musician and should have gone round the back.

"Yes?" she asked sternly.

"Joe Simpson," I replied. No response. "I'm the trumpet player in the band." Continued silence. I gave in. "I'm from the Gazette," I confessed.

"Stay here," she said. I'd stuck my foot in the door expecting it to be lopped off when she slammed it but she disappeared leaving the door ajar. I strained to hear a whispered consultation. A moment later, the maid returned.

"This way." And led me through the entranceway to the library. The blonde woman held a fresh martini and seemed to be inhaling it. The three men examined an architect's model of the as yet unrealized Applewood Manor resort. Seamus O'Toole appeared intent on moving a pair of plastic boats into position, inching them up a channel leading to the proposed marina. Paisley O'Toole, slender and alluring in a black cocktail dress wore a string of pearls long enough to skip rope. She jumped up to greet me with a dubious expression. One thing about the upper classes, they kept their manners in the face of rudeness.

"Joe!" she exclaimed in faux wonder and surprise. "Look who's here, darling," she said turning to her husband who'd allowed himself to be distracted by the intrusion, bushy ginger brows and moustaches bristling as he ambled over and took my hand in a crushing grip.

"Hello Joe," he said in a soft Irish lilt. "Didn't know you were coming round." He shot Paisley a quizzical glance.

"I wasn't invited," I said. "I heard there was some kind of powwow going on here this evening and felt it would be of interest to the community to investigate. After all, it's always news when the town's most prosperous businessmen gather together."

"I see," Seamus replied. "So you're on the record, is that it?"

"Naturally."

Seamus nodded. "Well, then, can we offer you something to drink?"

"Lemonade will do in a pinch."

"Fine," Seamus replied. Paisley summoned the querulous maid and placed the drink order. No one else had spoken.

"Let's take care of the introductions, then, shall we?" said Seamus. He reminded me of a buccaneer in a suit. Paisley demurely took my left arm and walked me to the centre of the room. She wore a sweet-scented musk cologne.

"What the hell do you think you're doing?" she hissed.

"Working," I hissed back. Her ruby-tipped claws dug into my forearm. I flinched and resisted the urge to yank my arm out of her manacled grip. The blonde woman watched us approach holding tight to the martini glass afraid it might float away. This time, she arched both eyebrows. I could see she recognized me.

The larger of the two men had coppery hair shorn in a stiff brush cut. His powerful physique had fled to fat years ago but he still retained the calloused hands and crude manner of a day labourer. Red O'Brien, local businessman and owner of a great deal of lakefront property including a number of motels. Because of his holdings, it was only natural that Red would cut himself into a deal like the resort. The other man, taller and slimmer with dark wavy hair and the smooth looks of an ambassador—Phillip Rothwell. Last time I'd seen him, he wore his hardhat and a snide expression. Now elegantly attired in a pale blue summer suit that showed his tan to good advantage. I wondered how he'd gotten on with Chief Mckie and Arne Guenther. As far as I was aware, the vandalism at the job site had continued unabated. The dissipated blonde, I took it, must be Mrs. Rothwell, heir to a tobacco fortune that gave Phillip some of the necessary capital to launch his voracious career. Mrs. Rothwell's name was Roberta, as I'd learned listening at the window. Her fingers felt cold and troubled. A crack in her make-up and she'd crumble to dust.

I said, "A pleasure to see you again, Mr. Rothwell." Rothwell handled my palm carefully as if he feared vermin and Red, who I'd run into more than once, merely tried to pulverize several fingers.

"How ya doin, Joe?" Red asked.

"Good thanks, Red."

Red turned to the group. "Better watch what ya say with a reporter in the house. This hack'll steal your thoughts." Which elicited some nervous laughter but Red guffawed as if he'd heard a dirty joke in some bar.

Within two months I'd be writing Red O'Brien's obituary. He'd be killed largely as a result of his own temper and pig-headedness getting into a tangle with a trespasser on his property, who, accidentally backed over him with a pick-up as Red bashed the rear end with a baseball bat. But for the present, Red O'Brien looked very alive exulting in the status he now claimed.

Rothwell spoke languidly but he fought to control his anger.

"I'm not sure I cared for the article you wrote about the coroner's inquest, Mr. Simpson," he said.

"Phil please, you promised you wouldn't ruin another party," said Mrs. Rothwell. Her speech came out mottled. Her lipstick smeared. I saw red lines in her eyes.

"Stay out of this Roberta, I'm talking to Mr. Simpson. Well, Simpson?" he asked. I could see how women might find a man like Phillip Rothwell attractive but the autocrat in him irked me in ways I couldn't begin to fathom.

"Write a letter to the editor, Mr. Rothwell. I'm certain it will be reviewed with interest," I replied.

Rothwell's face drained of its colour. Obviously, he wasn't used to being spoken to that way and certainly not by hundred buck a week reporters. Rothwell's voice sounded taut. He spoke with a rasp.

"There might not be a newspaper after I get through with it," he said.

"Oh?" I replied, putting out my best ho-hum look. "Do tell."

Paisley looked horrified. Mrs. Rothwell smirked discreetly into her drink glass. She seemed to enjoy her husband's discomfort. Rothwell took a step toward me and I girded myself for a confrontation. Red O'Brien stood there grinning hugely, enjoying the show. I thought I saw greenish hues in Rothwell's face as he clenched well-manicured fists, brought them up chest high and stepped forward. Before he could do anything, however, Seamus stepped in front, cutting Rothwell from my view.

"Maybe you'd like a quick tour of our new resort before we head into dinner, Joe?" he asked me in his soft voice sweeping his thick arm toward the glass case. "I'm sure you'd like to write up our promising plans for the community and describe how the town will benefit from such a development?" Rothwell turned back to his wife where they exchanged quiet but terse words.

"That'd be swell, Mr. O'Toole."

The maid returned with a sloshing glass of lemonade on a silver tray. As I picked it up, Seamus said, "I squeeze the lemons myself," and grinned hugely.

I grinned back at him. "Must be very satisfying."

"It is," he replied.

"Oh, for god's sake," Rothwell exclaimed. "Why don't we just chuck this intruder out the door? He barged in here unwanted."

I took a sip. The lemonade curled my palate. "Be my guest," I said.

Rothwell reddened and Red O'Brien licked his lips in anticipation.

"Now, Phillip," Seamus said. "Joe here was just doing his job when he was reporting at the hearing, right Joe? And it never hurts to be accommodating with the press, now, does it?" Before I could reply, Seamus took my arm and propelled me toward the scale model. "Take a look, Joe and see how the entire waterfront of Applewood is going to be transformed. Right now, it's a ragbag of isolated beaches mottled with seaweed and driftwood. We're going to clean it up and bring the community down to the waterfront. It's going to become a vibrant place where people from all over the region can bring their families and enjoy an outing or even better, settle here permanently."

Red nodded at me happily although I'm certain he would have preferred to see a few fists fly. I took out my pad and pen.

"Okay, Mr. O'Toole, shoot. Give me the update about this new development. I want the readers of the Gazette to hear it from the horse's mouth. To be the first to get the full story, all the details. And don't leave anything out."

Seamus smiled. "Excellent. Your timing's a bit, shall we say, inconvenient but I'm happy to tell you all about it." He glanced over at Paisley. "Darling, why don't you take our guests in for dinner while I finish up with Joe here. I don't want to keep the rest of you waiting while I blather on. No point in letting good food sit uneaten."

"I'd rather stick with you," Red O'Brien said. "I'd like to hear the official gaffe myself."

"And if you think I'm going to let you talk to the press without me, O'Toole, you've got another think coming," Rothwell said. "I mean that in the best possible way, of course."

Seamus nodded and swallowed. Paisley shrugged. "We might as well stay too. Dinner can wait a while."

"So, who's doing what here?" I asked and pointed at the neat, trim model of a cleaned up beach, cartoon storefronts and homes, toy boats and buildings. "What's everyone's role in the development?"

"I own this strip of beach," Red O'Brien said and planted a stubby finger on top of the case. "So, I'm right in the middle of it." Extorting cash for the land was more like it, I figured.

"And I'm working with the banking community to raise the financing for the development," Seamus said. "We're providing the capital to make it all happen."

"How much money are we talking about, Mr. O'Toole?"

He shrugged. "Thirty million or thereabouts. This isn't a slapdash project, Joe. We mean to do this right and to the highest standard, isn't that right, Phillip?"

Rothwell nodded and managed to swallow his bile. "The building and actual development work is being done by my company in partnership with Seamus. We will also be providing some of the funding in the form of additional grass-land and a community centre for the new residents and the townspeople."

"You see, Joe," Seamus interjected. "This is quite revolutionary if I must say, a new concept in community planning where everyone benefits."

"What are these here?" I asked and pointed.

"They're called townhouses," Rothwell answered. "It's a European concept where the living space is somewhat more compact than a detached house yet every unit has its own front and back yard and direct access to the beach, the marina, the stores and the community centre. It becomes self-contained. But you still have privacy if you want it. You can socialize with your neighbours or not."

"Looks a bit squeezed," I said. "I mean, we're out in the country here. Plenty of space."

"Not around the beachfront," Rothwell said. "That is prime real estate and there's a limit to it, you see?"

"So how much are these townhouses going to sell for?"

Rothwell glanced at Seamus, who pursed his lips. "Well, we're still working on the final pricing scenario, Joe but the range could be thirty-five thousand at the lower end up around forty-five thousand at the higher end for the larger units."

I whistled. "That's a lot of scratch." Heck, I'd already heard they sold out the first phase of the development.

Seamus smiled. "But see here, Joe, this is really the best bit and the most, er, beneficial. We can also provide the financing for the mortgages and we'll offer a better rate than the banks."

I paused from my note taking. "You're cutting out the banks?"

"No, not really," Seamus said. "Most purchasers will get their mortgages in the usual way but as an alternative we can provide the funding if necessary."

"You saying, Mr. O'Toole, that you can beat a five and a half percent loan from the banks?"

Seamus nodded. "In certain circumstances, I believe we can."

I scratched away for a second. "So, who's sabotaging the equipment? Who do you think the vandals are? Seems like they want to put a stop to all of this." And I gestured to the scale model. "And why do you think that might be? Any ideas?"

"We're working with the police on that, Simpson," Rothwell answered. "As you well know. When we have anything further to share with the press, I have no doubt that Chief McKie will contact you."

Both Red O'Brien and I snorted at the same time.

Seamus cleared his throat. "I'm sure Chief McKie is on top of it."

"Someone is willing to take pretty extreme measures to stop this development," I said. "Why? Any further thoughts on those who might disagree that this revolutionary concept, might not be welcome here?"

"It's a matter for the police, Joe. Simple as that," Seamus said quietly. "No reason for us to take it further when they have the means and resources to deal with the situation. We're builders. We are not policemen."

I'd set the glass of lemonade on top of the glass case. I picked it up and drained it. "Well, thanks for your time. I appreciate it and my apologies for barging in unannounced. Say, do you mind if we send our shooter, Dusty Rhodes, out to take some snaps?"

O'Toole and Rothwell exchanged looks. "I'm sure that would be fine, Joe," O'Toole answered. He reached into his jacket pocket and removed a slim leather wallet. He dipped in and took out a business card. "Just have him call the office and we'll arrange it."

I took the card and shoved it into my chinos. "Swell." I flipped the pad closed and tucked the pen behind my ear. "Well, thanks again. Sorry for busting in but you know, the news never stops."

I looked at Rothwell who found a convenient spot on the floor to examine. "Nice seeing everyone." Red O'Brien sweated. Roberta Rothwell's upper lip trembled as she downed the last drops of the martini. Only Paisley and Seamus remained cool. "I can find my way out. Thanks for the lemonade. Home squeezed, huh? I guess that's why it tasted so fresh." I took my leave.

Before kicking over the engine, I sat in my car for a moment, leafing through the notes I'd taken. The plans for the resort development sounded aboveboard although the vandalism bothered me. Somebody wanted to bring it to a grinding halt. I couldn't think of who might benefit. No rival firms had come forward. No competitors complaining in the wings. I had attended some of the town council hearings and Rothwell had been above board in his presentations and hadn't made any outlandish claims. So far, most of what he'd outlined in those meetings had come to pass except for the construction schedule. It remained in danger of going off the rails because of the vandalism. If other corporate interests weren't involved, that left mischief and mayhem as potential motivators. No motions or writs had been filed against the development and it came through clear as mud as to who might benefit. At this point in its development, halting the construction aided no one. All of which seemed to me to fall within the parameters of the general weirdness that seized the town. I couldn't shake the feeling all of this connected to Norma somehow, not how she died since the facts had come clear in the inquest but why. The mystery chemical found in her bloodstream troubled me no end. Cindy Lou said she'd had an older boyfriend, one who'd gotten her pregnant. I'd just left three prominent, wealthy, older men in the O'Toole's library. Couldn't see Red O'Brien fitting in somehow. Too much of a buffoon but he could be mean and dangerous. That left Rothwell and Seamus O'Toole. Powerful and charming each in his own way. Norma hadn't been without charms of her own. Clearly, Rothwell junior had been besotted.

I drove down to the Two-Tone hotel and decided to drink my supper. Dark moods haunted me, reached back to my violent childhood. Many of us drank to numb the pain. I was no different. Delaney Truscott stood guard at the door as usual. He saluted as I drew abreast. His shrewd eyes appraised my mood.

"Come to collect that drink?" he asked.

"If it's not too much trouble."

"No trouble, kid." He turned and signaled to the barman, Sam. "Go ahead, kid, drown your sorrows if that's what you're after."

I nodded. "Thanks. It just might be at that." He patted my back as I went in and took a seat at the bar. Sam waited. "CC on the rocks, Sam and don't spare the horses."

"Sure thing, Mr. Simpson." He replenished the peanuts before he grabbed the whiskey bottle and poured out a generous measure. Still early and the joint wasn't crowded. The pace would pick up later as the cottagers and resort goers came in for dinner. After the third hit, I felt the glow light me up. The peanuts disappeared then reappeared like magic. When I drank I thought about him, the old man. By drinking, I told myself I could understand him better and figure out why the fists came out. Why he looked for any reason to use them. I wanted to ask him, man to man, how he could act that way but I never got the chance. I know he got what he deserved. I know it deep in my heart. Then how come I couldn't forgive her for killing him? Answer me that one, Joe. You should have thanked her for saving your life. Instead, you turned away. Maybe that's why I didn't really care what people thought of me. Couldn't be worse than what I thought of myself. I had a letter from her, one she wrote me from prison. I kept it in my side pocket. But never opened it.

"This isn't the answer, Joe," a gruff voice said.

I lifted my forehead off the bar and looked blearily in the direction of the voice. "Teddy. What are you doing here?"

"Came in for a drink and found you holding up the bar all by yourself." He took the time to light up the stogy and draw on it carefully. "A young man like you should be out having fun instead of drowning your sorrows in this gloomy place."

"I happen to like this gloomy place. Suits my mood."

"You're not doing yourself any favours, Joe."

I snorted. "That's what my shrink says." I noticed the surprised expression on his face and stuck my peter pointer in his kisser. "Ha. Had you fooled there for a second. There is no shrink. As you can see." I spread my arms and almost tumbled from the stool. Teddy placed a steadying hand on my shoulder.

"You're a laugh and a half, kid."

I nodded. "I know. Haven't I told you umpteen times? Say, you'll never guess where I was earlier tonight."

The beetle brows clumped together. "Maybe you should just tell me."

"Crashed a dinner party at the O'Tooles. The Rothwells were there and Red O'Brien too. Got a private tour of the toy version of the new resort they're building down at the waterfront. Toy homes. Toy boats. Toy people."

"You don't say."

"I do say, Teddy. That's what I have been saying. There's got to be some connection to Norma. I know it. I can feel it."

"Got any proof, kid?"

"Uh…no. But I…"

"Then you gotta keep digging but be discreet, okay? These are powerful guys who…"

"…are advertisers in the Gazette?"

Teddy's face clouded. "That too but you can't go around accusing anyone of anything just because you don't like them and I certainly won't allow you to publish anything like that, either."

"Okay, Teddy. I'm not some amateur you know." I signaled Sam to fill me up again.

"Maybe you've had enough to drink for one night." He laid his powerful hand on my arm but I yanked it away knocking over the empty glass beside me. It rolled along the bar before dropping off the counter on to the floor. Fortunately, it stayed in one piece. Teddy bent down and picked it up.

"One thing I can handle is the booze," I said.

"You still carrying the letter?" Teddy asked. In a moment of weakness once, I'd told him about it.

"Yeah."

"Why don't you open it?"

"Can't."

"Why not? She wrote it eight years ago. Don't you want to know what it says?"

I looked at Teddy and suddenly sobered up. "I know what it says."

"What?"

I sighed. "The letter says that she stabbed the old man to death because it was him or her. And she wants me to forgive her."

"Have you?"

I stared at Teddy for a long moment. His round face flushed red. Sweat pooled in the seams of his thick neck. His small eyes slitted against the cigar smoke.

"You know, Teddy. I think I'd better head home. Got an early start tomorrow. Going fishing." I stood up feeling weary, like an old man who could barely walk. The booze. Drained you of energy. All it left you was the strength to take one more drink.

"See you, Teddy."

"I want to see those pages on this gathering of the powerful first thing Monday morning," he said.

"You got it, boss."

On my way back home, I passed by Sky High Records and Tapes. The door was closed but a light shone out from the back. I rapped on the frame and a moment later, Wishbone appeared wearing a quizzical expression. His face lit up when he saw that it was me and I didn't wear a uniform.

"Who you expecting, the fuzz?" I asked.

"I always expect those vigilantes," Wish said. "Come on in, Joe. I'm just clearing a few things up." He closed the door behind me.

"I was passing. Saw the light on."

"From the smell on you, I'd say you stopped by the Round House bar too," Wish said.

"That obvious?"

"Hey, I didn't say it was a bad smell, did I? But my drinking days are long gone. Just a quiet beer every now and then," Wish said as he busied himself behind the counter collecting pieces of paper and stuffing them into a folder. He unlocked a drawer behind the counter and shoved the folder inside, then relocked it.

"Pretty tight security for a record shop," I said and lit up a Sweet Cap.

"Competition's growing every day," Wish said lightly. "Gotta keep on top of things."

"I guess," I said.

"You know it, Joe. Business don't grow on trees. You gotta work for it or some corporate asshole will come in and scoop it away from you."

I sat in one of the two hardback chairs Wish kept in the store. "You don't like the Establishment much." It didn't come across as a question and that's the way I meant it.

"What's to like? Their profits don't help anyone but themselves. Those fat cats just stuff their pockets."

"By fat cats, you mean guys like Phillip Rothwell?" I watched him closely.

His pupils dilated and the narrow nostrils flared. "That's exactly who I mean. The guy's a predator sucking the blood out of people..." Realizing he may have gone too far, then added, "...well, he's not the only one. There's plenty of 'em out there. I'm just trying to make my own way, make a stand."

"Tilting at windmills, Wish?"

He grinned and the fly-away moustaches shot out from his cheeks like wings. "Yeah, maybe. I get the soapbox out too quickly sometimes. Sorry, about that, Joe. Preaching's finished for the night. The right Reverend Wishbone Jones has retired."

"Sure." A fly lazily buzzed around his face and he swatted at it several times.

"Damn," he said. I took a good look at his right hand. It caught the pale light.

"That's some kind of ring, you got on there." I hadn't really noticed it before.

Wish looked at his hand and grunted. "Oh, that? Yeah, school ring from my deep dark past."

"Mind if I take a look?" He hesitated then quickly shook his head. I got up and went to the counter. Wish held his hand out. A signet ring with an elaborate heraldic design and a Latin script. "What's it say?" I asked.

Wishbone shrugged. "Latin ain't my thing really but it's something like—'Never lost, always found'—something like that anyway."

"Wouldn't take you for a preppie," I said.

He game me an embarrassed grin. "We're not always responsible for where we came from or who we used to be, don't you think, Joe?"

Thinking of my own history, I couldn't help but agree. We said our good-nights then. Wish locked up the store. I continued on home. When I got there, I sketched out what I had seen in as much detail as I remembered. Fortunately, I'd sobered up.

Chapter Twenty-Two

The phone rang. In my current dream, the handle had grown tall as a two-storey building and jangled loud enough to rattle my brain. I couldn't wrap my hands around the receiver and it weighed half a ton. Someone had slipped it one of Alice's growth pills, I guess. But then it started to shrink and the jangling became sharper and more penetrating. I reached over and made it stop.

"Hello?" I croaked.

A female voice thick with crying and booze said, "He just beat me up again."

"Huh?"

Now it came back full of hate. "That bastard. One of these days I'm gonna kill him."

The guy with the razor sharp mind said, "Kill who?"

She kept going, like I wasn't there. Just some convenient ear.

"If it weren't for my baby, I'd do it too. It's just that I don't want him to grow up without a father. I can't stand the thought of him being an orphan. Even if he's rotten through and through," she said.

"Cindy Lou?"

The wailing cut itself off in mid-cry. "Darlene was seeing him too."

"Darlene?"

Now she was all business. The self-pitying ended. "Yeah. That's what I said, ain't it?"

"Who was it?"

"I don't know," she breathed.

"Come on, Cindy Lou."

"I tell you, I don't know, jerk. All I know is, that he's an older guy and some kind of big shot. Darlene and Norma both were protecting him."

"They knew about each other?"

"Yeah, they knew," she snorted. "That's a kick, huh?"

"Why're you telling me this? We didn't exactly finish our last conversation on a fond note."

"Because of Darlene. She liked you though I'm having trouble seeing it. She told me you had a damaged soul." Ouch. Darlene had been more perceptive than I thought. "Besides, all this shit has to stop. Larry's been on the warpath all day. He's riled up about something."

"What?"

"He won't say but it started when I passed on your message about the Meadows."

"What about the Meadows? Did he talk about it? What's going on up there, Cindy Lou?"

"I swear, I don't know. And I don't want to know. But whatever it is, it isn't good. He had that look on his face."

"What sort of look?" I asked.

"The sort of look that makes people sorry they ever tried anything."

"Okay, you're saying something's going to happen up there."

"I'm not saying anything like that. Jesus Christ can't you understand? He'll kill me if he finds out I even talked to you."

" Okay, what about Darlene or Norma? Did they say anything else? Anything at all?"

"Oh shit," she said.

"What?"

"He's coming back." Her voice faded out then back in again. "I gotta go newshound. And another thing, remember to forget I called you. Just forget about it." There was a long pause. I thought she'd gone but perhaps she was watching out the window for the Viking. Her voice came back tense and throaty, choking to get the words out. "One more thing. No cops. You give me away and my son won't have a mama. Something's happening up there and even though he scares me sometimes, I don't want Larry to get hurt."

"You mean the Meadows? Cindy Lou?" She slammed down the phone. I held on to it for a while searching for some answers. Almost as soon as I replaced the receiver, it jangled again.

"Who you talking to so early?"

"What?"

"It's five-thirty and I'm on my way, so get ready," growled Hal Bigelow, perky as a mountain-sized budgie.

I groaned. "Oh God, no. Right, don't your boxers in a twist, I'll be ready."

Hal laughed. "Look. You don't have to do anything fancy. Just haul your ass out of bed, take a shower, get dressed and basically, stay conscious. I'll do the rest. See you soon." And he hung up while I stared at the phone in disbelief. The wires were burning up this morning.

Why was I going fishing? I hate fishing. I don't like fish. You have to get up too early. I can't stand the feel of worms and I was squeamish about baiting hooks. I'd rather sweep up after horses on parade. Then again, maybe while I had the line cast into the free-flowing river and my thoughts quieted, some clarity would appear about all the loony happenings in this little nowhere berg. I wanted to tell him about Cindy Lou and what she'd told me. As for what happened with Darlene and Norma and the goings-on at the Meadows so far, I possessed only Cindy Lou's say so. Though she'd been scared plenty about something.

Six a.m. on the dot found me slumped on the front steps of my landlady's humble abode. I needed caffeine in the worst way. I shivered through my denim jacket feeling the damp. Forlorn rays of sunlight began to squeeze through swirling gaps in the mist. First, I heard the asthmatic engine then saw the lights of Hal's pick-up as it stuttered along Vine Street then turned up the driveway. Hal gave me a big grin, stuck a paw out the window and beckoned. As I climbed in, he slapped the seat and said,

"Boy, am I looking forward to this."

I said, "Me too. Wake me up when we get there. Better yet, wake me up when you're done fishing."

"Joe. I always figured you for a true sportsman."

"Yeah. That's me. Goodnight." I burrowed into the seat.

"Hey, put your seatbelt on. Safety first."

I grumbled. "Stop being such a cop." But complied with his request ramming the buckle into the clip. "Happy now?"

Hal wrenched the gearshift into reverse and backed down the drive laughing. "So, I hear you've been seen around town holding hands with a certain wild-haired young lady."

I sat up and rubbed my eyes. "Okay Bigelow. You got your gun handy? I might just have to use it."

"Aw Joe, don't be so sensitive. I think it's very sweet. A nice boy like you should be dating."

" You can let me out now. I'll walk home." Hal was killing himself with laughter. "Watch the goddam road, willya, Bigelow? Jeez. The last thing I want to do is die on a fishing trip."

The cab felt small and cramped. We'd run out of oxygen so I rolled down the window. Just the illusion of extra space made me breathe a little easier. The heavy air smelled of worms and wet leaves.

"Say, didn't I hear you were up in Brigsby yesterday?"

"Does the whole town have me staked out?"

"Relax Joe. Teddy told me. I ran into him at the old Courthouse. He was covering for you at the inquest, remember?"

"Yeah, okay. I went up to Beech to see Ellis Boston."

"Did you find out anything? I guess you heard that McKie has decided not to lay charges against old Ellis."

"No, I didn't hear that. Well that's as good as a life sentence for him. It'd almost be better if he was brought to trial."

Hal frowned, then fingered a razor nick along the right edge of his jawbone. A jawbone big enough for a steer. "How's that?"

I related the tale of my experiences at Beech, of Dr. Rumplemeyer, what Lawrence revealed without stating his name and the remarkable interview I had with Ellis himself. Hal's brick red face lit up in amazement.

"Boy," he said. "That's some story. I feel sorry for old Ellis, though."

"What about the guard's allegations, Hal?"

"That's all they are, Joe. You need more than that to bust in and stir things up. Remember, you're dealing with a government-run facility here."

"But there's got to be something that can be done."

"Look, I'm just a PC first class with an asshole for a Chief who doesn't know dick about law enforcement, okay? Besides, Brigsby is policed by the province. They're out of my jurisdiction."

"Sorry."

"Sure. Listen, maybe that guard can get you something to back up his story. Like a report or some memos or something. Then you can go to the crown attorney or even the health minister with concrete evidence. But if you rile those guys, be prepared to take a lot of heat. That means Teddy and The Gazette and everybody who works there too. Not to mention us, the cops, and the town."

"I knew it wouldn't be simple."

"Simple?" Hal snorted. "Fishing is simple. Writing a parking ticket is simple. Running drunks into the tank is simple. Well, so much for getting my mind off things. Damn job. Just never leaves go."

"You didn't have to ask me to tag along, you know."

Hal glanced over at me with a sour look. "I was just thinking the same thing."

"Er, speaking of which. You asked me earlier on the phone who I'd been talking to?"

Hal glanced over at me suspiciously. "Yeah?"

So I laid it all out for him, the mystifying chronicle of events, the tenuous connections and suspicions, rolled out in a jangly, caffeine deprived narrative.

"That's quite a story, Simpson. Makes one for the funny pages."

"Ah hell, I knew you wouldn't take me seriously." And I slumped further into the seat.

"Now, hold on. I didn't say you're as crazy as Ellis Boston, did I? Although sometimes I think so. But..." And he raised a forefinger the size of a chili dog before I could protest. "...we need to gather some evidence if any of this is to be believed."

"Okay, how do we do that?"

"I don't know...yet," Hal replied. At least I knew he was on my side. That counted for something.

We lapsed into silence and I stared out the window. The jack pines grew thicker and denser out here crowding the roadway. Rolling hills disappeared into scrub and brush. Steam radiated off the slick tarmac. We passed a broken down one-and-a-half storey farmhouse that fronted a laneway. The roof was crumbling and half-caved in. The windows had been papered over with tin foil. That made it a junkie motel.

Huddled on the rotted, peeling stoop shivered a miserable-looking figure, steadying himself. He stood, eyes closed, barely hanging off the metal railing. It existed as near to a slum dwelling as you'd find in Applewood. The trembling heap took a drag on the cigarette jutting from his pouty lips, spat it out and let the smoke dribble out of his mouth, as if he didn't have the strength to blow. All without lifting his head. So much for the life of the privileged. The leather jacket looked new.

"Pull over a second," I said.

"What?"

"Just pull over."

Hal wrenched the truck to the side of the road with a look of annoyance, the kind you'd see on a Brahma bull when it got riled. He pounded the wheel hard enough to crush the steering column. I opened the door and got out, then started to walk back to junkie heaven. After a moment, Hal got out too, cussing under his breath and trailed behind. If Blake Rothwell heard me come up, he gave no indication. He didn't flinch, didn't blink. Seemed barely alive.

I spoke harshly. "Rothwell." He didn't answer. "Rothwell. Look at me, Rothwell. Over here, man."

Blake lifted his chin just enough to give him a line of sight. He squinted. His voice rasped sounding tired and old. "What for? What do you want?"

"I just want to know how you're doing. How're you feeling this morning."

"Leave me alone." The pompadour slumped a little.

I started forward. A clamp on my shoulder that was attached to Hal Bigelow's arm held me back. "Take it easy, Joe," he said.

Some sort of crazy, irrational hate went to work on me. I tried to ignore it, tried to push it away but no soap.

"Leave me alone. Get outta here," Rothwell said working up to a feeble snarl. But it required a tremendous effort from him. The pretty lips looked bruised and pulpy—like grey worms on a wet sidewalk.

"Or what? Going to tell your daddy on me? Huh?"

"Joe. Knock it off," said Hal. "Can't you see the kid is sick?"

I turned to him. "Sick? Is that what you call it? Hopped up is more like it. Sick. That's a good one."

"Go back to your rag, newshound," panted the kid.

I started up the stairs.

"Why you little punk..." I got exactly two steps. Bigelow had a grip on my belt. He stopped me cold. "Leggo Hal."

"No one's on trial, here, Joe. It's time to move along. Let's get to the fish. Before we're all sorry."

I backed down the steps. Rothwell, in anticipation of my arrival had lifted his head off the rail and looked at me, grey face shining with sweat, eyes eager and unnaturally bright.

"Come on up and get it, newsboy." He brought his hand up showing a flick knife. "I'll cut you up, good. Believe me, it'd be a pleasure."

"Something else you learned at prep school?" I sneered.

"Lose the stick son, or I'll have to take it away from you," said Hal, as he shouldered me out of the way moving up the creaking stairs like a slow surge of the tide. Rothwell got up now on the balls of his feet, drawing himself up to a crouch position, coiled to strike.

"Hiding behind the cops now, Simpson," he hissed. My body stiffened. Hackles went up on the back of my neck.

"Easy Joe. I've got him. There's not going to be a lick of trouble here. No trouble at all", Hal murmured in his mesmerizing way. "Better drop the blade, sonny boy."

"Make me."

Hal sighed in a sad, hound dog way, letting his big frame sag a little, hands the size of a catcher's mitt swinging loosely at his sides. From my angle, I saw the hint of a curl on his upper lip. Rothwell's face beaded with sweat. A dark lock of hair hung low on his forehead. His mouth sloped down and he breathed with a slight whistling through his lips. And then in a sudden motion, he sprang forward arcing the knife in a vicious sweep. Hal's left hand darted up encircling the kid's wrist as he twisted his body sideways and caught him in mid-air, snapping the kid's hand back. Rothwell yowled in sudden pain, the knife clattered down the stairs and landed at my feet. I picked it up. When I looked around, Rothwell was pinned to the railing with his hands twisted behind his back, whimpering now.

"You broke my wrist," he screamed.

I said, "Smooth work."

Hal looked at me sourly. "Just routine, Joe. My job is to protect the public even if that includes you."

"Uh-huh. I expect so. Hope it didn't put a damper on your fishing."

Hal didn't bother to reply. "Do you want to take down this joint?" I asked, gesturing with the knife.

"What for?"

I thought about it. "Suspected operations base for illegal narcotics?"

Hal snorted. "It's my day off." He glanced at the kid, then cuffed him to the rail. Hal turned out the kid's pockets and not surprisingly, found his gear. A syringe, spoon and a baggie containing some white powder. "Now I gotta call it in. I've got no choice," he said sadly.

Rothwell cackled. "Barely enough to charge me with possession. Just a misdemeanour."

I bristled. "So you're a lawyer now?"

The kid just sniggered in response.

Hal radioed for a squad car from his truck and I guess it was no surprise when, after about half an hour, the lean form of Arne Guenther, deputy chief, slid out. Guenther had a still manner and the look of a man hardened by the plow and the sun. He was a man with no sentiment. None at all.

"What you got?" he asked, then spat on the grass.

Hal explained what happened. He showed him the kid's gear. Guenther listened quietly, head cocked slightly at an angle. Guenther hesitated, examined the syringe, spoon and powder, touching it like he may contract some disease, then jammed one of his boot heels in the ground. He turned to me.

"Sounds like you stirred things up, Simpson. Maybe nothing would have happened if you'd kept your nose out of other people's business." His voice dribbled out flat and slightly nasal.

I said, "Maybe so. But while we're spinning yarns in the dust, here's one for you. And it's free. Maybe young Rothwell here was all hopped up when he took out his daddy's boat. You remember. The night Norma Jennings went over the side. Maybe that accounts for the six-hour lapse in time before her disappearance was reported. And maybe that accounts for the lack of alcohol in his blood. Most junkies can't take the two together. They've got no stamina, no tolerance for booze. 'Course that's a lot of thinking and I don't want to do your thinking for you, Guenther. You've filled your quota for today."

The deputy chief set his expression in cement. I could see it harden before me. "Don't like reporters much myself," Guenther said.

"I'll try not to lose any sleep over that," I replied.

Hal nudged me. "Watch it, Joe."

Guenther then smiled with about as much warmth as a wax dummy in a glass case. He was hoping to get me on something. Anything. Jaywalking. Parking ticket. Picking my nose. Anything would do. So maybe, he could bang me around in the line of duty. "As long as we understand each other," he said.

"Oh yeah. We sure do."

Guenther looked at Rothwell for the first time.

"Come on, son. Time to go." Guenther unlocked the cuffs. Did it to piss me off. As Rothwell swaggered down the steps, he sneered.

"I'll be sprung in about ten minutes," he said. Then cackled to himself.

With a firm but detached politeness, Guenther bent along the tight crease of his uniform to help the kid into the back seat of the cruiser, slammed the door and strolled around the front. Tipping his hat, he said," Boys." Got in, gunned the engine and peeled away.

Hal appeared somewhat grumpy. "Thanks for squaring things with my boss," he said.

"Anytime."

Hal paused on the stair. "You know, the Rothwell kid's right. It'll take about ten minutes, if that, to get him sprung. They'll dump him into some treatment program. He'll get probation, anyway, first time."

I shrugged. "I know. 'Course you could charge him with attempted murder or at least, assault with deadly intent."

Hal grinned tightly, then shook his head. "Not a chance. Good thing you got me to risk my career over it, though, isn't it?"

"Don't worry, Hal. I've got some pull in the Mayor's office."

Hal squared his shoulders and set his jaw. "Well, Joe. Just keep it to yourself, will ya? Now. Let's get us some fish before the whole damn day is gone." But he stopped himself before getting into the truck. "What is it with you, anyway? You just couldn't leave well enough alone."

I felt a bit sheepish. "Reporter's curse, I guess."

Some sort of sense of realization suffused Hal's expression. He regarded the ramshackle house then turned his attention on the road. "You knew about this, didn't you?"

"Knew about what?"

"This place here. You knew we'd be passing it by on our way." He took a menacing step toward me with a finger the size of a baton pointed at my chest.

I kicked at the dirt a little. "Might have."

"Don't tell me. You were hoping the Rothwell kid would be here, weren't you? Something else to use against him and his old man, I'll bet."

I shrugged. "Well, you know, rumours. I'd heard this was a hang-out for junkies and you know, last night was the start of the weekend."

"I'm surprised you didn't have Dusty come along so he could snap some photos too."

"Thought about it," I said. "But there wasn't any guarantee we'd actually see anyone here."

Hal spat into the dirt. "Just got lucky I guess. None of this goes in the paper. I'll deny any of it ever happened." He climbed into the truck and slammed the door. And didn't say a word for the next 20 minutes.

We'd been following Highway 26 and just passed the turn-off to Brigsby when Hal eased his foot off the accelerator and peered to the right.

I asked, "What are you doing?" Cops don't always know who they are or what is right. We ordinary citizens take for granted that a uniform, badge and gun gives them some constitutional authority. Or we assume they're right more than wrong. What an idea.

"Looking for the turn-off. It's easy to miss." And just around the next curve in the road, he found it, a rutted gravel track that most would ignore unless they knew, like Hal, that it led to the best fishing in the entire county, again, according to Hal. Maybe even the province. And let's not forget, the universe. Hal wheeled the pick-up around and we started traveling inward.

"Time for a new pair of shocks," I said as we bucked along the trail in our mechanized appaloosa. "Yee-haw! Yip. Yip. Yip. Go get'im buckaroos," I sang.

"I liked it better when you were asleep," Hal groused. "Hmm," he murmured as we continued on, "the water's awfully high around here." And so it was.

To the point of the narrow, grumpy road becoming soggy with silt-laden pools filling the ruts and holes dotting the route. The surrounding bush had settled uncomfortably into a swamp as the earth had begun to disappear under the rising tide. Then Hal slammed hard on the brakes. I slapped the dash with my palms to keep from smacking my forehead against the windshield.

"What the hell?" he cried and we both stared incredulously like a couple of open-mouthed dummies.

"I don't believe it," I exclaimed. We got out of the truck and squished gingerly forward. For there, before our very eyes, weighing a good five pounds, flopped a speckled trout smack in the middle of the road.

"Holy shit!" cried Hal.

"Where'd it come from?" I asked.

Hal shook his head. "I can see the water is high but hell, it's not that high."

"Holy shit!" Hal cried again. "Look at this, Joe."

I looked. "What is it?"

"It's dead."

"What?"

"The fish is dead."

"But how come it's still moving?"

"I don't know. Muscle twitches maybe?"

"Bizarre," I said in wonder.

"Let's put it in the bag," Hal said.

I nodded, thinking hard now. "You can pick it up. I'm not going to touch it."

Hal looked at me. "Sissy."

"You said it."

Hal gingerly picked up the dead, twisting speckled trout, carried it over to the truck and stuffed it into his fishing bag. Then we drove on. The water remained high, parts of the road had submerged and I could see some tree frogs swimming from pool to pool and forest animals, rabbits mainly, stopping to take a drink. The heat had started to climb too. Hal's grating truck motor gusted hot vents of air into the sticky cab. After half an hour of continued bumping, grinding, and lurching, we arrived at our destination, Coca-Cola Falls. I heard the roar of throbbing water before I actually saw it. We parked the truck, took out all the gear and trudged down a narrow trail, crossed a crude wooden bridge that looked as if it might hold the weight of a starved alley cat. Just beyond a huge boulder lay the Falls itself. It took its namesake from dark water, black almost and churned up bubbles and foam so thick it looked like it came out of a soda fountain. The darkness of it gave me a chill. The thought of drinking from it, made me choke. The Falls cascaded in smoky sheets over a 30-foot drop where the water crashed onto the jagged rock outcrop below. Let's just say, it wasn't the ideal spot for recreational swimming or boating. Suicide maybe. Or drowning.

Sport fishermen might have preferred the swift flowing stream up above the Falls itself, dragging their hip waders out into the water to cast a fly and fight for balance. But the best fishing lay in a series of calm pools downstream a couple of hundred feet away. That's where the fish hunkered in groups and the current flattened out, making it relatively peaceful too. After a while, you started to think the roaring of the water actually belonged between your ears if you stayed too close. Hal had brought two pairs of hip waders but you didn't need them farther downstream where the current picked up because a three-sided granite rock face slowed the water right down. It climbed over the river's edge like a manmade wall. Besides, Hal's waders came up over my head. All you had to do was drop your line straight down about eight or ten feet and wait for them to bite.

Hal got me set up with a rod and since I was there I decided it was foolish not to indulge.

"Boy am I looking forward to this," he said again, full of glee. A big overgrown kid on a camping trip. But you had to know something weird was going to happen. We weren't disappointed. We stepped to the edge of the rock face and Hal took a deep breath staring out over the river at the fast flowing current and admired the scene. He sucked the clean air into his huge lungs and reaching out a hand felt the fine spray on his fingers. At that moment, the clouds parted and a bar of sunlight struck the water with force, lightening what was dark to a tenuous pale green. Like a glowing, phosphorescent marker, I followed the path of light down. Uh-oh.

"Hal. You better look at this," I said and pointed.

The contented smile on Hal's broad face froze as he followed the line of my forefinger. "Good Christ!" he cried. And jerked his line right out of the water.

It was either a fisherman's nightmare or fantasy. We stared slack-jawed at the sight. And what a sight. Masses of fish rolled and undulated, moving in a lethargic dance, about as energetic as Seniors night at Grossingers. I saw smallmouth and largemouth bass, carp, pickerel, speckled and rainbow trout too. It looked like the beginnings of a Baptist, fundamentalist revival meeting before the fever takes when everyone is just hot and sweaty under the canvas tent. Of course, this was fish we were talking about here not Baptists. Swooning from the heat of movement and the closeness of their bodies. It was enough to make even a catfish claustrophobic.

"What are they doing?" I asked myself more than anything. But Hal felt obliged to answer.

"I don't know."

The water teemed with the numbers of them. Packed so tightly you could just reach down and pluck them from the surface. It would have been child's play. A three-year old could catch his quota in about 90 seconds.

Hal looked worried. " I hope nobody else sees this, " he said.

"Why?"

"Because every yahoo and his mother will come up here and haul them out with a net. Forget about quotas. They'll take all the fish they can carry and then some. You can just guess what that'll do to sport fishing around here. It'll kill the stocks for sure."

"I wonder what's causing this?"

"Damned if I know. Sun spots or moon tides, maybe?" said Hal scratching at his scalp under the bill of his cap. "God damned if I know," he repeated shaking his head.

Since the challenge had fled, Hal felt too disgusted to fish and so we sat, drinking coffee, eating our sandwiches—tuna in honour of the occasion—and stared at water that took on a light and colour and movement of its own as the ranks of the lazy, discombobulated fish continued to swell like some piscatorial army on the move.

"Wish I'd brought my camera," I said wistfully.

By noon, we'd both had enough and drove back to town deep in our own thoughts. The dead fish in Hal's bag had finally ceased its jumping. What we'd seen didn't strike me as some natural phenomenon. I was convinced it was manmade. I asked Hal to let me off in town outside the local library. He didn't seem surprised just disappointed in the outcome of the day. And waved feebly as I slid out of the cab. Something twigged in the recesses of my memory and I went to leaf through the card catalogue in the medical science stack of the library. The usual mothers and kids prowled the shelves looking for happy tales to read. The section I wanted lay deserted. I found the reading material I'd looked up and settled down to some light entertainment.

* * *

Later that day, I walked into Doc Seaton's office, saying, " I've got something special for you." He sat at his desk filling out some complicated forms, looked up surprised but had the presence of mind to ask, "What's that, Joe?"

I plunked the brown paper-wrapped carcass on his desk. Doc froze for a moment, alarm spreading across his soft face. "What's going on?" he asked.

"It's a present for you. Go ahead and open it."

With a surgeon's precision, Doc unwrapped each layer of paper as if he were peeling skin. His face lit up in delight as he saw the handsome fish.

"Why Joe! You didn't have to do this. What a lovely surprise. This one's a beaut."

I hated to spoil it for him. "Uh, Doc. I don't want you to eat it. I want you to perform an autopsy on it."

"What? An autopsy on a fish?"

"That's right."

"But Joe, I, uh…"

I held up my hand. "It's very important Doc. I can't emphasize that enough." Doc removed his spectacles, rubbed the lenses shiny with a flap of his lab coat, put them back on his face, then sighed.

"All right, Joe. But it'll be the first fish autopsy I've ever done."

I grinned. "Think of it this way, Doc. It'll round out your career."

Since I had extra time on my hands, and layers upon layers of thoughts to peel off, I dropped by The Gazette offices. The Saturday edition had already come out and Monday was traditionally a slow news day since the world took a deserved break on Sunday, and would be put together tomorrow morning. Usually, we held back a few columns just in case something monumental broke. About fifty percent of the paper's content came from wire services; Canadian Press, UPI, Reuters, AP etc. and the rest of the space was filled by news and local advertising.

Teddy sat in his office, his little legs stretched out onto his desk, chewing on the cold stogey running his thumbs up and down his suspenders. Engrossed so deep in thought I don't think he heard me come in. Not until the door banged behind me did he look up. He motioned me over. His appearance surprised me—not in a good way, hair uncombed, face rough and red-rimmed eyes from lack of sleep, not to mention, bags large enough to pack a family of five inside.

"How was the fishing, Joe?" he asked quietly.

"Teddy. You look terrible. What's wrong?"

He nodded, massaging his temples. "First, tell me about the fishing."

"Well, Teddy, it was the strangest thing I've ever seen. Stranger even, than finding Ellis Boston on that pole. Stranger than the disturbed mob out in the square yesterday. Did you see them? A bunch of holy rollers led by Mr. Personality himself, Evan Beatty, preaching the end of the world, speaking in tongues and all that nonsense?"

"I did," Teddy replied. "I wrote it up for today's edition." And he gave me a quizzical look.

"Oh yeah," I said. I related the morning's bizarre events in sequence. "Anyway, we finally left around noon. I took the dead fish over to Doc Seaton for an autopsy."

"An autopsy on a fish? Now Joe. Maybe you've been working a little too hard lately."

"I don't blame you for thinking it but I've got a hunch, Teddy. Anyway, that's my story. What's yours? What's on your mind? I hope the editorial I wrote didn't cause you to lose any sleep."

Teddy shook his head, waving his hand in front of his face, coughing as if the cigar was lit. I saw the sallow pallor of his skin and the bitter look in his eyes as if he and I both realized, he was slowing down. The fire within him, that burned so bright these many years, had begun to lose its heat and turn to ashes.

"No Joe, it's not that. In fact, I think that piece is a pretty good piece of writing, not that I'd publish it, of course. You know we can't caterwaul like that. We go after news not speculation. I've been telling you every day for the past three years, haven't I? But you're just too damned stubborn to listen. Why can't you listen? Why?"

"Now look, Teddy, it's time for us..." but then I stopped, the heat I'd felt seeped away. Something was wrong. "What's going on?"

Teddy leveled me with a dead-on gaze, bringing those bushy eyebrows together in a grey clump and forming a deep furrow that ran the length of the bridge of his nose. "Someone's taking a run at us, Joe. They're trying to buy The Gazette."

I felt the need to sit down suddenly as the news hit me like a bludgeon and finally it all seemed to make some kind of sense. I said, "You have no idea?"

"All I know is it's a numbered company."

I shook my head slowly, to focus my thoughts and let the information sink in. "Those bastards. Those bastards. Don't you see, Teddy? It's coming into view now. Thompkins coming up from Toronto. The lavish dinner at the O'Toole's last night, talking up the development project down at the waterfront, influencing the merchants association, they must be behind it, Teddy. Who else is there?"

"You mean Rothwell and O'Toole?"

"Of course. Who else would benefit from favourable, local press coverage talking up the virtues of resort living? Can they really take over?"

Teddy nodded his tired head, eyes drooping, mouth slack from worry and fatigue. "That's why I was up all night. I was calling the other shareholders to see if they'd been approached yet or worse, to see if they'd sold out."

"How did you hear about it?"

"Angus McGee called me up. Said a lawyer acting on behalf of a client wanted to know if he'd be willing to sell his shares. Angus turned him down flat. Since then, I've discovered that two others have already sold theirs. They were paid an unbelievable price too, three, four times more than they're worth. Whoever it is now has thirty percent. And if they acquire fifty percent, according to the share agreement, they take effective control of the paper. So, at fifty percent, it's pretty much a stalemate situation. You see, ordinarily, shares couldn't be sold without the approval of the other shareholders but there was a small clause hidden away somewhere that rescinded that requirement once a shareholder reached the age of fifty. Now that agreement was drawn up about 30 years ago. And I'm the only shareholder under that age but just. I'm 49, so all the others can sell if they want to."

"How many shareholders are there?" I asked.

"Ten. The paper's made money from day one. We're audited every year. It hasn't been a fortune but it hasn't left anyone destitute, either. And we should improve on that pretty well this year too."

I thought for a moment, my mind racing, thinking how good life had been lately. In a way, The Gazette represented Applewood as it should be before all the eruptions took place. And it had to stay that way if it was going to continue to represent the community.

"We've got to get the other shareholders together and rally them around the cause, Teddy. Make sure no one else crumbles or gets greedy. Say. Why don't you make anyone thinking of selling a counter offer?"

"I thought of that but the bid is so high now I just can't match it, Joe. The bank would lend me some of the money but I'd probably have to use all my savings and sell my house too, just to come up with the cash."

I nodded glumly. "Well. Who do you think you can count on then?"

Teddy rubbed his grizzled chin. "Angus is solid. I'm pretty sure I can count on Frank Scopes, George Parkinson and Delaney Truscott. That's seven of the ten, eight including me. The other two are Felicia Burghardt and Alec Alameda. Felicia is a shrewd businesswoman and Alec, you know, is 93 and in a nursing home. His only heir is a grandson, Ricardo and I have no idea which way he may go."

"Well, why don't the rest of you get together and buy Alec out first?"

"We'll have to move awfully fast."

"Listen, Teddy. Organize a meeting for tonight. I'll give you a hand. Anything I can do to help, I will. You know this old rag means a lot to me."

The old Teddy of yore started to re-emerge. He set his lips into a straight line, jaws tight, eyes narrowed and alive.

"All right, Joe. We'll give 'em a fight. We'll make it so hard, they'll have to pay a million bucks before we'll crack."

I laughed with glee. "You said it. We'll fight 'em like they've never seen."

Chapter Twenty-Three

And that's how Beverly and I spent our first Saturday night together, organizing a shareholder's meeting at Shady Acres rest home where Alec Alameda lay confined to his bed. I felt some pangs of guilt doing this. It had only been a few days since Darlene had disappeared and I hadn't given her much thought. She deserved better. Her parents organized a memorial service called for in a few days time.

We had to bend the rules a little bit since residents are allowed only two visitors at a time. Crammed into the close space— myself, Bev, Delaney Truscott in his tuxedo, Frank Scopes, George Parkinson, Ricardo and Alec Alameda and Teddy—eight of us.

Alec Alameda lay in bed breathing heavily, labouring as if each draught of air might be his last. He'd shrunk to a reed and his swarthy skin had turned yellow. But his dark eyes burned brightly showing the world that an alert intelligence lay within the captive, desiccated frame. His grandson, Ricardo, sat at his bedside. Alec had built a tractor repair business into one of the largest farm equipment dealerships in the county. Ricardo ran it now and the neighborhood whispering said the fields weren't as fertile and more money poured out of the silo than came in. Teddy knew that Alec's shares were pledged to Ricardo, his only living male heir.

The small, stuffy room smelled of medicines and liniments and hardened cafeteria food. Beverly nudged me, then I felt her lips on my ear.

"This is a great idea for a date, Joe," she whispered. "I've never spent a Saturday night in a rest home before."

I whispered. "I thought you'd enjoy the atmosphere."

"It's very romantic," she whispered.

Teddy cleared his throat and moved through the compacted throng to Alec's bedside, and stood, facing out, so he could look everyone present straight on. "You all know why we're here. Someone is trying to take over The Gazette and we're the remaining shareholders. I was told this evening that Felicia Burghardt sold out raising their stake to forty percent. All they need is one more block and the paper is technically theirs, whoever they are."

"Any ideas on that," Delaney Truscott asked in a quiet, almost sinister way.

"Nothing conclusive but we've got our suspicions. Right Joe?"

"That's right," I said. "The purchased shares were issued to a numbered company. But it's pretty clear who would benefit from owning The Gazette for use as a propaganda mouthpiece to serve their own interests."

"Spell it out for us," said George Parkinson, a short, wiry man with a shock of white hair standing straight up from his scalp. He had the leathery look of a dedicated lawn bowler.

"Well," I replied, hesitantly. "It could be one of two parties, really. We suspect that the developers in town, RSC Developments, that is Rothwell, O'Toole and Red O'Brien are likely candidates. The other possibility is the Toronto Herald-Dispatch. Phillip Rothwell sits on the board of directors of the Herald-Dispatch too and its holding company, Crown Communications."

"How much are they offering?" asked Frank Scopes, in a loud, grating voice. He held out a transistor radio-like device—his hearing aid. Frank perpetually shoved it at people to better pick up what they were saying. Teddy looked distinctly uncomfortable now. He didn't want to answer Frank's question. He hemmed and hawed a little.

"Well… uh…they started off with $25,000 but Felicia drove a pretty hard bargain and pushed them up to $35,000 for each block of shares," Teddy said.

Delaney let out a low whistle. "That's a lot of jack."

"It sure is,"agreed Teddy. "A lot of jack. But fellows, I'm asking you to stand firm on this one. We all could use the money, no question about that. But as you also know, a lot's been happening in Applewood lately. There's been rapid growth, an influx of new people, new buildings and developments. The town's fast becoming a year-round resort and that's good news for all the merchants. But I ask you, do we want a group with vested interests controlling the only free and independent voice we've got? That's the issue here. Say a man dies in a construction related accident and there's an investigation. Do we cover it fair and square or will it be soft sold because the company happens to own the paper? Suppose we elect a Mayor who favours the developers? When that man falls flat on his face or makes a gaffe, we should report it as it plays, out in the open for citizens to hear about and make their own minds up concerning the person, not hand them spoon-fed pap because it serves another purpose. That's the type of thing I'm talking about here. It transcends the whole issue of money."

Ricardo resembled his grandfather but on a larger, more corpulent scale and his dark eyes and skin flushed with anger. Vinegar hung in the air.

"You gonna have a big fight, Teddy. A lot of the merchants would side with the other guys, you know. They bring in business and jobs for them. You could lose some of your advertising and then what good is this paper, huh?"

Teddy nodded curtly but I could see him grow angry as purple clouds gathered in his expression, knotting his face in repressed fury. Before he could spontaneously combust, I jumped in.

"Look Ricardo. A paper is more than just advertising. Sure, you need advertising to survive, no question. Everyone does. And I think we'll work very hard to keep them with The Gazette. But Teddy's right when he asks who should control the main source of information in this town? That's the issue here."

"Besides," Teddy interjected, "The Gazette has contributed a handsome profit to the shareholders over the past 30 years and that's not going to change. And you can take that to the bank."

"All the same, Teddy. A war could hurt everyone's business," screeched Frank. "And if they paid Felicia $35,000, who knows, for a controlling interest they might go up to $50,000? That's serious retirement money. And none of us here, you included, are exactly bare-chested Tarzans now, are we?"

Bev whispered, "Thank God for that."

"True enough, Frank," Teddy conceded. "I can't argue about the money. I can only ask you to side with me and keep your shares. Think about this: If the shares are worth this much now, what will their value be in five years or ten? That's a beautiful legacy for your families, your grandchildren."

"Ah, phooey on them," piped Frank. "I want to enjoy myself now. They've got their whole lives ahead of 'em. I've helped them out plenty."

"That's right," said Ricardo. "I could use the dough now. I don't want to wait five or ten years. My family's still growing."

"But the shares aren't yours, kiddo," Delaney said through his teeth. "They belong to Alec."

Ricardo pointed a finger. "Stay out of my business. It is between my family, okay? Don't stick your nose in, Delaney."

"I will when it affects the rest of us, Ricardo. You can bet on that."

"Oh, this is very nice," Ricardo said, rising and holding his hands pugnaciously. "You wish to start this in front of my grandfather while he lies ill in bed? Come on then, we will go outside and see who is right. Come on."

"That'd be swell," Delaney replied and actually looked happy, as if he were doing something useful, something he enjoyed for a change. And he shot his cuffs to show how swell it was. Before either man could make a prominent move, however, a stream of Italian invective poured out from the sick bed. Alec worked his mouth grotesquely, speaking in harsh, guttural tones. Ricardo dropped his hands helplessly to his sides, hung his head down in what appeared to be genuine shame and obediently sat down in his seat not looking up.

Alec licked his lips, then sipped from a glass of water on the night table next to his head. He spoke slowly and with great effort to be heard.

"You must forgive my grandson," he said hoarsely. "He is only 51 and still young and foolish. The same as his father, God rest his soul. Our family is known for its temper." He paused to draw strength. "I haven't got much time left and I must think about what I want to do. I must provide for my family. Ricardo is my only heir and there is no question he will receive the shares after I'm gone. But Ricardo doesn't always use his head, eh Ricardo? The shares have been a good investment. I've made my money back like all of you, many times. And I believe that Teddy is right. And maybe it is time to give back a little? People are moving in here who don't care about things like we do. People who don't have their roots here. I came to this place as a young man from Sicily in 1897. This is my home. I don't like what I see happening around me and think maybe it's a good time to die. I've seen many things. Cars. Airplanes. Wars. And now they're talking about putting a man on the moon. A man in the moon! That's more in one lifetime than I could have ever hoped to see. Let me think, I ask you, to let me think about what I must do. And I will let you know. Right now, I'm tired. You phone me later, Teddy, tomorrow maybe. I will tell you, okay? And now I must rest. I say goodnight to you and god bless."

Teddy said, "Thank you, Alec. I'm sorry we put you to all this trouble." The old man spread his hands in supplication and smiled angelically. The rest of us began shuffling out and my last memory of Alec was that of a wizened Jesus, absolving us of sin, melting slowly into his bedclothes. Ricardo remained behind with his grandfather, bent in prayer.

Beverly looked as if she were on the verge of tears.

"You okay?" I asked. She nodded without answering but swiped at her eyes quickly. We crept along the corridor. The lights had been dimmed and the infirm residents slept their restless sleep, the stillness broken by sighs, moans and pitiful cries of anguish raging over lost youth. I looked over at Teddy. His brow furrowed, his short body hunched as he trudged along in the dim flute of light cast by a single, weak bulb stationed like a lighthouse beacon over the entranceway.

Outside, we all shook hands in solemn procession. I said to Teddy. "Try to relax. Don't worry about things. Alec is on our side."

He ran a hand through his matted hair. "You could be right, Joe. You could be. I hope so. Anyway, I'll see you later. Nice to meet you, Beverly." And he swung his stocky body into one of the 19 cars he's owned, turned the ignition wearily and drove carefully off, holding the wheel rigidly as if it might suddenly leap out of his hands.

The others simply melted away into their cars and trucks and the rattle of sudden engines shattered the clear night's quiet atmosphere. Even the crickets and frogs and grasshoppers were momentarily startled ceasing their shrill cries. None of us were to know that Alec Alameda would die peacefully in his sleep later that night.

Only Delaney Truscott remained, leaning up against the clean side of my car, smiling thoughtfully, looking as if he belonged somewhere else. He looked up sharply as Beverly and I approached.

"Some meeting," he said.

I replied, " Sure was. If it were up to Ricardo, those shares would be history right now."

Delaney nodded. "You said, it Joe. Things are changing around here. Applewood used to be a nice quiet little place and now the smell of money is everywhere. It makes people do strange things. Makes them act in ways they never thought they could."

"I know what you mean," I said. Beverly hovered behind me like an embarrassed but excited bobby soxer waiting to meet her teen idol. For some reason, Delaney fascinated her. "I'm sorry, Delaney, I don't think I introduced you to Beverly."

Delaney delivered his Hollywood smile and took her hand. "How do you do, kid?"

"Hi," was the best she could do.

Delaney then reached into the side pocket of his tuxedo jacket and pulled out a silver flask. He offered it first.

"Care for some Napoleon brandy? It's the absolute finest," he said. Beverly shook her head but I took hold of the flask if only to feel it in my hands, the weight and workmanship were sleek. I placed it to my lips and felt the amber liquid glide smoothly into my gullet where it ignited a warm fire.

"Damn fine brandy, Delaney," I wheezed handing back the flask.

He inclined his head slightly in acknowledgement, then put the flask to his lips and tipped it back steeply holding it there for what seemed a long time.

"Mickey and me are thinking of packing it in, Joe. Moving out."

"What? But why? You're doing so well. Your business has never been better."

"Exactly. For the first time in a long time, we've got money in the bank. Enough to retire in style. As a matter of fact, we've bought a little cottage on Cap Ferrat."

"Cap Ferrat? You'd be bored there, Delaney. Besides, if you think you've seen rampant commercialism here, wait 'til you get there. All the Palm Beach phonies have adopted it."

"Maybe," Delaney conceded. "But it's what Mickey wants. She wants to take our stake and get out. We've had an extremely generous offer for The Round Table, more than generous."

"From Rothwell?"

Delaney flicked some ash at his polished feet. "Yup."

"You know the place will change. It won't be the same. Not even sitting in the bar will feel the same."

"It's not for me, Joe. It never has been. People like me don't seem to have a place in the world anymore. Years ago, when I was bootlegging, it was different. That was a time when it felt like I fit into things. Not now. Mickey doesn't know it but I kept a stash from the old days."

Beverly's eyes widened. "You mean loot?" she asked.

Delaney laughed and held up his flask to the light where it shone.

"Something better. One hundred year old brandy and there's enough of it to fill every snifter in North America. That stuff is worth more than the restaurant.

Let's just say it was a very long term investment I made and it's about to pay off very handsomely."

I was skeptical. "And Mickey never knew?"

Delaney nodded and said, "She never knew. I didn't want to touch it and believe me there were times I was tempted, kid. But I also figured that it was my ticket when the time was right. And now it is. So, so long Applewood." And he took another drink.

"I'll be sorry to see you go, Delaney. You and Mickey brought a little class to this place."

"Ah, the town'll survive. It's got too much going for it. I'm sure Applewood'll come out okay. But there's a dark mood in this little berg right now, Joe. I've seen it before…when you're on the edge of something new…it's exciting and sickening at the same time. I prefer the old days. You knew where you stood. A guy'd stick a rod in your kisser but at least it was all square. Now, who the hell knows? Who the hell knows anymore?" Then he smirked and ground the cigarette out under the heel of his polished loafer. "Well, it's late and I've got to do my dummy routine in the morning," he said with a trace of bitterness that I could taste right through the brandy. Then he turned and walked to his car.

Delaney moved beyond the perimeter of light and disappeared into the shadows. He got into his little red XKE, kicked the powerful engine to life and tore out of the parking lot, squealing his tires like a reckless dragster. I heard his laughter over the roar of the engine fade into the night.

Beverly spoke with a touch of awe in her voice, "What an elegant and charming man."

"You're probably in love with him. Every woman over the age of six falls in love with Delaney Truscott, eventually," I said. "He's dangerous. Women feel it and get excited. You think that maybe he's capable of anything, good and bad."

Beverly gushed.

"And he walked off into the night beautifully dressed in his tuxedo, flicked the glowing cigarette end into the gutter, hopped into his red sports car and drove out of their lives forever. Now, that's romantic."

Beverly continued to surprise me.

"You're right, Bev. I'm beginning to think you're always right. Say. Speaking of driving?" And I held up my keys. "Feel like doing the honours? All of a sudden I'm feeling a little drained."

Bev took the keys from my hand. "Let's go", she said.

No sooner had I slumped back in the seat my head hitting the support, than I disappeared into muted oblivion. Images of jumping fish, falling water, silver flasks, gold lighters and frightening tattoos swam around in my head like a school of stoned trout. I let Beverly keep the car so she could get home. I barely made it in the door. And like the very old and kindly Alec Alameda, I slept the tranquil sleep of the dead.

Chapter Twenty-Four

When I awoke the next morning it felt as if the night before hadn't happened. After my father was killed and my mother went to prison, I never really had my own place. I hadn't parked anywhere until now. Suddenly, I felt like a bona fide citizen rather than a guest waiting for his visa to expire. I lay prostrate in bed this Sunday morning, sounds of the new day crept into the room.

I shuffled into The Gazette about ten a.m. to prepare Monday's edition but to take a fresh look at the thing causing all the fuss—something that pitted decent citizens against each other.

As I drove in, I noticed that each day the presence of the Jersey Jokers became more visible. Peace symbols began appearing all over town; spray-painted on blank walls and the tarmac of public parking spots. Someone had festooned Chief McKie's personal patrol car with a fascinating nature scene; a layer of sod had been stuck to the roof with a variety of shrubs and shrubbery growing out of it and a bevy of plastic pigs blissfully grazed on this prefab, mobile pastureland. Wishbone Jones started running a very active T-shirt business out the back of his record store and what he called his "tie-dyed" designs sold like hotcakes all over town. In fact, kids from neighbouring towns came in just to scoop some up. At five bucks each, Wish again illustrated his business flair.

Balloons wavered from every lamppost and fence railing. An increasing number of young children showed up on the streets with their faces painted in clown colours. But then there were the more serious incidents too. After Rothwell had lit into Hal that day, a tool shed on the RSC resort site caught fire late one night. The fire didn't spread and the fire department contained it easily. No one got hurt. The gearbox of two of RSC's earth-moving machines had been stripped rendering the lumbering vehicles virtually inoperable. Wishbone

Jones joined the merchants association, just to add his solo voice to the chorus of business babble, I supposed.

Surveying this modest paper kingdom turned out to be a sobering experience, I must say. I sat on my chair whose springs rusted out long ago and swiveled this way and that peering intently. The premises looked dowdy and cramped. A few desks, some old typewriters and a mildew-infested library in the back summed up most of it. We had no typesetter as yet, second hand photographic equipment purchased from a camera buff who wanted to sell his used stuff cheap. Apart from salaries, the single greatest expense comprised subscriptions to wire services. A retired librarian, Wilma Jenkins, came in one day a week to shuffle the archives about and wrestle them into some kind of ragged order. She complained bitterly about the lack of space and proper means for storage.

I continued to swivel for quite some time feeling a little like Lear surveying the crumbling landscape when I was startled by a jauntily whistled tune. Out strode Dusty Rhodes from the darkroom, a cig behind each ear, examining a soggy photo newly plucked from the bath. He stopped dead in his tracks then grinned boyishly when he realized it was me.

"Hello, Joe. Didn't hear you come in," he said.

"What're you up to, Dusty?"

Pulling one of the cigarettes from behind his ear and sticking it between his lips, he sauntered over and leaned toward me in a conspiratorial manner.

"Glad it's you and not Teddy, Joe. I was just developing some shots for my portfolio. You know, I'm doing some night photography, nature stuff. Anyhow, up at Buttermilk Creek, there's a deer run, see, and I set up a trip wire, just to see what I'd get, you know? For fun."

"So. What'd you get?"

He grinned.

"A doe and a fawn stopping to nibble the grass by the riverbank." Dusty went to a cabinet and pulled out a glass sheet. He laid the photo on top of it, then brought it back for me to look at. At first, it seemed like just an ordinary shot. There'd been a bright moon and its light infused the general grayness of the scene with what I'd imagined was a bluish tint. It was nature; trees, river, branches but no animals to speak of. The detail was good, sharper than I'd expected.

"What kind of camera are you using, Dusty?"

"A four by five view…that's why the static stuff looks so sharp. But if anything is moving too fast, then it'll come out blurry. It's great for blow-ups, though. I'd love to do moon shots with this baby but I'd need a different set of lenses, which we ain't got."

I took another look. The river flowed longitudinally up the centre of the shot and in the foreground, you could see the texture of the stones in the water where it was lit. I followed the trail of water upward carefully like I would an arrow on a road map and that's when I saw the two deer. "Nice. Really sharp images. I like the way they're in silhouette against the moonlight."

"Very good, Joe. Good eye for detail."

As I looked at the photograph, an idea began to form. Sometimes I actually had a few.

I said, "Dusty, I need a favour."

He nodded, flicked some ash, took another drag, then replied, "Sure Joe. You don't have to ask. What's it to be?"

"Ever done any night shooting up at the Meadows?"

Dusty thought with an air of studied concentration, actually furrowing his smooth brow. "Can't say I have."

"You took this deer shot using a flash, didn't you?"

Dusty picked up the photo and held it to the light. "Sure I did."

"Is there anyway to take some night shots without using a flash?"

Dusty rubbed his chin. One or two hairs had sprouted. "Sure there is."

"How?"

"Well, there's new film on the market and you can really push the exposure in lower light. It helps if you've got a bright moon like in this shot here."

"What about the camera?"

Dusty grinned. "You're right. Can't use the four by five but as it happens I've just picked up a nifty 35 millimeter. Took me over six months to save up for it and I'm dying to try it out."

"Doing anything tonight, Dusty, say around midnight?"

He shrugged. "Can't say that I am."

"Then we've got a date. I'll pick you up around 11:30."

"Sure. Be there or be square."

"One more thing." Dusty looked at me expectantly. I took the crumpled piece of paper out of my pocket. "It's not a very good drawing but do you think you could find out where this came from?"

Dusty examined the drawing. "Sure, shouldn't be too hard. I used to have one of these myself. This is a fancy one though, Joe."

"Thanks."

Dusty gave me a funny look, then shrugged. "No problem." He then picked up the photograph and sauntered back to the darkroom. He dropped the cigarette, mashing it into the floor with the toe of his shoe. I winced a little whereas before, I wouldn't even have noticed. We'd have to introduce a strict policy around here enforcing the use of ashtrays.

Teddy dragged himself in looking more fatigued, more haggard and slumped over than ever. His fierce eyes were shot through with despair and he'd worn a crevice into his forehead. But he was shaved and neatly put together at least. His voice sounded grave.

"Better come into my office, Joe," he intoned, as he dragged by me, unleashing the spirit of doom about him as he set down his things and slumped into his seat.

"What is it, Teddy? You make the grim reaper look like Cary Grant."

In response, Teddy pounded his fist into the desk hard enough to make me wince for him.

"We're finished, Joe. Alec Alameda died in his sleep last night. Apparently, he made no provision in his will about the sale of his shares. They passed automatically to Ricardo."

"Don't tell me. Ricardo's sold out already."

Teddy nodded. "The buyer now holds fifty percent, so we're stalemated. That's it. We're done. Finished."

"I wouldn't say that, Teddy."

"Ah, Joe, it's no use," Teddy replied in a weary voice. "Maybe it's time to pack it in. Maybe it's time I retired."

I said, "You've still got fifty percent. Don't die on me now, Teddy. We need you in this. You give up on it and everybody else will too. And what about the readers in this town then? Aren't we fighting for them, really?"

Teddy nodded but I could see something flickering behind the bloodshot eyes—maybe just mad hope. But whatever it was, any energy brought to this fracas was welcome. Then, Teddy's eyes began to spin in their deep sockets and his face came more than halfway back to life. His voice took on a bit of froth.

"Well, Joe. I guess we'll just have to see what we see." He started to move about the room now, working his shoulders, flexing and feinting like a boxer coming off the ropes, trying to work some life's blood back into limbs that were bone-tired. Because of his short but wide stature, Teddy reminded me of a body puncher snapping crisp shots that drained the life out of you, took the bounce out of your knees. Perhaps it was time for a comeback at that. I left him in his office doing the shadow dance.

I put in a call to Doc Seaton at home figuring he'd be out dissecting plants in his garden by now. Nonetheless, Doc's wife answered in her no-nonsense voice.

"Hi Mrs. Seaton. It's Joe Simpson. Is Doc around?"

"Hello Joe. Now what do you want to bother him on a Sunday for? This is the first Sunday in weeks he hasn't been working."

"I know and I apologize. I just have to ask him one question. It won't take long, I promise."

"Well don't make a liar out of yourself, Joe Simpson. Just a minute and I'll get him."

I could see why Doc spent so much time at work.

"Thank you," I replied as sincerely as I could. But I guess Doc was lucky to have someone like Martha running interference for him. Not a few people in town have received a tongue lashing from her and it was an experience not quickly forgotten. After a moment or two, Doc picked up the receiver.

"Hello Joe. Martha tells me you can have exactly one minute of my time."

"Sorry to bug you Doc. But I wanted to know about the fish."

"Well, it was a beauty, Joe. But I guess you're interested in what I found out. The first autopsy I ever performed on a trout apart from cooking one up on the barbecue and filleting the bones, I mean."

"So you said, Doc," I replied dryly.

"So I did," he chuckled. "Well Joe. You've got good instincts, I must say."

"Then I was right about the chemical?"

"On the money," Doc breathed. "On the money," repeated. "Say, you don't handicap horses, do you Joe? You could make a lot of scratch if you did."

"Not yet, Doc. But then, if I do, you'll be my first customer."

"You're going to have to talk to McKie whether you like it or not, Joe. Or I will for you."

"Ah, it's hard enough to talk to the Chief at the best of times but when he's driving around in a car that looks like the twelfth hole of the Willowdale Golf and Country Club, it's much harder. Not to mention those hideous moose antlers stuck on the hood."

"I know. But still, it's a matter for the law now. And whether we like it or not, McKie's the law in this town."

"Okay, Doc. Point taken. Well, I guess I'll talk to you later. Enjoy the rest of your Sunday."

"Thanks for calling, Joe. Oh by the way, I'll be getting the lab report from Toronto sometime tomorrow. Didn't take as long as they thought."

I paused for a moment letting the significance of his words sink in. "That'll be very interesting, Doc. Very interesting indeed."

"It will, won't it? Talk to you later, Joe."

"Bye Doc. And we both hung up. Doc was eager to get back to his garden while I remained still, pausing to reflect on what was yet to come. I came to when I heard the buzzing of the disconnected line coming through the receiver. I hadn't replaced it properly on its stand.

Darlene and Norma were seeing the same guy, someone older, Cindy Lou had said. If it turned out that Rothwell had been Norma's lover then I wanted to find out more about him, to understand who he was and how he made his money. Did the odor of power and influence make him feel like he was invincible? He wouldn't have been the first tycoon to diddle around behind his wife's back. Or to find himself in the middle of a scandal either. Would Rothwell use his own son, a junkie and a weakling, to help him get rid of such a problem? Is that how Norma ended up at the bottom of Rattlesnake Bay? Stay tuned. And what about Seamus O'Toole? But then I looked at the two wives. Roberta Rothwell—tortured and long-suffering. Paisley—cool and calm. Paisley acted like an equal in her marriage. She was vibrant and mouth wateringly attractive. A man would have to be a fool to two-time her, in my opinion. Seamus didn't strike me as a fool. I puzzled over these thoughts as I headed into the backroom dungeon.

The archives, where we kept stacks of clippings from days gone by exuded the sour, stale odour of decaying paper, the air thick with dust and the paper files greasy with mildew. It reminded me of a hothouse in a thunderstorm. At least the clippings had been reasonably well-ordered, catalogued by year and broken down by month. I guessed at the year I wanted—1949, but not the month. Since many publications were clipped as a matter of course, each month's load held a sheaf of paper thick as a rhino's buttock. What was I looking for? Anything to do with Rothwell. He'd had such a high profile career the clippings had been abundant. I wasn't disappointed. But still, I didn't find exactly what I needed, something about his personal life rather than all of the corporate bumpf. So I began working my way back successively through each year.

Paul Devereaux founded The Gazette and served as publisher and editor until 1928, when his son, Foster took over. Foster who sold the paper to the original ten shareholders in 1937, who've owned it ever since, until now, that is. Paul Devereaux died in 1931 and Foster passed away in 1950. Foster had married but spawned no children. All remnants of the Devereaux family died away, none left in Applewood. Their sole legacy to the town—The Gazette.

File after file lay spread on the table as I rapidly thumbed my way through the yellow-brown pages, some of which crumbled at my impatient touch. What I found mainly chronicled Rothwell's early triumphs. Rothwell capitalizes on the post-war boom. Rothwell builds housing for returning vets. Rothwell puts up tallest office tower in the city of Toronto. Rothwell given the key to the city by Mayor Zuzu Plotnik. And so on. And so on. You'd have thought that Rothwell was the only one doing anything constructive in the entire province but obviously he knew the value of good public relations, while privately disdaining the small folk, of course. I came across photos of Roberta Rothwell too, by her husband's side, gallantly holding onto his arm attending the opera or symphony, looking younger and prettier, her features smaller and fresh, free from the trouble that would affect her later on in her life. Her face showed the plumpness of youth and the glow of prosperity. Rothwell already exuded a lean and voracious air. Showed an acquisitive intensity in his eyes. Fascinating really, how much the old flash cameras revealed. You could see the ambition dripping off him. Poor Roberta. She never had a chance. How can a woman compete with that?

I kept roving back and back in time—1947, 1945, 1944 and finally, I found something in the December, 1943 file folder. The day of the Rothwell wedding. A seemingly innocuous family portrait and there they all were, resplendent and shining. December 19, 1943. A sumptuous affair held at the elegant Casa Loma in Toronto.

Here's what the Toronto Tribune, a paper that folded in 1965, said of the wedding:

"Up and coming man about town, Phillip Rothwell, 25, tied the knot on this day. The prominent developer wed his blissful bride, the former Miss Roberta Endersby, 20, of Toronto whose family are of the banking and tobacco Endersby's. The gala event was held at Casa Loma decorated with all the trimmings and tinsel befitting the festive season. The groom wore black tie and tails while the bride donned a sweeping white gown of lamé and brocade. The train alone trailed some 20 feet behind her. Two young bridesmaids made certain no one got caught up in the flowing material. The ceremony, presided over by the right reverend Samuel Barrington was held at St. Paul's Cathedral earlier that afternoon. The blessed bride and groom will be honeymooning in Palm Springs, California…"

A family portrait taken on the steps leading up to St. Paul's also appeared in the Tribune. The aristocratic version of murder's row—Roberta, 20, Mrs. Ralph Endersby, Mr. Ralph Endersby, sister Eloise, 13 and brother Reginald, 10. The Rothwells—Phillip, 25, Mrs. Martin Rothwell, Mr. Eric Rothwell, uncle, and brother William, aged 11. Hmm, didn't know about the brother. I figured he'd be in his mid-thirties today.

Rothwell's father, Martin had died under mysterious circumstances the year before. I read the articles and it was more informative trying to read behind the lines than what they actually said in their sensationalist manner. It had been big news. Prominent financier found dead, possible suicide but then the police had detained Phillip Rothwell for 'questioning'. I'd been a young kid at the time but I remember the old man harping on about it. Apparently, he'd been scooped on that one and my mom and I suffered the consequences of his ill-humour. In other words, the bottle went up and the fists came out. Rothwell had been released and no charges laid but one article in particular that appeared in the Toronto Enquirer—a tabloid rag built on sensationalist headlines and lurid stories—implied there should have been. I noticed too, there was quite an age gap between Rothwell and his younger brother, William; a pale, skinny child with the look of a private school boy. I'd never known a private school kid, well-dressed in their uniforms, seemingly polite, who wasn't a devil at heart. William had that look. An impish expression, a cocking of the eyebrow. Then, bingo, another clipping jumped out at me. I grabbed it along with the others. Shaking the dust out of my nostrils, I replaced the musty old folders. I wanted to suck in some air. I wanted a cigarette.

I caught Dusty just as he was stepping outside. We lit up together. He noticed the envelope in my hand.

"What have you got, Joe?"

"A photo from the archives. Think you could do me another favour?"

"Whaddaya need?"

I took it out and showed it to him. "Just a blow up of this wedding photo and keep it as sharp as possible, okay? Then one more of the kid, as big as you can, especially here and still keep it in focus."

Dusty scrutinized the picture. "Gotta love those old flashbulb jobs," he said. "At least this one was taken in decent daylight. Lemme see what I can do. Shouldn't take long."

"Thanks Dusty, Appreciate it."

Dusty disappeared back into the darkroom. I decided to go for a stroll, maybe buy myself a coffee.

When I returned, Dusty had left the photographs in an envelope on my desk. I took a look at the original Rothwell wedding photo, then the new ones Dusty had re-worked and whistled. He'd done a capital job. The kid could make big bucks in the city doing airbrushing work. The photo and ad agencies would be all over him. I slid the photos back into the envelope and wedged it under my arm. I searched around the desk among the wad of clippings I'd pulled from the archives, found the one I wanted about the brother and slid it into the envelope too. I had a stop to make. Dusty had gone home. Only Teddy was left, sitting absently at his desk, sucking on the cold cigar, deep into the musings of a man whose life had gone off the rails without explanation. Teddy would have been happy and utterly content to live out the remainder of his active life as a resident of Applewood and run its newspaper. The paper represented his existence, it gave him an identity. If it was successful, then it reflected on him. If it wasn't he would work harder to make it so. But having it snatched from him meant that the core of his being had been chopped away. That's a hard thing to stomach for a man of middle age.

"Teddy. Get out of here, already. Things will work out."

He looked up at me thoughtfully, "Maybe you're right, Joe. I know I can't have it end like this. I'm not ready to move on yet. Dammit, I've lived in this town for 35 years."

I replied, " I've only been here for three but sometimes it feels like thirty-five."

"Ah, it gets into your blood Joe, this way of life. And then it's like a fever. Not the violent, raging kind but one that's mild and makes you feel giddy and light-headed at times, the kind of fever that makes you fall in love. It comes and goes but you know it's there, because like an affectionate puppy, you live for it. I drive home, Joe, and I see the beauty of the azaleas and wisteria in bloom. I smell the honeysuckle and buttercups and just let the warmth of the sun sink into these crusty old bones. And it's magic. Pure magic. But you don't have to believe me, you know. You may find out for yourself one day. In time, you just might."

"Maybe so. Maybe so," I said, pausing to resume the mantle of the busy young man on the run.

"But I've got to go. Go home, Teddy. Get some rest. Store up a jug of that restless energy 'cause I think we'll need it. I'll see you bright and early in the morning."

As I left Teddy waved at me but I knew he'd be there, feeling the air, speaking to the ghosts who'd helped him along on his way.

Chapter Twenty-Five

Walking to my car in the mid-afternoon sunshine, I noticed the Jersey Jokers working out in full regalia, drawing an increasing and fascinated crowd to the square. I stood on the perimeter for a moment and watched the acrobats toss different objects back and forth in succession. First it was the traditional pins, then rubber balls, then grapefruits that they peeled a bit after each toss and finally, split the pieces and tossed them to the crowd much to everyone's delight, then eggs, canvas-backed chairs and finally, ball peen hammers. Quite a spectacle, I had to admit and clearly the audience lapped it up. One of the jugglers lay on his back and the other stood on the bottom of his feet tossing balloons filled with water. At the end of the routine, he broke each of the balloons in turn, soaking the two of them. This elicited screams of delight and high-pitched laughter from the children and like-minded and fervent applause from everyone. The two long-haired jugglers in their pantaloons and striped jerseys and white-face, solemnly bowed low to the crowd as the pretty young girl circulated through the throng requesting donations in a clear and sincere voice.

I spotted both Damo and Wishbone lolling on the grass taking in the show. They smiled and joked about something. Wish looked in my direction, cocked an eyebrow and waved me over but I shook my head and pointed to indicate that I had to get on my way. He sent back an exaggerated shrug like a circus clown who found himself in a ticklish predicament and after some comic disaster, accepted it as part of the way things were. And that's how I felt about what I thought would happen soon. It was part of the way things were.

Striding away off the grass, I lost the feeling in my feet, as if the soles had gone numb. The shrieks of the children expanded in my ears. And just for a moment, the world stopped and I lived in a bubble where sound lost its volume and I could touch nothing, not even myself. A crackling roar welled up within me, starting from somewhere inside and then like a fountain, gushed outward. It was then that I heard those wondrous voices from the time on the Beatty's farm and they came on a rainbow of colour, a solid beam of sound and light burning its way through the air, through the bubble that had become my prison and I was suddenly liberated, free to move, free to resume myself again. It faded away and the earth resumed its motion, the laughter and applause came back as if on the rebound of an echo and life itself restarted.

The episode lasted only a few seconds and yet it had stretched like an elastic band until the moment had come for it to snap back to the sting of normalcy. I now knew from reading some medical studies in the library that this other dimension of experience always existed underneath the one we lived day to day. Was it spooky? You bet. A part of me, the rational being, didn't want to admit to it, and felt afraid of the consequences if I did.

Once again I drove out along the edge of Rattlesnake Bay buffeted by the stiff breeze blowing onshore. I could see the white sails heeling over in the distance, then springing sharply back as each gust suddenly died—and longed to be out there with them, riding the wind, moving with the firm chop, letting the cold spray run down my face, feeling the vibrating hull sing out. Maybe I'd buy myself a dinghy this summer, if I could find one cheap and in decent condition. Then I'd have something to look forward to on the bright early evenings and long weekends until the days grew short, snappish and cold. A place where I could go and forget about things, paying attention only to the wind and the water. Nothing else.

I steered the Chevy up the long, dazzling drive and parked beside the gleaming Rolls Royce. The surface of the marble slabs glittered in the sunlight and I felt like I was approaching royalty for an audience. I rang the bell expecting to be welcomed by the same surly maid who looked as if she spent her time off sucking lemons.

Instead, Paisley opened the door and the contrast couldn't have been starker. She wore a black bikini and a yellow chiffon peignoir, loosely sashed over her slim figure. Picasso had done her toenails in bright red. Gold lamé sandals cradled her feet. Her lightly bronzed skin gleamed with sun oil.

"Hello Paisley."

"Why Joe. What a nice surprise. Seamus and I are just sitting out in the back. Come join us. Let me give you a drink, you look thirsty. How about some iced tea?"

"Thanks. Iced tea would be lovely."

Paisley led the way but stopped abruptly in the hall, so abruptly that I bumped into her. Her hair was pinned up in back and wisps floated at the base of her slender neck. I stood close enough to smell her and I inhaled an intoxicating mix of oil, cologne and heat radiating from her skin.

She said coyly, from over her smooth shoulder," I don't mean to be rude, Joe. But what brings you around? It seems like you are stopping by quite often lately, not that I'm unhappy to see you, of course. Even though you were a bit rude barging in the other night." She turned, then reached out and touched my cheek, smiling more to herself than to me. Instinctively, I stepped back a foot.

"I came to see Seamus, actually. To pick up on our discussion."

She lapsed into a mock pout. "I'm hurt, Joe. I thought you came to see me," she said and now the angle of her face tilted coyly up. The way the sunlight streamed in from a high window made her make-up seem overdone, even garish, as she clowned around, the contours of her face cracking as the mask she wore stretched out of its carefully preserved form.

I didn't want to see that and didn't even want to think it but I did.

I said, "I'm always happy to see you, Paisley. You know that."

Seamus sat beached on a lawn chair, under an umbrella, reading a large book bound in leather. A straw hat wide as a sombrero covered his head and face while he looked as if he'd been dressed by leprechauns in a tartan short-sleeved jacket and shorts made of thick, absorbent terrycloth. His skin radiated white. Even his feet were wrapped in a large, orange bath towel. When he heard our voices, he looked up and I saw he wore dark glasses. His eyebrows went up over the dark frames.

"Joe," he said civilly enough. "I'm surprised to see you, I must say. But have a drink. Paisley, get the poor bugger a drink, will you?"

"I've already offered him iced tea", Paisley replied with a noticeable layer of frost in her voice.

"Iced tea?" retorted Seamus in disgust. "Have a real drink, Joe. What about a gin and tonic or even a beer, for god's sake?"

"Ice tea is fine, Seamus. Thanks anyway."

"Ach, what kind of newspaperman are you? You're supposed to be an alcoholic, it's the code of the trade, you know."

"I'll work on it," I replied as Paisley handed me a tall, dripping glass of iced tea. I took a sip. Delicious. The Sahara had appeared in my gullet. Paisley pulled up a lawn chair and sat opposite. She'd put on a pair of sunglasses set with rhinestones and looked again, quite glamorous. She shook her hair free, saying, "Isn't it a glorious day? I just love the summer, don't you Joe?"

"Let's just say, it's been a very interesting summer, so far."

Seamus took that moment to peer at me more intently over the top of his glass, slipping the shades down the bridge of his nose a notch. I knew his glass wasn't filled with ice tea. More likely whiskey and soda.

"So, what's on your inquiring mind, eh? To what do we owe this pleasure? Our last encounter was quite illuminating," he said acidly, as his eyes turned a chiller shade of blue.

I took a long sip of the cool drink and just to annoy him, began chomping on a piece of ice delaying my reply while I mused on my purpose here. But it was Paisley who became exasperated.

"Joe! Must you do that?" she complained. "It's so irritating."

"Sorry, Paisley. Actually, Seamus, I do want to know something."

I paused for effect, then said, "Someone is trying to scuttle your business. I'd like to know why."

Seamus dropped his jaw to half-mast in mild surprise.

"Is that a fact, Joe?" he asked, with just the hint of suspicion in his voice. "I s'pose you're referring to those little pranks out by the construction site. They're hardly worth a thought. Minimal damage done. Besides, the police, as I said, are on to it now."

"That's part of it, Seamus. But not all of it. I think the pranks are a warning. But it goes deeper. Much deeper," I said.

He mulled that over but came to no hard conclusions apart from the need to take a long gulp of his drink. "Go on, Joe," he said uncertainly.

"What do you know about Rothwell's old man? His death, in particular," I asked, rolling the cubes around in my glass. In a melodramatic gesture, Paisley brought her blood red nails up to her mouth.

Seamus jerked his head up. "What's that got to do with anything?" he growled impatiently.

I said, "Maybe nothing. Maybe everything. Can you just answer the question?"

Seamus prickled, ruffling himself up in his lounge chair like an irritated rooster. "Now listen here. You come barging into my home on a Sunday afternoon asking all kinds of rough questions. Who the hell do you think you are anyway?"

I shook a Sweet Cap out of its pack and fired it up. "Maybe I'm the guy who can save your business, Seamus old boy. Before all the tourists run like frightened rabbits and go back to Toledo or wherever they came from. Before RSC Developments crashes down from the mountain top."

Seamus knocked back the rest of his drink like any good captain of industry would in a sticky situation. "You're saying some damn peculiar things, Joe. Damned peculiar."

Paisley said, "Joe. I think you've simply lost your mind. It's that girl, isn't it? She's the one. You've gone soft in the head."

"Stay out of this Paisley, darling," Seamus said regretting he had to reprimand his fine-looking wife. He lifted his face out of the glass.

"Rothwell's father committed suicide many years ago. His investments had gone sour. He couldn't stand the shame and shot himself."

I said, "Maybe that's what Rothwell wants everyone to think."

"What are you saying?" Seamus demanded.

"I'm not sure," I admitted. "But it doesn't all make sense. I trolled through our archives and a couple of the articles on Rothwell senior's death suggested that it wasn't as simple as a depressed man mourning over some lost dough. Phillip may have been more involved than he wanted people to think."

"Think how?" Paisley asked.

Seamus groaned. "Paisley. Stay out of this."

I said, smiling at her. "I'm not sure. And what about William Rothwell? What became of him?"

Paisley said vaguely, "William?"

Seamus merely shrugged. "Haven't a clue. He disappeared some time ago. At least, Phillip hasn't seen him in about 20 years, maybe more. Why?"

I said, "Well, it occurs to me that William could be mixed up in the vandalism at the construction site, somehow."

"What makes you think so?" Seamus asked, putting his gingery beetle brows to good work.

"Just this," I said, holding up a small, single-columned newspaper clipping, yellowed with age. "Let me read you a bit of this. It's dated, September 30th, 1950. ...Neighbours called police to 129 Admiral Rd. in downtown Toronto when a gunshot was heard in the early morning hours. There, police took into custody, William Rothwell, aged sixteen, who, apparently had threatened to shoot his older brother, prominent real estate developer, Phillip Rothwell. Mr. Rothwell, visibly shaken, stated that his brother William was high-strung and had been depressed since the death of their father six years earlier. No charges were laid. William Rothwell was later released into the custody of an uncle..."

"What exactly are you thinking..?" Seamus stammered.

I nodded. "Well, what's happened to William? Did he just disappear? Seems a bit odd. I wonder where he is now?"

"What are you suggesting?" he asked.

"Nothing yet," I said. "Look Seamus, Rothwell is your partner in what I can see is a pretty important project. There's some question about what happened when the old man died and now the brother, that's all. Why would a kid grab a gun and try to shoot his older brother? Sounds like a pretty intense sort of hatred. Goes beyond the usual sibling rivalry, I'd say."

"I trust Phillip Rothwell," Seamus said. "All of our dealings have been proper and aboveboard. If you have some accusations to make, why don't you make them to the police, or have you already done so?" I shook my head. "Why not?"

"I only just thought of it," I replied.

Seamus stuck out his paw.

"Get me another drink, will you, my darling?" Paisely took the glass from him sullenly and marched off into the house. Seamus watched her go. "I don't want to alarm her Joe, but this business about William... it's been such a long time. He's changed no doubt."

I drew on the cigarette forcefully and nodded again. "I'd say so."

"I must tell Phillip, right away. And hire some additional security, naturally." The man of action was coming to the fore. When in doubt, buy it. The sun beat down. I sweated through my shirt. I plucked it away from my skin.

"You know Norma Jennings, Seamus?"

The blue eyes glassed over. The square jaw stuck out.

"I knew of her. Never met the girl in person." Those brows could knit a shetland sweater.

"What about Darlene Norris? You know her?"

"Only from the bank. I do a portion of my banking there. But I deal with many banks. Now why are you asking me these questions? I get the feeling I'm not going to like what you have to say."

" But you'll take it just the same. Norma and Darlene were seeing an older man, someone in business. I've got that confirmed, both of them, the same one. I'm guessing this guy is the father of Norma's child. All of a sudden Norma conveniently slides over the side of a speedboat and Darlene disappears."

If eyebrows had springs in them, then Seamus's did a grand impression.

"I thought the Jennings girl's death was accidental."

I replied, "It was, more or less. Before Norma jumped on that speedboat, she was hopped up, high as a kite."

"I also formed the impression that Blake was the child's father. That he, that he—well, you know—got her up the duff."

"Maybe," I said. "But I don't think so. Blake's a junkie, Seamus and junkies only think about one thing…junk and getting more of it. He's in pretty rough shape physically. I doubt if he's capable."

"I see," Seamus replied.

" Listen, I'm doing you a favour letting you in on this. Think about it, Seamus. There's only a couple of other guys in this town who fit the bill."

It took a moment to sink in, then the lion awoke. "You'd better get the hell off my property, Joe Simpson. I had nothing to do with either one of them," he roared just as Paisley appeared with a drink in her perfectly smooth, perfectly manicured hand. She stopped short. She looked very confused.

I swirled the ice around in the glass, then drained it. "I wasn't suggesting you had, Seamus. Thanks for the iced tea," I said, shoving the glass at Paisley, who closed her slim fingers around it automatically. "Don't worry. I'll show myself out." I knew I'd left a bomb in the drawing room. Wonder if it'd explode before I made it to my car.

I marched up the quartz tiles to the French doors, opened them up and disappeared into the cool black and white marble hallway. Big enough to play chess using life-sized pieces. I shut the front door that was only high enough for a giant to duck under as carefully as decorum required. Not too carefully.

I went back to my apartment, stared at the pages on the walls, added a page for Coca Cola Falls and wrote, dead fish, underneath. Then I drew some more arrows. Not so suddenly, a number of people and places had become interconnected. I added a page for Seamus O'Toole, linked him to Phillip Rothwell and added William Rothwell with a question mark and one for Darlene and Cindy Lou. On the 'Darlene' page, I drew an arrow to Norma and placed a question mark. Who connected the two of them together? So I drew a line back to Rothwell and O'Toole, the likely candidates. I had a pretty good idea who was behind the vandalism at the construction site but I still wasn't sure why. I looked at Wishbone Jones' name again and underlined it heavily three times with an exclamation mark.

Chapter Twenty-Six

"Why did I let you talk me into this," Hal said, big as a grizzly bear and just as prickly, jamming my front seat. "I'm off-duty for Christ sake."

"Because I can be very persuasive, that's why." I glanced at my watch and the luminous dial told me it was a few minutes shy of midnight. What would the old man do? He'd sit here all night if need be just to get the scoop. "Let's give it an hour. If nothing happens, then you, me and Dusty will go home and get some shut-eye."

"I'm on shift at eight," Hal said. "So how did you come by this information again?"

"Confidential informant," I replied.

"So who was it?" Hal asked.

"Note the term, confidential," I replied. "Besides, I don't really know."

"You shouldn't have told me that," Hal said.

"Why?"

"Because now I think less of you. Before, I actually thought you had a source you were protecting."

"I do," I said. "I just don't know who they are."

Hal looked like he was going to growl but instead he turned to Dusty. "Say, what kind of lens you got there?" The kid huddled in the back having laid out his tools and assembled them as quickly as he could in the dark.

"I've got a 250 millimeter telephoto zoom lens. It's the type they use for shooting football games, you know to get those shots right in the action," Dusty replied. "I've already loaded up the high speed film. With the bit of moon we've got tonight, we could get lucky. The shots will probably be grainy but I hope to be able to get pretty good detail with it."

"Swell," I said. "Isn't that swell, Hal?"

"Yeah, it's swell. Got any more coffee?" I handed him the thermos and he poured himself a cup. We sat awhile in silence except for Hal's slurping.

"What's that?" Dusty asked.

"What?" I replied.

"Thought I heard a boat."

We all listened in silence.

"He's right," Hal said. "I hear a boat motor."

"Good ears," I said. I didn't hear a thing apart from the water lapping up on the shore and a crazed hooting owl.

We eased out of the Chevy, clicking the doors shut. A slight breeze rustled the leaves in the trees. We took care as sound carried down by the water. The Meadows lay, oval-shaped and grassy, surrounded by a perimeter of birch and fir trees. The land sloped down to a beach with a sandbar that made for easy boat landings as long as the motors were pulled up before they chewed up the lake bottom. We crept up to the tree line and flattened out waiting to see if anything would happen. Dusty peered through the long lens on the camera sweeping his view along the perimeter of the shoreline. Wispy clouds danced in the sky letting the crescent moon shine through, its light sparkling the low chop as the current cascaded toward the beach.

"See anything?" I whispered.

"Not yet," Dusty hissed back.

"I see something." Hal had brought his night vision binocs, the pair he'd used during his military service. "Boat's approaching."

I could hear the put-put of the motor now as it slowed then idled and finally, cut out altogether. The prow nudged into the sand. "Four guys just stepped out of the boat," Hal said.

"Got'em," Dusty replied. "Let's see if we can get a little closer."

He began to inch forward crawling commando style on his belly, holding the camera aloft. I looked at Hal who shrugged then followed suit. Didn't have much choice but to follow. We crawled for about 20 yards and stopped where the ground had broken away forming a crevice with a bunker up above. We crouched behind the bunker making sure to keep low. Dusty had the camera out and clicked off shots. The shutter sounded like firecrackers to me but no one challenged us. The wind whipped up spewing swirls of sand. Dusty cursed and rubbed the end of the camera lens with a shammy. Hal kept his eyes peeled to the binocs scanning the scene down by the shoreline. By now I could make them out in silhouette and when the moon broke through I got a bit more detail. They hauled the boat up on to the shore and began unloading, humping kegs on to the beach. Six kegs in all.

"Make out any faces?" I whispered. Dusty shook his head.

"Still too dark and we're still too far away," Hal said.

I craned my head and peered forward. The ground spewed open with no cover all the way down to the beach. Our current position would have to do I guessed.

"I hear another one," Dusty hissed.

"Another what?"

"Outboard," Hal said and pointed. "Coming from the direction of the point." The others must have heard it too, since the action on the beach appeared to have stopped as the four figures remained immobile.

"Turn around," muttered Dusty, as a sliver of moon sliced through a cloud. Even I could see now that their backs were to us as they waited. After a few minutes, the second boat's engine became more distinct and as the moon dipped behind the cloud cover again, I caught a glimpse of a snub-nosed silhouette. Hal hadn't lowered the binocs for a second.

"Four more," he whispered.

"This isn't any good," Dusty said. "We gotta get closer. When the moon comes out I'm getting flare from its reflection off the water."

Hal continued to scan the ground before us. "I see a ridge," he said. "About 30 yards down to the right. That's the only cover out there."

"Great," Dusty said. "Let's go."

"Wait a second. What if these guys head that way, we'll be caught out in the open. Think deer. Think headlights," I said.

"It's okay," Hal said, "I've come prepared."

"Prepared how?"

"With this." He yanked something out of his windbreaker.

"What is it?"

"Flare gun," he said. "Got it along with the binocs."

"Great," I said. "That makes me feel a whole lot better. Eight of them and we have a flare gun."

"Let's go," Dusty repeated and wriggled off to the right. Hal gestured and reluctantly, I followed. Hadn't felt this foolish or gotten this dirty since I was a kid playing rangers in the neighbour's backyard. Dusty was a fast wriggler and made the ridge quickly. Hal and I crawled behind him. It was a better vantage point. We heard their voices now as the first four greeted the new arrivals. Still couldn't make out what they were saying. After what appeared to be handshakes, the figures made their way up from the shore toward the kegs and gathered round. Someone leaned in and began to twist off the top of one of the kegs. One of the newcomers dipped into the top and brought some of the contents out in the palm of his hand. He said something to the guy next to him and a penlight clicked on so they could take a closer look. I caught the outline of a bearded chin and long hair before the penlight snapped out.

"Gotcha," Dusty hissed.

The first figure set the cap back on the keg and twisted it shut. They repeated the same procedure for each of the kegs. Only two of the figures took part in the examination. The others stood around the perimeter, keeping lookout. The examination finished and the first guy gestured to someone behind him. The second guy handed the first what looked like a satchel. He set it on the ground in front of the kegs. A figure bent low over the satchel. Again, the penlight snapped on and the contents were examined. Just as the guy straightened up holding the satchel in his right hand, the air shrieked and growled driven by the thrashing of gears exploding out of four-stroke engines. From across the open ground, I saw headlights bouncing over the grass as a brace of motorcycles raced toward the group of men. The bikers uttered war cries. Taking a second to assimilate what was happening, the eight men broke into action. Three picked up two kegs each and awkwardly sprinted for one of the motorboats. The others followed sprinting in the opposite direction. It seemed clear, though, that the motorcycles intended to cut off their path before they hit the shore.

"Jesus," Dusty exclaimed. "What the hell is happening?"

"Somebody's unhappy," Hal muttered.

"That's right," I said. "Looks like somebody's decided to bust up the party."

The roar of the bikes boomed as the riders revved and wheeled closer and closer. I saw something metallic glint in the moonlight and realized that the bikers wielded chains as they jounced forward. A pair of them blocked the path to the boats. The first guy sprinting toward the shore, leapt into the air and knocked one of the bikers out of his saddle, hurdled over the bike and kept on going, racing for the beach. The guys with the kegs floundered. The weight and awkwardness of the baggage slowed them down and before they could get very far, the bikers encircled them. The bikes swooped and swerved closer and closer slashing with the chains. I heard a boat motor start up. Someone had made it down to the beach as a motorcycle and rider tore after him. The riders came off the bikes and a melee ensued in the darkness. We heard yells and grunts and curses and the thud of fists. Dusty fired off shots like a demon. Hard to tell who was who or who was getting the better of whom but I suspected the chains tilted the balance in favour of the bikers.

"Hmm," Hal said.

"Use your secret weapon," I said.

"Good idea," Hal replied.

"Dusty," I said. "Get ready. Your close-up awaits."

Hal aimed the muzzle of the flare gun at a point above the flailing figures. He pulled the trigger. A whooshing sound accompanied by a high whistle followed the flare as it reached the upper point in its trajectory. Then a loud crackle and a bang as the phosphorescence lit up the night sky. The combatants froze in mid-action, fists poised, as the battle stopped on a dime. There was a moment of utter stillness. A second later, it all came unstuck. Bikers raced for their machines. The others took off toward the boats, dragging the kegs behind them as fast as they could. The motorcycles bounced off along the field toward the main road. Three guys splashed into the water where the first boat idled. They clambered aboard, dropped the motor and opened up the throttle. The others loaded the kegs and followed suit. The second motor kicked alive. The boats spun around and surged off in opposite directions bouncing on the current heading for distant shores.

"Man," Dusty said. "Nice touch with the flare. Really spooked them."

Hal turned to me. "You know any of those guys?"

"I've got an idea who some of them might be."

"Let's go take a look. See if they left anything behind," Hal said.

"They must have thought they were surrounded," Dusty exclaimed as he stood up and slung the camera over his shoulder.

"If only they knew," I replied.

"You worry too much, Simpson. I would have just arrested them," Hal said.

"Using what? An empty flare gun?"

"If I had to," Hal replied indignantly. "Come on."

We trudged over to the spot where the first group had congregated. Hal shone his penlight on the area. We could see where the grass had been trampled and the indents of the kegs. Hal flicked the light around. "Doesn't look like anything is here," he said.

"Wait a second." I got down on my knees and began to feel around in the grass. "Shine it over here, will ya?" The tight beam moved toward my groping fingers. "Ah," I exclaimed. "You little beauty."

"What'd you find?" Dusty asked excitedly. I held it up between thumb and forefinger. "What is it?"

"Looks like a purple pill," Hal replied disgustedly.

"More than that," I said. "It's a lot more than that." Carefully, I wrapped the pill in my handkerchief and slipped it into my pocket. "Come on, Dusty. You've got some developing to do."

"Another long night," Hal groused.

"I can drop you at home," I said. I checked my watch in the moonlight. "It's gone just past 1:30, you can still get a couple hours of shuteye."

"Funny, Simpson. Let's see what Dusty's got in his camera."

Dusty laid the photos side by side on the composing room table, the one where Stumpy plied most of his trade. He'd managed about a dozen prints that revealed some murky detail. The three of us took our time examining them.

"Who do you know?" Hal asked me.

"Who do you know?" I asked him.

"You first."

I sighed. "Fine. This guy here, the one rummaging around the satchel is, Johnny D'Amato aka Damo, an American. He heads that troupe, the Jersey Jokers. We've all seen them around town. Standing just behind him is a fat biker named, Bobby Ross. I've had a few words with Bobby in the past. Next to him is Wishbone Jones, proprietor of Sky High Records and Tapes. There's only one other guy I recognize and that's because he's unmistakable." I plopped my forefinger down on the tall, broad-shouldered figure Dusty caught slamming his fist into one of the other hapless guys. "The Viking. He and Bobby Ross lead rival biker gangs. They don't care for each other too much."

"Recognize anyone else?" Hal asked.

I shook my head. "That's it. Can't make out any of the others and even if I could, I'm not sure I'd know them anyway. You?"

"The same," Hal said. "Those boys from the second boat must be from another county. I know most of the miscreants and criminals that are local."

"So what do you think was going on?" Dusty asked. "Quite a hullaballoo out there tonight."

"Why don't you spell it out, Sherlock?" Hal drawled.

I cleared my throat. "Sure. Well, it seems one rival biker gang was invading the territory of another. That's why The Viking showed up, to tell Bobby Ross the Meadows is his turf and maybe muscle in on what he was doing. That brings us to the second thing. The first group of guys from the boat was selling something to the second group who handed over what I figure is some cash in the satchel. So, a financial transaction took place."

"What were they selling?" Dusty asked.

I reached into my pocket and pulled out the handkerchief, unfolded it and picked up the little purple pill. "This."

"Which is what?" Dusty asked.

"I'd like to know that too," Hal said.

"Hands of fire. Taller than a tabernacle," I murmured. In my mind, I flashed on the paper collage in my apartment. Mentally, I drew an arrow from Ellis Boston connecting him to Damo and Wishbone Jones.

"Huh?" Hal and Dusty looked bewildered. "Start making sense, Simpson. It's too late and my nerves are on edge," Hal said.

"Sorry. I was thinking about something else," I replied. "If this is what I think it is, then it's called LSD or Lysergic Acid Diethylamide."

"What's that when it's at home?" Hal asked.

"It's a hallucinogen and when taken causes the user to experience vivid dreams and visions, crazy fantasies. It's been used in experiments by the American military. It's said to distort reality and sometimes the dreams are visually beautiful and sometimes they turn into nightmares. I remember that Damo mentioned he'd been involved in some medical experiments run by the military, so he'd know all about it."

"I don't understand," Dusty said. "People take it for what? For fun?"

I nodded. "Sort of. It alters perceptions of reality, distorts what people think they are seeing and experiencing and for some that's a desirable thing."

"Even if it ends in a nightmare?" Dusty asked.

"Uh-huh."

"What you said before," Hal interjected. "What was that all about?"

"I was thinking of Ellis Boston. He had a vision of some sort of monster. Hands on fire. Tall as a tabernacle, he said. It was attacking Lizzie and he went to defend her, beat this thing off with a hoe."

"Ellis thought Lizzie was being attacked by some kind of monster?" Hal asked.

"That's right."

"And you're thinking," Hal said. "That Ellis was on this LSD stuff?"

I shrugged. "Kind of makes sense, don't you think?"

Dusty snorted. "I can't see Ellis Boston taking any hallucinogenic drugs, can you? Straight as an arrow is Ellis, er, was Ellis, I mean."

"I know," I replied. "That's what doesn't add up. Now listen, Norma was found to have some sort of chemical in her system, as yet unidentified. Okay?"

"Okay," said Hal, pensively.

"I spoke to Doc Seaton a while ago. You remember that fish we found flopping on the road?"

"Yeah. Five-pound trout. Dead as a door nail."

"I had Doc Seaton run some tests on it and guess what?"

"What?" asked Dusty and Hal in unison.

"Same chemical found in the fish as in Norma." I held up the pill. "I think it was this chemical."

"But how?" Dusty asked.

"Someone gave Norma the LSD," I said. "Maybe it was the Rothwell kid, I don't know but I guess it could have been anyone. Maybe she took it herself, thought it was just kicks, take a pill do something wild and crazy," I said bitterly.

"Still doesn't explain Ellis," Hal said.

"Or the fish," Dusty chimed in.

I sighed. It had been a long day. Parched, I walked over to the water cooler. I pulled the cup and the bottle let out a gurgle. I watched the air bubble float to the surface of the water. I pressed the lever to fill the cup. Another fat bubble floated to the surface ending in an elongated belch.

"Joe," Hal said.

Startled, I looked over. "What?"

"Water's pouring on to the floor."

I looked down at my feet. A nice puddle had formed and spread around my toes. Suddenly, I had my answer. The common denominator.

Chapter Twenty-Seven

The cacophonic blast of a motorcycle revving its engine woke me out of a deep sleep. I looked over at the travel alarm clock that I used for everything but traveling. It read 4:33 am. Jesus. That meant I'd been asleep for all of an hour. The gangs were dragging up Nottawasaga road again. Couldn't they just give it a rest like those of us who don't sleep in leather? Those people had a strange orientation in relation to time. Wasn't it supposed to be the early hours when they slept off the soddening effects of the nightly beer and booze fest? They had no business turning up now, early on a Monday morning but there they were and here was I; awake before dawn and little chance of drifting off again. Bad habit. Once awoken, my brain automatically plugged itself in and began to hum as the rest of the organism started to warm up. Unfortunately, in a small community, any loud noise seemed ten times louder than it really was, since you lost the ability to tolerate such things when you left the city. Must be the clarity of the country air, noises piercing the night amplified as they traveled from the source to your ear. Or more likely, I was a little bit jumpy these days.

I made my desk before eight o'clock, which, in the summer, was a rarity. Teddy had left me a note. The Crown had decided there existed sufficient evidence to charge Blake Rothwell with criminal negligence relating to the death of Norma Jennings. No mention of assault charges from the day before. As I suspected, the fix was in. That made me happy—hearing the kid faced charges on something but it surprised me too. I truly thought he'd be slapped on the wrist, called a naughty boy and fined. But if convicted, he might do a couple of years jail time, though a year to eighteen months in a minimum security facility seemed more likely, maybe even probation or rehab. I put a call through to

Horatio Bongard figuring he looked the diligent type who showed up early to work. Crown attorneys complained constantly of being bogged with cases.

"Horatio. Joe Simpson here."

"What can I do for you, Joe?" came the laconic response and I could hear the sigh in his voice and the plaintive inquiry in his tone. That of, what does he want from me? What does anybody want from me?

"I'm fine, thank you for asking. Anyway, Horatio, I just wanted the scoop on the Blake Rothwell charges. Need to write a follow-up to the inquest."

"Uh-huh. I see. Uh-huh. I see." He cleared his throat noisily.

"Come on, Horatio, quit stalling. I'm surprised as hell, frankly. No one thought he'd be charged."

"Uh-huh, Joe. Well, there was some reluctance, I'll admit."

"From McKie?"

"Now Joe. I'm not going to tell you that. You seem like a smart guy and capable of figuring out deep, meaningful events. Anyway, anything pertaining to a fellow law enforcement member, you wouldn't hear it from me and it couldn't be attributed directly to this office, either. No matter what it was. Or how derogatory."

"Got it, Horatio. Where's it going to be tried, by the way?"

"Brigsby."

"Brigsby? Why Brigsby?"

"They've got the available space and a judge, that's why. All the other slots are filled. Besides, we do want to avoid a repeat of any the shenanigans that took place during the coroner's inquest. It's been a pretty busy summer, Joe, from a law perspective that is. The prelim is June 20th and then we'll find out the trial date."

"So, why was the Rothwell kid charged?"

"I felt there was enough evidence to go ahead. Particularly in light of his own testimony at the inquest," Horatio replied. "And other things come recently to light."

"But you know Oliveira's going to use that, saying it is prejudicial to his getting a fair trial, not to mention, he testified of his own free will at the inquest."

"Oh sure, Freddy'll use that and more. But there are no deals made. Blake Rothwell agreed to testify at the inquest, period. What happens after is what happens after."

"I gather, Horatio, that these other things you're speaking of may relate to the fact that the kid is a junkie and was likely juiced-up while tooling his Daddy's speedboat around Rattlesnake Bay? And that's why there was a six-hour lapse in reporting the accident. The kid had to get a grip. Get cleaned up before checking in with the cops? Probably, he panicked and ran home to get Daddy-o and his lawyer to make it nicey-nice for him. Now what do you think of that scenario?"

Horatio answered dryly. "I'd rather not say. But I'm certain all the pertinent facts will come out in the trial, okay Joe?"

"Oh, come on, Horatio. You wouldn't have known any of this if it hadn't been for me in the first place. And if I hadn't suggested a similar possibility to deputy chief, Guenther. Or did he tell it differently? To make himself look smart, which would take some doing, I must say."

"No comment at this time."

But my questions must have revitalized him as Horatio sounded almost ener-getic. "Look Joe. I gotta go. Try not to be so tough on the coppers. They're working with the best they've got. Now maybe you and me don't think that's a heck of a lot. But that's just a very private and personal opinion. So, I'll see you around. Brigsby maybe." He slammed the receiver down and I thought I heard him sniggering over the line before it went dead. All of which, made me wonder if Horatio hadn't lost his marbles along with everyone else around here but then when I thought about it, it really wasn't surprising.

The receiver still clung to my stunned hand when I heard a commotion com-ing from the front door. Nadine Morgan— surrounded by Wishbone Jones, a mirthless Damo and half a dozen of the Jersey Jokers in full regalia. No won-der she looked spooked. Wishbone had a grip on Nadine's claw-like hand that clasped her set of keys. I had locked the door behind me. They struggled over the keys, Nadine, fiercely refusing to give them up. Certainly not to the likes of the rabble confronting her, not even if it meant forgoing her life itself.

Nadine must have thought that an assault was in progress but Wishbone, while grabbing at the keys, tried placating her.

"Quiet, lady. Will you be quiet? For god's sake, you're going to wake up the whole damn town. We just want to get in, that's all," he exclaimed.

Nadine continued to yell. "No. No. No. Help, somebody, help," she wailed like Nell, jammed into a barrel about to plummet over Niagara Falls.

I flung open the door. Nadine cut off in mid-scream, quickly putting her fingers to her mouth. Wishbone gave me a look of pure exasperation. Damo stood silently, a lurking presence behind Nadine while the rest of the gang remained still and mute.

Wish said, "Thank God, Joe. I'm trying to get in here."

"What's going on? What are you doing here?" I demanded.

"Hey, let us in and I'll tell you, okay?" Wish said. "Really, it's fine. We just got off on the wrong foot here. Let us in, Joe. Come on."

Nadine said, "Don't do it, Joe. They're trouble. I can smell it."

"Yeah sure, they're trouble. But what's a little trouble now and then?" In my mind, I saw the image of Wishbone captured by Dusty illuminated by the light of the flare.

"Are you crazy, Joe? These hooligans?"

Wishbone took umbrage at her remark. "Hey lady. I got a right to be here. And that's what I've been trying to tell you if you'd shut up for a second."

I said, "Okay everybody. We'll deal with this inside. No need to create a spectacle for the entire town."

Nadine glared at me but marched in. The rest of the troop followed in behind her.

Damo pointed, then spoke for the first time. He wore a sleeveless vest and no shirt. His tattoos looked menacing and the muscles on his arms rippled as he moved.

"Is that the editor's office?" he asked.

I nodded. "Yeah, that's right." Something seemed odd, even sinister about the question.

Damo said, "Good." He went to Teddy's office and tried the door. Locked. "Where's the key?" he asked casually.

"What are you doing, man?" I asked. Meanwhile, any semblance of order crumbled as the jugglers started with the staplers, then progressed to the In baskets and from there to the garbage cans. One of the acrobats stood on his hands and walked along the edge of my desk. The other practiced handstands on my swivel chair. Letting out a crackling, high-pitched roar, Stumpy Butler charged out of the composing room, his inflated arms tattooed in ink, gripping in his raw-boned hands, a scarred sledgehammer. He bore the wild-eyed look and countenance of a man bent on destruction as the hammer swung through the air. The Jersey Jokers scattered like a bunch of ten pins, a few hit the floor rolling.

"Get outta here you hoodlums. Get outta the office," he yelled stomping toward his increasingly cornered prey.

"Wait a second, man, take it easy," Wish pleaded. Damo rushed forward as Stumpy raised the hammer above his head with the intention of crushing someone or something.

"Stumpy! No!" Nadine commanded. Stumpy halted in mid-air.

"But these people are causing a ruckus, Miss Morgan. They need to be stopped."

"That's not the way to do it," she said and eyed Damo as he stood poised to launch himself at Stumpy given the slightest quiver.

"She's right, Stumpy. We need to talk this out, not smash up the place. Give me the hammer." I held out my hand. Stumpy looked around slowly. Disappointment wormed its way into his features. Reluctantly, he lowered the hammer and I grabbed the handle away from him.

"We just need to calm down," I said. "All of us, before someone gets hurt."

"Tell that psycho," one of the Jokers called out. "He's the one that's crazy."

Damo smiled. "I can dig crazy."

I patted Stumpy on the back. "It's okay now. Let's just get back to work." Once again, Stumpy's shoulders slumped as he trudged back to the composing room. He cast a furtive, furious glance over his shoulder then disappeared. I breathed a sigh of relief. "Now, where were we?"

Damo held out a large, powerful hand. "The key," he repeated flicking his head toward the office.

"I don't have the key. Only Teddy has it. But even if I did, I'd eat it first."

"Okay. We'll wait," Damo replied and sat in Paisley's chair.

I turned to Wishbone. "You want to tell me what is going on here, Wish? What are these people doing here?"

"I'm sorry, Joe. Really. But the thing of it is, you see. Aw hell, why'nt you read it for yourself." And he reached into the inside pocket of his suede jacket and pulled out an envelope. He handed it to me.

Worried and troubled suddenly, I opened the envelope and unfolded the paper found inside. I gazed at a legal document, with an impressive looking seal and notarized by a ritzy Toronto law firm, stating clearly that fifty percent of the shares accrued to The Applewood Gazette Co. Ltd., were in the possession of Ontario 656778, the sole proprietor of which—Wishbone Jones!

Talk about the surreal usurping the present. I thought for a second I might faint but as my senses went momentarily woozy, they also came back quickly on a razor thin wedge of anger.

"The record business must be more lucrative than I thought," I said, while Wishbone smiled, cocked an eyebrow and rubbed one of his moustaches. But it wasn't the record business I thought of, far from it.

"Must be," he agreed.

"You think you know how to run a newspaper?"

Wishbone shrugged. "Not really. But you do."

"Teddy's the editor of The Gazette, nobody else."

"We'll see."

"What do you want with a newspaper, anyway? If you've got so much damn money, why not expand your store or buy more stores? Buy a whole chain if you want."

Damo spoke for him. "A newspaper is the voice of the community. Let's say we want to influence the pitch of that voice, Joe Blow. Can you dig that?"

"Influence or control?"

Damo flexed his biceps again, then popped a knuckle. "What's the difference, Joe Blow?"

"People won't read it. They'll think it's a joke. You'll lose all the readers and then the advertisers. How are you going to operate it then? There won't be anything left to run."

Wishbone looked a little sheepish.

"Don't worry about the money, it doesn't matter. But Joe, understand see, we want to do something meaningful here. Something people will thank us for in the end."

"Leave the paper alone then, and let us do our jobs."

Wishbone shook his head. "Can't do that Joe. You see, you're not doing your jobs very well. There's a whole constituency out there you've been ignoring and that's got to stop. The community of youth. Young people are the key factor in society today, Joe and you guys here just don't get it. We're gonna make this paper over for them. Radical, yeah. But relevant? You'll see. They're the ones making things happen. They're the ones who are gonna be in charge. They're the ones who control a lot of discretionary bucks, if you want to look at it in your terms. Your so-called advertisers haven't gotten hip to that fact yet. It ain't their parents anymore, Joe, it's the kids who represent the significant market here. And that change in influence represents everything that is happening. You've missed the whole damn thing," he said in a disgusted tone, shaking his head, mourning for the unhip, the uncool and the flat out hicksterism of our lost souls.

I had to admit, that listening to Wish's words, I couldn't entirely disagree. In fact, I had been mulling some of the same ideas myself, albeit more slowly perhaps. But this was a small town paper, hardly the harbinger of change in the midst of a conservative population.

"You're trying to create a revolution in the wrong place, guys. This is a small burg not a cosmopolitan metropolis like New York or London where there's ample room for an alternative voice. Here, we represent fairly, I think, the ma- jority. And if a growing force in the habits and culture of youth comes to the fore, believe me, we'll recognize that. But you have to know, change, particu- larly radical change, comes more slowly in the countryside. We're not the urban hip. Most people here still think that beatniks are some kind of dangerous sub- versive subculture. I bet there's not a person within twenty miles of here, apart from the local English teacher or one romantic student who's read On the Road or Catcher in the Rye," I said, getting into the rhythm of the argument. "There's nothing to say we can't do more, cover more of what you think we ought to be interested in, Wish, if it's a legitimate issue for this place, right here and right now. But you have to understand, there is also the business of running a suc- cessful newspaper. Something you know absolutely nothing about. Wishbone, you've bought into a valuable asset here. You just gonna goof it up? Let it die?"

Damo looked at me intently. "Believe me, Joe Blow. It is legitimate and there's no time to lose. No time like now to start."

I said," Just a minute, Damo. I was talking to Wishbone. Now, who's the co- owner here? You or Damo? With ownership comes responsibility, baby. So, I want to know, who's calling the shots? And don't forget, the syndicate still controls 50% of the shares. You've got a stalemate on your hands."

Before either could answer, Teddy burst in with a bewildered look on his face, as if he were trying to wake up from a devastating dream.

"What's going on here? What do they want?" The tension notched up as all the unblinking eyes in the room had swung first from me to Wishbone, to

Damo, then back to Wishbone and me. Then collectively, all the visual heat turned directly on Teddy who was more than slightly taken aback.

Not looking forward to this, I stepped up to him and patted him on the shoulder of his seersucker jacket.

"Teddy," I said, sweeping my hand across the room pointing at Wishbone. "Meet the new co-owner of The Applewood Gazette." Teddy's mouth popped open but I was totally prepared. I caught the cigar butt before it could hit the floor.

* * *

The situation looked dire. A rift in the attitude of the two major players, Damo and Wishbone Jones had emerged. Wishbone expressed a willingness to work with the staff of The Gazette although he proposed a radically new editorial agenda. Damo, on the other hand, represented something more destructive, wanting to tear the whole thing down. I wasn't entirely antithetic towards the proposed agenda, that is, if The Gazette had been a student paper or been created by some underground urban guerilla movement. But our old time press went back over sixty years and instantaneous policy changes were not in the offing. The proposal came forward to dump things like gardening, recipes and the lovelorn section and devote swollen column inches to things like rock'n roll, youth affairs, street fashion, and polluting the environment. I can't deny I wasn't attracted to it. What didn't wash however, was the adoption of a biased, left wing, anti-establishment outlook damning outright everything considered traditional, hierarchical, conservative, religious, government, military-related and so on. Damo wanted to confront the community and foment reaction, get people from vastly different walks of life dropped into a fish tank so they'd communicate. I thought they'd asphyxiate in short order.

Upon hearing these strange proposals, Teddy popped more than a few blood vessels in his brain. It took a mighty effort to restrain him. Everything he'd ever done, ever stood for, was being diminished and attacked. But I took it a little more calmly because I had a better idea how things would turn out. Ironically, exposure to this turned out to be a good thing. Maybe, we were too complacent. Maybe we should open our eyes a little more.

"Guys," I said. "What you're proposing here is just not going to work. And I'll tell you why. You're trying to take a viewpoint that exists within a subculture according to you, and impose it on the mainstream. People will shrug it off, won't take it seriously. You've got to let these views percolate up from the bottom if you want people to believe and sympathize, not impose your will from the top down. Instead of opening up the lines of communication, you'll drive a wedge between people and polarize the community. Not only that, it will alienate the span of generations. God knows, parents and kids have a tough enough time getting along without us telling kids to dropkick their parents' values off a cliff marked Rock'n Roll. How about this instead? You get to prepare a column, an editorial each week on a topic of your choice. In the meantime, we'll expand our coverage of what's happening with youth, you know, music, and all that. Maybe we'll set up a youth bureau and hire a student or apprentice to cover that beat. In fact, Wish, you can nominate someone to write the stuff, since you're paying the bills."

Wishbone nodded thoughtfully. "I like that idea, Joe. It's cool. Very cool. In fact, I know the perfect person for the job." And he let out a piercing whistle blast by putting his fingers to his lips. The front door opened and in walked Beverly, smiling cool, calm and collected. She looked professional in a crisp white blouse and slacks, a leather bag hung over her shoulder, pad and pen, in hand and at the ready.

"Meet your new youth affairs reporter, guys."

This was totally unexpected. "Hi Bev," I said.

"Hi Joe."

"But he's go to go," Damo said, pointing at Teddy.

I shook my head. "No. No way. Teddy's the only one who can run this place. If you want to achieve your aims here, that's the way it's got to be. You have any experience running a daily newspaper, Damo? Do you know what it takes to put it together? We all need each other here. Otherwise, you may have bought into a paper but your high-priced investment isn't worth a penny."

"He goes," Damo repeated.

I turned again to Wishbone, who was lounging beside Teddy's desk with his feet up, bouncing his dirty sneakers off the wall.

"It seems to me Wish, that Damo here is exhibiting signs of a militaristic establishment kind of persona-based attitude. Now, you'd better ask yourself. Who's the new co-owner here? You or Damo? Who put up the dough? I can tell you this. If it's Damo, then we'll all walk and you're on your own as of now. You'll have an empty building. Not only that, Teddy and me can pull together enough capital to start our own paper and drive you out of business. We can be up and operating within days. Think about it."

Wishbone laughed nervously. I had him and he knew it. Damo emanated a potent kind of charisma, able to persuade those around him to do what he wanted through the force of his personality, his self-assurance and a hully-gully kind of pseudo-wisdom. So, he'd been in prison and the funny farm? So what? He could use that to manipulate the naive kids in his pack. I think Wishbone sensed this but may not have been looking for a confrontation believing in some sort of wrong-headed peace and love and let's talk about it, approach to life. But Wish was a businessman too. He'd demonstrated that pretty clearly with Sky High.

"Interestingly put, Joe. Very interesting indeed," said Wishbone.

Damo said, "Wishbone, you listening to this codswallop? Jeez, my daddy never shoveled this much shit on his farm."

"Just a second, Damo. You're just a visitor in these parts, right? I live here, man and I got to think about that, dig?" Wishbone turned to me. "I'm not sure about the old guy here, Joe. I don't think he likes us much."

I replied, "Won't stop him from doing a damn good job, Wish. Let me talk to him for a second, all right? You guys clear out and then we'll get back together tomorrow."

"You're stalling," Damo said.

"Hey, you think you can just walk in and change everything instantly? Not going to happen. I'm just asking for a day, that's all."

"He's right," Beverly said. "A day's not going to make a difference, right Wish?"

Wish stared at Damo then nodded.

Wishbone and Beverly stood up. "Let's go," Wish said. Damo glared at me and suddenly, I felt real fear. His personality oozed intimidation. They filed out and closed the door behind them. As soon as we were alone, Teddy exploded.

"Are you insane, Joe? Negotiating with these delinquents? Have you completely lost your senses?"

"Calm down, Teddy. Just calm down, for god's sake. I know what I'm doing."

"How the hell can I calm down? A bunch of long-haired revolutionaries have marched in here and taken control of The Gazette for Christ's sake."

"You know, Teddy. Some of the things they're suggesting make sense. Not the way, maybe but the content. Maybe we've closed our minds a little to what is going on out there. Maybe we need a bit of a broader perspective. And I think hiring an apprentice is a solid idea."

Teddy slammed his hand down on his desk, took the cigar out of his mouth and pointed it at me.

"Now I know you've really lost it, this time, Joe. It's that girl, Beverly. She's got you tied up in knots. She stole your brain in the night."

"Now leave Beverly out of this. It's got nothing to do with her, Teddy. Nothing. Teddy, I want you to clam up a second and listen to me, okay? We will go along with these people. Wait and hear me out. We will placate them, do you hear? Soon, everything will be back to normal. It will be as if nothing happened, like it was just a bad dream. That's my solemn promise."

Teddy continued to glare at me and I looked right back at him. He ground the cigar between his teeth. Finally, he looked away, unsure now.

"What do you mean exactly, Joe. You know something I don't?"

"Yes."

"What is it?"

"I'm not telling."

"Come on."

"No."

Teddy sighed and shook his head slumping into his chair. "Ah Joe, I don't know what's going on here. Maybe you're right. Maybe I'm out of step with what's happening in the world. Maybe I don't deserve to be a newspaperman anymore."

I said, "That's utter nonsense and you know it. As a veteran newspaperman, you're supposed to keep an open mind on things. So, for god's sake, let's just do that and work with what we've got today. Tomorrow, who knows?"

Fear shone in his face and for once he seemed completely incapable of using his grumpiness as a defense. He stood there, looking like a vulnerable, middle-aged man standing at the brink where he could lose everything he held dear. He glanced around and where most would see a few rickety desks and wobbly chairs, Teddy saw ideas and life and issues and arguments and above all, stories.

"I love this little hovel, Joe," he said quietly and sincerely. "I don't want to lose it. It's all I've got."

"You won't Teddy. And that's a promise."

All I had to do was make good.

Then I left. I left because I had to calm my nerves and I needed to find some courage to talk to Delaney, the kind that came out of a bottle. I walked up the street instinctively heading for comfort. The Round Table. I didn't have to think, just park myself on a stool, prop my elbows on the bar and order a Johnny Walker Black, no ice. Sam, the barman gave me a look but made no comment, just poured it out and set the glass in front of me in one smooth, easy motion. The place looked barren, just one out-of-towner nursing a bloody Mary reading the newspaper. Not The Gazette. I could tell. I took a sip and it went down like a volley of fire. Just what I needed.

"You got troubles, Joe?"

I looked up over the rim of the glass. There must have been surprise all over my face because I heard a peal of laughter. "Mickey....?"

She eased on to the stool beside me. "You expecting someone else?"

"No, not really. It's just that..."

"I'm never seen during the light of day? Is that the rumour now? That I'm a vampire?"

"Of course not. I'm just used to seeing Delaney down here, that's all."

"I spend too much time in that damn office, upstairs. I get the feeling I'm missing out on things." She fished a Dunhill out of her satin bag. "Got a light, Joe?"

I fumbled with my lighter but got it going. She looked at me over the flame. Her emerald eyes sparked. I almost forgot to snap it shut but Mickey tilted her head away blowing out smoke.

"Thanks," she said. "You look like your puppy just died."

"Wish it were that simple, Mickey."

"Tell me about it."

I shook my head. "Maybe one day. I was hoping to find Delaney here, though."

"He's out. Dealing with some suppliers. Any message?"

I shook my head again. I signaled the barkeep for a refill and he topped me up. Mickey remained calm and unruffled. I placed a five on the bar top but she pushed the bill back to me.

"Your money's no good here, Joe, and that's my say-so."

"Thanks." Which left me wondering how to start the question I wanted to ask. But then she made it easy for me.

"Go ahead," she said but then glanced at the elegant Cartier on her wrist. "If you're quick about it. This place never stops and I have things to do."

"I was just wondering about the old days... you know, before the war."

"What about them?"

"Did you know him then?"

She took a long drag on her cigarette, then shook her head. "I met him after... 1947. He was running a bar in Montreal. I came in as the office manager and the rest, as they say, is history. Why do you want to know, Joe? Are you writing an exposé on local businessmen?"

"The word is you're selling up."

"We're thinking about it. Why not enjoy life while we can? While we're still young enough? Things are changing around here and we just don't fit in, anymore. There's nothing wrong with that, is there?"

"I suppose not."

"But you have doubts?"

I shrugged. I really didn't know how to answer her without giving too much away.

"You think we're a strange match, Delaney and me?"

"I wouldn't know."

"We suit each other. We're a team and work well together. Without both of us, this place wouldn't have been a success."

"And RSC Developments wouldn't have been interested?"

"That's right. Best time to get out is at the top end of the market."

"And that's now?"

"Could be... or maybe not. We'll just have to see, won't we?" She slid off the stool, then straightened her skirt.

"About Delaney... "

"Yes?"

"What was it that...?"

She crushed the fag end into an onyx ashtray. Mickey was a cool customer. "It was the element of danger I found exciting. I went to a convent school, you know? All those girls in a cloistered environment. We used to talk about the ideal man, our romantic hero. That's Delaney. Sometimes, I think he's capable of just about anything and that keeps a girl interested. On her toes. You just never know what he's going to do some days. Know what I mean?"

Again, I shrugged. "Don't know much about convent schools... or girls for that matter."

"Well, if you meet one...watch out. It was nice talking to you, Joe. See you around." Then she floated away from the bar. I watched her go, then gulped the rest of my drink.

Chapter Twenty-Eight

Monday, June 16th, 1966. Barely one week after I first saw the wretched body of Norma Jennings sprawled in the sand and felt an impotent surge of outrage and despair.

Night had descended and I drove my car through a wooded drive keeping my thoughts sheltered from the consequences ahead. The story. Finding the truth pushed me forward. I hoped I was wrong. Top down, wind streaming in over the side but I felt rock solid with a granite sense of purpose, unmoved and unmovable. There'd been some rain and the tires hummed as they spun along the tarmac prior to turning down the dirt road. The moon above was shrouded in cloud and I could almost hear the Wagnerian music in the treetops and the shrieks of carrion fowl piercing the night air. Inexplicably, I thought of a purple prose poem I'd read in school:

The moon was a ghostly galleon
Tossed upon cloudy seas
And the Highwayman came riding, riding
The Highwayman came riding, riding...

And now, I did the riding, a different steed, however, but my future and that of the fabled Highwayman were fated to merge or diverge. The poetic hero had been shot down by the Sheriff, lured from safety out of love for a woman. And me? I didn't know. Poetic irony. I hated poetry.

Under a lone streetlamp stood a forlorn phone booth. Probably the only one for thirty miles. I pulled up and pushed my way in. The glass had been punched out but the receiver still hummed like a reassuring pulse. I made a call.

The farmhouse looked shabbier and more dilapidated than I remembered but this time I came in sober; paint peelings hung in strips like shriveled banana skins. Underneath, menacing cracks splintered the wood. Holes had been punched in the flesh of the screen door and the windows had a nice coat of cooking grease. The yard had been left untended—unkempt, baling baskets full of refuse had been tossed in a heap spilling rotted food, broken bricks and fire ashes.

Nonetheless, the trees stood tall, proud, almost contemptuous. Boulders hunched in shadowy outcrops like stolid, silent scouts, guardians of the night. As I parked my car under the dense overhang of a willow tree, a rumble came out of the heavens accompanied by the first splattering of rain. I left the top down and walked toward the house, then ran as the rain upped its tempo. I sprinted the long driveway and my hair flattened as the wet soaked through my windbreaker and streamed into the thin T-shirt I wore underneath. The weather's oppressiveness mirrored my own forebodings. The closer I drew, the more my heart accelerated its beat. My lungs couldn't pull in enough air. Around back, I spotted a hazy shape. I crept up to it. Seemed to be a car covered in a canvas sheet. I lifted up a corner but all I saw was ink. I pulled the canvas away then slipped on wet leaves going down in a heap and by doing so, dragged the sheet off the body. I cursed under my breath, grabbed hold of the door handle and pulled myself upright. I ran my hands along its trim exterior, savoured the sleek contours, fingered the headlamps in front and whistled to myself. Black Corvette. Fantasy car. I stood there in the wet, admiring it for a moment, then turned to go. Same car that ran me off the road.

By the time I'd traveled to within feet of the front door, my breath came out huffing. I desperately wanted a smoke. I thought I knew what I was doing. In fact, I had played the scenario out in my mind casting the villains as characters in a story of my own making. *Most of the arrows connected in my head. I saw the old man and he laughed at me but I told myself I'd beat him this time. He'd never have gotten the story I was going to write. I'd put him out of my life and thoughts for good.* But certainty didn't exist when dealing with personalities that thrived on unpredictability. I don't mean physical danger necessarily, although there was that too but the mind itself, cut its way through to new ideas and experiences butchering the old standards left behind. Some might think it a serious threat to one's existence. I didn't share that view. This pursuit of the new and unusual fell out of grace fragmenting the innocence of those harmed by it, twinned by the motivating selfishness and self-interest of those who operated under the facade of a new movement. There were victims. Who was going to make it right? In the cases of Norma Jennings, Darlene Norris, Lizzie and Ellis Boston, the answer popped up as a cipher. Nothing to be done. No way to make it up. I held out a dim hope for Ellis but nothing more.

They wouldn't be expecting me and that calmed me somewhat. I'd let them think we'd capitulated and that they had won. That our ignorance came compounded by fear. We had cowered and let them take just enough of a lead on the leash. What was I thinking?

I rapped sharply on the windowpane. I heard a sudden exhortation from within, a drawn out AAAhhhhh sound. Voices started up and a pale face appeared shiftily at the window, full of suspicion and anger. He fumbled with the lock and the door swung open.

Wishbone Jones, clad only in soiled jeans, pulling on his fly-away moustaches blocked the entranceway.

"What are you doing out here at this time of night, Joe?" I didn't answer and he could see I appeared serious-minded and purposeful. Maybe I spooked him a little.

"Oh, what the hell, you'd better come in," he said and stepped aside. His long hair hung limply about his face. On his chest I saw a dagger tattoo, its sparkling tip poised to prick his heart. Stepping further in, I shook off loose droplets of water. I saw Billy Ross and Damo. Neither spoke but exchanged looks while they sat on low chairs around a coffee table, its formica top ringed with stains and bubbled with holes burned by misplaced butt ends. The room was lit only by a small, brass floor lamp, the kind you pick up at flea markets for a buck. The corners had sunk into shadows.

I nodded to them. "Gentlemen."

"Looks like it's been raining," said Bobby Ross by way of a joke and laughed for a long time over nothing until the sound died away in his swollen throat. Damo retained his composure.

"Have a seat, Joe," Wishbone Jones said looking anxious. "Can I get you something? You know, coffee or beer, something?"

"No thanks," I replied.

"Joe's got something to tell us, isn't that right, Joe?" Damo said and I could picture him preparing to take some action only I had no idea what that might be.

"Listen Joe. I hope you're not sore about what happened at The Gazette today. We'll work it out, right? Everybody'll be happy," Wishbone said, nervously running thin fingers up and down his sinewy arms.

I shook my head. "I don't think so, Wish. I just don't think it's going to play."

"Why not?" And I could see he looked genuinely puzzled as if he really thought everything would go according to some idealistic plan.

"I think you know why," I replied.

"Oh, I get it, Joe," Wishbone said putting his hands on his bony hips. His chest was so skinny I could count his ribs. "Your real boss wouldn't like it, huh? You and Graff are in the pockets of the developers right? Rothwell and that bunch? That's it, isn't it? They've got you on a string. Oh boy, Joe. I sure had you figured all wrong."

"You still do. Where'd you get the money to buy The Gazette, Wish? You paid a lot for those shares—close to $200,000, I reckon. You've only been in town maybe six months. I know Sky High's doing well but not that well."

Wishbone made out as if he wanted to laugh but it came out like a strangled whinny.

"Hey, don't you know that I'm an eccentric millionaire, Joe? I thought you knew that. It was family money. Money I inherited."

"Maybe it was, maybe it wasn't," I said.

Damo and Billy Ross remained rigid as statues.

Wishbone exclaimed, "What don't you think, huh? You don't believe me, Joe? Well, it's true." And he laughed, a high, tinny laugh that gave me shivers. Damo's face had gone white, pinched with anger. Bobby Ross's eyes glowed unnaturally bright. He licked his lips in anticipation of some madness about to begin.

I shrugged. "Maybe you do have family money, Wish, but that doesn't change the fact that you and Damo and Bobby Ross here, are dealing." The tension squeezed up a few points. Bobby Ross glared at me with a hunger, salivating at the thought of causing me some harm. But he knew, or thought he knew that I wasn't going anywhere, either, and could wait for the right time. A cold sweat broke out across Wishbone's face.

"Selling what?" he sneered, frightened now.

"Oh you know, Wish. It's called lysergic acid diethylamide—aka LSD, a powerful hallucinogen, right? You boys have created a nice little market for yourselves out here in tourist land. Flying kids to the moon. Stirred up the competition too, a little bit. Stay away from the Meadows, eh fat boy? And the Viking wasn't threatening to horn in on your action, was he? Looks like you've got a nice little war out here."

"You're crazy, Joe. Crazy as a jaybird." Wish turned to his companions. "He's crazy. Totally crazy."

"You know all about it, don't you Damo? You were given LSD up at the funny farm, weren't you?"

Damo smiled radiantly. "That's right, Joe Blow. I know all about it."

"So, you teamed up with Bobby here, the local boy who made good, am I right, Bobby? You had a hot commodity here, a growing market to tap. That night, when I stumbled in here. The strong chemical odour I smelled wasn't cleaning solvent spilled by accident. You gentlemen are brewing the stuff right here. Or nearby. You've got your own little laboratory out here in the sticks. It's perfect. Isolated. Easy for dropping off and picking up, either by land, by boat or even air."

Wishbone started to plead now. "Joe. Don't say that, Joe. You don't know what you're saying, really, you just don't know. Don't say anymore. For god's sake."

Bobby, in his Neanderthal-like brain, decided now was the time. He stood up.

"So, you just walked in here? That's good for us, I guess. And bad for you."

Damo put out a hand to restrain him. "Hold on. There's more. Am I right, Joe Blow? Let's hear the whole damn story first. There's time. We'll hurt him later. I love a good story."

I said, "Oh yeah. There's more. Have a look at this. I'm sure you'll find it interesting." And I tossed a brown manila envelope on the table. Damo picked it up, curious now, ripped the flap and pulled out one of the photographs Dusty had taken down by the Meadows. He examined it for a long moment, then dropped it.

"Old news," he said.

Wishbone rushed over. "Lemme see that," he cried grabbing it up. He picked up the photo and went rigid, turning to chalk. He drew his right hand down his face as if it were the monkey's paw.

"This was all you, wasn't it Wish? You thought, let's burn the brains of the entire countryside. Raising or in this case, exploding the consciousness of the community. Beautiful. Except for a couple of things, of course. Took me a while to figure it out. You have a number of events seemingly unconnected. Norma in the drink, Darlene disappears, Ellis Boston, some of the townsfolk picket the main square proclaiming the end of the world and evil prevailing, fish affected and even me, having bizarre dreams and feelings. The Jersey Jokers show up and lo and behold it's all going down. But I couldn't see the connection. Then it hit me. Water. I did some research in the library. A small amount of undiluted chemicals dumped in Buttermilk Creek will affect anyone drinking the water or using it for irrigation like the dozens of farms in the area. Like Ellis Boston's farm, for instance. That's the common denominator. Water. Simple. Effective. Easy."

Wishbone broke in, stammering, sniffing danger. "No one was supposed to get hurt, Joe. I swear it. It was supposed to be a joke. A prank."

"Shut up, Wishbone," sneered Bobby Ross.

I nodded. "That's right, Wish. This was your way of getting back at what you hated—the developers and big business interests. Blow the minds of the townsfolk and screw the development by gumming up the machinery. Then along the way what happens? Lizzie Boston is dead. Her husband's mind is locked away somewhere in Beech Mental Hospital. Thousands of fish have gone weird. And then there was Norma and Darlene. You supplied them, didn't you? They started coming to your parties, and hanging out. Isn't that how it all started? They were good looking, young, and eager to experience new things."

"It wasn't supposed to happen like that, I swear it, Joe."

"Norma couldn't handle it," Damo said. "Didn't take the right approach. She was a lamebrain, you know? And she drank too much at the same time. A real downer. That's what went wrong. It was her approach, her attitude. She just didn't get it. So, she got cut off. Darlene just came along for the ride."

"Well, I guess Norma kept something for a rainy day, Damo old buddy, because her blood was hopped with the stuff."

Damo shrugged. "That's just the way it is, sometimes."

I sneered, "You're all heart. Big man when it comes to rhetoric and platitudes. Revolutionary…bullshit…hype…artist…con man. What do you think of that, baldy?"

He shrugged. "It's not gonna make a difference to you, not here, not now."

I turned back to Wishbone. "What about the kid, Blake? Was he in this too?"

Wishbone backed away. "No. No. He wasn't involved. No way. Only Norma. The kid didn't know a thing. I mean, look, Joe. I couldn't do that, you know…"

One more arrow to draw, a through line from Wishbone intersecting Phillip and finally, to an eleven-year old prep school boy. "To your own clean cut nephew, Wishbone? Your nice preppy junky boy?" I paused while he stared at me in that stupefying, mouth wide-open kind of way.

"Am I right…William?"

His mouth opened and closed like a fish but no sound came out as he swallowed several times trying to work something back into his palate.

"You don't know that. What would…?" he whispered.

"I got another snap here," I said, drawing it out of my soggy pocket. "It's one where everyone is playing happy families. Take a look, Wish. It's a wedding shot, Phillip Rothwell's wedding." I held it out to him and Wishbone snatched it from my hand but held it like it contained a deadly virus. His expression looked as if he'd just contracted one. "I started thinking about why these things were happening in the town. What was the point of driving people loony? And why target the resort development and sabotage the equipment? I did a little reading and came across an item about Philip Rothwell, discovered he had a younger brother who seemed to have disappeared, a younger brother who, at the age of 16, tried to shoot him. Not much resemblance left to that prep school kid, is there? Except for the way you cock your eyebrow. That's exactly the same." I pulled out the blow-up Dusty made showing William's right hand and threw it at him. I grabbed his right hand and held it up to the light. "And then there's this, of course. Fancy school ring. Finally. A clue to the background of the mysterious Wishbone Jones. I couldn't resist checking it out after I saw it the other night at the shop. Guess what? I looked it up. This ring belongs to St. Gerhard's College for Boys—an exclusive boarding school. 'Never Lost, Always Found'. Kind of profound, isn't it? And who was enrolled as a student at St. Gerhard's in 1941? Let me fill in the blanks for you. One William Rothwell, brother of Phillip. Some coincidence that you happened to have the same ring, isn't it, Wish? You being William is the only thing that makes sense. Where did William go after he disappeared? And now he's turned up here in Applewood. Hippie. Record store proprietor. Drug dealer. You must really hate your brother a lot," I said. Even Damo and Bobby Ross looked surprised.

Wishbone dropped his hands to his sides and looked straight up at the ceiling. He was the walking dead now. And knew it.

"Oh shit," he said. "Guilty as charged, Joe." Then he looked down at me and I could see bitter tears welling up in the corners of his eyes. "You gotta know something, Joe. You see, I have dedicated my life to undoing everything my brother has ever done. I mean everything."

I shook my head in disbelief. Blind fury. "Enough to do all this?"

He balled his hands into enormous fists and brought them together on his skinny chest. He gulped for air. He'd explode in a second. Then he screamed,

"You don't understand. Nobody does. He killed my father."

And the sound of his pain echoed in the lonely room. Then he spoke quietly, whispering, trance-like.

"Phillip's hand was on the trigger. The thing of it is, Joe, I heard the shot. I found him, lying there, with his blood all over the walls, the carpet, the ceiling, everywhere. Can you imagine that? Eleven years old and seeing your own father like that, huh? It messed me up real good. I swore I'd pay him back. But first, I had to get away. When I felt ready, I came home. It took a long time and some years before I could make that happen. But I made it, man. I pulled myself together. The only things he cares about are money and power. Power corrupts right? Well it did a helluva job on Phillip, that's for sure." The truth was, I could imagine it, more than Wish would ever know.

He was down on his knees now. "You gotta believe me...no one was supposed to get hurt. It wasn't supposed to be that way, I swear it. Oh God, I swear it."

"Well Wish," I said. "That's the problem with money. Someone's always trying to take it away from you." Tears flowed into the furrows of his seamed face splattering his naked chest, running down the blade of the tattoo. They looked like drops of blood leaking from an open wound.

"Guys...we can make this right. No one has to get hurt, right? No one has to get hurt anymore...."

Damo cracked his knuckles and the muscles in his biceps jumped and twitched. "Now Joe Blow," he said quietly. "Just where does all this leave you, huh?"

Bobby Ross eagerly nodded his shaggy head. "Just what I was thinking."

I said, "Don't be stupid. You think I haven't written all this out and sent a packet containing the photos to the police?"

Damo put back his head and roared.

"To McKie? That incompetent birdbrain? He wouldn't know what to do in a laundromat. What would you have us do, Joe? In our position, what would you do?"

I shrugged. "I never said it was McKie," I said. "There's more. There always is. You see, boys, I've been thinking about this whole thing long and hard. Now, it seems to me this operation required organization. The kind of organization you boys weren't really capable of handling. That meant an older hand. Someone with the know-how and experience to run things like distribution, pricing, and lest I forget, fixing the cops. Someone who enjoyed keeping young girls like Darlene and Norma on a string." I paused. But then I just had to show off. Show them how intelligent I was. How thorough an investigator I could be. "If you're a student of history, kinda reminds me of the booze wars in the 20's and 30's." The room lapsed into deathly silence. Wish stood shivering and hugging himself off to the side. Bobby Ross and Damo went still.

Out of the gloom, I heard the snap of a lighter and caught a glint of gold. I saw the flare as a Dunhill flamed, then caught fire. The fire died quickly into the hot coal of a burning ember, it brightened then dimmed with a quick exhalation of smoke.

I said, "Hello Delaney."

His polished shoes gleamed in the dim light. He moved forward and the click of his heels on the broken wooden floor tapped out in rhythm. He drawled casually. "Hi Joe." He stepped into the circle of light. The other three half-turned towards him and waited. He rotated the fancy gold lighter, playing it with his slim brown fingers, so fastidiously manicured. Delaney shot me a weary smile. Somehow, the teeth didn't seem as white or pearly.

"What are we going to do with you, Joe?" he asked thoughtfully.

"How about cement overshoes in Rattlesnake Bay?" I sneered.

Delaney laughed. "I think we can do better than that, kid." He paused, then frowned. "You know, this was a foolish move. I was hoping you had more sense."

"I figured it out. Others will too."

The smooth shoulders came up, then down. "Maybe. But we'll be cleared out. Long gone."

"Tell me why, Delaney. You had a good deal. A pretty fine life, it seemed to me."

He grinned, stretching his fine lips into a tight mask.

"Oh you mean playing the smiling host to a bunch of tight-assed tourists? You call that a life? To a stooge maybe but not me. It was choking me, Joe. I wanted my old life back. But of course, it's never the same, is it?" And rubbed his chin thoughtfully.

"And you hooked up with these clowns? To peddle LSD? To mess up the lives of innocent young girls?"

"I'm a peddler from way back, Joe. Booze. Drugs. The girls are always part of that kind of show. They don't matter. They never do. Besides, they weren't so innocent. Let's just say, I saw a market opportunity—that's what the business guys call it, don't they? I needed supply, courtesy of old Wishbone here, distribution, Damo's line and then, some muscle, Bobby Ross and his boys. Not quite like bootlegging but not half bad, either. It was fun for awhile."

I said, "You forgot the cops."

Delaney grimaced like he'd eaten something sour. "Right. And the cops. McKie was cheap but he's a dummy. Guenther had a little more on the ball but not much. Still, they were useful in their own way."

In my mind, I saw the jugglers and the acrobats sliding tabs to pimply kids in corners while children screamed with laughter and delight. Concealing powder in the balloons they handed out.

"Norma was pregnant with your child?"

He shrugged. "Didn't know about that. Too bad."

Delaney took a long drag on the Dunhill, allowing himself to forage in his memories, then flicked some ash onto the floor. When he came to, his eyes were dark and hooded. "It never lasts, of course."

"There is that," I said.

"What are you going to do with this guy?" screeched Bobby Ross.

"Shut up," Delaney said.

"But I…"

"I said, shut up," Delaney growled, baring his teeth.

"That's right. What's the play now?" As a reporter, I had to know. The phone call I'd made. I'd left a message for Hal letting him know where I'd be headed and what I'd be doing. Figured he'd ride in with guns blazing. As a potential victim, I was scared to death.

Delaney slid his right hand inside his left armpit. The elegantly tailored tuxedo jacket fell open revealing brown leather straps—a harness. Delaney jerked his arm back quickly and I heard the scrape of metal on rawhide. A pretty looking .45 automatic service revolver appeared in his strong hand. It was pointed at me. The weapon looked old but well-cared for, freshly oiled and ready-to-use.

A laugh as thin as an eggshell cracked the silence. Wishbone shuffled forward, shaking his head, hair swinging from side to side.

"No way, man. It's not going to happen. No way."

The snout of the .45 shifted direction slightly, the barrel pointing now at Wishbone's bare chest. The distance between them—about sixteen feet. Wish continued to shuffle toward Delaney, inching almost, talking as his feet scuffed the floor. Delaney stood there silently, looking calm and relaxed, the cigarette drooping off his lips, smoke curling lazily upward in the humid air.

Wish rapped, "I've been in the jungles. I've been in the cities. I've looked in men's faces when they've been afraid. Of everything. Of me. I've seen death. I've delivered it, man. I'm sick of it. I just can't let you do that," Wish said, laughing nervously. "I just can't," he pleaded. "Don't you see? It just screws everything up. I mean, everything I've been trying to do here." He contorted half-laughing and half-crying as he spoke, whimpery and joyful.

They stood six feet apart now. Damo and Bobby Ross froze into statues. Damo had a wild, excited look in his eyes. Wishbone reached now, fingers groping, almost touching Delaney, hoping to mesmerize him into giving the weapon away. That's when the shot rang out. Boom. So loud. Louder than anything I've ever heard, shattering the room with thunder and smoke. Wishbone's body recoiled from the chest downward in a vibrating pulse. His tangled head recoiled, hair springing from his scalp like a string curtain, his arms flew up and the momentum slapped him flat on his back. His right leg bent at the knee tucked neatly under the left, as if he were about to curtsey. His head rolled twice, then lay still, features slack, eyes rolled upward in a glassy stare. The tip of the tattooed dagger had been shot away, leaving a gaping hole. Only now, the drops of blood were real.

"Jesus!" exclaimed Bobby Ross. "Sweet Jesus." Wish's blood splattered his face. He clawed at it like a wild animal.

Delaney coolly looked at me. "Too bad. He was a good chemist. But things got out of hand and all good things come to an end. Wishbone had a weak heart and a conscience. He really thought he could change things for the better through the paper. He was a dangerous fool and that's bad for business." He paused, contemplating the barrel of the gun then looked up. "You got any tabs stashed here?" Damo forced his gaze away from Wishbone's body. He nodded mutely.

"Get me a couple."

Damo disappeared into the back.

"So that's how it is," I said bitterly.

"That's how it is, Joe." Damo returned and held out three small purple tablets in the scarred palm of his hand.

"Take them, Joe." I took them. "Wash them down with this."

Delaney handed over his elegant flask. He flicked the barrel of the gun. The knuckle of his forefinger tightened on the trigger. I unscrewed the elegant little top, threw the pills into my throat, took a pull and swallowed.

"Damo, make sure Joe's not playing hide-a-boo."

Damo forced my mouth open and prodded my tongue with his thick fingers. He would have made a lousy dentist.

"Looks okay," he said.

"How long?" Delaney asked.

"About ten minutes, maybe less." Damo replied.

Delaney nodded.

"Tie him to a chair but not too tight."

Damo forced me down into one of the vinyl, padded kitchen chairs, the kind that stick to your back and make you sweat. I sweated plenty. Bobby Ross flinched spastically clawing at his face until Damo went over and slapped him hard with the back of his hand. Bobby stopped then, coming back to his senses. He stood up then slipped a cotton jib sheet over my head, binding me across the hips and chest. He tied my hands behind my back. My head began to balloon.

Damo said, "It's done."

Delaney nodded again, checking his watch.

"Time to go. Too bad about all this, Joe. I really did appreciate the write-up on the restaurant."

"It was a pack of lies," I said.

Delaney grinned.

"Oh Joe, I'm wounded." The grin died. "So long, kid. See you in Cap Ferrat, or hell, maybe."

The three of them left only the echo of their footsteps. They stranded me with my own thoughts, the sight of poor Wishbone stretched out on the floor and the rattling of the windows as the rain lashed at the broken down farmhouse, pounding the tin roof in a fury. I thought I heard a tinkle of glass and a crackling sound. Out of the back bedroom, I saw a sheath of fire. Tendrils of smoke two-stepped across the room.

I giggled. Nice fire. Warm me up. Nice, nice fire. Campfire. Out in the woods. We could sing some songs. The line of fire drifted forward and formed itself into fingers, then hands, and then sprouted a leering, shimmering face. The crackling and popping jumped inside my head. Kernels of sound caromed around inside my skull. Rivets of pain shot through every nerve end, down my neck, along my shoulders and through my arms. A green field of electricity radiated out of my fingertips. I held them up and I could see right through them, see the skin melting away and the bones crumbling to dust. I screamed out in a strangled, horrible voice. A voice made eerie and strange by the dope. Wishbone's body floated up off the floor. I screamed again, then, as the sound came back at me, laughed for no reason other than it seemed to make some kind of sense. I tried it again and it felt good. My ribs undulated with the exhortation of breath. Wishbone's bare feet were pointed toward me now, then swiveled back and forth unsteadily like a compass point finding its pole.

A voice talked very fast. My voice.

"Hands of fire. Tall too. Taller than a tabernacle. Hands of fire. He speaks to me. So I slew him. I slew him with a hoe. Why not? It was a perfectly good hoe. Wishbone, spin me a disc, man. Make it a good one. House of the Rising Sun. Yeah. My soul lies heavy tonight…I see dead fish…dead fish…jumping in the road."

Wishbone's corpse then commenced to spin. The compass had gone haywire as the motion picked up speed pushed by some centrifugal force and I heard the whine as his feet, then head, hair flying straight out, whizzed by, a sound like a rotor cranking up, catching on, then spinning faster and faster until it formed a rounded shape that bled orange and green and violet—the colours splattered the room like globs of paint or blood.

Beyond the blur, moving and yet not moving oozed a blanket of fire, it crept up and over like an animal, putting its paws on Wishbone's body forcing the spinning to slow until he came fully into view. The fire then wrapped itself cosily and magnificently around him as the voices…those magic voices came back to carry me away. They hummed, "AAAHHHHH…" and the power and tension of the music swelled horribly, filling the room, filling me, digging into my arms and legs like rivets driven into flesh and I screamed in agony as the notes swelled carrying my voice with it. It grew and grew like a helium balloon, pressing my chest, squeezing the air out of my lungs until I felt the heat and the room with me would explode, the pressure building, pushing beyond pain, beyond gravity, beyond being. A great roar filled my ears and bashed and beat me about the temples. My eyes rolled back in their sockets. I felt my body begin to lift off like a rocket in its first stage. A tremendous force carried me up and up and then, like Ellis Boston, I sprouted wings, the front of my face stretched, then elongated into a beak, and I flew for what seemed like miles and miles. Soaring on the wind. I looked down. Far below were the thin ribbons of roadways and tall grass wavering in the breeze, reeds and golden rod bent to one side. Suddenly, I felt cold. I tucked my head under my arm and tumbled from the sky. That's all I remember. It seemed like plenty.

* * *

A hard-edged instrument beat my face. I wanted it to stop. Stop, I said but the beating continued. Like talons clawing my cheeks. I tried to raise my arms. Fend it off, whatever it was. I remained helpless. There was nothing I could do, couldn't resist. The beating wouldn't go away.

"Joe?"

I opened my eyes. Through a sheen of sparks and flames, Beverly's face shimmered before me. It changed colours. First green, then orange, then purple. The instrument of torture had been her hand caressing my cheek. I moved my limbs. They seemed to be functioning. I looked around and sniffed. Smelled ether and ointments. Starched sheets. Empty walls. Had to be a hospital room. That meant I lived and functioned.

"Bev?" She nodded and gave me a cloudy smile.

"You've had a nasty time of it, Joe. But you're going to be okay," she whispered in her strong, vibrant way. And the clouds and sparks and flames slowly began to dissipate and drift away. I took a good look, blinked and looked again. She wore a smart suit and her hair was neatly groomed. Her fingernails looked professionally tapered and polished. I glanced down and spotted fashionable high heels and an expensive looking leather bag at her feet. Then her manner. A bit cold, distant. She wore glasses. In her lap lay a newspaper. She handed it over. I recognized it as a copy of the Toronto Herald-Dispatch. "Take a look," she said. "Sadly," she continued not sounding remorseful at all, "we scooped you on this one. It wasn't my choice, Joe, you've got to believe that."

I read the headline, saw the photo of Wishbone's burnt out house, scanned down to pictures of Phillip Rothwell, the scale model of Applewood Resort, Wishbone as an adult and a blow up of him as an 11 year-old at his brother's wedding. "Nice byline," I said. "Good for you, sister. Looks like the only way you could scoop me was having me blown up and left for dead."

She actually smiled at that. "I admire that about you, Joe. You're persistent and brave. Foolhardy, but no one can doubt you've got guts."

Although my brain had been mashed like overcooked linguine, bits started to gel. "The note about the Meadows. That was you?"

"Uh-huh."

"Why?

She sighed. "Believe it or not I was trying to help you get the story. I found out what Wish and Damo were doing at the Meadows but when you ended up here, it left me no choice. I had to file it. I'm sure you understand. I think we're alike in that way. It's all about the story, isn't it?"

"And the rest of it, all that guff about your family, leaving your sisters, wanting to go to university...?"

Beverly cleared her throat. "Well, part of it was true, the stuff about my sisters. I didn't get along with my dad. Just another one of those mean drunks, so I had to get out."

"Right. So, this was just another assignment to you?"

"Barrett's idea. He figured I could fit in quickly. After he heard about the Rothwell kid and the inquest, he decided I could do a little bit of undercover reporting, so he sent me up here from Toronto to check out the situation. You turned him down, remember? He wanted you first, Joe. I came second. I was his back-up plan," she said with some bitterness. "Like I had to prove myself to him, so I made sure that's what I did. The whole thing with Wishbone just happened. I was looking for a job and he had one available. I didn't know he was into the other things, I mean, not the extent of it."

"And you and he were...close?"

Beverly paled and stared into her lap. But to her credit, she finally faced me full on. "When you're undercover, Joe, it needs to be convincing so, things happen. I'm not always proud of it. Wishbone was a gentle soul underneath it all. I really liked him. And for what it's worth, I liked you too. Wish got badly screwed up when his father died."

"So, I was just the roadkill, crushed under the tires of the story." I made it a statement not a question. Her eyes widened but she didn't say anything but finally, a terse nod blew my way. Can't say it didn't hurt, hurt plenty. "Uh, you know, I have fragments of memory, pieces coming back to me. That night at Wish's party, I seem to recall you and he arguing. What was that about?"

Beverly sighed. "It was about the drugs."

"What about them?"

"He and Damo were selling them to the kids at the store. The kids who came to buy records. When I found out, it made me angry so I asked him to stop."

"Never thought about telling the cops?"

"No."

"The story came first. Well, you're a real pro, kid. Had me fooled. Guess I'll get you next time."

"I know about you, Joe. Barrett told me...about your folks, how your mom killed your father and went to prison for it."

"Pitying the downtrodden, Beverly? How noble." Suddenly all the arrows in my head dissolved, went to mush. "I think you should go now, Beverly. You've had your moment. Gloating time is over." My head felt like an old banger and what energy I had left bled away from the verbal sparring with Beverly. My eyelids slipped and she just disappeared from view.

An eon later, Teddy Graff appeared. His head seemed unnaturally large, swollen like a balloon.

"Scared us plenty, Joe," he boomed through an echo chamber.

"If I'd known what you were up to, I would have stopped you. Damned crazy thing taking on those boys. Why, you're lucky to be alive. And then where would I be? Have to break in some young reporter from scratch. Inconsiderate, Joe. Damned inconsiderate."

I nodded. "Wishbone..?"

Teddy shook his head sadly. "We know about that too. Found what's left of him in that burned out shack. The others got away...for now."

"How did I..?"

From a crane attached to the ceiling, Hal Bigelow's head lowered into view. "Damndest thing. You got blown clear, Joe. You must've been sitting near a couple of propane tanks. When they ignited, you were launched right out of the place and landed in some bales of hay and garbage outside. Doc Seaton says it's a miracle you didn't break your neck. As it is, a fractured ankle, two broken ribs and some singed hair ain't too bad. Though it kind of smells like a summer barbecue in here."

"Funny," I muttered. "Quit the force. Become a comedian." I drew a breath and didn't know breathing could be so painful. "Didn't you get my message?"

Hal frowned. "Message?"

And then I dropped back again into the pit of sleep.

Chapter Twenty-Nine

The mist shrouding my heart evaporated. The fog cleared from my brain. Once the mystery had been revealed, the town of Applewood was left to itself. Left to cope with the challenges facing it. Rebellious youth. Erosion of traditional mores and values. Rampant development. Influx of tourists and new money as Applewood embodied a microcosm of upheaval, both good and bad in its continuing search for clarification of its identity. I simply believed the town suffered through a personality crisis. But what a week it had been! Just mere days after Norma Jennings' body had been fished from the water and I felt as if I'd shed an entire life.

A week later, I managed to get up and around on crutches, feeling well enough to go to Wishbone's funeral. His remains had been released by Doc Seaton, after the usual autopsy with the usual results, of course. Some of the hair from my eyebrows and sideburns started to grow back. A good sign. But still, I looked like someone who'd strayed a little too close to an A-bomb test site in Nevada five seconds before detonation. Patches of skin dropped away from my forehead and chin leaving a pink and brown cross-hatch effect. Suddenly, I was in style.

Hal reluctantly helped me into my grey suit and drove me in my car.

"Is this a date?" he asked.

"Why Hal, honey, never thought you'd ask," I replied through chapped lips. Even my tongue felt sore.

Like everything else, Mount August Cemetery wasn't very far away. Situated up the flat top of Bascomb's Canyon overlooking Rattlesnake Bay. The day broke cool and dry with a touch of wind. I could feel the autumn in it. The Bay shimmered in the sunlight, its dark waters moving restlessly. Something restless moved within me too. I felt in the pocket of my suit coat for the clamshell and caressed its smooth cool surface. Norma had died stupidly but I decided to remember her vitality and youth. The clamshell would echo that for a long time to come.

A small crowd of mourners gathered. Phillip and Roberta Rothwell. Blake hovered restlessly behind his parents, wringing his hands, scratching his palms. Seamus and Paisley O'Toole. Teddy. Hal. Me. Doc Seaton. Barrett Thompkins appeared on the crest of a hill. Smiled beatifically and threw me a salute. I stuck out my tongue at him. Beyond the rise, in the Johnson section, sat a group of long-haired, scruffy kids who'd frequented the record store, those who'd adopted Wishbone as some kind of pop icon. They watched the proceedings with open and silent curiosity.

After the parson spoke his piece, rather dryly, I thought, the diggers lowered Wishbone's casket into its lonely pit. I looked up to see Phillip Rothwell bearing down on me. I was in no condition to escape. He appeared nervous and fluttered his hands.

He said, "I suppose you don't think much of me…" Before I could answer, he went on.

"Can't say I blame you, Simpson. But I want to tell you the truth. William did hate me. He believed, mistakenly, that I killed our father. The truth is, that father was a dying man. His doctors had discovered a brain tumour, inoperable, they said. It was a matter of months at the most. He'd be in pain, and gradually lose all his faculties, slip into a coma and eventually die in a vegetative state. Our father was an extremely proud man. It was intolerable that something like this should happen to him. He told no one of his condition except myself. On the day he died, he'd had some kind of seizure. This was several weeks after the doctors delivered their, uh, analysis to him. He called me into his room. His right side had become paralyzed. It was all happening faster than he'd thought. He was panic-stricken. When I went in, a pistol was lying at his feet. He'd dropped it and couldn't hold the grip. He then ordered me to pick it up, place it in his right hand, put the barrel to his temple and pull the trigger. He begged me to do it. The thought of it was horrific to me, of course. But out of love and respect and maybe, fear…I did what he asked of me. I did it for him. You must believe that. It all seemed to happen so fast. William heard the shot. I didn't even know he was in the house. He came racing into the room and saw my father on the floor, the gun at my feet and drew the obvious conclusion. Nothing I could do or say altered his belief that I had murdered our father in cold blood. He wouldn't listen to me. And after all these years, you can see what it has brought. Duty. Obedience. Discipline. All my life I've done what I thought was right and proper, Mr. Simpson. And I suppose, in light of all this, it seems a sham, doesn't it? And where does it end? My son..."

He broke off and looked rather pathetic for a high and mighty industry baron. He looked up at me and smiled weakly. "I'm sorry. I'm sorry you have suffered on my brother's behalf. I don't know if I can make it up to you but..."

I managed to raise a bandaged hand.

"It's okay, Mr. Rothwell. A lot of this is my own doing. Pig-headedness. Well, I guess, it's something that you bothered to explain it all. No hard feelings. Good luck to you."

Rothwell knit his jaw, then nodded curtly.

"So long, Simpson." Then he gave me an ironic smile. "Oh by the way. I've resigned my seat on the board of directors of Crown Communications."

As he turned, his wife came up and touched my hands carefully. Her limbs shook and lips trembled.

"Goodbye, Mr. Simpson. I'm so glad you're all right."

Then her husband took her arm and they walked stiffly away. Blake sneered in my direction and I knew their tribulations weren't over yet.

The light wind felt fine on my face. I turned to Hal.

"Come on. Let's put the top down in that old heap of mine and go for a long ride by the shore. We can watch the boats."

He smiled, punched my arm with just a bit of sting and said, "Aren't you the romantic?"

He grabbed my elbow and we too, walked awkwardly away.

Three days later, pieces of Delaney's XKE, washed up on the beach of Rattlesnake Bay. His body may be floating in the bay somewhere. But somehow, I had a feeling he and Mickey were quaffing champagne on the Riviera. Some place like Cap Ferrat. She sold the restaurant and quietly left town. Damo and some of the Jokers surfaced in Mexico where they got busted for drug smuggling and ended up serving a long prison sentence. Bobby Ross became a born again Christian. Now, he rides for the Lord. The sight of Wishbone dying scared Jesus right into him. Chief McKie and Arne Guenther left the force in disgrace, although no evidence saw daylight against them. And now, Hal Bigelow r the show.

A month later, I managed to get up and around like a normal person. I threw away the cane and hobbled just a bit. My hair had grown back. Most of it, anyway. A letter came in the mail postmarked, Stanley Island, British Columbia. Darlene. She was living on a commune out there. She'd disappeared she'd said because it seemed the best way to rid herself of some pressing problems. And she said she was sorry for causing anyone pain or uncertainty. But her life was starting to turn itself around now. She'd discovered the holistic way. It was a brand new day, she said. I doffed my hat to her. I'd toast her silently when I bought the next round at the Round Table. Or maybe, I'd just giving up smoking and drinking for good. 30.

About the Author

W.L. Liberman believes in the power of storytelling but is not a fan of the often excruciating psychic pain required to bring stories to life. Truthfully, years of effort and of pure, unadulterated toil is demanded. Not to sugarcoat it, of course, writing is a serious endeavor. It is plain, hard work. If you've slogged away at construction work, at lumberjacking, delivery work, forest rangering, sandwich making, truck driving, house painting, among other things, as I have, writing is far and beyond more rigorous and exhausting. At the end of a long, often tedious, usually mind-cracking process, some individual you don't know pronounces judgment and that judgment is usually a resounding 'No'. This business of writing is about perseverance and stick-to-it-iveness. When you get knocked down and for most of us, this happens frequently, you take a moment to reflect, to self-pity, then get back at it. You need dogged determination and a thick skin to survive. And an alternate source of income.

W.L. Liberman is currently the author of eight novels, two graphic novels and a children's storybook. He is the founding editor and publisher of TEACH Magazine; www.teachmag.com, and has worked as a television producer and on-air commentator.

He holds an Honours BA from the University of Toronto in some subject or other and a Masters in Creative Writing from De Montfort University in the UK. He is married, currently lives in Toronto (although wishes to be elsewhere) and is father to three grown sons.

Also by the Author

- Dasvidaniya

- The Global View

- Looking For Henry Turner

Lightning Source UK Ltd.
Milton Keynes UK
UKHW011055120920
369780UK00006B/209